Heidi Swain

The Winter Garden

**SIMON &
SCHUSTER**

London · New York · Sydney · Toronto · New Delhi

First published in Great Britain by Simon & Schuster UK Ltd, 2020

Copyright © Heidi-Jo Swain, 2020

The right of Heidi-Jo Swain to be identified as author of
this work has been asserted in accordance with the
Copyright, Designs and Patents Act, 1988.

1 3 5 7 9 10 8 6 4 2

Simon & Schuster UK Ltd
1st Floor
222 Gray's Inn Road
London WC1X 8HB

Simon & Schuster Australia, Sydney
Simon & Schuster India, New Delhi

www.simonandschuster.co.uk
www.simonandschuster.com.au
www.simonandschuster.co.in

A CIP catalogue record for this book is available from the British Library

Paperback ISBN: 978-1-4711-8572-4
eBook ISBN: 978-1-4711-8573-1
Audio ISBN: 978-1-4711-9210-4

Typeset in the UK by M Rules
Printed and bound in Great Britain by CPI Group (UK) Ltd, Croydon, CR0 4YY

To
Amanda Preston,
agent extraordinaire and fabulous friend.
Merry Christmas, my darling!

Chapter 1

Before I moved to the Broad-Meadows country estate in Suffolk, I'd never celebrated either the summer or the winter solstice, but meeting octogenarian estate owner Eloise Thurlow-Forbes had soon changed that, along with a lot of other things.

'In order to garden successfully,' she had told me the day we met, which just happened to fall on the summer solstice three years ago, 'one has to be in tune with nature, the seasons, Mother Earth, the moon and all their cycles.'

I had been tempted to mention how the human race, global warming and the rising sea levels were set to change all that, but thought better of it. Even though I'd only just met her, Eloise Thurlow-Forbes, with her elegant white bun and refined features, looked to me like a woman who knew her own mind and I wasn't long in her company before I realised my hunch was right. It came as something of a surprise, however, to discover that she knew my mind too.

'Come on, Nell,' I said, pulling my thoughts back to the

present and climbing out of my van. 'We need to hurry or we'll miss it.'

With much stretching and yawning, the fawn-coloured Bedlington Whippet cross reluctantly levered herself out of the passenger seat and trotted along behind me. We weren't the only ones who had taken the journey to Ness Point, the most easterly spot in the UK, to watch the sunrise, but we stood a little apart from everyone else and I gazed in awe as the sky turned gold before the sun appeared majestically over the horizon, the few clouds in front of it turning the beams into something akin to an art deco sunburst.

'What shall we do now?' I asked Nell once the spectacle was over. She responded by leaning heavily against my legs and pushing her damp nose into my hand. 'Shall we go and see Eloise?'

Her tail thumped and her eyes brightened a little at the sound of her mistress's name.

'Come on then,' I said, turning back to where I'd parked the van. 'Let's go.'

By the time we arrived, I had mixed feelings about the visit. I couldn't talk to Eloise without mentioning what it was that I had lain awake half the night trying to find the words to say, but I knew I couldn't put it off much longer, no matter how unpalatable it was.

'I really hope I'm mistaken about this, Eloise,' I swallowed, pulling my thick, dark plait over my shoulder in a gesture she was sure to recognise as me seeking courage and comfort, 'but I have a horrible feeling that Jackson's gearing up to sell the estate. I might be wrong,' I quickly added, 'but there's a couple of things he's said during the last few weeks and I get the feeling . . .'

My words trailed off and I flicked my hair away again. Eloise was a great one for trusting her instincts and she had taught me how to rely more on mine, so there was really no point trying to sugar-coat the situation. Nell sighed, rested her head on her paws and stared at me. Her gaze struck me as reproachful.

'It's no good looking like that,' I told her. 'It's nothing to do with me. I'm hardly going to be able to change his mind, am I?'

I wondered what would happen to Nell if Jackson did sell up and move back to America. I couldn't imagine for one second that the comfort of his great-aunt's rescue dog would be high on his list of priorities.

Given that, if he did cut and run, I could well lose not only my job but my home too, I really had more pressing things to worry about, but I was fond of the dog and, unlike me, she had no say over her fate.

Little had I known when I first went to visit Eloise that fate had led me to her beautiful house and garden not to size the place up as a potential venue for my forthcoming wedding, as was the original plan, but as somewhere, for want of a less clichéd phrase, where I could find myself.

Within hours of my arrival I had broken off my engage-ment and accepted Eloise's offer of a gardening job and a place to live. The last three years had been an education, both personally and professionally, and even though I didn't feel ready to graduate, circumstances, this time beyond my control, suggested that I was going to be moving on again.

'I'm sorry not to come with better news,' I said, leaning over the grave to rearrange the flowers I had brought the week before and which were still holding their own in spite of the hot September days. 'But I wanted you to hear it from me, Eloise, and I know it's a lot to ask, but if you have any thoughts as to what I'm supposed to do now, I could really do with a sign because I have absolutely no idea at all.'

I sat back on my heels and listened to the silence in my head. My thoughts were still too clouded with grief to see the path ahead for myself. I could hear Nell starting to snuffle about, a blue tit twittering and somewhere in the distance a tractor at work, no doubt preparing the ground for next year's crop, but that was it. There was no inspirational thunderbolt, no flash of enlightenment to reignite my creative spark.

'Not to worry,' I smiled, trying to sound stoic as I got ready to leave, 'I'm sure I'll come up with something and besides, I might be wrong. I'll see you next week.'

It was hot back in the van so I turned over the engine, let down the windows and flicked on the radio. Nell drank her fill from the doggy water bottle I always carried with me while I tried to decide whether to head back to Broad-Meadows or make the most of my day off and explore further afield.

'That's not right, is it?' I said, reaching to retune the radio which had somehow switched from BBC Suffolk to BBC Norfolk. 'Come on, Nell. It's time to go.'

I had hardly driven any distance at all before the radio crackled and slipped back to Norfolk news again but I couldn't change it because the road ahead was busy.

'*The beautiful gardens here at Prosperous Place are already serving the local community, aren't they?*'

My brain tuned in at the mention of a 'garden' and I risked turning the volume a little higher, which resulted in missing a gap in the traffic.

'*That's right. In the old walled garden, we have the Grow-Well, which is a community space used by the residents of Nightingale Square. We raise fruit and vegetables there and have a few hens.*'

'*And I understand the Grow-Well recently won an award, didn't it?*'

'*Yes, we won the community garden award and that gave us enough funding to set up another garden and wildlife area and pond just behind the local youth centre.*'

'*That's wonderful, and what exactly is it that you're planning to do here now?*'

'*Well, the gardens around the house here at Prosperous Place are already open on certain weekends during the summer, but I'm planning to make use of them over the winter too. There aren't all that many big green spaces within walking distance of Norwich city centre and I want to open the place up so people can come and enjoy getting outside even during the bleaker months of the year.*'

'*You were diagnosed with seasonal affective disorder last year, weren't you?*'

'*Yes, yes I was, and that's what's prompted the idea really. It's all too easy to stay inside on the long, dark days when the weather*' is cold and the skies are grey, but getting outside, even for just a few minutes, can make all the difference.'

'So, your idea is as much about mental wellbeing as physical health.'

'Exactly, and that's why I'm opening the garden up today to invite people to come and take a look . . .'

I didn't get to hear the rest of the interview as a car tooted impatiently behind me and I realised I had been holding up the traffic. I waved in apology, turned on to the road and then into a layby to have a bit of a think.

I didn't need long. I had a whole day at my disposal, Norwich was less than an hour away and I was a firm believer in embracing nature and gardening for mental health, especially during the 'long dark days' as the person being interviewed had described them. It would be fascinating to see what this garden in the centre of the city looked like and what they had in mind to do with it.

A quick online search led me to the Grow-Well website where I discovered, along with details of the open day, that the owner was a Mr Luke Lonsdale. Before I could talk myself out of it, I keyed the postcode into Google Maps and found the quickest route to take me there.

'Right then, Nell,' I said, jamming my phone into the holder on the dash so I could follow the directions, 'how do you feel about going on a bit of an adventure?'

Her lengthy yawn suggested she didn't care for the idea at all, but I ignored her and carried on regardless.

*

Prosperous Place was easy enough to find, but as I approached the gate, it struck me that I might not be allowed in with Nell. I lingered outside as a few people wandered up. Some had pushchairs and an elderly gentleman zipped by on a mobility scooter, but no one had a dog.

'Are you going in?' asked a voice behind me. 'The gardens are open to everyone today.'

I turned to find a friendly-looking man in his late sixties, wearing a padded green gilet and a name badge (which informed me that he was called Graham), holding a large picnic basket.

'I had planned to,' I told him, 'but I didn't think about the dog. I'm not sure if I can go in with her. I'm guessing you work here. Do you think it would be all right?'

'I don't actually work here,' he smiled, stepping around me and through the gate. 'I'm just helping out the owner today. Let's go and ask him about your companion, shall we?'

'Thank you,' I said, following him inside.

My eyes were quickly drawn to the beautiful Victorian mansion and what looked like a very large garden and grounds that surrounded it. I don't know what I had been expecting, but the photos online really didn't do the size of the place justice. I was certainly surprised to find somewhere like it, privately owned, in the middle of a city.

'Luke!' Graham shouted, beckoning over a man with dark curls and intense brown eyes.

If this was Luke Lonsdale, then he was also a surprise.

I had assumed the owner would be someone much older. I tried to quieten the voice in my head, which was keen to remind me how dangerous assumptions could be, and sounded very much like Eloise's.

'Graham,' said Luke, bounding over and looking somewhat flustered. 'What can I do for you?'

'This young lady,' said Graham, rather unnecessarily pointing me out, 'wants to come in, but isn't sure if she can bring her dog.'

'Well now, let's see,' said Luke, his brow smoothing as he took a look at Nell, who stood, as always, just a little behind me and out of the limelight.

He squatted down on his haunches and held out his hand. To my utter amazement Nell stepped out of my shadow and allowed him to make a fuss of her.

'I don't think she's going to cause too much havoc, is she?' Luke smiled up at me.

'And I've got biodegradable poo bags,' I said, pulling a handful out of my pocket. 'You know, just in case.'

I had no idea why I'd said that and I could feel my cheeks flaming.

'In that case,' said Luke, straightening back up and looking amused, 'it's got to be access all areas, hasn't it?'

'Thank you,' I said, stuffing the bags back into my pocket.

Fortunately, I was saved from further mortification by the arrival of a television crew who were keen to interview Luke for their lunchtime show. He certainly seemed to be a draw for local media and I couldn't help thinking, as I thanked Graham, and Nell and I took the path further into the garden, that he looked vaguely familiar.

However, once I was deeper inside, my thoughts didn't linger on the handsome owner because I was mesmerised by everything else. The garden, I worked out, given the size of the trees, was easily as old as the house, with long sweeping herbaceous borders, a hidden fern garden, rose garden, pet cemetery, what looked like a meandering stretch of river and sizeable lawns. Everything was enclosed by a high brick wall, beautifully bleached and softened by time. It was an absolute gem of a place, or it had been once.

To the untrained eye, it was probably perfect, but I could see what was hidden beneath. The lawns might be in check, but the shrubs hadn't been properly pruned, the roses scaling the walls were almost out of control and in some parts weeds had run rampant through the borders. This was a garden on the cusp. That said, it wouldn't be too difficult to restore it to its former glory and as a potential proper winter garden, it held endless appeal.

I wandered for an hour or so and was lost in my thoughts until Nell stopped dead in her tracks.

'What is it, you silly dog?' I asked, pulled up short as she refused to budge.

I couldn't see anything which could have spooked her, but she could be a funny old thing. Eloise and I had often speculated on the life she had led before being welcomed into the Thurlow-Forbes fold.

'What does she think?' shouted a man's voice.

I turned to find Luke striding across the lawn towards me with a little girl sitting comfortably on his shoulders.

'Does she approve?' he grinned, coming to a stop and lifting the girl down.

'She loves it,' I told him, patting Nell's head as the child craned to look at her hiding behind my legs. 'Although she's just stopped here for some reason and is refusing to move.'

Luke looked at the magnificent cedar tree behind me.

'Could be the tree,' he commented, squinting up into the branches.

'I doubt that,' I laughed. 'She's much better with trees than people.'

'But this tree has a history,' he said seriously, scooping the little girl back up again. 'This is my daughter, Abigail, by the way,' he added, 'my youngest.'

'Pleased to meet you, Abigail,' I said, and she dissolved into giggles, burying her head into her dad's shoulder.

'And what do you think of the garden?' he asked me.

I took a moment before answering. 'It's stunning,' I said, looking around again.

'But?'

'But?' I echoed.

'I could sense there was a but coming.'

How disconcertingly intuitive of him. I wrinkled my nose and tried to phrase my response in a way that wouldn't cause offence, or at least I hoped it wouldn't.

'Well,' I said, clearing my throat, 'the lawns are great.'

'And so they should be,' said Luke, looking at the mown

grass beneath his feet, 'given how much I pay a contractor to keep them cut. What about the rest?'

'Would you like my personal or professional opinion?' I asked him.

They weren't all that dissimilar, but I could easily soften the personal one a little.

'Are you a professional horticulturalist then?' Luke asked, raising his eyebrows.

'More or less,' I said evasively.

I wasn't sure my experience warranted such a lofty title, but gardening was the job I had been happily employed to do for the last three years and I had kept Broad-Meadows beautifully. Jackson might have taken every opportunity to point out that I didn't have a formal qualification to back up my expertise, but he hadn't yet worn me down enough to stop me sharing my thoughts.

'Professional then,' said Luke, biting his lip. 'Tell it to me straight.'

After giving Nell some encouragement to move – a treat from my pocket – we walked around the gardens together and I pointed out a few of the things I had already noticed. The herbaceous borders warranted the most comment. Had they been regularly deadheaded, they would have continued flowering far longer, and it would have been better to stake the delphiniums in the spring to hide the supports, rather than leaving it until they were fully grown and then lashing together canes and twine Heath Robinson style to try and keep them standing.

'I do what I can,' said Luke, sounding gloomy, 'but for most of the time it's just me and a volunteer, and she's only here a couple of days a week. I know I could ask my friends and neighbours, but they already have their hands full with the Grow-Well.'

'In that case,' I said, keen to make amends for my pronouncement on the place, 'you do very well indeed. There's nothing here that couldn't be salvaged, given the right attention, and its potential as a proper winter garden is immense.'

'You really think so?'

'Definitely,' I said firmly. 'A full-time professional would have it all back on track in no time.'

Luke nodded thoughtfully. 'And what do you mean,' he asked, 'by a *proper* winter garden?'

'One that showcases shrubs, bulbs and trees that are at their very best from late autumn through until spring,' I explained. 'These dogwoods over there for example,' I said, pointing, 'with the right pruning they could be a blaze of colour again and there are lots of winter shrubs that could easily be incorporated and which flower on bare stems and have the most delicious scent.'

Luke looked intrigued. 'That does sound wonderful,' he said, looking towards the borders with fresh eyes, 'and much more spectacular than what I had in mind. I was just planning to open the place up. You certainly seem to know what you're talking about. I don't suppose you want a job, do you?'

12

I went to laugh the suggestion off, but he looked as if he meant it. His expression rather reminded me of the one Eloise had worn when she offered me a position practically within minutes of meeting me. Nonetheless, familiar though it might have been, it was still a surprise to be faced with it for the second time in my life.

'Thank you, but I already have one,' I told Luke, aiming to keep my voice steady. I didn't add that I had no idea for how much longer. 'I manage a garden in Suffolk, over near Beccles, on the Broad-Meadows estate.'

'Shame,' he tutted. 'Sorry, I didn't catch your name.'

'It's Freya,' I told him. 'Freya Fuller.'

'Well, Freya Fuller,' he said, setting Abigail back on her feet again. 'If I can't give you a job, would you consider leaving me your contact details at the house?'

'What for?' I asked.

'So, I can pick your brains,' he smiled. 'In an advisory capacity.'

'All right,' I agreed, 'I don't see why not.'

Later that afternoon, having enjoyed a picnic lunch for the masses made from produce grown at the Grow-Well which was on the opposite side of the grounds, I called at the house and left my details with Luke's wife, Kate.

She was every bit as kind as Luke and, as I walked back to the car park where I'd left the van, I couldn't help thinking that Eloise and the summer solstice might not have provided me with a sign about my long-term future, but my trip to Norwich had been a welcome distraction nonetheless.

Should Luke ever get in touch, I was going to enjoy being involved in the winter garden at Prosperous Place, even if it was only in an advisory capacity.

Chapter 2

I had left my phone tucked away in the glove compartment of the van and, when I turned it on again to help me negotiate my way back to Broad-Meadows, I found there were four missed calls from Jackson's mobile to tug at my conscience, and by the time I arrived home there were another two.

I did have a hands-free set-up but, in spite of my loyalty to Eloise and the estate, I didn't want to talk to him on my day off and certainly not while I was driving. I was more tired than I would have expected and needed to concentrate.

I hadn't much noticed it during my quiet working days and even quieter evenings and weekends, but I had become accustomed to spending time alone, sometimes not talking to another living soul from one day to the next. I hadn't thought it was an issue, but my day at Prosperous Place talking to Luke, Graham and Kate had been exhausting and highlighted the fact that I was perhaps in danger of becoming a little too comfortable with my own company.

Nell and I enjoyed a light supper and then I had a long bath with the intention of turning in before my usual bedtime so I would be bright-eyed and bushy-tailed, ready to start work early the next morning. However, Jackson had other ideas. I had barely finished tying the belt of my bathrobe when I heard him hammering on the door. There was no question of it being anyone else because we were so isolated and besides, Nell only ever growled when he was about.

I opened the door and peeped out, my still damp hair snaking almost down to my waist. If I didn't dry it soon, there would be no taming it.

'Oh, you *are* here then, Freya,' he frowned, his sarcastic tone and sweeping gaze making my hackles rise as high as Nell's. 'I've been trying to reach you on your cell all day.'

I couldn't help but wince at the sound of his southern drawl and closed the door a little. It wasn't the sight of him that rubbed me up the wrong way – just a couple of years older than me, he was tall, solid, dark-haired and handsome. Quite possibly fanciable if you didn't mind the slightly too white teeth.

And it wasn't his accent either – I was as receptive to a cowboy as any fluttering southern belle thanks to watching my fair share of Sam Elliott movies – but it was more the *way* he said things, rather than the voice in which he said them.

'You knew I was taking today off, Jackson,' I recapped for him. 'We talked about it last week, remember? I wanted to honour your aunt's memory by celebrating the solstice.'

'That's today, is it?' he said, sounding amused.

'Yes,' I sighed, 'it is and, as today is my day off, I'm free to come and go as I please.'

'But you're working next Saturday to make up for taking the extra day, right? I have remembered that correctly, haven't I?'

'No,' I said patiently. 'I worked last Saturday to make up for it. I put the hours in before I'd taken them. We did discuss it at some length.'

'Oh yeah,' he nodded. 'I do recall now you come to mention it.'

He certainly should. He had tried to make a pass at me when we were in the glasshouse talking it over and I had been forced to resort to some nifty tactics with the hosepipe to ward him off. Accidentally, of course. Not.

'So,' I said, raising my eyebrows. 'We've established that I'm here, so if you don't mind . . .'

I went to shut the door, but he took a step closer and I stopped. Shutting the door in his face wouldn't do anything to enhance our working relationship and besides, one day I might need a reference from this guy.

'Actually,' he said, 'there's something I need to talk to you about. Can I come in? Just for a minute.'

'Can it wait until the morning?' I asked, trying to sound friendlier. 'I'm just about to turn in for the night.'

I was determined not to let him cross the cottage threshold, even if it was only for a minute. I didn't trust him and I certainly wouldn't have felt comfortable talking to him wearing nothing more than my flimsy cotton bathrobe. Nell's low-level growling behind me told me that she was reluctant for me to let him in too.

'How about we meet in the office at eight and we'll talk then,' I suggested. 'We can have a coffee.'

He narrowed his eyes but thankfully stood down. 'All right,' he said. 'I'll see you at eight. Sweet dreams.'

Even though the bath had soothed my body and settled my busy brain after my unusually sociable day, my brief exchange with Jackson meant that falling asleep was impossible. There was no doubt in my mind that he was going to tell me he was selling up, and the more I thought about it, the more awake I stayed.

Consequently, rather than feeling rested and refreshed the next morning as planned, I flung back the duvet feeling cranky, looking puffy-eyed, with untameable locks and feeling thoroughly unhappy about having to grant him an early audience. At least I'd been canny enough to suggest we meet in the office, where I could keep the heavy old desk between us.

'Good morning,' he called, right on the stroke of eight. 'How did you sleep?'

One look at my face and it should have been obvious that I hadn't.

'Fine,' I said tightly, pushing my chair further under the table. 'What did you want to talk about, Jackson? I have a lot to get on with this morning.'

'Making hay while the sun still shines, hey?'

'Something like that.'

It had been a hot and sunny September so far and the garden was still wearing its beautiful late-summer bloom.

The borders Eloise and I had revamped and replanted together were filling out nicely. I had known, when she suggested the project, that she was planting for the future and it saddened me to think that I most likely wouldn't see them flourish.

'You promised me a coffee,' Jackson reminded me.

'Sorry,' I apologised. 'I've run out. I thought there was a teaspoon or two left, but the tin's empty.'

I don't know why he looked so put out. He had told me on more than one occasion that he hated instant anyway.

'Right,' he said, eyeing me for a moment before lowering himself into the seat opposite so we were at eye level.

My disturbed night had left me feeling cranky and my bad mood was putting me in danger of sabotaging the reference I had a feeling I was going to need, but in that moment, faced with his smug expression, I didn't much care.

'In that case,' he began, cocking his head to one side, 'let's get straight down to it, shall we?'

I swallowed and looked him dead in the eye. I had been dreading this moment ever since he turned up after Eloise's funeral and took over. I had known from the very first moment I clapped eyes on him that he wasn't going to take the place on and continue to run it as my dear friend had hoped.

I had never fathomed why she had such faith in him, but now, faced with the inevitable, I couldn't help thinking that him selling up to someone else was probably for the best. Surely, it would be better for the house, garden and grounds to be owned by another family, a family who would love it every bit as much as Eloise and her ancestors had.

'The sooner the better,' I therefore encouraged.

'Okay,' he nodded, letting out a long breath and making a great show of adopting the role of a doctor about to break bad news. 'I don't quite know how to tell you this, Freya . . .'

'Do you want me to say it for you then?' I asked, keen to give him a hint that I had worked it out already.

He didn't appear to appreciate the interruption and leant forward in his seat.

'I've been giving this a lot of thought,' he continued, 'and it hasn't been an easy decision to make, but I've looked at the estate accounts and talked to the bank and,' he paused for dramatic effect, 'I've come to the conclusion that I have to sell the estate.'

'I see,' I said, my voice pleasingly steady and calm.

'Of course, I know this is the last thing that Aunt Eloise would have wanted,' he carried on, 'but I can't manage the place from the States. It really needs me here full-time to keep a handle on things, but I can't commit to that. Looking at the paperwork, it's obvious that my aunt lost her way a little during the last couple of years and I'm looking for damage limitation here now.'

I bit my tongue. I had been with Eloise for longer than the last couple of years and her business mind was as sharp as a packet of pins. Her ability to run the place as efficiently as she always had, had never waned. It was her body that had failed her, not her mind.

'With regards to what your aunt would have wanted,' I told him, 'I think you've made the right decision.'

'You do?'

'Yes,' I said, 'I'm sure she would want the place to be loved as she loved it, and as you've said on more than one occasion, it's not somewhere that matches everything else in your impressive property portfolio.'

It felt good to be able to fire his words back at him.

'And of course,' I added for good measure, keeping my chin held high, 'you really don't have to justify your decision-making to me, Jackson.'

'I'm not,' he said, sounding further disgruntled. 'That's not what I—'

'I'm just the gardener,' I shrugged, cutting him off. 'What you decide to do with the place is entirely up to you.'

'I know that,' he blustered, turning red. 'I just thought that you might—'

'Please,' I said, smiling sympathetically, 'you have more than enough to be thinking about. Don't concern yourself with worrying about me on top of everything else.'

He sat up a little straighter and fiddled with the cuffs of his shirt. Why he still persisted in dressing as if he was working in his city office was a mystery, but the steely glint in his eye was a sure sign that he was frustrated that I hadn't reacted how he had wanted me to. If he'd been hoping to offer a shoulder for me to cry on, then he was well and truly out of luck.

'I've already had the estate valued,' he then said, suddenly all business, 'and it will be going on the market in the next couple of weeks. My realtor has said it might take a while to sell. In the current financial climate, it might not be easy to find someone who can afford the place.'

'Estate agent,' I interrupted.

'What?'

'In England, it's an estate agent, not a realtor.'

'Right,' he said, drumming his fingers on the desk. 'Estate agent.'

'Sorry,' I said, 'go on. I didn't mean to cut you off.'

'Well, I just wanted to keep you in the loop really. In case you were wondering why I was having the place photographed and showing strangers around.'

'Thank you,' I said. 'I appreciate that.'

I didn't want to have to ask the next question, but I needed to know where I stood.

'And what about me,' I said. 'Do you want me to stay on?'

'Of course,' he smiled, latching on to my one show of vulnerability. 'It's more important than ever that the gardens look good now.'

I nodded.

'You will stay, won't you?'

'Yes,' I said. 'Of course.'

It wasn't as if I had anywhere else to move to and it felt important to keep the place exactly as Eloise had loved it, right up until the moment it became someone else's. I had no idea what I would do after it was sold, but that could be a worry for another day. Eloise had taught me that it often didn't pay to look too far ahead.

'So, that's that then,' Jackson said, pushing back the chair and standing up.

'Yes,' I said, 'that's that.'

'Oh, no,' he casually added, 'there is just one more thing.'

'What's that?'

'I want you to move out of the cottage.'

'What?'

'I've checked the paperwork,' he carried on, looking down at me, 'and the place isn't officially part of your contract, is it?'

'Well, no, but ...'

I was pleased I was still sitting down because I wasn't sure my legs would have held me. They had turned to jelly and Jackson would have loved the spectacle of seeing me stumble.

'Not that you've actually got a contract,' he pushed on, 'not a legally binding one anyway.'

I couldn't argue with that. My arrangement with Eloise had been above board when it came to paying taxes and so on, but beyond that our business association was pretty casual.

'And given how long the sale is likely to take,' Jackson pushed on, 'I've decided to let the cottage out. God knows I need to try and generate some sort of income from the estate. I've already got tenants lined up who are willing to pay the market rent.'

'But where will I go?' I stammered. 'And why didn't you ask me about paying the market rent?'

'I don't quite think the pittance you're paid would make that a feasible option, Freya.'

'Eloise and I agreed that figure on the basis of me being

provided with a roof over my head,' I said firmly. 'I do have certain rights, you know.'

'And so do I,' he retaliated. 'And which particular roof is over your head has never been specified, has it? There are plenty of empty servants' rooms in the house. You can move into those. Think how convenient it will be for us to be living closer together.'

I opened my mouth, but no words came out, which was probably just as well, given the profanities I could have resorted to. When Eloise first broached the idea of me living and working at Broad-Meadows, she had offered me the choice of either living in the cottage or taking rooms in the house. She was pleased I'd gone for the little cottage.

'It will give you some space and privacy,' she had said kindly.

And it had. It was going to be a blow to leave it.

'And just to prove I'm every bit as generous as my aunt,' Jackson added, with a nauseating smile, 'how about I give you today off so you can move your things. After all, there's no time like the present when it comes to getting stuff done, is there?'

Given the little I had, it had taken me no time at all to move my things from the cottage into the house. Most of the furniture belonged to the estate and everything else I could squeeze into the back of my van. I picked a couple of rooms furthest away from the wing Jackson was lording it up in and both Nell and I did our best to avoid him, but it wasn't easy.

Whenever our paths crossed, I would paste on a smile, resolute that I wouldn't give him the satisfaction of knowing how much I was missing my cosy little bolthole and the privacy it had afforded me, but suddenly the days seemed to drag and autumn felt like it was taking forever to land. That said, I had found one way to keep my spirits up, and thanks to Nell, mine and Jackson's contact to a minimum.

When I first moved into the house, Jackson had insisted on me coming to the kitchen at the end of every day to talk through what I had been doing, but one night Nell's strange behaviour ensured I would no longer have to endure his daily interrogation.

'I'd rather you didn't bring that damn dog with you in here,' Jackson had grumbled, when he noticed her circling and whining in front of what had been her old spot next to the range. 'It's not hygienic, and what's the matter with her anyway?'

I knew Nell wanted the loo, but I wasn't going to tell him that.

'It's Eloise,' I said, looking about me and into the distance over Jackson's shoulder.

'What?' he snapped.

'Nell senses her everywhere,' I said, trying not to laugh as the colour drained from his face. 'But especially in here.'

'Don't be so ridiculous,' he swallowed, his eyes darting around.

I called to Nell and shrugged. 'It's true,' I said, making for the back door before Nell embarrassed herself. 'I've heard her footsteps at night, haven't you?'

He avoided me and Nell after that, but I still found the change to our residential circumstances difficult. Had I somewhere else to go, he wouldn't have seen me for dust. However, my only real option would have been to phone my parents and ask if I could stay with them, and I couldn't face that. Besides, the commute would have been impossible.

Consequently, I had no choice other than to keep my head down and get on with my work, but all the while I was resentful of the fact that my halcyon days and treasured memories of life with Eloise at the Broad-Meadow helm were becoming increasingly tainted.

There weren't many places in the garden that attracted enough mobile signal for my phone to ring, but on the first Tuesday of October, just as I had finished inspecting Eloise's beloved borders and was getting ready to start raking leaves, I must have hit a signal hotspot.

'Hello,' I said, standing stock still for fear of losing the connection.

'Hi, is that Freya?' asked a man's voice. 'Is that Freya Fuller?'

'Yes,' I said. 'Who's this?'

'Luke.'

'Luke?'

'Luke Lonsdale,' the voice elaborated, 'from Prosperous Place in Norwich.'

It had been a while since my visit and as I hadn't heard from him straightaway, I assumed he wasn't going to call.

'You came and looked around my garden a couple of weeks ago,' he carried on, no doubt assuming I'd forgotten who he was. 'We talked about making a Winter Garden.'

'Of course,' I said. 'Hi.'

'Hi,' he said again.

'So, how's it going?'

'Good,' he said, 'really good. Well, in theory. In my head, it's all perfect, but not much has happened outside yet.'

'There's still plenty of time to make a start. The weather's being very kind this year.'

'It is,' he agreed, 'but I really want to get going with it. I'm sorry I haven't called you sooner.'

'That's all right.'

'I misplaced your number, you see.'

'It's fine.' It wasn't as if we had made solid arrangements to follow my visit up.

'So, what can I do for you?' I asked.

'Well,' he said, 'I know it's a bit cheeky, but I was wondering if you would consider coming back to have another look around and help me make some notes about planting and stuff. I'd pay for your travel costs and time, of course.'

'Oh,' I said. 'I see.'

I was delighted, but his request had taken me by surprise. Having established who he was, I thought he might just want to talk a few things through on the phone.

'I know it's a lot to ask, but I'd really appreciate it. You seemed to have a good grasp of what it is that I want to do when we talked before.'

I spotted Jackson striding purposefully towards me and thought some time away from Broad-Meadows, even if only a few hours, would be most welcome.

'I'm more than happy to help,' I keenly told Luke. 'I could come this Saturday, if you like?'

'Really?' he sounded over the moon.

'Yes,' I confirmed, 'I can be there around eleven if that suits you.'

'Absolutely,' he said, and I could tell he was smiling. 'That would be perfect. And drive straight up to the house. I'll open the gates so you can park here.'

'Fantastic.'

'Great. We'll see you then.'

'See you Saturday.'

I hung up just as Jackson reached me, a scowl etched across his forehead.

'Were you on the phone?' he grumbled. 'I don't pay you to make personal calls during working hours, Freya.'

I went to snap back but was distracted by the back of the magazine he had tucked under his arm.

'What's that?' I frowned.

He tutted and looked at what had caught my attention. 'What's what?'

'That,' I said, pointing.

'*Esquire* magazine,' he said. 'Why?'

I squinted at the aftershave advert adorning the back

cover and the half-naked model aesthetically draped across a very sleek-looking boat. The model looked very much like Luke Lonsdale.

'Have you never seen a half-naked man before?' Jackson quizzed, examining the detail more closely. 'This ad is a few seasons old, but it's still doing the rounds. I can't believe you've never seen it.'

'Well, I haven't,' I said in wonder, 'but I have just made a date for Saturday with the guy featured in it.'

'Of course, you have,' Jackson laughed, striding off again. 'Of course, you have, Freya. You're beginning to sound as barmy as Aunt Eloise!'

I quickly turned away to hide my laughter as he tripped over the rake and Nell took a passing nip at his ankles for good measure.

Chapter 3

Every evening that week I stayed in my rooms, trawling through my books and making notes on prospective plants and ideas which would enhance Luke's vision for the Winter Garden. The project might not come to anything for me, but it was a welcome distraction and stopped me pining for the cottage and missing Eloise.

Towards the end of the week, the weather took a decidedly damp turn and it was raining steadily as I turned into the open gates at Prosperous Place on Saturday morning. I gathered my file, clippings and bag together and told Nell we would make a dash towards the house. She wasn't a fan of wet weather and would have stayed curled up on my bed, but there was no way I could have left her at Broad-Meadows all day. Jackson wouldn't have given her needs a second thought.

'Good morning,' said Luke as I stepped out of the van and he appeared with an umbrella big enough to cover at least four people.

'Good morning,' I smiled up at him.

He might have looked a little older than the guy on the back of Jackson's magazine, but it was definitely him. I didn't know whether to mention that I knew who he was or not.

'I think we'd best start with coffee in the house,' he suggested, with a nod to the rain. 'According to the forecast it's supposed to be sunny in about an hour, so there's no point getting wet now.'

Given the thick blanket of cloud above our heads, I wasn't sure I agreed with his prediction but gratefully ducked under the brolly, with Nell on my heels, and followed him inside.

'Come into the kitchen,' he said, having shrugged off his coat and taken mine before leading me through the impressive house. 'It's warmer in there.'

The temperature was a little chilly, but the cavernous kitchen, which was almost as big as Eloise's, was surprisingly cosy.

'Freya,' smiled Kate, standing up to greet me as if I was a long-lost friend, rather than someone she'd briefly met during a very busy day. 'Come and have a seat.'

'I hope you don't mind me bringing Nell,' I said in an apologetic tone, 'it wasn't practical to leave her behind today.'

I was beginning to get the feeling that it was never going to be practical to leave her. I'd recently overheard Jackson muttering something which sounded a lot like 'take you back to where you came from', and if it was her that he was talking about, then there was definitely trouble ahead.

'She's more than welcome,' said Kate.

'I'd have been disappointed if you hadn't brought her,' said Luke, squatting down to make a fuss of her.

Nell rolled on to her back, putty in his hands.

'Yet another woman falling for your good looks,' said Kate, rolling her eyes.

'Yep,' he winked. 'I've still got it.'

I didn't think I'd ever get a more opportune moment to ask the question which was beginning to burn.

'Were you once a model by any chance, Luke?' I asked. 'Only I saw this aftershave advert on the back of a magazine the other day and the guy in it rather looked like you.'

'I was,' he said, turning endearingly pink. 'It was a while ago now though, and I was only ever in it for the money.'

While he made us coffee, he explained how it had been an easy way to pay off his student debts and become solvent enough to make buying and restoring his ancestral home, Prosperous Place, a reality.

I was fascinated to discover that it had been a distant Victorian philanthropic relative, Charles Wentworth, who had owned one of Norwich's shoe factories, who had built the house along with those just across the road in Nightingale Square, for the benefit of his workers. Buying the house back had been Luke's father's dream, but after his death, Luke had soon become equally fascinated with the story and determined to reclaim and restore what he could and also do as much good work locally as his ancestor had.

'Hence the Grow-Well,' smiled Kate.

'And now the Winter Garden,' Luke added.

'Wow,' I gasped, feeling in awe of both the past and the present. 'I've spent the last few days researching winter gardens,' I told the pair, 'but now I'm thinking I should have been googling Prosperous Place and your family, Luke. I'd love to know more about them.'

'Well, that's no problem,' he said, setting down a mug in front of me. 'Kate and I can fill you in on what you want to know as we go along.'

I felt a pang of disappointment that I wasn't going to be properly involved with the project because it all sounded absolutely fascinating.

'So, what have you discovered in your research?' asked Kate, looking keenly at the pile of papers and my bulging file.

I ran them through the notes I had made, expanding on the list of shrubs and trees I had previously mentioned to Luke and again emphasised the importance of scent as well as all the other senses and how using form and structure would enhance what was already established.

'Talking of structure,' said Luke, once I had stopped to draw breath, 'I've also been thinking about adding some sculptures.'

'Oh,' I said, wondering what he had in mind.

Was he talking about commissioning something bespoke or popping down to the garden centre for a few gnomes? I seriously hoped it was the former. Not that I had anything against gnomes, but I wasn't sure how they'd fit into the elegant scheme of the Prosperous Place Winter Garden that I had in mind. Not that it was my vision that was going to be created, but still.

'What sort of sculptures?' I asked.

He didn't have the opportunity to answer as the kitchen door flew open and in ran two little girls, followed closely by a woman with flushed cheeks. Nell tucked herself further under my chair and I leant my leg against her to reassure her that everything was fine. Clearly, I wasn't the only one who had become a little too accustomed to my own company.

'We're starving!' groaned the eldest girl. 'Is it lunchtime yet?'

'Sorry,' apologised the woman, scooping up the little one I recognised as Abigail. 'They wouldn't wait.'

I looked at my watch and was amazed to see that it was actually well past lunchtime. We had been talking far longer than I'd thought.

'That's my fault,' I said. 'I think I've got a bit carried away.'

'Not at all,' said Kate. 'Your enthusiasm is contagious, Freya.'

'And you certainly know what you're talking about,' said Luke, taking Abigail from the other woman before settling her in a high chair and handing her a breadstick which she immediately annihilated by bashing it against the tray.

'This is Carole,' said Kate, introducing me to the woman. 'She lives in Nightingale Square and is one of the Grow-Well gang.'

'You met her husband, Graham,' put in Luke, 'on the open day.'

'Of course,' I said, standing up to shake the woman's hand which was a little formal, but I got the feeling that she was someone who appreciated a good first impression. She was dressed almost identically to how her husband had been. All that was missing was the name badge. 'Pleased to meet you.'

'And you, my dear.'

'She's also the glue that keeps the Grow-Well committee on track, the girls in line, and pretty much everything around here running like a well-oiled machine,' beamed Luke.

Carole looked pleased. 'I don't know about that,' she flushed, 'but I like to do my bit.'

'More than your bit,' said Kate, 'and we all love you for it.'

'And I'm Jasmine,' said the older girl, holding out her hand for me to shake and mimicking what I had just done with Carole.

'And I'm pleased to meet you too,' I said, shaking it but not quite as firmly.

'How do you do?' she asked, in a silly, posh voice.

'Very well,' I mirrored back, making them all laugh. 'And how do you do?'

Jasmine dissolved into giggles and Abigail offered me the soggy end of her breadstick, making me feel very much at home.

'I'll come back for the girls in a bit,' said Carole, 'which will give you three a chance to look around outside in peace. It's stopped raining by the way, but it's wet underfoot. You'll need wellies.'

Fortunately, I had put mine in the van. I rarely travelled without them and none of my clothes objected to a bit of mud. My creased old Barbour and well-worn jumpers and jeans were generally as sophisticated as I got.

'Thanks, Carole,' said Kate.

'Have you seen the cats?' Luke asked her, handing Abigail another breadstick because she had started to clamour for her sister's as soon as she had handed me hers.

'Both asleep in the bothy,' said Carole. 'See you in a bit.'

After lunch of homemade soup and delicious bread, which Kate told me came from a wonderful bakery just up the road and had been baked by another Nightingale Square resident, Carole returned for the girls, and the three of us set off into the garden. It was very wet, with puddles pooling on the paths and everything now looking soggy, forlorn and in need of some proper deadheading and general tender loving care.

'This weather has certainly helped the weeds along,' commented Luke, bending to pull up a particularly large specimen.

'I think we've definitely seen the end of the summer now,' I agreed. 'It will be time to put things to bed before we know it and hopefully for you guys, wake the Winter Garden up.'

They both looked excited at the prospect, even if they weren't all that sure how to go about it.

'Are you absolutely sure I can't tempt you with that job offer?' Luke asked, as we finished the tour, having looked at an area I had missed before and which Kate said was a carpet of snowdrops in the spring. 'It still stands, you know.'

'We'd love to have you on the team,' said Kate, linking her arm through mine.

My heart skipped in my chest as we made a dash for the house when the rain started again. I was sad not to have seen the Grow-Well, but at least it would be the perfect excuse to come back for another visit.

'You said you manage a garden in Suffolk, didn't you?' asked Luke, offering me a chair at the kitchen table once we'd pulled off our muddy wellies by the back door and picked the conversation up again. 'On the Broad-Meadows estate.'

He had a very good memory.

'That's right,' I confirmed.

'And do you love it there?' Kate asked, sounding very much like she hoped the answer was going to be no.

'I do,' I sighed, 'but it's complicated.'

Over tea and a slice of Victoria sponge – another treat from the bakery – I explained about how my job was potentially set to come to an end and how I was currently living in tied accommodation. I didn't go into details about how I came to meet Eloise because it wasn't relevant.

'So, the upshot is,' I told them, 'I'm soon going to lose both my job and my home, and I can't consider another position unless it offers me somewhere to live.'

No one said anything for a few seconds but a look passed between the couple. Luke raised his eyebrows and Kate nodded. I had no idea what the silent exchange meant, but clearly, they did.

'Would you excuse me for just a moment?' said Luke, standing up and walking out.

He was back before I'd drunk the second cup of tea Kate

had pressed on me and he was looking really rather pleased with himself.

'Well?' Kate asked.

'We can go over when we're ready,' he answered.

'Assuming Freya wants to,' she pointed out.

'Assuming Freya wants to what?' I asked, putting down my cup.

Luke turned to look at me. 'Okay,' he said, taking a breath. 'Let me just make sure I've got your current work and accommodation situation perfectly straight in my head, Freya.'

'Okay,' I said, looking between him and Kate.

'From what you've told us, I'm thinking that you might be interested in coming to work here and helping us set up the Winter Garden, yes?'

'Yes,' I quickly said, because I was *extremely* interested. 'If it wasn't for the fact that I'd have nowhere to live,' I hastily added for further clarity, 'I'd be here like a shot.'

'And do you think you'd be happy to stay on to manage the garden and grounds once the Winter Garden is established?'

'Of course,' I said, feeling confused. 'It's a beautiful space. Any gardener would be proud to maintain it, but that still doesn't alter the fact . . .'

Luke shook his head. 'Come with us,' he said, holding out his hand for Kate, who stood up to follow him.

'And don't look so worried,' she said to me, 'because I think we might just have found the perfect solution.'

It stopped raining as we made the short journey across the road into Nightingale Square, where I could see there were half a dozen or so lovely houses built around a green. They all looked in good repair and the green was well maintained.

'This is the one we want,' said Luke, opening the gate of the second house on the right. 'How would you like to live here, Freya? Rent-free as part of your salary.'

'I don't understand,' I said, as the door opened and an elderly gentleman ushered us inside.

'Get in before it starts again,' he insisted. 'And wipe your feet. What a lovely dog,' he added, patting Nell's head.

She was looking as unsure about everything as I was.

'Come into the front room,' he said, steering us inside before I had a chance to gather my wits, 'and we can talk properly. From the look on your face my dear, I daresay you haven't got a clue what's going on, have you?'

'No,' I swallowed, 'I haven't.'

'Not a Scooby,' he laughed. 'I'm Harold, by the way.'

Having politely refused Harold's offer of yet more tea, and a cold sausage leftover from his lunch for Nell, the four of us sat in the living room, which had a large bay window overlooking the square, and Kate insisted on explaining everything because she knew Luke's enthusiasm would get the better of him and he'd end up missing bits out.

'You see the house next door,' she said, beckoning for me to look out at the lovely house next to Harold's.

'Yes.'

'Well, I own it,' she told me. 'I bought it when I moved here from London before I met Luke. Then, when I moved in with him at Prosperous Place, I decided to keep it and rent it out. A lovely young woman called Poppy lives there now with her brother, Ryan.'

'Okay,' I said, still not seeing how that was anything to do with me, or how it explained why I was sitting in Harold's house when I should be thinking about heading back to Suffolk.

'As it was part of the original Wentworth empire, for want of a better word,' Luke couldn't resist butting in, 'Kate decided it would be lovely to keep it and view it as an extension of Prosperous Place.'

'Right,' I said.

'And now I'm moving into assisted living accommodation,' chimed in Harold. 'I'm selling my house, which has been lived in by my family since Charles Wentworth built it, back to Luke.'

'So, it's another piece of Mr Wentworth's legacy that's being returned to the fold?' I guessed. 'It will be another extension to Prosperous Place, like your house, Kate?'

'Exactly,' she said. 'And the plan was to rent it out, but . . .'

'But, as you need somewhere to live, Freya,' put in Luke, 'and Kate and I *really* want you to take the job as head gardener and Winter Garden project manager, we're thinking that it would be perfect for you.'

It sounded wonderful in theory and my heart leapt at the prospect, but if I accepted, was I going to be jumping from the frying pan into the fire? After all, as lovely as Luke and Kate were, the set-up might end up leading me into the same mess that I was currently facing if things didn't work out.

'It would all be above board,' said Kate, clearly picking up on the reason for my reluctance, 'we'd have a contract properly drawn up, along with a tenancy agreement.'

'It's not that I don't trust you,' I began to say.

'We know that,' she smiled, 'but we also appreciate that the circumstances you're dealing with now would make you wary of potentially facing a similar situation in the future, so we can take steps to ensure that wouldn't happen.'

I nodded and let out a breath, trying to take it all in.

'But you don't really know anything about me,' I said, still determined not to get swept along. 'You haven't asked about references or qualifications, my experience or anything really.'

'We know enough,' said Kate. 'We're great believers in gut instinct.'

She sounded just like Eloise, and again I thought how this offer of a job and home echoed my last.

'And I have to admit I have found out a bit about you, courtesy of a quick search online,' Luke admitted. 'I found some information about the Broad-Meadows open day last summer, along with your interview in the local press. It made for impressive reading and the photographs were wonderful.'

Eloise had opened the garden up for charity and insisted the focus of the newspaper article was on the garden and my work in it, rather than her life story.

'I see,' I said.

'Look,' said Luke. 'Don't say anything yet. Let Harold show you around and then come back over to the house. I know it's a big decision for you.'

'Huge,' agreed Kate.

'And there's no rush,' Luke added, with a twinkle in his eye.

'But you would like to start the Winter Garden project in time to have something to show this winter,' I smiled, making a calculated guess. 'Am I right?'

'Exactly,' he grinned, as Kate shook her head.

'We'll see you in a little while,' she said, ushering him out. 'And in spite of what Luke says, there really is no pressure.'

Harold showed me proudly over the house, pointing out the room where he had been born and explaining that most of the furniture and some of the contents would be staying as he wasn't going to have room for them.

'I don't know how you'd feel about that,' he said, looking about the kitchen. The room clearly hadn't been decorated for a while and featured an abundance of orange pine and Hornsea pottery containers. 'I don't suppose any of this is in style now.'

'On the contrary,' I told him. 'This kitchen is the height of fashion, Harold. The retro look is very popular right now.'

'So, it wouldn't all go straight in a skip then?' he sniffed, his voice a little shaky.

'Absolutely not,' I reassured him. 'None of it would. Not if I moved in, anyway. Between you and me, I haven't got an awful lot in the way of furniture and material possessions. I've always travelled light, so anything you left would be very much appreciated.'

Harold was clearly much cheered by the thought as we walked through the dining room and back into the living room where he had kindly turned the electric log-effect fire on for Nell because he thought she looked a bit chilly.

'So, what do you think?' he asked. 'Are you going to take the job?'

'I'm certainly going to give it some serious thought,' I told him.

'If I were you, I'd snatch their hands off,' he said firmly. 'You won't find a better place to live or a better family to work for.'

I thanked him for showing me around and Nell and I walked back over to Prosperous Place. If I did accept Luke and Kate's offer, then my daily commute would be barely longer than the one I had now. The pair had certainly given me plenty to mull over.

After Luke's call asking me to come back, I had wondered if the job offer would still stand but I hadn't for a single second speculated that there might be accommodation to go with it, and certainly not an entire house set around the pretty green in Nightingale Square!

'So,' said Luke, rocking back on his heels, from where he was waiting for me on the drive. 'What do you think?'

'The house is lovely,' I told him, 'and it's a very tempting offer.'

'And I can email you with salary details and holiday entitlement and so on, this evening, if you like.'

Kate came out of the house to meet us with Abigail in her

arms. The little girl's cheeks were flushed as if she had just woken up, which she probably had.

'That would be great,' I nodded. 'Thank you.'

'So, there is some hope then,' said Luke, biting his lip.

'There's always hope,' I told him. 'And I promise I won't keep you hanging on,' I added, addressing them both.

'I really hope you say yes, Freya,' Luke reiterated.

'And of course, we're more than happy for you to bring Nell,' Kate added.

If only she were mine to bring.

'You two look very much like you come as a pair and she would be a lovely addition to our community here, as would you.'

I thanked them both, kissed Kate on the cheek, before remembering to collect my wellies and paperwork, and then climbed back into the van, settling Nell next to me.

'See you soon,' Luke said hopefully, as they waved me off.

I waved back and pulled out on to the road before turning on the radio. It had somehow switched back to Radio Suffolk, even though we were definitely in Norfolk and in spite of the fact that I hadn't re-tuned it since it had mysteriously reset itself after I had asked Eloise for a sign.

'Thanks, Eloise,' I laughed into the air around me. 'Message received and understood.'

Chapter 4

I'd never been much of a one for lying in late, not even when I was on holiday. I'd never seen the point of getting out of the habit of setting my regular alarm. If I was awake, I'd get up and get on, no matter what day of the week it was. However, having had such an overwhelming start to the weekend, I did allow myself a slow start on the Sunday. Not that it wasn't productive.

Luke and Kate had wasted no time in emailing the promised details about salary, holiday entitlement and numerous other perks I would enjoy, should I decide to take up their offer of starting a new life at Prosperous Place. The finer details made for very pleasant reading.

My only real concern about accepting their offer came from the fear that I might not be up to the job and that I would let Luke down. When Eloise was alive, I always felt more than capable, but Jackson's barbed comments about my lack of formal training and qualifications nagged away at me in low moments when I was missing my friend most.

Deep down I knew he had sown the fear to keep me in place and toeing the line while he sold the estate off, but he had done his job well and my confidence had dipped right when I needed it most. I would have to dig deep if I didn't want to pass up Luke and Kate's generous offer.

'What do you think?' I asked Nell, hoping for some encouragement as I stretched out my legs to where she was curled up at the end of the bed and gave her a gentle nudge. 'Do you think we should go?'

She thumped her tail and I wasn't sure if it was wishful thinking on my part or not, but there did seem to be something of the old twinkle in her eyes. She hadn't looked this engaged since she'd lost her mistress and entered her period of mourning.

My gaze returned to the details currently filling up my phone screen and I let out a groan as a reminder to ring home flashed up. As loath as I was to do it, I knew I couldn't keep putting it off. It had been six weeks now since my fortnightly calls to my parents had tailed off and if I left it any longer, they'd most likely start calling me, or worse still, turn up in person. Dreading the thought, I hastily pressed the number for home.

'Freya,' answered my mother, her tone full of relief. 'At last. We'd all but given up on you. We were planning to drive up this afternoon and find out what was going on.'

I could hear my father's deep voice agreeing in the background and thanked my lucky stars that I had got myself together and called just in the nick of time.

'I have been meaning to ring,' I fibbed, avoiding Nell's knowing stare, 'but I've been so busy, what with the warm weather.'

'I can well imagine,' Mum surprised me by saying.

Usually when I made any sort of comment about my workload her standard retort was that it was my own fault for taking on such acreage single-handed. My parents ran a very upmarket landscape design company and were well aware of how many hours of weekly maintenance and what sized team it took to efficiently run somewhere the size of where I was working.

Neither she nor my father had made any secret of the fact that they had been deeply disappointed when I stopped working for them, ditched my horticultural design software and picked up my spade. These days, they didn't go in for getting their own hands dirty, opting instead for remote project management, whereas I had discovered I still needed the closer connection to nature, the daily dose of green things growing, to keep my mind balanced.

They had never forgiven Eloise for offering me the opportunity to go, quite literally, back to my roots, after I had broken off my engagement. It didn't matter how many times I told them she had nothing to do with my decision not to marry, they wouldn't believe me. To their minds, it was all too much of a coincidence and I had long since given up trying to convince them otherwise.

'I daresay you're having to go all out to keep things pristine now, aren't you?' Mum carried on, surprising me further by sounding almost sympathetic. 'Well, as pristine as one person can in grounds of that size.'

That was more like it.

'Jackson won't want anything out of place when he starts showing prospective buyers around, will he?'

Clearly, word about the sale had already reached her. I shouldn't have been surprised, she and Dad had contacts everywhere when it came to property sales which included more than a few acres. They were always on the lookout for the next potential project and clients with pockets deep enough to turn their visions into reality, so they were bound to find out sooner rather than later. Definitely sooner, in this case.

'I can't deny,' Mum wistfully carried on, 'that I had been wondering if, thrown together in grief, you and Jackson might have formed some sort of an alliance.'

I didn't waste my breath telling her that Jackson hadn't been grieving, but I was keen to cut her off because the thought of forming any sort of alliance with him made me feel quite bilious.

'When did you find out he's selling up?' I asked.

'I heard a rumour a couple of weeks ago,' she told me. 'And your father and I have been waiting for you to call ever since.'

'Why?' I shot back. 'I wouldn't have rung to tell you, even if I had known, you know gossiping isn't my style.'

'I wasn't suggesting that,' she tutted, sounding snippy.

'Why then?'

'For you to ask if you can come home, of course. I also heard that Jackson's already moved you out of that poky little cottage, so he can make a bit of money out of it, hasn't he? So, I'm guessing your services are going to be surplus to requirements soon too. He's bound to contract your job out. Where has he put you? In the stable block?'

It never ceased to amaze me what she could find out. I bet she'd somehow picked this titbit up via the cleaning agency Jackson had employed.

'There's no way he'll contract out,' I told her. 'He wouldn't want the expense and, for all you know,' I added, more for the sake of my dignity than anything else, 'whoever buys the place might want to keep me on. And I'm not in the stable block, I have rooms in the house.'

'Even if they did want to keep you,' Mum pointed out with annoying accuracy, 'I can't imagine you'd want to work there for someone else, would you? What if they wanted to change things? Goodness knows, the place could do with an overhaul, but I can't imagine you'd want to be involved with it, would you, Freya?'

Seeing Jackson sitting at Eloise's desk in the morning room was difficult enough, the thought of someone else instructing me to make changes in the garden was unbearable. Even if they did love the place, like Eloise had, they were bound to want to put their own mark on it, weren't they?

'Of course, I wouldn't,' I sighed, feeling the fight leave me. 'I'd hate that.'

For a moment, I'd forgotten all about my potential fresh challenge and possible new home. Thank goodness I had such exciting prospects and, should I be brave enough to accept them, I wouldn't have to wait to find out what was going to happen to the estate once Jackson had banked his fortune and headed back to the States. In fact, according to my informal contract with Eloise, the one he was so keen to keep waving in front of me, I wouldn't officially be obliged to wait barely any time at all before leaving.

'Well, there you are then,' Mum said smugly. 'You'll have to come home, won't you?'

She sounded a little too happy that my time at Broad-Meadows was coming to an end, but I wasn't in any way tempted to tell her about what I might be doing next. I wouldn't be telling anyone until I had given it more thought and shared my answer, whatever that might be, with Luke and Kate.

'And when you do,' she carried on, 'you'll soon find out that your dad and I have just the thing to get you back on track.'

I wasn't aware I'd fallen off it.

'We've got a project currently taking shape in Wellington that you can work on,' she told me. 'It's going to be an eighteen-month contract.'

'At least,' I heard Dad say in the background.

'At least,' Mum reiterated, in case I hadn't heard him.

'Wellington,' I repeated.

'Yes,' she said. 'You know, the capital of New Zealand.'

Of course, I knew where Wellington was. It was only a week or so ago that I had been video-calling my ex who had relocated there.

Peter's family firm was in the same industry as mine and we had met through a work project. I knew full well that our mutual business interests were one of the reasons why my parents had been so keen for us to get married. I think they rather fancied a future merger that mingled more than blood.

I got the impression that now Mum knew Jackson was a no-go, she was hoping I might consider reforming my *alliance* with Peter. If that was the track she was hoping to shove me back on, then she was going to be in for a shock. We might have managed to stay friends, but there were no romantic feelings between us whatsoever.

'Well,' I said, fiddling with my hair and deciding now was not the time to set her straight, 'I'll certainly think about it.'

'Yes do,' she said, sounding pleased. 'A fresh start away from Suffolk is just what you need.'

She was right of course, but I was considering crossing the county line, rather than travelling halfway around the world.

'Come on,' I said to Nell, once I'd finally got Mum to hang up and fired off a text to Peter warning him to look out for any hints of rekindled romance that my parents might be about to start sending his way. 'Let's go and talk to Eloise.'

It was too soggy underfoot to sit in my usual spot next to Eloise's head, so Nell and I made use of the nearest bench instead.

'Thank you for the sign, Eloise,' I said aloud, grateful that there was no one else about to hear.

The morning service had finished and everyone had no doubt rushed off to tend to their Sunday roasts.

'As I'm sure you know, it's led me and Nell to somewhere really rather special.' I imagined my old friend smiling and nodding. 'And as wonderful as it is, and as excited as I am to even have the chance to be thinking about taking it on, I am still very sorry about Jackson and his decision to sell up. I know how keen you were to keep the estate in the family. My only hope now is that the next owner will love the place just as much as you did, Eloise.'

I let my thoughts drift, mulling over what Mum had said, and listened to the soft susurration of the trees, enjoying the feel of the gentle breeze stirring my hair as I turned my face to the sun.

'And that's exactly why,' I eventually carried on, having come a little closer to making my decision, 'I won't be offering to stay on when Jackson makes his sale. The new owners are bound to want to make changes,' I swallowed, 'and even if they do end up being wonderful, I don't want to be in any way responsible for them.'

The fact that the sign I had asked her for had been sent was evidence enough that Eloise did understand, and I couldn't help thinking that the tone of my little monologue made it sound very much like I had found my courage, set aside Jackson's attempts to knock me down and decided what I was going to do.

It felt as if a great weight had been lifted from my shoulders as I took a deep breath and walked back to the van.

'Luke, hi,' I swallowed, 'it's Freya.'

I had planned to make the call when I got back to the house, but having made up my mind, I couldn't wait a second longer so rang him from where I'd parked at the church.

'Freya,' he said, 'hello. We weren't expecting you to ring so soon. Kate's here. I'm going to put you on speakerphone. Hold on.'

'Hey, Freya,' said Kate. 'How are you?'

'I'm good,' I said, nodding even though she couldn't see me. 'Great actually. I'm not interrupting your lunch or anything, am I?'

I could hear the girls in the background.

'No,' said Kate, 'we're eating later.'

'Okay,' I said, 'great. I'll probably do the same myself today.'

There was a beat of silence and then Luke spoke. 'Look you two,' he said, sounding flustered, 'as lovely as this small talk is, can we please just cut to the chase?'

I couldn't help but laugh and Kate did too.

'Sorry,' I said.

'We are actually on tenterhooks here,' Kate said, and I could tell she was smiling. 'Luke's even got his fingers crossed.'

'Really?' I laughed again.

'Really.'

'So,' he said, 'are you ringing with good news or bad?'

'Good,' I said, deciding to put him out of his misery. 'Well,' I added, 'good for me and I hope good for you.'

I quickly batted away the fear that I might not be good enough, which was still determined to rear its ugly head.

'You're coming?' Luke questioned.

'I'm coming,' I said firmly. 'I'd like to take you up on your offer of a job and a home in Nightingale Square.'

Luke let out a very loud cheer, which started Abigail, at least I think it was Abigail, crying.

'Oh, that's wonderful Freya,' said Kate. 'Fantastic news.'

It really was, so why I found myself on the verge of tears, I had no idea.

'And were you happy with everything in the email?' she asked as Luke made soothing noises in the background. 'The salary, terms and so on.'

'Yes,' I said, 'more than happy, which is more than my current employer will be when I tell him that I'm leaving.'

I had told Kate a little more about my time working with Eloise and how it contrasted with working for Jackson.

'Don't worry,' said Luke. 'We won't be expecting a reference. Your experience speaks for itself.'

'Along with your gut instinct,' I reminded him, brushing away a happy tear and sitting up straighter knowing that he was right; I was up to the task.

'Exactly,' he laughed. 'So, when can you come?'

'Well,' I said, mentally flicking through dates, 'as long as we can get all the paperwork sorted and Harold is happily settled in his new place, I can come at the end of the month. I only have to give a week's notice for every year I've worked at Broad-Meadows, so that's three weeks in total.'

'That's Hallowe'en weekend,' said Kate, shuffling papers. 'We can get everything drawn up and signed by then and

Harold is moving next weekend, so that will give me time to sort the house out a bit.'

'Oh, please don't worry about that, Kate,' I insisted. 'Everything there looked fine to me.'

'Perhaps I'll just fling the hoover about a bit,' she said.

'I can't tell you how pleased we are, Freya,' said Luke.

I really couldn't believe this was happening. These wonderful people had landed in my life and solved my employment and housing problems in one fell swoop!

'I won't let you down,' I told them both, my tears gathering apace. 'The Winter Garden is going to be wonderful.'

I could hear Abigail cranking up the volume again and felt as if I might be about to match her.

'I really don't doubt it,' said Kate, raising her voice above the din, 'and I can't wait to see it. I'll email you with more details about everything later today, okay?'

'All right,' I said, 'and thank you.'

'Bye for now,' they said together.

'Bye,' I said, 'see you at the end of the month.'

'See you on the thirty-first.'

I ended the call and had a bit of a sob before driving back to Broad-Meadows. Nell rested her head on my lap and I wondered what I was going to do about her now I had made up my mind to move.

Back at the house I tried to creep up to my room, but my plan was thwarted as Jackson was in the kitchen and insisted that I join him for lunch. He made it sound like a pleasant invitation to socialise, even including Nell in the party, but

I was on my guard, which was just as well, because he had barely finished carving the joint of beef – badly – before I realised that this was very definitely a working lunch and the thrilling thoughts I wanted to indulge in about my new job and home were going to have to wait.

'I think that should be enough to be going on with,' Jackson smiled, once he had finished reeling off a list of tasks for the following week, very few of which had anything to do with the role that I had been employed for.

'I should say so,' I said, puffing out my cheeks. 'I only hope you can find someone at such short notice to undertake them. I've more than enough to keep me occupied in the garden and of course, you let the housekeeper go, didn't you?'

Jane Taylor had worked for Eloise for decades but Jackson had dismissed her within days of his arrival. He had reckoned, long before he had got the measure of the place and the work involved in looking after it, that it didn't require live-in domestic staff. The agency he had since employed to clean, and who I suspected of gossiping, were slapdash to say the least.

'I'll be expecting you to muck in, Freya,' he told me, with a challenging look in his eye. 'You're living here now too, after all.'

I bit my lip, determined not to tell him yet.

'In lieu of charging you rent, I need you to help out in the house.'

What he really meant was, do most of the work that Jane used to do.

'And you'll have to go,' he said, looking at Nell and addressing her in a completely different tone to the one he had only minutes before welcomed her with. 'I can't be doing with you cluttering up the place. Can you remember which rescue home she came from, Freya? With any luck they might take her back.'

That was it. I threw down my napkin and pushed back my chair. My determination not to share my news had flown straight out of the window.

'Don't worry about Nell,' I told him. 'I'll be taking her with me.'

'Taking her with you?' he frowned. 'What do you mean? Where are you going?'

'I'm handing in my notice, Jackson,' I said. 'I was going to tell you tomorrow when I'd had a chance to write my letter of resignation, but your abhorrent attitude has forced my hand.'

He opened and closed his mouth a couple of times, turning redder by the second.

'But you can't leave,' he blustered. 'I need you here to look after the garden. I'm going to have prospective buyers coming around in a few weeks' time and the lawns will still be growing.'

'Not my problem,' I shrugged.

'You can't have another job lined up,' he said, eyeing me with an expression of annoyance and curiosity, 'you haven't had time and I haven't been asked for a reference.'

'Where I'm going and what I'm going to be doing is no concern of yours,' I told him, 'and you needn't panic, I'm not leaving with immediate effect.'

'Of course, you aren't,' he said, sounding further nettled, 'you can't because you've got to work notice.'

'That's right,' I agreed.

'That's right,' he repeated.

'Three weeks,' I smiled.

'Three weeks,' he choked. 'That can't possibly be right!'

'One week for every year that I've worked here,' I reeled off. 'That's what your aunt and I agreed and that's what I'll honour. It's all in my contract – not that, as you're so keen to keep reminding me, it's legally binding.'

I was certain I would be getting something far more formal from Luke and Kate and, given what had happened here, I was pleased about that. I supposed I had been a bit naïve when I moved to the estate, but then neither Eloise nor I had ever envisaged a situation like this occurring when she took me on.

'I'm going to check that,' Jackson said bitterly. 'I'm going to check that, right now.'

He jumped up from his chair and stormed out of the kitchen.

'And get that damn dog out of here!' he shouted over his shoulder.

'Gladly!' I shouted back, rushing to give Nell a hug.

Chapter 5

Even though I knew in my heart that I had Eloise's blessing to leave Broad-Meadows and embrace the new challenge of living in Nightingale Square and working in the gardens at Prosperous Place, I did wonder how I was going feel when the time came to finally hand over my keys.

I had learned so much about myself during the last three years and I loved the garden like an old friend. It had offered me solace on darker days and a quiet, gentle support that I wasn't sure I'd find anywhere else, and certainly not in the bustling city. However, I needn't have worried about how I was going to cope with all the extra company, because for almost every second after I had told Jackson that I was leaving he had been just half a step behind me, watching my every move and clocking me in and out of every task.

Whether he was concerned about getting his wages' worth, or that I might leg it with the family silver (not that there was any to speak of), I had no idea and I certainly wasn't going to give him the satisfaction of asking, but I did find his shadowing unnecessarily invasive and when the day to leave did finally dawn, shrouded in an autumn mist which stole my last view of the place, I was feeling more than ready to go.

'Come on, Nell,' I said, opening the van door and ushering her into the passenger footwell as another vehicle spookily appeared out of the mist, 'it's time to leave.'

There was no room for her in the back, not that she liked riding behind me. She had always preferred shotgun but the plethora of boxes containing our worldly goods and few bits of furniture meant that she had no choice but to curl up under the dash for this ride to Norwich.

Amongst my scant belongings, I had also added a collection of cuttings, garnered from Eloise's favourite plants. We had taken them together before planting out their parents in the revamped borders as a sort of back-up and gap filler, and now they were coming with me to Nightingale Square to be nurtured and help fill the Broad-Meadows-shaped hole in my heart.

'We'll see if we can stop and have a stretch when we're halfway there,' I told Nell as she curled her lithe limbs around her and I gently closed the door. 'Not that it's all that far, but we don't want you getting cramp, do we?'

The other vehicle, a van I unfortunately recognised, drew to a stop beside me, and Jackson raced down the front steps from the house, a look of victory lighting up his smugly arranged features. He had obviously been poised to pounce, hiding in the hallway and biding his time to inflict maximum impact.

'Just a minute, Freya,' he barked at me.

'Hello, Peggy,' I said to the stout woman who had climbed out of the van wearing work boots and a muddy waxed coat, while I ignored my almost-former employee. 'What can I do for you?'

'She's here to do something for me actually,' said Jackson. 'Now, where's that damn dog got to?'

'It's a sad business this, Freya,' said Peggy, the manager of the rescue centre where Eloise had plucked Nell from. 'I don't know how the poor old girl will cope with going back into kennels. She hated it last time and now she's grieving too.'

'You aren't serious?' I said to Jackson.

'Well, I don't want her,' he said nastily. 'I haven't got time to look after a dog. Peggy and I have discussed it and this is the only solution. Isn't that right, Peggy?'

'I'm afraid so,' she sighed, looking every bit as miserable as Nell would if she caught sight of her former gaoler.

Peggy was a wonderful woman with a heart of gold, but as far as Nell was concerned, she meant other dogs noisily barking, a concrete kennel and a lengthy, possibly infinite, wait. No fireside, no treats, no home comforts and limited walks.

'We have to do what's right for Nell,' said Peggy, opening up the back of the van to reveal a large metal crate. 'And if Jackson says he can't manage her—'

'But I told him—' I interrupted, shooting Jackson a look.

'And now you're leaving too,' Peggy carried sadly on, 'the poor love won't know what's hit her.'

'Which is exactly why,' I said, raising my voice, 'I told Jackson that I was taking her with me!'

In the days following my resignation announcement, I had made it more than plain, on more than one occasion, that even though he didn't want her, I did.

'What?' said Peggy, stopping in her tracks.

'Nell is coming with me,' I reiterated.

'No, she's not,' said Jackson, turning red, 'because she's not yours to take, is she? She belonged to Aunt Eloise and therefore, like everything else here now, she belongs to me.'

'But you don't want her,' I said angrily.

'Which is why, I'm getting rid of her,' he shot back. 'My dog, my decision.'

Peggy slammed the van door closed again, making us jump, before adjusting the belt on her coat and drawing herself up to her full height which wasn't far off six foot. Jackson shrank in response, and were the situation not so dire, I might have laughed at his cowed reaction.

'You're taking Nell with you?' Peggy asked me.

'Yes,' I said, 'there's no question of that. I would never have left her here with him.'

'You should have told me, Freya,' she said. 'As Nell came from the centre, I should have been informed of any change in her place of residence or ownership.'

I hadn't thought of that. I had foolishly assumed that Jackson would be relieved to have one less thing to deal with when I had told him what I was planning to do, but apparently not. It turned out that he wanted to make as much drama out of the situation as possible.

'Exactly,' said Jackson petulantly. 'But don't worry, Peggy, because there hasn't been a change of ownership. The mutt's still mine. Unfortunately.'

'Where exactly are you taking her?' Peggy asked me, holding up a hand to quieten Jackson again.

I looked at him as he craned forward to hear what I was going to say and bit my lip. Thanks to Luke and Kate's willingness to forgo a reference I had managed to keep my new abode and place of work a mystery and that's how I wanted it to stay. I hadn't even furnished my parents or Peter with the finer details. They knew I had a job in Norfolk, but not exactly where. I wanted time to settle before I filled them in.

I beckoned Peggy to follow me until we were out of earshot and then in hushed tones explained the situation, asking her not to pass the information on, especially to Jackson.

'I see,' she said, marching back around to where Jackson was standing.

I quickly followed, hoping she was satisfied that I had told her enough to keep Nell out of the metal crate.

'Have you any idea how busy I am, Jackson?' she angrily asked. 'Have you even the slightest inkling how hard it is to feed, clean up after and arrange a schedule of walks for seventeen dogs with just three volunteers?'

'There's no need to take that tone,' he pouted, sounding hurt, but Peggy was in full flight.

'You have called me out here this morning on false pretences,' she stormed on. 'You knew that Freya here – who, by all intents and purposes, has been Nell's sole care-giver since your aunt's death – was willing to take the dog on full-time, and yet rather than simply ring to explain what was happening and request a transfer of ownership you insisted I came in person – and not with Nell's best interests at heart, but because you wanted to make mischief.'

Jackson looked astounded and then angry, but not particularly contrite.

'You should be ashamed of yourself,' she scolded.

'Now look here . . .' Jackson scowled.

'Why don't you get off, Freya,' she then said, turning to me and smiling. 'Before that poor creature catches on that I'm here and goes into a decline, and I'll take Jackson here,' she added, marching him back up his own steps, 'into the house to discuss the donation he wants to make by way of apology for wasting my precious time.'

There was no opportunity to say goodbye but the look on Jackson's face was enough to make my departure from my old life less maudlin and more amusing and I set off down the drive with laughter on my lips and feeling surprisingly light of heart.

It was only an hour's drive to Nightingale Square, but as promised I stopped en route to let Nell stretch her legs while I checked my phone. There was a message from Kate telling me to go straight to my house because she and Luke were having to make an unexpected trip into the city. She also explained that she'd left my key in the safe which Harold had had fitted inside the little brick porch. She had already sent me the code in one of the many emails we had exchanged and I couldn't help thinking that it would be nice to see the place for myself and settle in, in peace.

I was just climbing back behind the wheel when my phone vibrated again. It was another message, this time from Luke, telling me not to start unloading boxes on my own because they would be along later to help. Having already managed to pack everything on my own, and carry it down four flights of stairs, I was certain I could cope with the straight run up the garden path, but it was nice that he had thought to offer. As I turned the key and set off again I already knew that I was much going to prefer having considerate Luke rather than suspicious Jackson as my boss.

'Here we are then,' I said to Nell, pulling on the handbrake and turning off the ignition once I had driven around the square and parked up outside the house. 'Home sweet home.'

The square looked a little different to the last time I had seen it. There were far fewer leaves on the trees for a start and every house was adorned with at least a pumpkin or two. I had forgotten it was Hallowe'en.

I was grappling with the key safe when I heard someone clear their throat behind me.

'You must be Freya?' asked a man's voice.

'That's right,' I said, twisting round.

'I'm John. I live next door with my wife, Lisa, and our little brood.'

'Pleased to meet you, John,' I said, abandoning the safe for a moment and turning to look at him properly.

He was a big, solid bloke with a smile as broad as his

shoulders and he looked as friendly as they come. The black and red checked shirt he wore made him look like a lumber-jack and the size of his hands suggested he would have been useful in the role.

'These things can be a bit tricky,' he said, reaching around me and lining up the numbers in double time and with sur-prisingly nimble fingers. 'There you go.'

The little door dropped down and there, as Kate had promised, was the key.

'We'll come over in a bit,' he said, with a nod to the van, 'and give you a hand to unload.'

'That's very kind of you,' I told him, 'but there's really no need. I haven't got all that much.'

'It's no bother,' he insisted. 'We'll make short work of it, and save you the bad back.'

I went to let Nell out of the van and it was only then that I realised that he had said 'we'. I wondered who the 'we' would be. If I wanted to settle in, in peace, then I had better be quick about it.

With my heart hammering in my chest, I turned the key in the lock and pushed open the door. The layout was exactly as I remembered it, with the stairs ahead and the sitting room to the right with the dining room and kitchen behind it, but there were a few gaps on the walls now and the shelves were mostly empty.

With the absence of some furniture, the rooms felt bigger too. Not empty though, just big. There were bunches of fresh flowers and foliage in vases in every room and a 'welcome to your new home' card from the Lonsdale family propped up against the kettle in the kitchen and another from Harold, with a note explaining about the noise the hot water pipes made. There was even a bowl of water already set out for Nell and, after flicking on the kettle, I discovered not only milk in the fridge, but eggs, bread, ham, a cold cooked chicken and some leafy salad – no doubt from the Grow-Well – too.

'My goodness, Nell,' I said happily. 'I think we've fallen on our feet here, don't you?'

She thumped her tail in response as she drank her fill before wandering back into the sitting room and curling up in front of the fire, even though it wasn't turned on.

I took my tea upstairs and checked out the rest of the rooms. Everything was sparkling and fresh and there was a welcoming scent of lavender as I sat down on the bed. Clearly, Kate hadn't been able to resist giving the place an autumn clean after Harold had moved out. Not that there had been anything amiss with his housekeeping skills, but she obviously wanted to make the house feel a little different and I was grateful that she had gone to so much trouble to make me feel welcome. There were just enough gaps and vacant spaces for me to add my own things and then the place really would feel like home.

I banished thoughts of the cottage I had left behind, and the cramped rooms I had more recently been holed up in and went back downstairs to think about where I was going to put everything. I had barely started when Nell began to bark and someone rang the doorbell.

'Welcome to Nightingale Square,' beamed Kate, holding out a bag for me to take once I had opened the door.

'Come in,' I smiled back, 'and thank you. What's all this?'

I led the way down to the kitchen and turned the kettle on again before peering into the bag.

'Sweets,' I said, looking at her again. 'Thank you.'

'They're not for you,' she laughed. 'It's Hallowe'en. They're for the trick or treaters. Jasmine's helping Luke to carve a pumpkin for you. They'll bring it over in a bit.'

'That's great,' I told her. 'Thank you so much.'

I couldn't remember the last time I'd been actively involved in the spooky goings-on at Hallowe'en. Broad-Meadows was too isolated to attract door-to-door visitors.

'And thank you for making the house so welcoming,' I added. 'I've just finished looking around and everything is wonderful.'

'It's my pleasure,' Kate told me, 'and I'm so excited that you've moved in today of all days.'

'Why is that?'

'Because I moved into the square on Hallowe'en too,' she told me, 'and Lisa from next door gave me *exactly* the same welcome gift,' she added with a nod to the bags. 'My life has been completely transformed since I came here, Freya, and I've got the feeling yours is going to be too. I'm not suggesting it's going to be all plain sailing, but we're a great community here and everyone looks out for each other.'

Right on cue, and as if to prove her point, the doorbell

went again. I shut Nell in the kitchen, in case she was beginning to feel a little overwhelmed. I knew I was.

'Shall we get cracking then?' John beamed, rubbing his hands together. 'And get this stuff into the house?'

He wasn't alone this time. Graham and Carole had been drawn in as reinforcements and I could see Luke crossing the square carrying a very impressive, if slightly wonkily carved, pumpkin, with the two girls in tow. Kate came to stand behind me and I got the feeling that telling them I'd rather manage on my own would either offend them or be ignored and actually, seeing the kind look on all their faces, I found I didn't want to manage on my own. For now, at least, I'd had enough of flying solo to last me a lifetime.

'All right,' I said, tossing John the keys to the van, 'let's make a start.'

Chapter 6

I didn't manage to either set foot in the garden, or do a scrap of work during my first two days living in Norwich. Having ferried my things from the van to the house, Luke and Kate then insisted, with the others backing them up, that I should take time to settle in, find my feet and take stock of the changes happening in mine and Nell's lives.

Although keen to forge ahead, I had to admit I was both physically and mentally exhausted by the end of the day. Having unpacked my things in the house, lined up the cuttings in the back porch which was tacked onto the kitchen, and then spent ages handing out the sweets to the trick or treaters, when I climbed into bed I swiftly fell into a lavender-scented long and dreamless sleep. I had no idea whether or not the water pipes made any of the noises Harold had suggested, because I was well and truly out for the count.

Waking late, I followed everyone's advice and set Sunday aside for pottering about, and much of Monday was commandeered by Kate as 'orientation day'. By the end of it, we had sorted out utilities and other bills and then walked for what felt like miles.

By teatime I was registered with the nearest doctor's surgery, Nell was acquainted with the vets and I knew where Blossom's the bakers and Greengage's the grocers were located as well as the pub, fittingly for Norwich, called The Dragon, and a couple of other interesting-looking shops, including a second-hand bookshop and a vintage emporium.

'I'm sorry we haven't had time to explore further,' Kate said as we arrived puffing and rosy-cheeked back in the square, 'but at least now you've got the gist of what's closest.'

'I have,' I told her, 'and very lovely it all looks too. It's going to be a novelty being able to walk to the shops for milk and freshly baked bread. At Broad-Meadows I had to drive everywhere.'

'So, you're happy?' she asked.

'Ever so,' I honestly told her.

I was still happy the next morning when my alarm went off, but I was a bit jittery too. I hadn't felt first-day nerves when I started work for Eloise, but I had them by the time I slipped my feet into my wellies and crossed the square to Prosperous Place. It felt like there was so much more at stake here, what with the Winter Garden to plan and plant, but that was exciting as well as scary.

'You got in all right then?' called a voice from an upstairs window as I walked around the side of the house.

I looked up and found Luke leaning out of it.

'You scared me half to death,' I called back, my hand on my chest.

'Sorry,' he grinned.

'Yes,' I told him. 'I disarmed the alarm and reset it when I closed the gate.'

'Great,' he said, 'then you shouldn't have any problems opening up the sheds and office. I'll come out and find you later.'

'There's no rush,' I insisted. 'I'm looking forward to having a proper look around on my own for a bit, if that's all right?'

He gave me a thumbs up and disappeared back inside, and Nell and I carried on.

The sheds Luke referred to weren't sheds in the wooden garden storage sense, but a sturdily built brick collection of what had possibly once been stables or garages. Two were set aside for the garden. The largest stored the bulkiest equipment – an ancient ride-on mower, chainsaw, hedge cutter and the like – while the smaller one was reserved for a comprehensive selection of hand tools, buckets, pots, labels, etc with the end being given over to what Luke called the office. Basically, an old table, a couple of chairs, a grubby kettle, a pile of invoices and a stack of gardening magazines.

I spent the first couple of hours inspecting everything, checking service dates on the machinery and generally acquainting myself with what I had to work with. Everything looked to be in good order, aside from the ride-on, but the hand tools, which were wonderfully old, could have done with a good scrub and sharpen as well as a coating of linseed oil to protect the wooden handles. I noted that down as a wet-weather task. There were always things to do when managing a garden, even during inclement weather.

By the time I had finished going through everything, Nell was getting restless.

'Come on then,' I said, pulling my coat back on, 'let's go and see what the garden has to offer, shall we?'

In much the same way as I had worked through the tools and equipment, I made notes on every aspect of the garden, prioritising those areas which needed the most work and marking out, on a rough hand-drawn design, points of interest which we could highlight when the garden was open in the winter. There was already a lot that we could utilise and some obvious spots where we could further and easily enhance what was already planted.

The only thing missing was a functioning greenhouse. The original ones were little more than shells, their wooden frames rotting and empty. Broad-Meadows had heated space in abundance and I knew I was going to have to broach the lack of it here with Luke at some point. A garden of this size really needed a glasshouse, even if only a small one.

'Here you are,' said Luke, when he later caught up with me in the fern garden. 'We thought you'd come to the house for your tea-break, but there was no sign of you.'

'Crikey,' I said, straightening up from the crouched position I'd been in, trying to read a faded plant label, 'is it that time already?'

'Not tea-break time,' Luke laughed. 'You missed that completely. It's almost twelve now.'

'Is it really?' I gasped, amazed that the morning had run away with me and I hadn't realised.

'Yes,' he said, 'and Chloe, our trusty volunteer, is going to be here any minute. She's looking forward to meeting you.'

I was looking forward to meeting her too. I hoped she was, at the very least, willing and able because I had plenty lined up for her to do. My list-making was supposed to make me feel more organised and help settle my nerves, but it was getting so long, I was starting to wonder if just the two of us would be able to tick even half the things off in the time we had to get the garden ready to open.

Chloe turned out to be about my age, with a healthy can-do attitude and closely cropped auburn hair. She arrived by bicycle, with a bag from Blossom's tucked in the basket and a warm and welcoming smile lighting up her striking amber-coloured eyes.

'Oh, look at your gorgeous hair!' was the first thing she said to me as I pulled my heavy plait over my shoulder for reassurance. 'Kate told me it was long, but I thought she was exaggerating. Sorry,' she then apologised, shaking her head as she climbed off the bike and thrust the bag from Blossom's into Luke's arms. 'Rolls for lunch,' she told him before turning back to me. 'Let me introduce myself properly, I'm Chloe.'

She was shorter than she had looked when she was sat

on the bike, but no less full of enthusiasm. She was exactly what the garden, and I, needed. I was surprised Luke hadn't been making better use of her, what I could already tell was, boundless energy.

'And I'm Freya,' I smiled back.

'Of course, you are,' she grinned, 'with your pretty blue eyes and Rapunzel tresses you couldn't possibly be anyone else. And this is lovely Nell.'

Nell was doing her best to stay hidden behind my legs. I reached behind me and patted her head.

'It is,' I told Chloe. 'I'm afraid she's a bit shy.'

Chloe nodded. 'I can sympathise,' she said, looking at the little she could see of Nell's head, 'I'm a bit that way myself.'

Luke rolled his eyes and led us into the house while I tried to work out if she was being serious and braced myself for the first of many unusual working lunches.

As the three of us (Kate was away for the day), ate our way through the soft filled rolls, and then some delicious cakes, I, at Luke's request, talked them through the notes I had made so far.

For the most part, he and Chloe sat and listened, encouragingly nodding along, with the occasional '*I told you we should have been doing that,*' thrown in from the eager volunteer.

'So, Chloe,' I said, once I had finally finished and the clock on the wall was telling me we had talked way beyond the thirty minutes I usually allotted myself for lunch, 'can you remind me how many days a week you're here?'

'Just two,' she said. 'All day Tuesday and Thursday. I missed this morning because I had an appointment, but as a rule I'm here from eight until four.'

There was plenty we would be able to get done in that time and I felt my shoulders relax a little.

'And if push came to shove,' she went on, 'I'd be happy to give up the occasional weekend.'

'That's very kind of you,' I said, thinking that I would definitely be taking her up on the offer ahead of the Winter Garden opening and wondering if any of the Grow-Well team could spare a few hours too.

I knew that Luke had said he didn't like to ask them, but if it did get tight for time, I was sure they would help, Graham especially. I was feeling much better now we had talked the tasks through. I might not have had the formal qualifications Jackson would have preferred, but I did have the skills and experience. I could do this. I would do it, and what was more, I would do it well.

'And is there anything you really enjoy doing in the garden and anything you absolutely hate?' I asked Chloe.

She shook her head. 'I'm happy doing anything,' she told me. 'I come here for the exercise and the fresh air. This place has worked wonders for my mental health, so I'm happy to undertake whatever task you assign me.'

Just as I thought, Chloe really did have a great can-do attitude.

'I work as a teaching assistant at the local primary school the other three days of the week,' she elaborated, 'so you might even be able to talk me into some extra hours during the holidays.'

I noticed she was wearing a wedding band.

'And I can see you're married,' I said with a nod to her left hand. 'Do you have any kids of your own?'

Luke started gathering the dishes together and I felt my face go red. The older I got, the more often I had found myself being asked the same thing. Given how much I resented the sympathetic looks I received when I said no, I didn't have any children, I felt awful for letting my mouth run away with me and asking the same thing of Chloe, especially when I noticed the look on her face.

'No,' she said, with a suddenly less than convincing smile, 'no kids, and no husband actually. He died before we got around to it.'

I didn't know what to say but I wished Nell would start digging a hole in the floor for me to crawl into. That was the last time I was going to let my mouth overtake my brain.

'I'm so sorry,' I whispered.

She was far too young to be a widow.

'You've not been living in Norwich all that long, have you, Chloe?' said Luke, kindly coming to my rescue.

'No,' she said, 'what is it now? About eighteen months, I reckon. I moved here six months after Ade died. Completely against the advice of my mother, of course,' She tutted, sounding more like herself again. 'She wanted me to stay put. Same house, same town, same life, but I couldn't do it. I didn't want to do it. Once Ade had gone, I realised I had nothing of the same life left and so I decided to build myself a new one.'

'That was very brave,' I told her.

'My mother prefers to call it stupid,' she told me, thankfully sounding far happier again. 'She said I was making a mistake and that I'd regret it.'

'And have you?'

'Not yet,' she beamed.

'I can sympathise,' I said, 'on the opinionated parent front, I mean. My mum and dad have never been backwards in coming forwards when it comes to expressing their views about my life choices too.'

Mum had been completely thrown when I told her I had a new job in Norfolk and that I wouldn't be taking up her and Dad's offer of a fresh start with an old flame in New Zealand. She had wanted details, but I told her the same as Peter; I'd fill them in properly as soon as I was settled.

'That's something we have in common then,' Chloe laughed. 'Not all that long ago we would have had long hair in common too, but I cut mine off. I didn't do it myself,' she hastily added. 'I paid someone to cut it and I loved it straightaway but my mother thought I was having a breakdown. My Britney phase, she called it, and was all for staging an intervention.'

Chloe's mum sounded even more of a handful than mine.

'Anyway,' said Chloe, shaking her head, 'sorry. I didn't mean to overshare.'

'You haven't,' Luke and I said together.

'I think you two are going to get along very well,' he carried on.

'So do I,' Chloe and I then piped up in unison, and we all laughed.

Once Luke had loaded the dishwasher, we walked around the garden together and I assigned the pair a number of jobs to be getting on with straightaway. I also offered a list of prospective plants, bulbs and shrubs for Luke to consider buying, which he eagerly embraced. Given how mild the weather still was, should anything I'd suggested take his fancy, there was still time to get it planted.

'And these three silver birch trees,' I pointed out as we wove our way back towards the office, 'they'd look even better if they had a wash and brush up.'

'What?' frowned Luke, looking up into the branches.

'Are you being serious?' Chloe laughed.

'Yes,' I said, 'look at the bark. It's such a beautiful colour and it would look even better if it was clean. The National Trust and RHS gardens are all doing it now,' I added. 'Google it tonight and you'll see what I mean. If you fancy it, you could even illuminate them in different coloured lights once they've been cleaned up a bit.'

Luke nodded and I got the feeling that I would find him out early the next morning with the power washer.

'Warm water and a nice soft brush will do the trick,' I told him, just in case he was really considering giving them a blast.

With our schedule of work for the next couple of weeks

agreed, Luke headed off to collect Abigail from Carole and then Jasmine from school, leaving me with Chloe.

'I'm sorry I asked if you had any children, Chloe,' I said to her, because it had been bugging me all afternoon. 'I hate it when people ask me and I'm sorry if I upset you. I don't know why I did it.'

'It's the ring,' she said, holding up her hand. 'It was a logical assumption.'

'Even so,' I apologised, 'I am sorry.'

'I keep telling myself it's time to take it off,' she said, staring down at it. 'Because it's not as if I haven't come to terms with it all. It's not as if I'm stuck in the past or anything, I'm living a completely different life here and a happy one at that, but I just can't bring myself to take it off.'

'Then there's absolutely no reason why you should,' I said firmly.

'You know what,' she said, linking her arm through mine, 'Luke was right, you and I are going to get along, Freya.'

I felt the same way too. My own new life was going to be very different to the one I was used to, but it was going to be fun working with other people for a change, and I was about to say as much, but was distracted by a sudden blast of music in the courtyard.

'What on earth's that?' I frowned.

I hadn't thought I'd seen a radio in the office, so I was certain I hadn't left one playing but the sound definitely wasn't coming from the house. It was too far away, even if the volume had been cranked right up.

'It's coming from over there,' I said, setting off at a pace with Nell still shadowing me as she had been all afternoon. 'You don't think someone's broken in, do you?'

'What, and alerted everyone within a ten-mile radius by blasting them with music?' laughed Chloe, rushing to catch me up.

She had a point.

'It'll be the artist guy in the studio,' she told me.

'What studio?' I frowned, coming to a stop.

I couldn't remember seeing an artist's studio.

'It's in the space next to the machinery store, and it's not what you'd generally think of when describing an artist's studio. It's much more rough and ready.'

I was intrigued. 'Let's go and have a look,' I said, setting off again.

'Best not,' said Chloe, catching my sleeve.

'Why not?'

'I've been warned that he's not all that keen on being disturbed,' she told me, making me feel even more curious. 'You'll meet him soon enough because he's moving in too.'

'Is he?'

'Yes, he's converted the space above into a little flat. It's a bit basic, but from what I've heard he was desperate. Luke thinks he's an absolute find.'

She had to raise her voice as the sound of a grinder rent the air making Nell whimper.

'What sort of an artist is he?' I asked, pulling Nell close.

'Some sort of sculptor I think,' Chloe frowned, 'I'm not

all that sure, to tell you the truth. I've never seen any of his stuff.'

We had reached the door now and could see the glass panels were lit up in a shower of sparks.

'Looks exciting though, doesn't it?' Chloe grinned, wide-eyed.

'Noisy,' I said back, covering Nell's ears.

If this guy was making the sculptures that Luke had suggested he wanted to display in the garden, then I would have bet good money that they weren't going to be common garden gnomes.

I knew I should have felt relieved about that, but listening to the combined racket of music and grinding metal, I didn't feel soothed at all.

Chapter 7

All was calm and quiet when I went back over to the garden early the following morning and I was soon so immersed in my work that I forgot all about the noisy artist and the fact that, according to Chloe at least, he was set to become another new neighbour.

'Morning,' she beamed, as she hopped off her bike early on the Thursday morning. 'How's it all going?'

'Good,' I told her, trying to stifle a yawn.

'Tiring?' she ventured.

'A bit,' I admitted. 'It's been a hectic few days.'

And if I was being honest, I had found some of it rather overwhelming. I was immensely grateful that Luke, Kate and Prosperous Place had landed in my life right when I needed them, but the move to the city, the late-night clanking of the water pipes and the general busyness made me miss Eloise and the tranquillity of Broad-Meadows. I knew it was early days, and that it would soon settle down, but it was challenging nonetheless.

'I found city life exhausting when I first arrived,' Chloe said reassuringly, 'and I hadn't taken on anything like you have here. Give yourself time,' she smiled, 'and be kind to yourself.'

'I'll try,' I promised.

'Good,' Chloe continued, happy to have said her piece. 'Now, where's my bucket and hoe? I've been chasing these weeds in my sleep!'

By the end of the day Chloe had emptied endless buckets. I surreptitiously watched her, deadheading nearby and doing a little light pruning as I worked through the herbaceous border a short distance away. I was relieved to note that, not only was she a hard worker, she also did the job properly. There was no pulling off of leaves and leaving the root behind in her haste to make things look better. The weeds were completely eradicated.

'I've been meaning to ask,' I called after her, just as she was making off with another load towards the end of the afternoon, 'what's the composting set-up like here? I haven't seen any bins.'

'We've got bays, rather than bins,' she told me, 'and they're behind the wall at the back of the Grow-Well.'

'That's something else I haven't seen.'

'What?' she gasped. 'Not any of it?'

'No,' I said, 'not yet. Luke and Kate haven't had a minute to show me and I haven't wanted to just venture over there on my own.'

'Come on,' said Chloe, looking at her watch. 'I'll take you

now. Everyone will be starting to gather to get ready for the bonfire party tonight.'

I'd forgotten all about that. There had been an invitation to the celebration which was taking place on the green, waiting for me on the doormat when Kate and I got back on Monday. As lovely as it was to be included, I wouldn't be going because I couldn't leave Nell. She was bound to quake when the fireworks were let off and I wasn't sure I was up to meeting everyone all in one go. That said, given what Chloe had just announced, I was about to be introduced to them en masse anyway.

'Don't look so worried,' she told me, waiting until I caught her up. 'Everyone's really lovely.'

The Grow-Well was amazing. There were productive, packed raised beds, a tidy bothy, a few hens in a large run, fruit trees trained around the walls, a small glasshouse and an area set aside for socialising which included a long table, vast barbecue and brick-built pizza oven. It all looked far better than I had been expecting and a stark contrast to certain other parts of the garden.

'This is incredible,' I said in awe, once Chloe had acquainted me with the clever composting system.

'Thank you,' glowed Graham, as he caught my words, 'and I've been meaning to come and find you to say that if you ever need an extra pair of hands in the rest of the garden, you know where I am.'

'There's every possibility that I might take you up on that offer,' I told him.

'Do,' he insisted. 'Luke doesn't want anyone to feel obliged to lend a hand but I'm more than willing.'

'Duly noted.' I nodded. 'I'm certain extra help will come in very handy the nearer we get to opening the garden.'

'Let me introduce you and Nell to everyone properly,' he then offered, making my heart race.

Nell was practically welded to my side. She had coped better than I had expected with the changes so far though and I hoped this extra new experience wouldn't be a step too far for her.

'Thanks, Graham,' I said, as I took in the many unfamiliar faces. I hoped it wouldn't be too much for me too.

Lisa, John's wife, was present along with their brood of three and Heather, who lived in the first house in the square, and who also had three children, was with her. We had just started to chat when Kate arrived, back from the school run with the girls, and we were soon joined by more of the men.

Ryan, at about nineteen, was the youngest of the guys and he lived with his sister, Poppy, in the house on the right of mine. That, I remembered, was the one that Kate owned.

'We were working the day you moved in,' Poppy smiled. 'Otherwise we would have come and joined the welcoming committee.'

'That's all right,' I swallowed, thankful that they hadn't been around to further swell the numbers.

'I daresay you had a houseful even without us, didn't you?' Ryan grinned.

'Something like that,' I smiled back.

Next there was Jacob, a teacher and also Poppy's partner. He lived in the house on Poppy's other side and finally Neil. He and his husband, Mark the baker, lived in the last house as you left the square which was next to Lisa and John.

'Right,' I blinked, struggling to fit the names and places to all the faces.

We were missing Heather's husband Glen, as well as John and Mark and Harold of course, who was still considered as much a part of the team as he had been when he lived there. Which was only proper given that he had been born and raised in the square and had more connection to the place than the rest of us put together.

'So,' said Carole, 'have you got the measure of who lives where now, Freya?'

'Not really,' I said, biting my lip.

'Heather and Glen in the first house,' she said, holding up her hands as if she was driving around the square's one-way system. 'Then me and Graham, Jacob in the third, Poppy and Ryan next, then you, then Lisa and John and finally Mark and Neil.'

'I see,' I nodded. 'That's kind of what I thought.'

Lisa started to laugh. 'Simple, right?'

I shook my head and pulled a confused face. By that point, it wasn't a difficult expression to muster.

'Don't worry,' Lisa giggled, 'you'll soon get the measure of it. We won't make you learn the kid's names today.'

'I already know Abigail and Jasmine.'

'Just six more to go then,' she nudged.

I knew she meant well, but it really was a lot to take in and, as welcoming as everyone was, I did still feel very much the new girl and rather a meek country mouse, now I was faced with my tightknit town cousins.

'Where's Nell?' I said, suddenly realising that I couldn't feel her warm body pressed to my leg. 'She was here a minute ago.'

'Don't worry,' said Chloe soothingly, 'she's with Doctor Dolittle over there.'

My eyes darted to where she was pointing and I realised that Ryan and Nell had separated from the group and moved, with another dog, a little further away.

'He's a whizz with animals,' said a girl standing next to me. She sounded utterly in awe, or was it love? I couldn't be sure. 'I'm Tam, by the way.'

'My eldest,' Lisa elaborated, 'and the other dog with Ryan is Gus. He actually belongs to Colin, who owns the bookshop, but Ryan's kind of adopted him. Gus, I mean, not Colin!'

I was amazed to see leggy Nell and the stocky little French Bulldog nose to nose. Nell, with her tail wagging, looked far more relaxed than I felt. Clearly, I wasn't the only one making friends today, but I got the impression that she was taking it in her stride whereas I was still a bit nervous. For the first time ever, I envied her a little.

'Are you coming to the party tonight, Freya?' asked Heather, as she wrestled to clip one of her children into a double buggy.

'Now then,' said Lisa sternly, giving her friend a hand as I looked between the two boys and realised that Heather had twins. 'Stop messing about.'

Heather straightened back up, letting Lisa take over.

'No,' I said, 'afraid not. I know she doesn't look it right now, but Nell's of a rather nervy disposition and she's had a lot to cope with this week.' We both had. 'I don't want to leave her so I'm going to have to give it a miss.'

'We aren't having fireworks,' Heather told me. 'Just a bonfire and some sparklers. We recently decided not to have fireworks in the square. There are more than enough organised displays around and about.'

I was relieved to hear that.

'But that doesn't mean someone won't be letting them off in the next street along,' Lisa pointed out having secured the truculent boy back into his buggy.

'That's true,' Heather agreed.

'You do right to stay with Nell tonight,' said Lisa. 'I'll bring you round a hot dog later.'

Her attention was then pulled away from me by the arrival of Luke, who everyone stopped what they were doing to listen to.

'Sorry I'm late,' he said. 'I've been helping Finn move some of his stuff.'

'That's the artist guy I was telling you about,' said Chloe as she wandered back over to stand with me. 'Have you heard any more from him?'

'No,' I whispered back. 'Is he properly moving in today?'

'Sounds like it.'

'And I'm sorry I wasn't here to introduce you all to Freya,' Luke carried on, pointing me out and making my face flush. 'I take it you've all met her now.'

'Yes,' said Lisa, 'leave the poor girl alone.'

My hands automatically reached for my plait.

'Great,' said Luke, clapping his hands together. 'Let's crack on then.'

Graham and Carole then stepped up and started telling everyone what to carry and where to and Luke made his way over to me and Chloe.

'Sorry I hadn't managed to bring you over here sooner,' he apologised to me, 'but it's been a bit of week. And I'm sorry I haven't done much in the garden either.'

Kate joined him and transferred Abigail from her arms to his.

'That's what I'm here for,' I pointed out, 'and you made a great job of the silver birches.' That was one job he had been keen to embrace.

'Thanks,' he smiled. 'You were right, they do look good.'

'We're hoping you'll join us for supper tomorrow night, Freya,' said Kate.

'Oh yes,' said Luke, 'I almost forgot, I want to talk to you about positioning these sculptures and I've found some great historical plans and papers about the garden in the attic.'

'And have you told Freya about your other idea?' Kate pressed.

'No,' he said, 'not yet. I haven't had a chance and actually,

I don't want to tell anyone until I've got it all a bit clearer in my head.'

'I'm intrigued,' I said, looking at Kate, who was shaking her head. 'I take it it involves the garden.'

'To a certain extent,' Luke said mysteriously.

'But we're still pushing ahead with the plans for the Winter Garden?'

'Absolutely,' he smiled. 'I've already ordered most of what you had on that list.'

'Oh, my goodness,' I laughed. 'I wasn't expecting you to buy everything!'

'Well,' he said, 'we want to make an impact, don't we?'

'We do,' I agreed. 'And we'll need to make a decision on the final layout before it all arrives.'

'I'm thinking more of a wintry path through the entire garden now,' he said, his gaze drifting off, 'with highlighted points of interest including the sculptures of course, rather than one focused area. What do you think?'

Given that he had ordered so much of what I had suggested, I thought we could create enough of a spectacle to do that.

'As long as it isn't too patchy,' I pointed out, erring for now, on the side of caution. 'We wouldn't want to just dot things randomly about.'

'We can always buy more plants,' Luke said enthusiastically.

I wondered if I would be able to convince him to divert some of the garden budget in the direction of refurbishing the glasshouses or, if he couldn't run to that, possibly buying a new one. With the number of plants I could then raise under glass, it would pay for itself in no time.

'All right,' I agreed, 'that sounds great.'

'We'll talk more over supper, yes?'

'Definitely.'

'Luke!' called Graham. 'Can you give us a hand moving these tables?'

Luke gave Abigail back to Kate and rushed off again.

'He's in his element,' she said, watching his retreating back. 'It's such a weight off his mind having you here, Freya,' she added, turning back to me.

I understood that. A garden could be a burden, especially one the size we were working with, as well as a blessing.

'This summer has been an endless round of just trying to keep on top of everything,' Kate further explained, 'but now he can stand back and look at the bigger picture.'

'I don't know how he's managed to do as well as he has,' said Chloe.

'Because he's had you helping,' I told her. 'You obviously love the garden too, Chloe, and you've worked so hard today.'

I hoped that didn't sound patronising. I hadn't meant it to.

'I do love it,' she said. 'It's a sort of solace, isn't it? The repetition of pulling up those weeds today let my mind wander and my thoughts drift. Gardening really is soothing for the soul.'

I couldn't have put it better myself.

*

A little later, Chloe headed home and I wasn't all that many paces behind her. I thanked Ryan for looking out for Nell, who was saying a reluctant goodbye to her new best friend, Gus, and together we walked back through the garden to lock up the office.

There was no noise coming from the studio but there was a light on and another shining, in what Chloe had told me had been turned into a flat, above. I'd really had enough introductions for one day, but felt it would have been a missed opportunity to just walk by and not say anything.

The door to the studio was open and I peeped inside, pulled up short by what I saw. The place was filled with towering piles of what looked like, to my eyes at least, junk. It was an indoor scrap metal yard with something big being built on a plinth at the centre of it and some smaller pieces lined up on a workbench at the back. Intrigued, I took a step further in, with Nell still next to me and cocked my head to try and work out exactly what it was that I was looking at.

I still hadn't worked it out when I heard heavy footsteps thundering down the stairs which ran up the side of the wall at the back.

'Hello!' I called, as feet clad in heavy, dust-covered work boots descended and were swiftly followed by a pair of long, solid legs, encased in ripped, oil-stained jeans. 'I'm Freya,' I said, my introduction trailing off as a maroon linen shirt followed the bottom half and then a face sporting a beard and framed by long dark hair which was loosely tied back, topped the vision off.

The guy, Finn, I guessed, looked like every inch a Viking and his expression was every bit as fierce. All that was missing was an axe.

'What the hell?' he shouted as he jumped down the last few steps, making the floor shake.

His deep voice resonated around the space and I replaced my former idea of him wielding an axe for Thor's mighty hammer. There was enough electricity in the ether to make the air crackle.

'You can't bring a bloody dog in here!' he thundered.

Nell whimpered, turned tail, shot through my legs and pelted straight out of the door.

'Oh my God, Nell!' I called after her, completely taken aback and panicking that I was going to lose her if the garden gate was open. 'We just wanted to say hello,' I shouted angrily over my shoulder before taking off after her, 'and happy moving-in day!'

Chapter 8

Thankfully I managed to spot and catch Nell as she was doubling back around the lawn. She looked as panicked as I felt and was panting heavily. Graham happened to be ferrying the last of the things to the green when he spotted me trying to calm her, and kindly offered to lock the sheds and pop the keys through my letterbox.

I didn't tell him what had caused Nell's sudden sprint, because I didn't think I could explain without sounding irate and the last thing I wanted to infer was that having only just laid eyes on Finn, I already disliked him, even though I did.

A little later Lisa kindly dropped around some food and after that I heard the Guy Fawkes party in full swing on the green. I was thankful that there weren't too many bangs and cracks nearby, otherwise my poor companion would have slipped into a further decline. She barely touched her tea and her sleep was fitful that night, the slightest movement by me in the bed, instantly rousing her.

The next morning, and for the first time ever, she refused

to budge from her basket and I spent the day working alone in the garden and quietly seething. There was no one at the studio, no one who could be stirred by my early morning hammering on the door anyway. Given the strength of my annoyance, that was perhaps for the best.

After work, I checked the cuttings I had liberated from Broad-Meadows and took a reluctant Nell for a brief wander around the green. She was still wary, but thankfully calmer after her peaceful day at home. I spoke to her gently as she sat on the threshold of the bathroom while I soaked to prune-like proportions in the tub ahead of supper with Kate and Luke.

I had just pulled on my dressing gown when my phone started to vibrate on the nightstand.

'Peter,' I smiled, when his face appeared on the screen. 'You're up early.'

It must have been about five in the morning in New Zealand.

'Big work day,' he smiled back, 'and I wanted to get a run in early.'

'I don't know where you get your energy from,' I told him, stifling a yawn.

'The more exercise I get, the better I feel,' he laughed. 'You should try it.'

'Hey!' I retaliated, 'I get exercise all day thanks to my job, and so would you if you got your hands dirty on a project once in a while.'

'So, how's the job going?' he asked. 'You've been on my

mind this week. I know you said you'd call when you were settled, but I couldn't wait any longer. Is everything all right?'

I wondered how Mum would interpret his kind enquiry as I filled him in on how things were panning out and finished up with the details of what had happened when I went to introduce myself to Finn.

'He sounds like quite a character.'

'That's not quite how I'd put it,' I frowned, picturing the supersized god in human form barrelling down his staircase.

'Well,' Peter pointed out, 'as you're practically living in each other's pockets and going to be working together, you're going to have to find a way to get along, aren't you?'

I refused to admit that he was right.

'I'm sorry, Peter,' I said, noticing the time, 'but I have to go. I'm having supper with my bosses tonight.'

'No doubt you'll be talking shop all evening.'

'No doubt.'

'I better get going too.'

'I hope your big work day goes well.'

'Thanks,' he said, as he leant towards the screen to cut the call off.

'Oh, and Peter,' I quickly added, before he was gone.

'Yeah?'

'Thanks for calling.'

'No worries, mate,' he said, in the worst attempt at a New Zealand accent I'd ever heard.

'Still not nailed the lingo then,' I laughed, as he shook his head. 'And isn't that an Aussie phrase?'

He stuck his tongue out and signed off.

As I was running a little late, I gave my hair a quick blast with the dryer and left it loose before picking out one of my fancier, by which I mean, not workwear, tops and teamed it with a clean pair of jeans before heading off, leaving Nell looking decidedly put out, which suggested she was definitely beginning to feel better.

'Wow,' said Kate, when she opened the door to let me in. 'You look amazing. My goodness, Freya, your hair is long, isn't it?'

'Too long,' I told her, quickly offering the wine I had carried over in an attempt to brush over her compliment. 'I didn't know what we'd be eating so I thought I'd bring one of each.'

'You really didn't have to,' she told me, taking the bottles of red and white, 'but thank you.'

'You've given me a home and a job and now supper,' I said seriously, 'the least I can do is supply the wine.'

She shook her head and laughed as I closed the door behind me.

'And you've restored my other half's sanity,' she pointed out. 'I think that's already a fair trade. No Nell,' she noticed as I shrugged off my jacket.

'No, not tonight.'

It was warm in the house and the sitting room, which I hadn't seen before, had a fire burning brightly in the grate and was lit mostly by candlelight. It wasn't the grand, formal room I had been expecting and I felt my shoulders relax. I could already tell it was going to be a lovely evening, getting to know my new employers better and talking about our vision for the beautiful garden. My creative flame had almost been snuffed out when Eloise died and Jackson then stamped on it, but now, thanks to Luke's enthusiasm for the Winter Garden, I could feel it warming up again, poised to burn just as brightly as before.

'No Nell?' queried Luke, echoing Kate.

'No,' I said. 'She had a bit of a scare yesterday and is still feeling a bit unsettled. I thought it best to leave her at home.'

'I have a horrible feeling,' came a voice from the shadows, 'that might be my fault.'

There was no mistaking who the voice belonged to and I let out a long slow breath. So much for my prediction that it was going to be a great night. I wasn't much in the mood to spend an evening with the giant who had terrorised my four-legged best friend.

'Your fault, Finn.' Luke frowned. 'How so? Have you two already met?'

The Viking stepped into the light, towering above us all and making Jasmine, who he scooped up and held comfortably in his arms, look as tiny as her sister.

'We've sort of met,' I said, keeping my eyes on Luke. 'I went to introduce myself last night, but Finn bawled at Nell and me before I got the chance to say hello and Nell made a run for it. You know how sensitive she is.'

The words were out before I could check them and everyone's eyes, including Jasmine's, swung back to Finn. So much for my recent conviction to not let my mouth move faster than my brain.

'I'm so sorry,' he said, setting Jasmine down again. 'I really didn't mean to scare her.'

'Then you shouldn't have shouted,' I pointed out, unwilling to accept his apology, even if it did sound heartfelt. Clearly, I was on a roll. My love for Nell had awoken the lioness in me. 'You scared us both.'

I took my first proper look at him and found, like me, he had left his hair loose, but the sides were plaited to keep it off his face and surprise, surprise there was Thor's hammer hanging on a leather thong around his neck. Son of Odin, the god of thunder, really was standing among us.

'I didn't mean to,' he said, taking a step closer to me. 'It's just that I panicked. I hadn't cleared the studio floor all week and I was worried she'd stand on a shard of metal or something. The studio is no place for a dog with soft padded paws.'

'I see,' I swallowed, taken aback by the kindness in his eyes.

'I just didn't want her to get hurt,' he said, his voice softer but still deep.

'Well, there was still no need to shout,' I said. My tone sounded curt when pitched against his. 'If you'd just asked me to wait outside at normal volume, then she wouldn't have run off and ended up cowering in her basket all day, would she?'

'Oh, poor Nell,' gasped Jasmine.

I had forgotten that she and Kate and Luke were listening.

'She's feeling a bit better now,' I said for Jasmine's benefit, definitely not Finn's.

'You're right,' he said, still staring down at me.

When I risked a closer look, I could see that his eyes were curiously grey, but speckled with dark, almost black, flecks. I struggled to look away, momentarily mesmerised by what I had intended to be just a fleeting and accusatory glance.

'I shouldn't have shouted,' he agreed.

'And you didn't even come after us,' I swallowed. 'You didn't even come to see if I had found her.'

'I was going to,' he said, sounding even more remorseful, 'but I thought it might make the situation worse. I thought she'd carry on running if she saw me again and you were obviously angry.'

I opened my mouth to respond.

'And with good reason,' he quickly added. 'But I did find Graham a few minutes later and he said that you and Nell had gone home. I did think of checking on you both, but then I realised I didn't know where home was.'

At least he'd gone some way to finding out if we were all right. That was something I supposed.

'I'm living in the square,' I said, clearing my throat. 'In Harold's old house.'

He nodded. 'I'm really sorry we've got off on the wrong foot,' he then said, holding out a bear-sized hand for me to shake, 'especially as we're going to be working together. Can we start again, Freya?'

I looked at Kate, who was nodding encouragingly and

Luke, who seemed to be holding his breath. It was just as Peter had pointed out; given the circumstances, Finn and I were going to have to get along.

'All right,' I told him, 'as long as you promise not to shout at my dog again, and sweep the studio floor every now and again just in case she ventures in. Not that I think she will.'

'Deal,' he grinned, his face transformed, as he grasped my hand in his.

There was no mistaking the lightning shock of feeling which transferred from his fingers to mine. Under any other circumstances, I would have considered it a cliché, but as I was in the presence of a Norse god, the sensation felt thoroughly fitting. I didn't know if he felt it too, or if it was completely usual for him. His beguiling grey eyes might have been smiling, but they gave little away.

'Why don't you tell Freya what it is that you do, Finn?' suggested Luke when he finally began to breathe again, 'and I'll pour us all a drink.'

'Just a small glass for me, please,' said Finn.

Kate offered us the sofa and we sat at opposite ends, Jasmine jumping up on Finn's knee, the second he sat down. I got the impression that he was someone she knew well and certainly felt comfortable with.

'Where's Abigail?' I asked Luke as he handed round glasses.

'In bed already,' Jasmine answered for him. 'She was really tired and grumpy at teatime so she's had an early night.'

'Which means she'll be up at dawn,' said Luke, rolling his eyes.

'Fortunately, we're used to early starts,' said Kate with a smile, before ducking out to check on the food.

There was a beat of silence and I quickly filled it for fear that it would grow into something insurmountable.

'So, Finn,' I said, after taking my first sip of the crisp and chilled white wine, 'what is it that you do?'

'I'm a builder by trade,' he told me. 'I work with my dad and brother, half-brother, that is, in the family firm.'

That didn't exactly strike me as a job that would warrant a studio.

'So, where does the studio come in?' I asked.

I couldn't help but notice the colour rising in his cheeks.

'Finn's an artist,' said Luke. 'With an amazing talent.'

Finn shook his head.

'You are, mate,' said Luke, slapping him on the shoulder. 'If only you'd believe it. I'm just going to see if Kate needs a hand.'

Finn looked at me and puffed out his cheeks. Without Luke to speak for him, he had no choice but to carry on.

'I make things,' he said quietly, 'out of things that no one else wants.'

That went some way to explaining the scrap metal.

'Luke mentioned sculptures,' I said, trying to help him along.

Clearly, he wasn't used to talking like this. His self-effacing nature made me warm to him a bit.

'Yeah,' he said. 'He's asked me to make a few pieces for the garden. I think he wants the two of us to work together on that. I'll create them and between us we'll find the best place for them.'

I didn't mention my former vision of gnomes. Finn was definitely not a gnome type of guy.

'Did you go to art college?' I asked.

I could just imagine him surrounded by adoring students, seductively splattered with clay and paint.

'God no,' he laughed. 'Sorry,' he quickly carried on, 'if you knew my father, then you'd know why I'm laughing.'

'You said you worked for him.'

'That's right. The day after I left school at sixteen, he had me working full-time on a building site and I've been laying bloody bricks ever since. Sorry, Jas,' he added as his profanity earned him a frown. 'It was always my dream to go to art college, but Dad wouldn't hear of it. He said I needed to learn a proper trade. That messing about with paints and canvases wouldn't put food on the table.'

'Supportive then?' I said, taking another sip of wine and thinking how comfortable and relaxed Jasmine looked. Her eyelids were beginning to droop.

'He's old school,' said Finn. 'What you'd call a man's man and my half-brother is a chip off the old block.'

'But not you?'

'No, not me.' He sighed. 'I take after my mum.'

'So how come you're here?' I asked. I wanted to find out the rest of his story now. 'Making sculptures from scrap is a big leap from paints and canvases and laying bricks.'

'It's taken me a while to get here.'

'Go on.'

He shifted to get more comfortable and I handed him his glass because he couldn't reach it.

'Dad didn't know it,' he continued, 'but I always had it in the back of my mind that I'd go to college once I'd qualified as a builder and even though a few years passed, I was still determined not to give up on my dream, that is until I went to a couple of college open days. I wasn't there long before I realised how out of place I looked, how much older than everyone else I suddenly was.'

'What, even the mature students?'

I knew that plenty of people returned to education or had career changes.

'At the ages I was, I seemed to kind of fall in-between,' he frowned. 'Too young for the mid-life lot and definitely too old for the rest.'

'So, what happened after that?' I asked, leaning a little closer in my eagerness.

'I carried on doing various bits and pieces at home, and then one day we were helping this couple clear out a garage ahead of building an extension. We were filling skip after skip and I realised what a waste it was, sending it all to landfill just because it was unwanted or no longer fit for its original purpose.'

He looked at me and I nodded for him to continue.

'I took a few things home and reimagined them into something else. Took them apart and then put them back together in a totally different way.'

'I see,' I said, as the pieces began to fall into place.

'It was a complete fluke that Luke happened to see one of the pieces I'd made. He'd come to talk to Dad about some work we were doing here and arrived as I was moving it around in the garage.'

'Your dad was a bit miffed about that, wasn't he?' said Luke, as he came back into the room and caught the thread of conversation.

'Yeah,' grinned Finn. 'He was embarrassed, I think. His idea of what I should have been spending my free time doing wasn't quite the same as his.'

'But I could see that Finn had a real talent and a passion that wasn't going to be fulfilled in a tiny corner of his garage at home,' Luke told me, 'so, after we got to know each other a bit better, I offered him the studio here to work in and a commission to go with it.'

'When I told Dad,' Finn carried on, 'he went nuts.'

'So, we turned the space above the studio into a flat,' said Kate, joining us again, carrying with her a delicious smell and cheeks flushed from the heat of the kitchen.

'And now,' said Finn, bringing me up to date, 'I've just moved in.'

'And are you still working for your dad?' I asked. 'Or have you fallen out completely?'

'He's still not come around to the idea, but we're not completely estranged,' he said, wrinkling his nose. 'I would love to make a full-time living from the sculptures, but for now I'm working as a builder by day and in the studio at night and during the weekends. I don't want to fall out with the family so I'm trying to juggle things and I'm so grateful to you two,' he added, turning to Kate and Luke, 'for giving me this opportunity.'

I raised my glass to the pair of them too.

'I'd like to add my gratitude to Finn's, if I may?' I smiled. 'You've given me an amazing opportunity too. Thank you both so much.'

'That's one thing we do have in common,' said Finn, smiling at me and making me blush.

'That and really, really long hair,' said Jasmine, who was suddenly wide awake again. 'Did you bring my present, Finn?'

Finn's present turned out to be a tiny cat made from clock mechanisms and cogs. When you turned a key, its tail moved and its ears twitched.

'It's beautiful,' I whispered, as I admired the intricate detail and wondered how hands as large as Finn's could create something so delicate. 'How have you managed to give it so much personality?'

'Like I said,' grinned Luke, 'he's an artist.'

'This one is Violet,' said Jasmine, holding it up and turning it from side to side so she could examine all the details. 'I've already got Dash.'

I knew those were the names of the family's two cats and wondered if Finn might one day fashion something that would resemble Nell for me.

'I never would have believed hands the size of yours could

create something so tiny, Finn,' I said, my cheeks burning even brighter the second I had verbalised my thoughts.

'Oh, I'm pretty dextrous,' he smiled, making my temperature soar.

'Right,' said Kate, 'supper is ready.'

'I'm going to get ready for bed,' announced Jasmine.

'Make sure you put Violet on a high shelf, won't you?' said Finn. 'Abigail mustn't be able to reach her.'

'I know,' said Jasmine, giving him a hug. 'Thank you, Finn.'

'You're welcome,' he said, hugging her back.

Supper was a tasty risotto made with vegetables from the Grow-Well and topped off with generous shavings of pecorino cheese. Luke offered more wine to accompany it and by the time I'd finished I could have fallen asleep.

'That was delicious,' I said. 'Thank you, Kate.'

'You're welcome,' she said. 'It was no bother. Just the sort of cooking I like at the end of a busy week.'

She and Luke wouldn't let either Finn or me help tidy away.

'Why don't you go and get Nell?' Luke suggested. 'And then you won't have to worry about rushing back.'

'But what about your early start?' I reminded him. 'I don't want to keep you up.'

I wasn't sure how Nell would cope with seeing Finn, although I supposed she would have to meet him again at some point and perhaps being away from the studio, she wouldn't make the connection between the big bear of a bloke and the bawling voice.

'Like Kate said before, getting up early is par for the course with kids,' Luke shrugged. 'We're used to it.'

Finn was back on the sofa when I returned with Nell and he kept his voice soft and quiet as I led her over. She gave his slowly outstretched hand an exploratory sniff and then turned her attention to the fire. Finn looked at me and shrugged and I felt relieved that I wasn't going to have to worry about keeping the pair apart.

By the time I looked back at Nell, which was really no time at all, the cats had found her, probably because she was in their spot. Dash quickly curled up against her side and Violet pinned her down and gave her a very thorough wash.

'Right,' said Luke, 'as that's all settled, come and have a look at what I found in the attic.'

Spread out on the table in what I guessed was the formal, if somewhat chilly, dining room, were a set of plans. They were rather creased and battered but they were definitely the garden and in the corner was the name of a long since dead designer. From what I could make out, they had been drawn up to show the original hard landscaping features rather than planting schemes.

'I'm guessing,' said Luke as he pointed various sections out, 'that these are the points where there were once sculptures in the garden.'

'Yes,' I agreed, squinting to see the detail as the light wasn't all that bright. 'I think you're right. This definitely isn't a soft landscaping plan. It would look completely different if it was defining a planting scheme or something, and here look,' I pointed, 'this must be the bandstand next to the river.'

The building was rather grand for the size of garden, but I could imagine Luke's philanthropic ancestor hosting concerts there throughout the summer and inviting everyone along to enjoy them, including his workers.

'Have you got your mobile with you, Finn?' I asked. 'I've left mine in the other room.'

'Yes,' he said, pulling something that resembled a small brick out of his pocket.

'Oh,' I said, 'I was going to ask you to shine your torch on the key in the corner so I could decipher it.'

'Sorry,' he said. 'No can do, I'm afraid. This thing is pretty ancient. It doesn't have a torch.'

'So, I see,' I laughed. 'Never mind.' I turned my attention back to the design. 'Look at this bit here, the fern garden originally ran much further than it does now. That line there is the wall.'

'You seem to know what you're talking about, Freya,' said Finn, his voice surprisingly close to my ear. 'You clearly know your way about a garden design. I haven't had a chance to ask you about your work yet.'

I stood up straight. 'I'll fill you in another time,' I told him, keeping my eyes on the table. 'Not that there's much to tell.'

'Oh, I don't know,' said Kate who, having checked on the girls, now joined us, 'I think we all have a tale to tell.'

I wasn't sure I would call a broken engagement, my parent's disapproval, the death of a friend and arguable dognapping, a tale as such, not that I would actually be sharing very much of that with Finn.

'Well, I'll look forward to it,' Finn smiled, making my stomach feel as though it were filled with butterflies even though we were well beyond summer, 'whatever it is.'

Luke cleared his throat and we turned our attention back to the plans. He explained that he didn't want to replicate what had been on display before. Using Finn's modern sculptural pieces would allow him to stamp his own sense of style on the place, but we might want to consider utilising a couple of the garden's focal points, such as the end of the herbaceous border.

'And what about the dragon trail?' asked Finn. 'Have you thought anymore about that?'

'The dragon trail?' I frowned.

'Yes,' Luke grinned. 'As Norwich has great historical connections with dragons, Kate and I thought it would be fun if Finn could make some smaller dragon sculptures, ten or so, to dot around in the garden, for people to find and record on a map.'

'Oh, I like the sound of that,' I said, imagining them peeping out from hidey holes in the fern garden. 'It will definitely add an element of fun to the garden. The only dragon I've come across so far is the pub, and I haven't made it inside there yet. I'll have to do some reading up.'

'And do crack on with making them, Finn,' said Luke, answering his question, 'they're a definite yes. I got the trail idea from a family trip to a winter wonderland at Wynthorpe Hall near Wynbridge last Christmas,' he then elaborated.

'Amongst other things,' said Kate, with a wry smile.

'Oh?' Finn and I said together.

'I know that place,' said Finn. 'What was it that inspired you, Luke?'

'All will be revealed tomorrow,' our boss mysteriously said. 'I'm going to talk to everyone in the Grow-Well after lunch. There's a working party happening in the morning to have an autumnal tidy-up.'

I didn't think that would take long. Everything had looked pretty pristine to me.

'And I'll be sharing my ideas after that.' Luke grinned again.

'More ideas!' I laughed.

'Oh, he's full of them,' said Kate.

'And all of them are brilliant,' Luke beamed.

I wasn't sure if Kate agreed, but Finn and I looked at each other and carried on laughing, each of us obviously keen to discover what our kind employer had lined up for us next.

Chapter 9

As drowsy as I had felt, relaxed from the wine and cocooned in the warm and comforting rooms at Prosperous Place, the walk back across the road to the square in the crisp, chill air woke me back up and I found it impossible to fall asleep straightaway.

I lay in bed with Nell curled up next to me and let my mind explore everything that had happened during the last week. Was it really just a week ago that I had spent my last night at Broad-Meadows?

As the pipes creaked throughout the house, I realised how quickly I was settling into my new abode, how many friends I had made in such little time, how in love I was with the garden and my new job and my unexpectedly warm feelings for Finn. So far, he had turned out to be the biggest and most overwhelming surprise of all. I wondered what Peter would make of that. It was certainly a speedy change of opinion on my part.

I was pleased Peter and I had parted on good terms and

that I had been able talk to him, even if it was through a screen. Since I had lost Eloise I had struggled with the overwhelming sense of loss. My grief, for a while, had touched the very core of me and I needed a friend to turn to, albeit a long-distance one. Had Jackson been another man, I might have turned to him, but he was the polar opposite of his benevolent relative.

I was exceedingly grateful to now have kind folk I could talk to nearby, even if none of them were privy to what it was in my past that had led me to Nightingale Square. I felt a lump form in my throat as I acknowledged that Eloise was no longer my present or my future.

'Goodnight, Eloise,' I said, to the framed photograph of the two of us which stood on the nightstand. 'I'm sorry I can't be with you tomorrow.'

It was going to feel strange not going to visit her at the church, but I knew she would understand. After all, she was the one who had sent the sign and led me to this special place.

I didn't make it over the road early enough to help with the Grow-Well tidy up the next morning, because I had to do some shopping, but I did arrive in time to meet the rest of the team before Luke's announcement. Lisa reckoned I was looking even more bewildered once I'd added another few names to the mental list I was already struggling with, and she solemnly promised to set her kids to work making name badges for everyone to help me out.

'So, how are you settling into my old house?' asked

Harold, who had arrived on his mobility scooter just after me. 'Have those pipes been giving you a scare in the middle of the night?'

When I thought of some of the noises and whisperings I had been subjected to at Broad–Meadows, not all of them plucked from my imagination to frighten Jackson, I knew it would take a bit more than just creaky plumbing to spook me.

'Very, very well,' I told Harold, 'and thanks to your note, explaining what the noises are and when to expect them, they haven't given me too much bother.'

'Well, that's good,' he nodded. 'And have you got everything you need?'

I knew it must have been a wrench for him to leave so many of his possessions behind and his gentle enquiry confirmed it.

'I have, thank you and I'm very grateful to you for letting me have use of your lovely things. I'm looking after them all, I promise.'

'I don't doubt it, my dear,' he said, reaching for my hand and giving it a squeeze.

'And how are you settling in?' I asked.

'Just grand, thank you,' he said, his tone much brighter. 'Although there's never a moment's peace.'

I could completely empathise with him there.

'Oh?'

'Yes, it's either come and play dominoes here, or let's go and have a singsong there. Sometimes I have to pretend I'm not in,' he laughed, sounding like a much younger man.

I was pleased the move had suited us both so well.

'I had to creep out just now,' he confided. 'If anyone had heard me, I'd have been roped into helping set up tonight's bingo!'

We laughed together and I looked up just in time to see Chloe arrive with Finn. He bent to say something to her and she threw back her head in response and laughed so loudly, the sound carried all the way to where I was standing with Harold.

Considering Chloe had said she'd never met him before, they certainly seemed to have bonded with lightning speed. But then, for all I knew, perhaps that was how the god of thunder rolled when he found a woman he liked the look of.

'If you'll excuse me, Harold,' I said, quickly banishing the flash of green I felt must have been lighting up my eyes and which took me completely by surprise, 'I need to check on Nell.'

I soon found her and she looked happy enough, initiated into the gang which included both the Prosperous Place cats and Gus. For a previously solitary creature, she was swiftly finding her feet and I was pleased to see them all asleep out of the chilly breeze in the bothy. Even if the sight did make me feel irrationally redundant.

'So how do you cope with it then, Freya?'

I hadn't realised anyone had been talking to me and turned to find Graham standing close by.

'Sorry,' I said, tuning back in, 'I missed that, Graham. How do I cope with what?'

'The changing seasons,' he said, turning up the collar of the coat which had replaced his gilet now it had turned colder. 'Do you find the long, grey days a bit of a mood killer?'

I thought about it for a moment before answering.

'No,' I said, 'I can't say that I do, but that's probably because I'm always outdoors. If anything, grey days are generally dry days and that means I can carry on with my work without having to dig out the waterproofs. As long as it's dry, I don't always notice what the sky looks like.'

'You're lucky,' he said, sounding envious. 'I wish I could say the same. I never used to mind it, but now, the thought of the long dark winter stretching ahead does nothing for my spirit.'

'Luke's been diagnosed with SAD, hasn't he?' I said, looking over to where my boss appeared to be getting ready to say something.

'That's right,' said Graham, 'and I'm seriously thinking about visiting my GP to find out if I'm the same. I always enjoy helping out here, of course, but sometimes it's just not enough. Luke has been very proactive since his diagnosis and seems far happier as a result. As you know, that's been his inspiration to create the Winter Garden.'

'It's going to be a bright beacon of hope on those dull days that you hate so much, Graham,' I earnestly told him. 'I can promise you that. There'll always be something cheering to see. My planting plan practically guarantees it.'

Graham appeared rather buoyed up by the idea and I hoped Mother Nature wouldn't let me down. That said, if flowers, bulbs, bark and unexpected sweet scent weren't all enough to inspire happy thoughts, then Finn's clever sculptures hidden around the place certainly would be. I refused to allow myself to look back to where he and Chloe were standing. I knew they were still together because I could hear Finn's deep voice and Chloe's light laugh working in perfect harmony.

'And don't forget, it'll soon be Christmas,' I reminded Graham, as much as myself. 'We're on the countdown now.'

'That we are,' he smiled. 'Are you a fan of the season?'

'Yes,' I said, thinking of all the decorating and present-buying, mulled wine and general over-indulgence. 'Yes, I am.'

Living in the city was going to make shopping for Christmas so much easier and guarantee me access to as much over-indulgence and as many seasonal treats and traditions as I could wish for. The isolation at Broad-Meadows had made for a much quieter celebration than the one I imagined I would be facing here. I had always loved the peace and tranquillity that came with spending Yuletide with Eloise, but I was delighted, and rather surprised, to find that I was very much looking forward to finding out what noel in Norwich had to offer.

'What about you, Graham?' I asked, feeling my heart flutter at the thought of it all. 'Do you like Christmas?'

'Oh yes,' he smiled, 'I do. It's such a highlight.'

'Right,' said Luke, shouting above everyone's chatter and cutting mine and Graham's conversation off before I had a chance to mention helping me in the garden. 'Can I have your attention please?'

Everyone quickly fell silent and gathered around him. Chloe and Finn were practically opposite me now. Chloe waved and mouthed 'hello' and Finn looked surprised to see me when Chloe nudged him and pointed me out. He waved too and I smiled back, but admittedly, not all that warmly.

'Thank you all for hanging on this afternoon,' said Luke. 'I know you've all been working hard this morning and it's getting chilly now, so I won't keep you for too long.'

Carole and Poppy moved quietly between us all, handing out mugs of frothy hot chocolate. It smelt delicious and I gratefully wrapped my gloved hands around the warm mug.

'As you know,' Luke continued, 'thanks to the arrival of Freya, plans for the creation of the Winter Garden are now well underway.'

Everyone turned to smile at me and I smiled briefly back before turning my attention to gently blowing the froth on my hot chocolate. When I looked back up again, Finn was still looking at me, so I trained my eyes on Luke.

'And even though there will be plenty to look at this year,' he explained, 'the garden will still be very much in its infancy.'

I was pleased he understood that. Instant gardening, the sort you saw on television makeover shows, was not something I could apply to this project at Prosperous Place. There would, as Luke had just pointed out, be plenty to admire this year, but it would take a few seasons for the planting to really come into its own and look as spectacular as it already did in my head.

'And therefore, I've decided to organise something else for people to enjoy in the run-up to Christmas and possibly beyond. Something inspired by mine and Kate's visit to see her family in Wynbridge last year.'

'Does this have anything to do with the Winter Wonderland you mentioned last week?' asked Graham.

'It does,' said Luke. 'The grounds at Wynthorpe Hall, which is a large country estate, were set up with all sorts of activities for locals to enjoy in the gardens and woods and I want to do something similar here. There's no room for reindeer and we couldn't cope with a constant stream of visitors, so I've adapted the Wynthorpe Hall extravaganza and what I'm suggesting is four weekends of workshops and demonstrations, happening outside and in the house too, called Winterfest.'

'Winterfest,' Graham whispered next to me, trying the word on for size.

'What I'm imagining,' said Luke, warming to his theme, 'are six, possibly eight workshops initially, one on a Saturday and another on a Sunday, based around nature, food and the winter season, happening both in the garden and indoors, that folk can sign up to take part in.'

'That sounds like a wonderful idea,' said Heather.

'I agree,' added Poppy.

'So, where do we come in?' asked Graham.

I could tell from his tone that he was keen to play a part.

'Well,' said Luke, biting his lip as he looked around at his neighbours and friends, 'I know I said I'm going to organise it, but I'm hoping that some of you might consider running the workshops.'

'Us?'

'Yes,' said Kate, stepping up to stand next to Luke. 'We know that it's a big ask, especially in the run-up to Christmas, and that everyone's time is limited, but you're such a talented bunch, that we're hoping you'll consider sharing your skills and helping us come up with a programme of events.'

'We haven't got long,' said Luke. 'I had been looking to book demonstrators and instructors but they're either too expensive, too far away or already booked.'

'When are you hoping to start?' someone else asked.

'November twenty-eighth,' Luke announced, wincing a little as he said it.

'But that's just three weeks away,' gasped Carole.

'I know,' said Luke. 'I know.'

The level of chatter amongst the group began to rise.

'Why have you left it so late?' called the unidentified voice again.

Luke shrugged and Kate shook her head.

'It's impossible,' said Lisa. 'You'll never get anyone to sign up in time.'

'If we can come up with a programme,' said Luke, 'I can use my media contacts to spread the word and I'm hoping Ryan will help out with the Grow-Well social media accounts to share the news even further.'

'You can rely on me boss,' Ryan called back, giving Luke a thumbs up.

'I'm going to leave the idea with you over the weekend,' shouted Luke, but I wasn't sure anyone was still paying attention.

I listened to the excited chatter around me, especially from Graham who was already mulling over who could possibly do what, and the penny dropped. I looked back to Luke who grinned at me and winked, confirming what I had just worked out.

This was his way, I realised, right down to leaving it all until the last minute to give everyone, but especially him and Graham, a sense of purpose and something to focus on as the weather shifted from autumn to winter and the darkness crept in. If I did end up asking Graham to help me too, he certainly wouldn't have time to worry about, or even notice, the shorter days!

'Graham and I aren't the only ones who feel it,' Luke said, once he had made his way over to me, 'and I'm hoping some other locals who struggle will sign up to take part and feel better for doing it. I'm not expecting to turn a profit from the venture, but the mental health benefits are going to be far better than a healthy bottom line.'

'But why now?' I asked.

'Why not? Don't you think it's a good idea?'

'I think it's a wonderful idea,' I told him, 'but surely it would have been better timed to have it after Christmas. January and February can be pretty depressing, especially once the celebrations are forgotten and the twinkly lights are packed away.'

'I never said this was going to be a one-off,' Luke pointed out. 'If we can pull it off, then I'm planning to keep it going right up until the equinox in March. I won't be asking everyone to give their time again after this initial launch, unless they want to, of course, but if we can generate enough interest then Winterfest can run all winter long, especially the outdoor events.'

'Like I told you,' said Kate, with a smile as she linked her arm through Luke's, 'he's full of ideas.'

'He certainly likes to keep busy,' I laughed.

'Oh yes,' she agreed.

What with the Winter Garden *and* Winterfest, Luke was going to have his hands full for the next few months.

The pair moved off to talk to some of the others and I listened to the excited voices and flurry of suggestions that were beginning to come to the fore. I was in no doubt that there would be enough ideas to fill Luke's initial proposed weekends and probably sessions to spare. Which would be good if it did continue after the festive season.

'What do you think, Freya?' asked Finn, striding over, with his hands in his jeans pockets and a thick woollen scarf wrapped around his neck.

That he looked gorgeous was annoyingly my first thought.

'I think it's a great idea,' I told him, sniffing my half-empty mug in an attempt to stop the woody scent of his aftershave assaulting my senses.

'What are you going to do?' he asked, pinning me with a look.

'Me?'

My eyes momentarily flicked to his face.

'Yes,' he said, 'you, Freya. You're the gardening expert. Surely, you're going to offer to do something.'

I absolutely was not. There was no way I was going to stand up and instruct anyone to do anything.

'Have you come up with anything yet?' Chloe beamed, as she bounced over to join us.

Clearly Luke's plan had got her well and truly fired up, unless talking to Finn had put the smile on her face and the glow in her cheeks.

'Finn's going to offer to teach people how to make bird boxes and hedgehog homes out of wood offcuts, aren't you?' she enthused, digging him somewhere near his ribs with her elbow.

She wasn't quite tall enough to do it properly.

'I'm thinking about it,' he said, lowering his voice in case Luke got wind of the idea before he was ready to officially air it.

'It's a brilliant idea, isn't it?' Chloe said to me, her eyebrows raised. 'Just what Luke will be hoping for.'

'Yeah,' I said, 'great.'

Perhaps she would offer to step up and work as Finn's trusty assistant and they would fall in love over the woodpile. I let out a long breath, absolutely hating myself for even entertaining such a mean thought. That wasn't the sort of person I was at all. It was no business of mine whether or not they got on, and given everything Chloe had been through, she was entitled to a little romance. If that was even what was brewing.

'Well,' said Finn with a sniff, looking crestfallen as he let his shoulders drop, 'it was just a thought.'

He strode off again and Chloe turned to me and frowned.

'You might have sounded a bit more enthusiastic,' she tutted. 'He sounded really shy when he asked if I thought it might be a good idea, but I told him it was brilliant and that you'd probably snatch his hand off if he offered to make some for the garden. I bet he won't even mention it to Luke now.'

'I hardly think he's going to care about what I think,' I said, feeling my face flush as I watched him walk out of the Grow-Well without a backwards glance.

He hadn't stopped to talk to Luke, but that was probably because he had to be somewhere or had something else to do. I was certain his departure wasn't anything to do with me.

'Well, whatever,' said Chloe, 'you could have been a bit kinder. That was the first time I've spoken to him and he was really reserved to begin with. I got the impression that it took a lot for him to even come out here.'

She was right, I could have been kinder. I usually prided myself on being kind and consequently felt every bit as bad as I deserved to.

'He said you'd had some sort of falling out when you first met,' she carried on, making me feel even worse, 'but he was pleased to have it sorted because he thought you were really lovely.'

Given the speed at which he'd just left, I thought it was pretty safe to assume that he wasn't thinking that anymore.

Chapter 10

I made my excuses and left soon after Luke's announcement. Everyone was still happily chatting away as the hot chocolate mugs were rinsed and the last of the tools were cleaned and locked away. Nell was none too happy about being wrenched from her friends, but it was gearing up to rain and I wanted to get back to the house.

'Thanks for coming over, Freya,' said Luke when he spotted that I was about to go. 'I know it's your day off, so I really appreciate it. It was kind of you to find the time.'

But not nearly kind enough, according to some, I couldn't help thinking. And justifiably so.

'Any plans for the rest of the weekend?' asked Kate.

'Absolutely none,' I told her, 'it's going to be bliss.'

I kept my head down as I walked by the studio. Finn hadn't come to find me after our clash over Nell the week before and I had no intention of making the current situation worse by drawing his attention to it. I was sure Chloe had got the wrong end of the stick and he hadn't left because of me at all. At least, that was what I told myself.

I was hard-pushed to reach the state of 'bliss' I had told Kate my plans to do nothing would transport me to. In fact, I couldn't seem to get within miles of it. Having the chance to sit down and do nothing for two days always felt like a good idea in the middle of a busy working week when my muscles ached and there was rainwater trickling down my neck, but the reality didn't quite live up to expectations. When the opportunity for a lazy weekend did finally fall at my feet, the hours felt far longer than sixty minutes and I soon became bored.

Consequently, on Saturday afternoon I ended up changing the bed, catching up with the washing, vacuuming, dusting and scrubbing. Not that anything really needed doing. Kate had given the place a more than thorough autumnal spruce up, and it wasn't as if I'd been at home long enough to conjure too many dust motes, but the activity did go some way to occupying my mind.

By the time I had decided to take Nell for a walk, the light was fading and it had started to rain heavily. I pulled the curtains, then fired off a quick text to my father telling him my first working week had gone well and Mum needn't worry about airing out my old room, before cooking a less than comforting frozen pizza and taking myself off for an early night. I didn't message Peter to tell him about my change of heart about Finn because there didn't seem much point.

I woke early on Sunday, refreshed from a surprisingly good night's sleep and feeling pleased that the skies had cleared and the sun was back. There was a reply from Dad on my phone which suggested that he and Mum were appeased by my message, which was a relief, and I threw back the duvet, determined to make the most of the day and not waste a second of it by striving to reach nirvana by doing nothing.

'Come on,' I called to Nell, once I had tamed my hair into some sort of submission and was dressed. 'Let's go for a wander.'

The early morning air was chilly but invigorating, with the sun already shining, and our walk was long and brisk. Nell could easily keep pace with me and the grin on her face told me that she was enjoying stretching her legs every bit as much as I was. There weren't too many people about either, so our progress was unhindered and we returned to the square panting but both feeling much revived.

I had let my mind wander as I pounded the pavements and even though I still had no plans to offer to run any workshops for Luke, I did unpack a few boxes containing various craft projects that I had enjoyed during my time at Broad-Meadows. I wasn't going to be tripped up again by having nothing planned for the weekends and had just finished setting everything out on the table when the doorbell went.

My first thought was that it might be Finn and I checked the state of my hair in the hall mirror before answering. I was annoyed that that was who my thoughts had immediately sprung to. I had no idea why he would go to the effort of seeking me out, and I was further annoyed by the sense of disappointment which hit when I deciphered the silhouette on the doorstep and realised it wasn't him, but two of my new neighbours.

'Good morning, Freya,' smiled Carole, when I opened the door.

'Morning,' I smiled back.

It didn't escape my notice that she had a very official-looking clipboard tucked under her arm and I wondered what I was about to let myself in for.

'Hi,' added Poppy, who was standing just behind her, 'we're sorry to disturb you on a Sunday.'

Her tone was genuinely apologetic and I wondered if she had headed out with Carole to soften the older woman's intrusion into the generally lazier start most folk enjoyed on the seventh day of the week.

'That's all right,' I reassured her.

'Only we spotted you heading out earlier, so we knew you were up,' Carole said approvingly. 'Any chance we could just come in for a minute?'

'Of course,' I said, opening the door to let them and Gus, who was standing next to Poppy, inside. 'Would you like a cup of tea? I was just about to boil the kettle.'

'That would be great, thanks, Freya,' Poppy smiled.

I led them into the front room and by the time I returned with the tray of tea, Gus and Nell had stopped play fighting and were settled in a heap in front of the fire. The two women were keenly eyeing the bits and pieces I had set out on the table.

'Looks like you've been busy,' said Carole, with a nod

to the A4 journal which was open on a page depicting September at Broad-Meadows.

It was a particularly pretty layout with pressed flowers and illustrations as well as my thoughts on the weather and what was still in bloom.

'And these are amazing,' said Poppy, pointing out my pile of preserved leaves. 'Where did you buy them from? The colours are incredible, so vibrant.'

'I made them,' I told her, passing her a mug and offering the sugar bowl and a spoon, 'well, not the leaves, obviously, but I preserved them in glycerine to help them keep their colour and make them more durable.'

'Wow,' said Poppy as she stirred her tea, 'what do you do with them?'

'I've added some to my journal,' I said, flicking back through the pages to late summer the previous year, 'and others I've used for display by threading them on to cotton and hanging them up like a sort of natural bunting.'

Carole and Poppy exchanged a glance and I realised the visit was heading exactly where I had expected it to when I spotted Carole's clipboard, but I wasn't going to give in. There was no way I could stand up in front of a bunch of strangers and teach, instruct, tutor, whatever they were going to call it.

'So,' said Carole, all business after she'd allowed a beat to pass. 'You're probably wondering why we've called, Freya.'

'I think I might have worked it out,' I said with a sigh, my eyes on Poppy, who was still looking through the collection of leaves. 'You can take some if you like,' I told her.

'I'd much rather you showed me how to make my own,' she said, with a crafty grin.

I'd walked right into that one.

'The thing is,' said Carole, 'we've decided what we're doing for Winterfest, haven't we, Poppy? And so,' she carried on, not giving Poppy a chance to answer, 'we're doing a quick house to house to see if anyone else has any suggestions about how they'd like to help.'

At this juncture she looked pointedly at the table and back to me. She couldn't have been any more obvious, but I was still feeling adamant that I wouldn't give in.

'I'm sorry, Carole,' I said, shaking my head, 'but I'm really not cut out to stand up in front of a crowd—'

'That's exactly what I said,' interrupted Poppy. 'Selling my recipes on cards in Greengage's and in the little book Mark and I put together is one thing, but delivering a masterclass in person is something else entirely.'

'So,' I said, feeling relieved as I let out a breath, 'you know exactly how I feel.'

'I do,' she agreed, 'which is why I've decided to join forces with Mark. We're delivering our session together.'

'Poppy's going to demonstrate how to make her chuck-it-all-in chutney,' Carole elaborated, 'and Mark's going to come up with a simple festive loaf.'

'I won't feel half as nervous if I've got him working with me,' said Poppy. 'In fact, I'm really looking forward to it.'

She did sound excited.

'And you could join forces with someone else to show

them how to make these,' said Carole, holding up a leaf, 'and maybe offer some tips on how people could make their own nature diary.'

'That would make a great family winter project,' chipped in Poppy. 'The ideal way to keep people heading out and getting some fresh air during the bleaker months.'

Their ideas did sound wonderful, and I loved the thought of people being encouraged to get outside when the instinct was to hunker down and stagnate indoors, but their suggestions would have been even better if they hadn't directly involved me.

'That's great in theory,' I conceded, 'but I don't know who I could share a session with. I don't really know anyone well enough. I mean, I've only been here a week.'

'Lisa,' they both said together, cutting me off.

'Lisa?' I frowned.

'Of course,' said Carole, as if we were the most obvious pairing in the world. 'Lisa's going to run a nature-themed creative writing workshop.'

'She's an author,' added Poppy, helpfully giving the suggestion some context, 'a really good one.'

'And she's looking for someone to work with her,' Carole went on, 'because she thinks she can only fill a couple of hours, even with an inspirational walk before she gets the pens out and the creative juices flowing.'

'She'll be much happier working alongside someone else,' smiled Poppy. 'Just like me and Mark.'

From what I could work out, Carole had no qualms about

flying solo for her Christmas cake and pudding session, which came as no surprise at all.

'Lisa's creative writing combined with your clever craft and nature diary idea would be the perfect partnership,' said Carole, quickly scribbling something down on her clipboard. 'That could easily fill a day.'

'I'll have to think about it,' I said, feeling rather railroaded. I wasn't surprised by Carole's super-efficient tactics, but Poppy joining forces with her made her harder to ward off.

'There's no time,' said Carole, 'you heard what Luke said yesterday, if Winterfest is going to happen, then it needs to be sorted fast.'

'But the attendees wouldn't be able to take their leaves away with them,' I desperately added, 'they need to be immersed for a few days for the glycerine to work.'

'Folk could come back to collect them,' Poppy unhelpfully suggested, 'or we could send them on. They don't weigh much so it would be a reasonable cost to factor in. I'm sure we could work something out.'

'Is everyone else doing something?' I swallowed, feeling resistance was futile.

'Not everyone,' said Carole, consulting her notes again.

Phew. That would make saying no slightly easier.

'Heather might not be able to manage it because of the little ones, but almost every other household has come up with something.'

Bang went that theory.

'And even she said she'd be willing to assist in some things if she could juggle childcare with Glen's weekend work.'

That was that then. I had no one, other than Nell, depending on me, and even she was extending her boundaries and making the most of getting to know the Nightingale Square and Prosperous Place menagerie.

'So,' said Carole, tapping her pen on her clipboard. 'Can I put you down, Freya?'

'Yes,' I squeaked, feeling I had no choice. 'I suppose so. You'd better partner me with Lisa, hadn't you?'

'Great stuff,' said Poppy, fingering the pile of leaves again.

'Marvellous,' said Carole, finishing her tea and heading for the door. 'Luke will be thrilled to have you on board.'

I hoped everyone would. If I was going to put myself through it, then I wanted everyone to appreciate the gargantuan effort the new girl was making.

'Last stop is the new chap, Finn,' said Carole to Poppy, who was carrying Gus because he refused to get up, 'he'll be over at the studio.'

'You're going to ask him?' I frowned.

'We're asking *everyone*,' Carole said firmly.

'We'll come and find you tomorrow before we go and tell Luke,' said Poppy, rushing to keep up with her friend. 'As you'll be on site, you can help us share the good news. He's going to be so pleased.'

Which I guessed was more than Finn would be when Carole started hammering on his door.

*

As promised, just before lunch the next day, Carole and Poppy came to find me ahead of going to tell Luke what they had come up with so far.

'I can't be too long,' said Poppy, who was rosy-cheeked from her walk back from the grocer's where she worked. 'I've blagged an early lunch, but I can't be late back. Oh,' she added, 'what's all this?'

As easily distracted as a kitten with a ball of string, she wandered over to the potting bench where I had spread out a selection of leaves which I had gathered throughout the morning.

'I thought it might not be a bad idea to start collecting some leaves now,' I told her. 'If the forecast isn't great when Lisa and I have our session, then I'll already have some to hand that haven't turned soggy. They don't have to be dried out before they're preserved, but they do have to be intact – and it won't hurt to have a back-up plan.'

'You're all fired up by the sounds of it, Freya,' said Carole.

'I wouldn't go that far,' I told her, 'but I'm hoping I won't feel quite so stressed about it all, if I'm well prepared.'

'I'll share those words of wisdom to the others when Winterfest is officially announced,' said Carole as I gave Nell her lunch and locked her in the shed, just to be on the safe side.

I didn't want to take her with me and I couldn't risk her wandering off unattended and ending up in Finn's lair again. Not that given her first experience of the place, she was all that keen to go back, but you never know.

'Let's go and tell Luke what we've arranged then.' Carole urged. 'Kate said he's in his office.'

Luke was in his office, but we couldn't go straight in to see him because he was already talking to someone. The three of us sat on chairs in the corridor, with our backs against the walls like the three wise monkeys. I wasn't sure which one I would have been.

Poppy looked at me sitting poker straight and tried to stifle a giggle.

'I feel like I've been sent to the headmaster's office,' she squeaked, her shoulders shaking, with laughter.

'You've had a lot of experience of that, have you, Poppy?' asked Carole, which made her laugh all the harder and set me off too. 'Why am I not surprised?' she tutted, adding an eye-roll for good measure, which made Poppy crumple further.

'What's all the racket out there?' came Luke's voice from the other side of the door.

'There,' said Carole, sounding cross. 'He's heard you, and how does that look when he's got someone in there with him?'

The door was suddenly plucked open and Poppy bit her lip, her cheeks turning the brightest shade of red.

'I might have known,' grinned Luke. 'You'd better come in.'

'Sorry, Luke,' said Carole, 'we didn't mean to disturb your meeting. We can come back later if you like.'

'No, it's all right,' he said, beckoning us in. 'I'm not in a meeting. It's only Zak. He's doing a bit of measuring up.'

'Only Zak,' said the man's voice from inside, sounding offended, 'that's nice, that is.'

'Oh,' winked Poppy, 'now we're in for a treat. Watch yourself though, Freya, he's trouble, this one.'

'For pity's sake,' hissed Carole. 'Pack it in, the pair of you.'

Poppy giggled again and we followed our leader into the office. If I hadn't felt like a naughty schoolgirl before, I did then. Poppy had pulled me down to her mischievous level and as a result Carole had tarred me with the same brush.

'I might have known,' said the man who had to be Zak because he was the only other person in the room, 'don't you ever go to work, Poppy?'

'I'm on my lunch break,' she pouted, 'and what about you, you hardly sound hard at it.'

'Oh, I'm always hard at it,' he grinned, tossing and catching the tape measure he was holding.

It was tricky to make out what he looked like while he was standing in front of the window but when he moved aside to let Luke back behind his desk, I caught sight of a pair of impressive biceps in a slightly too tight T-shirt, sparkling blue eyes and a buzz cut.

'So,' said Luke, ignoring Zak's flirtatious innuendo, 'what can I do for you three?'

Zak turned back to his measuring but not before he'd winked at Carole. It was my turn to bite my lip and Poppy covered her mouth with her hand. Luke pretended he hadn't noticed anything, but he must have done.

'I'm hoping you've come to tell me that you've had some

ideas about filling Winterfest sessions,' he said, looking between us.

Poppy nodded and Carole, positively glowing with pride, handed him her papers.

'We've got plans for four Saturdays and three Sundays,' she said proudly.

I decided not to pay further attention to Zak, who was flexing and stretching more than was probably really necessary for someone simply wielding a tape measure. Carole and Poppy, but particularly Carole, had put a lot of work into the proposed Winterfest schedule and I wasn't about to be distracted by some silly bloke's behaviour.

'This is all amazing,' gasped Luke, flicking through the pages. 'Far better than anything I could have come up with. I knew I was doing the right thing handing it over to you guys. There's a fantastic mix of stuff here and, Freya, you've only just arrived and your name's down twice. That's wonderful.'

'Well,' I said, trying to sound blasé, 'it was the least I could do ... hang on ... twice?'

'There's so much variety,' Luke enthusiastically carried on. 'We can have some of the nature-based sessions in the Grow-Well and gardens, depending on the weather of course, and the cooking in the kitchen here. If the weather *really* puts a spanner in the works, I suppose we could even have some of the crafting inside too, after the initial foraging and gathering.'

'That's what we were all thinking,' Carole keenly agreed.

Clearly the discussions had continued after I'd added my contribution to the cause. I wondered what else I'd been signed up for in my absence. I was about to ask, but Poppy spoke up first.

'So, when are you planning to make it all official?' she asked Luke.

'Well there's no time to hang about,' he said, reinstating what he had said on Saturday. 'I'll ring the radio this afternoon and if you could ask Ryan to come over when he gets back from college, Poppy, then we'll set a page up on Facebook and share the details on Twitter.'

'He should be home by three,' said Poppy, looking at her watch. 'At this rate you could have everything online by teatime.'

'With less than three weeks until Freya and Lisa launch the project,' grinned Luke, making my stomach roll, 'that's no bad thing.'

'Finn was talking about all this at dinner yesterday,' said Zak.

My eyes flicked back to him.

'Finn and Zak are brothers,' Luke said to me, filling in the blanks.

'Half-brothers,' Zak was quick to point out. 'And your name came up too, Freya,' he added, pinning me with his blue eyes and making me blush.

'Is that right?' I swallowed, determinedly meeting his gaze.

I would have paid good money to find out what had been said and Zak's wide grin told me he knew it too.

'Mum and Dad weren't sure if he'd turn up yesterday,' he carried on, 'what with the fallout from him moving in here, but he arrived just as Mum was getting ready to serve up. He said he's going to be making bird boxes or something, is that right?'

His tone was a little too amused for my liking.

'Yes,' said Carole, with a sniff. Clearly, she'd picked up on Zak's tone too. 'He'll be making hedgehog homes as well. He's very talented, your brother.'

I was relieved that Finn had agreed to take part and that my unenthusiastic response hadn't put him off. Not that it should have done, but Chloe had made me feel guilty and I could hardly tell her that my lacklustre response to his plan was borne out of jealousy at seeing the pair of them together, rather than a dislike of his big idea, could I?

'If you say so,' said Zak, flipping and catching his tape measure again. 'Dad says he should be building houses instead of fannying about making bijou boxes for blue tits.'

'Well,' said Luke, sounding cross as I caught an echo of someone walking along the corridor, 'your dad always has had a way with words, hasn't he?'

Finn had said his half-brother was very much like his dad. If that was the case, I wasn't sure I'd like him. Zak struck me as a troublemaker and a mouthy one to boot.

'Gift of the gab, Dad's got,' Zak proudly said. 'Must be where I get it from. Finn's more arty-farty, like his mother was.'

I looked at Zak again. He was obviously aware someone

was outside too and it didn't take a genius to work out who he thought it was.

'Well,' said Luke, 'I think that covers everything. I'm going to double-check the rules the council have about this sort of thing and then it'll be all hands to the pumps.'

It certainly wasn't my place to, but I wished he had said something to shut Zak up as opposed to ignoring him, but then perhaps Zak was the sort who just wouldn't quit if paid any attention, negative or otherwise.

'Super,' said Carole, 'I'm pleased it's all working out.'

She didn't sound quite as thrilled as she had before and I guessed that presenting her and Poppy's weekend of hard work in front of Zak wasn't quite what either of them had had in mind.

'Me too,' Luke said. 'Is there any chance you could do me a favour this afternoon, Carole?'

The two of them walked out through a different door, leaving Poppy and me in Zak's somewhat overblown presence and the other visitor still waiting in the corridor. Luke obviously hadn't realised he'd got someone else waiting and I wished I'd said something.

Poppy and I stood up to go and Zak came around the table and leant against it. He put his tape measure down and crossed his arms, making his muscles ripple in the process. I don't know who he was trying to impress, but the posturing did nothing for me.

'So,' he said, looking squarely at Poppy, 'when are you going to let me buy you a drink then?'

'Never,' she said firmly.

Zak really did think a lot of himself if he was making a play for a woman who was already in a rock-solid relationship.

'Excellent,' he nodded. 'There's nothing I like more than a challenge.'

'Is that right?' she tutted.

'Hell yeah,' he laughed. 'I'll wear you down in the end.'

Poppy laughed and swatted him with the back of her hand and whoever was outside strode off.

'Come on, you,' I said, pulling at her sleeve, 'isn't it time you were getting back to work?'

'Bugger,' she said, looking at her watch, 'you're right. I'm going to be late.'

'I'll give you a lift in the van, if you like,' Zak offered, 'I'm heading that way.'

'No thanks,' said Poppy, following me to the door.

'Sure?'

Poppy rolled her eyes and shook her head.

'You're incorrigible,' she tutted.

I didn't think he'd know what that meant.

'She's sure,' I told him. 'She can jog.'

'And what about you, Freya?' he asked, turning his baby blues back to me. 'Can I tempt you to an afternoon in the pub?'

'Absolutely, one hundred per cent not,' I told him. 'Some of us have work to do.'

My eyes quickly scanned the corridor but the only evidence that someone had just been in it was the swinging door at the end.

'Damn,' I muttered.

'What's up with you?' frowned Poppy as she followed me out. 'I thought that went very well.'

I raised my eyebrows.

'I meant with Luke,' she added, as we headed outside. 'Don't take any notice of Zak. He's like that with everyone. You'll soon get used to him. He even flirts with Mark and Neil if he gets half a chance. He thinks he's God's gift, but he's harmless really.'

I didn't think Finn would agree and, to be honest, I didn't either. I got the distinct impression that Zak's mouth and cocky manner had the potential to cause plenty of harm.

Chapter 11

The next few days were the busiest I'd encountered for a while. Chloe went great guns with the tasks I'd assigned her on Tuesday, our brief clash over my misinterpreted lack of interest for Finn's part in Winterfest thankfully forgotten, and by the end of Wednesday the first specific planting area for the Winter Garden had been weeded and dug over, ready for the new scheme.

The already established and beautifully bright stemmed dogwoods were going to have their numbers doubled, and an array of early bulbs, aconites, violets and anemones were to be planted beneath. It was just about still mild enough to get away with putting the bulbs in and I knew it was going to look dazzling when the low winter sun hit it, but would still be impressive even on the dullest of days. I could already visualise the contrasting vibrant red and orange stems under-lit by a carpet of bright yellow and purple flowers, and if that clever combo didn't lift everyone's primal spirits, then nothing would.

That said, the mere thought of it wasn't enough to stop my mood dipping a little, but really that was down to my aching muscles. It had been a while since I'd done anything so intensely physical and Chloe and I were taking a much-needed break when Lisa came to find us on Thursday afternoon.

'Are you coming over to the house?' she asked, her head appearing around the door and making us jump.

'Already?'

I checked my watch; the afternoon had really run away with us. There was definitely no danger of time dragging during the working week at Prosperous Place.

'Yes,' Lisa said hurriedly. 'He'll be on in a minute. You are coming, aren't you?'

'Of course,' I said, grabbing my keys and encouraging Nell out of her basket. 'You're coming too, aren't you, Chloe?'

'Wouldn't miss it for the world,' she said, standing up and stretching out her back.

Luke had bagged a spot on Radio Norfolk to promote Winterfest and everyone who could was going to listen ahead of walking into the city together for the festive switch-on later that evening. I hadn't been all that keen to go and see the lights – a bath and an early night had been much more tempting – but Poppy had looked so disappointed when I turned the invitation down, that I changed my mind.

'I'm so pleased you've signed up to help with Winterfest, Freya,' Lisa said as we walked to the house. 'I wasn't all that keen myself, but when Carole said you weren't sure about doing it alone, I willingly stepped into the breach.'

'She said that, did she?' came Chloe's voice behind us.

'Yes,' said Lisa, twisting round to look at her. 'That is right, isn't it?'

'No,' I said, 'not really. I was nabbed by both Carole and Poppy. According to them, *you* were the one feeling jittery about flying solo and needed a partner to extend your session with!'

Lisa shook her head. 'The sneaky mares,' she tutted. 'I might have known, but never mind, hey?' she grinned. 'I think what we're planning will work really well together. I'm looking forward to it, aren't you?'

'I'm sure it will be fine,' I agreed, resigned to the situation now there was no going back. Luke was about to announce the event to the nation, well, the Radio Norfolk listeners anyway, so it was too late to change my mind. 'More than fine.'

'That's the spirit,' said Chloe with a laugh.

The three of us joined Carole and Graham, Ryan, Heather, Mark, Harold, Kate and a collection of children, cats and dogs around the radio in the kitchen and grinned as Luke's name was announced.

His smooth, deep voice was made for radio and the presenter was clearly smitten. She gave him far more airtime than I was sure was necessary and listening to him reminded me of the day I had asked Eloise for a sign and had been led to Norwich.

It brought a lump to my throat as I looked around the kitchen at everyone's faces as they listened eagerly to what

Luke had to say, and I wondered if there were any listeners about to find their own lives transformed by a trip to Prosperous Place, just like mine had been.

By the time the interview ended, Ryan, whose phone was set up to receive Grow-Well social media notifications, was inundated with messages, posts, shares and retweets.

'Something tells me we're not going to have a problem with numbers,' Carole beamed.

'Just as well you got so many of us to sign up to help out then, isn't it, Carole?' Lisa said meaningfully.

'Poppy helped too,' our clever coordinator quickly pointed out. 'And it will be wonderful to have everyone involved.'

I supposed I couldn't argue with that, although I would have been far happier taking a back seat and handing out materials and making tea.

'Right,' said Kate, once everyone had finished scraping chairs and chatting, 'Let's all meet in the square at four fifteen, shall we? That gives us an hour to get there before everything kicks off and hopefully time to grab some chips from the market.'

She and Luke had kindly offered to buy food for everyone and, from what I'd heard from Carole about the traditional switch-on, the city centre was going to be packed.

'Sounds perfect,' said Heather, gathering her brood together.

'Don't worry if I'm not there on time,' said Lisa. 'I will be coming, but it might be a stretch to get my lot back from school and changed by then. If I don't manage it, I won't be far behind you, and John's finishing early so he can help.'

'And I'll meet you all there,' said Chloe. 'I want to go home for a quick shower first.'

We all went our separate ways and I wondered if Finn would be joining us. I hadn't seen or heard him all week, aside from his shadow in the corridor on Monday and then I was still assuming that that had been him. I hadn't seen anything of Zak either, but I didn't mind about that.

In total, including children (but not dogs, as they were staying home because of the crowds and fireworks), there were well over twenty of us gathered together on the square by Kate's recommended time.

'It's nothing short of a Christmas miracle,' Lisa laughed as she and John ushered their beaming brood across the road.

'Just goes to show what can be achieved with the right motivation, doesn't it?' John joined in, giving his wife a squeeze.

'I wish it really could be Christmas every day,' said their little lad, Archie, as he jumped up and down.

'Now, don't start that,' said John with a grin. 'We'll all be sick of those words in a few weeks' time.'

'Not me,' said Archie, puffing out his cheeks and pulling off his woolly hat, which Lisa shoved straight back on.

A cheer went up as Luke jogged over the road from Prosperous Place, closely followed by Finn.

'It was mad trying to get back through the city,' Luke panted. 'I should never have taken the car.'

I hadn't ventured into the city yet, but I knew the radio

station was located in The Forum building which was next to county hall where a Norwich striker and his YouTube sensation girlfriend would be turning on the lights, so it was hardly surprising that he had found it busy.

'How did I do?'

Everyone began telling him at once and Ryan showed him his phone, scrolling through the social media feeds, the screen lighting up their faces in the near dark. From what I could make out, every session would be booked by the end of the week and if I pitched in, I wouldn't have to worry about twiddling my thumbs during the weekends for a good while to come.

'Not too shabby then?' Luke grinned, clapping his hands together. 'Right, who wants chips?'

We made our way along the already busy paths into the city like some overgrown and extra-long school crocodile. Most of the men had little ones on their shoulders, even Finn, who was looking even larger thanks to an oversized knitted sweater. He was carrying Jasmine on his shoulders and it made for a very striking tableau, though I hoped we wouldn't encounter any height restrictions along the route. I should have lent her the hard hat one of the builders had left back in the garden office.

Just as predicted, the city centre was awash with people and we had to queue for a while before everyone had their own cone of chips. The children had all been lifted down before we entered the market, which was made up of rows and rows of individual striped canopied permanent stalls.

From the glimpses I had seen, it looked as though you could buy anything you wanted, from practically anywhere in the world.

'You all right?' asked Ryan, coming to stand next to me as I sprinkled salt on my chips.

'Yes,' I nodded, letting out a long breath. 'I'm okay.'

'Sure?'

I looked at his young face and was surprised to find his brow etched with a frown.

'Only I know that look,' he said, giving me a sympathetic smile. 'I had a bit of a moment in here myself when I first moved in with my sister. It's tight for space, isn't it?'

The eagle-eyed youngster had picked up on my sudden feeling of claustrophobia and kindly rushed over to check up on me. He really was a kind-hearted young lad. No wonder Poppy always looked so proud when she talked about him.

'Yes,' I said, swallowing hard. 'It is a bit of a squeeze and I'm not all that comfortable in enclosed spaces.'

I had been doing my best not to think about it, but Ryan's observation and kindly meant intervention had kicked my awareness of the limited space up a notch.

'And what doesn't help is being stuck in here with a tree like him,' he added, giving Finn's arm a friendly thump.

'What's up?' Finn asked, awkwardly twisting around and looking down at us.

Now Ryan had drawn my attention to it, Finn did seem to take up an extraordinary amount of room. I looked up at him and felt my knees weaken as my chest started to flutter with a sudden palpitation. I should have stayed focused on my feet.

'Freya's feeling a bit hemmed in,' said Ryan as Poppy called for him to collect his chips.

Finn's eyes flicked back to my face and I wished Ryan hadn't pointed my problem out, even though he had meant it kindly.

'I'll be okay,' I swallowed again, looking around for a way out. 'I just need a breath of air, that's all.'

'Here,' said Finn, offering me a hand to hold, 'I can see the way, come with me.'

'I don't need to hold your hand,' I told him.

'Yes, you do,' he said firmly, 'otherwise I'll lose you. Come on.'

I did as I was told and my knees felt even wobblier as I slipped my hand into his, but I didn't think that had anything to do with the cosy confines of the market, because they didn't feel any stronger once we had eased our way out and were standing in the slightly less cramped spot on the steps with the best view of county hall. The only thing it could have been was his close proximity, but I wasn't prepared to consider what that might mean.

'How's that?' he asked, letting go of my hand, but still standing close. 'Do you feel any better now?'

'Much,' I lied, my cheeks flushed from the cold and my fingers tingling as a result of having his hand wrapped around mine. 'Heaps better, thanks, Finn.'

'It was a squeeze in there,' he said, looking back along the crowded rows, 'it's not usually as busy as this.'

'I haven't been able to cope with being boxed in since one of my cousins locked me in a cupboard when we were playing hide and seek,' I blurted out. 'I was only little, but I've never forgotten it.'

I don't know why I'd felt the need to justify what had happened. It wasn't usually something I talked about. Working outdoors practically guaranteed wide-open spaces and it had been a while since I'd been affected by the impact of my relative's nasty little prank.

'In that case,' Finn tutted, 'I'm not surprised you found it a bit much.'

Thankfully there wasn't time for me to further overshare as the rest of the Nightingale Square gang edged their way up the steps to stand near and around us and a cheer went up as Santa's sleigh arrived at the front of county hall having finished its tour around the city streets, where it had further fuelled everyone's excitement for the evening's entertainment. Music started to play somewhere and the noise level seemed to increase tenfold. Fortunately, I felt fine with the sky, rather than the canopied market, above me.

'Is that your phone?' Poppy asked, giving me a nudge as she went around with a bag, collecting everyone's rubbish.

I had no idea how she could have heard it, but I reached into my pocket and pulled it out. A text from Chloe had just landed, asking where we all were. There was no way I would be able to see her, or her me for that matter, so it was time to enlist the help of the tree, as Ryan had called him, again.

'Finn!' I shouted above the din. 'Chloe's somewhere in that direction, I think. Is there any chance you can spot her?' I knew it was a long shot. 'Or could you maybe wave that way and she might be able to pick you out.'

By some miracle, the plan worked and within a few minutes she joined us, laughing as she told everyone how she had spotted Finn's hand waving above the crowd and used him as a human satnav to reach us.

'You're coming in handy with those great bear mitts of yours tonight, mate!' laughed Ryan, clapping Finn on the back.

'What does that mean?' Chloe asked, turning to look at me.

'No time,' I said back, pointing to where a group of people had stepped out on to the county hall balcony and were preparing to start the countdown.

Lights, fireworks and more music filled the next couple of hours and as wonderful and exciting as it all was, I was grateful to be standing among friends. I had no idea what I'd been doing at Broad-Meadows on November the twelfth the previous year, but I knew for certain that it didn't involve anywhere near as many people or as much noise.

'You look as if you've had enough,' Lisa laughed, unaware of how I was really beginning to feel. 'Are you going to head back with us? Some of the others are stopping off at The Dragon en route, if you fancy it, the lucky buggers.'

The Prosperous Place crowd grew even larger as we walked back because Poppy and Jacob were joined by their friends Lou and Colin, who ran shops on the street next to Nightingale Square, and most people had bags of various sizes which further added to our bulk. I still wasn't ready to start my Christmas shopping just yet, not that I had all that much to get, but clearly some people were keen to get ahead.

'I think I'm going to carry on with the others,' I said to Poppy as we reached the pub and split into two groups.

Carole and Graham were going home, along with everyone who had children to get to bed.

'You can't go yet,' said Chloe, slipping her arm through mine. 'I've just spent the last half a mile convincing Finn to come in for a quick pint.'

I felt that horrible pang of jealousy prickle again. The pair had already walked most of the way back arm in arm, even though they were ridiculously mismatched height wise, and now Chloe was lining me up to play gooseberry. I really wasn't in the mood.

'That's as maybe,' I said, 'but I need to get back for Nell.'

'I thought Ryan said she had Gus for company tonight,' Finn pointed out.

I hadn't realised that he knew about that. Poppy had thought it would be a good idea to put the dogs together so if they were disturbed by the echo of any fireworks, they could console each other.

'She has,' I conceded.

'There you are then,' said Chloe, pulling me towards the

pub. 'A quick one won't hurt, will it? It's about time you were introduced to our fabulous Dragon!'

The Dragon was fabulous, but it was also pretty small, or at least it felt it by the time the nine of us had squeezed in to join the regulars and the rest of the post switch-on party revellers who were also heading home the slow way after an evening in the city.

'All right?' asked Finn, frowning down at me once he'd clocked how busy it was.

It was kind of him to ask, but I couldn't help wishing that I hadn't told him the real reason behind my wobbly moment back in the market. I didn't need him looking out for me every time there were more than half a dozen people in a room. I daresay my uncharitable thought was a bit ungrateful, but really, I just didn't want a fuss.

'Yes,' I said, doing my best to smile, 'I'm all good.'

Warm, dark and welcoming, the pub had low ceilings which felt all the lower because they were bedecked with festive garlands of greenery and lit with twinkling white fairy lights. There was a fire burning in the grate, which cranked up the heat, and smiling staff behind the well-stocked bar who added to the cosy ambience. It really was very lovely, but I knew I would have liked it even better if it hadn't been quite so busy.

I opted for half a pint of bitter from a local microbrewery which, I was told, was located on the outskirts of the city and was in such high demand it was going to have to lose the 'micro' moniker and move to bigger premises.

'Have you been in before?' asked the young woman serving.

'No,' I told her, counting out my money. 'I only moved to the area last week.'

'I didn't think I'd seen you before,' she smiled. 'You aren't Freya, by any chance, are you?'

'Yes,' I said, 'I am. How on earth did you know that?'

I thought the village closest to Broad-Meadows had the fastest bush telegraph in East Anglia, but perhaps I was wrong. I had expected at least a certain level of anonymity in the busy city, but clearly, I was mistaken about that too.

'I'm a friend of Chloe's,' she said, waving at the table where our mutual friend was making herself comfortable. 'She mentioned your gorgeous hair and I don't think there's anyone else in the vicinity with such a long plait.'

I supposed the length of it did make me a fairly recognisable resident.

'I see,' I said, handing her cash in exchange for my drink.

'So, welcome to The Dragon, Freya,' she said charmingly, 'I hope you enjoy your inaugural visit.'

'Thank you,' I said, taking a sip of the bitter, which was surprisingly light and refreshing. 'I love the atmosphere already and the garlands are very pretty.'

'The landlord came up with the idea,' she explained, 'because we haven't got room for a tree, and I'm not surprised you like them,' she added, 'what with you being a gardener, I mean.'

Chloe really had filled her in and I wondered how well the pair knew each other. Had my arrival been casual pub chat or was it more a case of exchanged news between close friends?

I don't suppose it mattered, but I did feel a little on the back foot as I looked around and wondered who else knew who I was and where I worked and lived.

'Sorry,' I heard Finn saying huffily as I inched my way through the bar and over to the table everyone else was squeezed around, 'but there's nothing I can do about him.'

'No,' said Poppy's partner, Jacob, sounding equally miffed, 'I don't suppose there is.'

'You can perch on here with me if you like,' Chloe said to me, shifting half off the bench she was already on the edge of.

'No,' I said, 'you're all right. I don't mind standing.'

I did really because my legs were aching even more after the walk into the city and back, but I wasn't planning on it being long before I made my excuses and left.

'I would offer you my seat,' said Finn, 'but if I stand up, there'll be even less room.'

He had a point.

'I really am fine here,' I told him, 'but thanks.'

It was weird standing next to him when he was sitting down. His face was far too close to mine and the heat from the fire was warming up that intoxicating aftershave he wore.

'Anyway,' he said, turning his attention back to Jacob, 'you won't have to worry about him hanging about for too much longer because there can't be much left for him to do and now I'm living on site, I've told Luke that I'm happy to see to anything that comes up.'

'I'm not worried as such,' said Jacob. 'It's just he always seems to hone in on Poppy.'

'I wish you wouldn't keep on about it,' she laughed. 'I'm perfectly capable of handling him and it's all bravado anyway. He'd run a mile if I gave him back as good as he gives me.'

'Well, let's not test that theory,' Jacob shot back.

'And it's not just Poppy,' Finn carried on. 'He met Freya on Monday and she got the same treatment, didn't you?'

Everyone's eyes turned to me.

'Met who?' I queried. 'And got what treatment?'

'Zak,' Finn elaborated. 'He came on to you in Luke's office, didn't he?'

'Actually, no,' I said, 'that wasn't me.'

I didn't want to further fuel Jacob's concerns about Zak flirting with Poppy, but I didn't want anyone thinking that I'd been bewitched by his muscly charms.

'I heard you,' Finn said, turning slightly red, 'you were having a bit of banter with him in Luke's office, but to be fair you did sound as if you were—'

'That wasn't me, it was Poppy,' I cut in, ruffled that he had jumped to a conclusion and the wrong one at that. 'Sorry, Poppy.'

Jacob's gaze swung back to his girlfriend and Finn looked up at me.

'Oh,' he said, 'I just thought . . .'

'I know what you thought,' I told him, 'but I wouldn't have talked to him like that. He's not my type. I'm not inter-ested in egocentric muscle–bound idiots.'

Finn's face split into a sudden smile.

'That's the best description of him I've ever heard.'

159

'Well,' I said, trying not to notice how attractively Finn's eyes crinkled when he smiled, 'that's as maybe, but don't tell him that's what I said, will you?'

'I won't,' he chuckled.

'So,' said Chloe, looking mischievous, 'what is your type then, Freya?'

I shook my head and refused to answer.

'Did you tell Zak where to go?' Jacob asked Poppy.

'Of course, I did, you loon,' she laughed.

They kissed and made up and everyone finished their drinks before getting ready to head home.

'I need to get back too,' I said, draining my glass. 'Nell will be wondering where I've got to.'

'No, she won't,' said Poppy. 'She'll be having a great time with Gus. There's no need for you to rush back. I'm only going because I want to make sure Ryan's all tucked up. He's got a college trip tomorrow and has to leave early.'

'You should stay and have a drink with, Finn,' Chloe whispered as she buttoned up her coat and pulled on her woolly hat.

I thought that was a strange suggestion, coming from her. If anything, I thought she would be the one hanging on to bag some extra alone time with him, because not only had they walked back from the city centre arm in arm, they had been squeezed next to each other in the pub too.

'What about you?' I asked her. 'You could stay.'

She shook her head.

'I'm walking back with Hannah,' she said, pointing over

to where the young woman who had served me earlier was getting ready to go. 'We live on the same street, but you two should stay and keep each other company.'

'I don't think so,' I said, looking over to where Finn was now leaning over the bar. I couldn't help noticing how broad his back was.

I felt as though I'd already shared enough with him for one evening; first I'd told him about my most traumatic childhood experience and now I'd given him my less than glowing opinion of his half-brother, which of course he had loved.

'Look,' said Chloe, 'I know it's nothing to do with me, but at some point, aren't the pair of you going to have to work together in the gardens?'

'Yes,' I sniffed.

'And wouldn't it be easier to do that if you got to know each other a bit?'

Given the amount I'd already said, I thought he was getting to know me plenty fast enough and we were only positioning sculptures together, we weren't exactly office desk buddies.

Nonetheless, Chloe looked at me in expectation of an answer, her eyebrows quizzically raised.

'Maybe,' I conceded, 'but not tonight.'

'Why?' she demanded. 'This is the perfect opportunity.'

Given that it was more than obvious that Chloe seemed to like Finn in a way that transcended the friends zone, I could hardly tell her how weak my knees had felt when he took my hand in his or how, when I was first introduced to him, the fluttery sensations in my stomach made me forget there was anyone else in the room, could I?

All of those feelings I had experienced put my interest in the man still standing at the bar way beyond the friend zone too. They were primal and disconcerting and certainly inconvenient. I had enough on my plate right now what with settling into a new home and a new job. I certainly didn't need the added complication of a new crush too, because that was all it could be. Chloe was going to be the girl for Finn, not me, but I didn't feel, knowing what I did about her tragic past, that standing in a packed and noisy pub was the moment to point that out.

'You need to stay,' she hissed, when I didn't answer, 'build on the good work you've already done tonight.'

'What do you mean by that?'

'Describing his brother as egocentric and muscle-bound has *definitely* got you off the hook for belittling his Winterfest suggestion.'

'I didn't belittle it,' I said, defensively.

'Just stay,' she practically begged, although I had no idea why. 'Oh God, here he comes. Just stay and get to know him a bit better. Think of it as furthering your professional relationship, if nothing else.'

There wasn't time to object.

'Are you not leaving, Freya?' Finn asked when I didn't follow Chloe.

'Not just yet,' I said, my voice catching as my so-called friend gave me a double thumbs up as she backed out the door.

'Looks like it's just the two of us then,' he commented, looking about him. 'Why don't you grab us a table now it's quieter and I'll get you another drink.'

'Thanks,' I swallowed, taking the pint he offered when he eventually came back from the bar again. 'You'll have to let me get the next one.'

I had no idea why I said that because I wasn't planning on staying. Finn nodded as he tried to work out where to put his long legs so that they wouldn't be in everyone else's way.

'I'm sorry about that mix up over Zak,' he apologised.

His tall frame wasn't easy to fold up and I noticed that he'd had to walk with his shoulders hunched and his head bent to avoid ending up wearing a holly crown. In the constricted space which was enhanced by the smell of wood smoke, he looked like a bulky extra from *Game of Thrones*.

'No worries,' I shrugged. 'And I'm sorry about what I said about him.'

'That's all right,' he chuckled. 'It was actually the highlight of my evening.'

'You were right when you said you were nothing alike, weren't you?'

'I honestly don't think you could find two blokes who are more different,' he confirmed, before taking a long pull at his pint, which I found myself mirroring. 'He's a carbon copy of my father and it's a nightmare when the pair of them get their heads together. For me, anyway.'

'What about your step-mum?' I asked. 'What's she like?'

'She's all right,' he told me. 'Nothing like my mum, of course, but we get on okay. To be honest, sometimes I can't believe she married my dad.'

'Are you talking about your mum or your step-mum?'

'Both,' he smiled.

'Well,' I said, 'just to reiterate, I wasn't flirting with your brother. As I said before, he's not my type.'

'Who is?' he asked. 'You never did say.'

I busied myself with my drink and Finn laughed.

'Fancy another?' he offered, striding back to the bar before I'd had the chance to say no.

I did manage to get in the round after that, to level things up a bit, but I made sure I had just a half. I was feeling wonderfully relaxed by then and I wasn't worried about getting back for Nell or anything.

'You all right?' Finn asked as I struggled to sit back down after a meandering walk to the loo.

'I'm fine,' I sighed, eventually dropping down on to the seat with a heavier than expected thud.

Finn grinned and I smiled back.

'Thanks for coming to my rescue in the market,' I said, leaning in a little. 'I had no idea it was going to be so packed, otherwise I wouldn't have followed everyone in.'

'It wasn't nice what your cousin did to you, was it?'

'No,' I agreed, 'it wasn't. I've never been able to ride in a lift as a result and the London underground is definitely out of bounds.'

'I'm not all that keen on it myself,' he admitted, 'all

those bodies packed together and no fresh air. It can't be healthy, can it?'

'No,' I said, feeling momentarily mesmerised as the light caught the Thor's hammer around his neck and I struggled to focus back on his face, 'it can't.'

In my slightly sozzled state, he looked even more like a god in human form. No wonder Chloe had made a beeline for him.

'I still don't really know much about you, Freya,' he said, 'other than that you have a very mean cousin and that you're a fantastic gardener. The night we had supper with Luke and Kate, you found out loads about me and now you've met my half-brother too, but you're still something of a mystery.'

I didn't think there was anything mysterious about me, but if he carried on flattering my professional skills like that, then I would be tempted to tell him everything there was to know, starting from childhood and working my way forward in minute detail. I pushed my glass further away, thinking I shouldn't have anything else to drink.

'What are your family like?' he asked. 'Any annoying brothers to wind you up?'

'No,' I said, 'I'm an only child. Hence the play dates with the cousin from hell.'

'Parents then?'

'Yes, two. Dad's all right,' I then blurted out, 'but Mum's a total pain in the—' I clapped my hand over my mouth. 'Mum and I have a tendency to clash,' I said, reeling my motor mouth back in. 'They're in the gardening trade too. Landscape design consultants, nothing hands-on like me.'

'Have you ever worked together?'

'Yes, I did work with them for a while, but it didn't work out.'

'What with your mum being a total pain in the—'

'Exactly,' I cut in and Finn smiled.

'So, you weren't working with them before you moved to Nightingale Square?'

'No,' I told him, 'I was managing the garden on a country estate called Broad-Meadows in Suffolk.'

'Why did you leave?'

'The owner,' I swallowed, 'my friend, Eloise, she died. She was actually much more than a friend,' I added, my voice thick in my throat. 'She was like a grandmother to me.'

'I'm sorry.'

I took a deep breath, refusing to give in to the wave of emotion the mention of her name still evoked.

'Her American nephew,' I carried on, 'Jackson, inherited, and let's just say we had different views on how the place should be run.' I was starting to think of him less often, but I could still recall his confidence-eroding comments. 'Actually,' I added, 'he'd give your Zak a run for his money, because he's a total narcissist too.'

'Not an easy person to work with, I take it?'

'No one works *with* Jackson,' I said crossly, 'you only work *for* him.'

'Nothing like Luke then?'

'Absolutely nothing like Luke,' I said, reaching for my glass again.

'So, how did you find out about Prosperous Place? When did you apply for the job there?'

'I didn't,' I told him, 'I just happened to hear Luke talking about his plans for the Winter Garden on the radio and thought I'd come along and have a look. My mum was fully expecting me to move home once I'd realised I couldn't cope with staying at Broad-Meadows and seeing the estate sold. Between you and me, she was probably pleased it was happening.'

'Because she wanted you to move home?'

'No, because she never forgave Eloise.'

'For what?'

I pushed the glass away again.

'Offering me an alternative.'

'To what?'

'The life she and Dad were expecting me to live.'

'Which involved . . .'

'Marriage,' I cut in. 'Broad-Meadows was my wedding venue. I was getting married there, but I realised I couldn't go through with it and broke it off.'

Finn looked as if he'd been punched in the stomach. All the colour drained from his face and he sat back in his chair. Perhaps I wasn't the only one who had gone heavy on the bitter. I was pretty certain it was stronger than the more commercial stuff.

'And what was the alternative Eloise offered you?' he quietly asked.

'A job and a cottage,' I told him, 'and the opportunity to

discover what I really wanted out of life, because it certainly wasn't marriage.'

'Or the groom,' Finn said tersely.

Fortunately, our engagement hadn't reached the point where Peter had been transformed into a groom and the fact that I still hadn't started looking at gowns, should have been warning enough for both of us that there was little point in viewing potential venues. Although if I hadn't, of course, I never would have found Eloise, or Nell. Nell . . .

'I think I'd better get back,' I said to Finn. 'I know Nell's got company tonight but this is the longest I've left her and if I don't get some sleep soon, I'll be useless tomorrow.'

'Yeah,' said Finn, sounding gruff as he shoved his glass across the table so it sat next to mine, 'I've got an early start too. Let's go.'

Chapter 12

Finn walked with me as far as the turning into Nightingale Square and then peeled off to Prosperous Place. He hardly said a word on the walk back and I couldn't manage to make small talk because I was too preoccupied with trying to focus on my feet. The cold night air had hit me like a brick when we left The Dragon and my legs and feet didn't want to work together, which was most distracting.

As Poppy had predicted, Nell and Gus were fine and I was grateful Gus stayed overnight because I somehow managed to sleep right through my alarm. If Poppy hadn't come to collect him and roused me by hammering on the front door, I probably wouldn't have made it into work at all.

'What the hell's happened to you?' she gaped, taking in my dishevelled and pale appearance as I held up a hand to shield my eyes from the light which streamed in when I opened the door. 'Oh God,' she whispered, 'you haven't got Finn in there with you, have you?'

'What?' I frowned. 'No, of course not, whatever made you say that?'

'Nothing,' she grinned. 'Where's Gus? Is he good to go?'

Sunglasses were hardly necessary on such a dull November day, but I kept them firmly in place and my thumping head down at work, avoiding all contact with anyone else and rushing back home, unusually for me, the very second the time ticked over to four o'clock.

Towards evening, I started to feel a little better, but I was still grateful that it was almost the weekend and I could take myself off for a very early night. I eventually managed to dismiss the thoughts about what Poppy had assumed and which had plagued me all day and slept soundlessly until late the following morning. Thankfully when I woke my head felt much more like my own again and I had an appetite to rival Nell's.

'Freya!' Chloe called, beckoning me over as I joined everyone who had started to congregate on the green Saturday evening. 'Do you want some mulled wine?'

'Just half a cup, thanks,' I said.

I didn't really want any, but neither did I want her to guess that my lack of enthusiasm for the festive tipple was the result of a hangover I had ended up with after staying on with Finn at the pub.

'There you go,' she smiled, handing it over.

We had all left the cosy confines of our homes and ventured out as a result of invitations from Luke and Kate which had arrived earlier in the day. Inspired by the switch-on in the city, Luke had arranged for a large tree to be erected on the green and he, Kate, their children and most of the other little ones who lived in the square, had spent the last few hours decorating it with lights and huge baubles.

Goodness knows where he had sourced those from and as I took the spectacle in, I wondered where he'd found the tree too because it was planted in a huge pot. Given the weight of it, it must have come on the back of a lorry. I really must have been out for the count, to have slept through the delivery of that!

The air was filled with the mingling spicy scents of mulled wine and warm mince pies, which Carole was hastily handing out before they got cold and it really was beginning to feel a lot like Christmas. I already knew my celebrations this year were going to be very different and, looking around at everyone's happy faces, I was pleased about that.

Life in Nightingale Square might have been a bit overwhelming at times, but it was an honour to be a part of such a close-knit community and I was about to realise just how integrated I already was.

'How did you and Finn get on on Thursday night?' Chloe asked.

'Oh,' I said, trying to remember the finer details. 'All right. We talked about family and stuff for a bit and then walked home.'

I thought the conversation had gone a little flat towards the end of the evening, but thanks to the excesses of microbrewery bitter, I couldn't get a clear grasp on why.

'Well that's good then,' said Chloe. 'You must be feeling relieved. There's nothing worse than having to work with someone you don't get on with.'

The cheeky tone of her voice didn't quite match what she was saying, but there was no chance to clarify what she was really getting at.

'Gather round folks!' Luke's voice rang out and we all huddled closer to the tree. 'Gather round.'

Taking in the numbers, I saw there were even more than just those of us who lived in the square.

'Who's that?' I whispered to Chloe, nodding towards a trio I didn't recognise who were standing opposite us.

'That's the Stanton clan. Zak and his mum and dad,' she told me, also looking over.

The two men were standing shoulder to shoulder, with a slightly shorter woman between them.

'I didn't recognise Zak with the hat on,' I whispered.

'Or the coat,' said Chloe, with a wry smile.

She had obviously been privy to his posturing and preening too. Thankfully it was too chilly for him have his biceps out.

'From what I can make out,' Chloe carried on, scanning the crowd, 'Luke's invited everyone who has helped out at the house this year, all the trade staff and their families, as a thank you for their hard work.'

It was a generous gesture, certainly one he wasn't obliged to make and, given the swollen numbers, I guessed there had been a lot of work carried out during the last twelve months.

Everyone was tucking into the mince pies, enjoying the wine and looking very happy to be there. As was I.

'Where's Finn?' I asked, 'isn't he coming? He's not with his family.'

'I'm here,' said a voice close behind me, making me jump and Chloe squeal.

'Thank you all so much for coming,' said Luke. 'After our trip into the city on Thursday night, I thought the square could do with a bit of festive cheer and as plans for the Winter Garden don't extend to here, we thought we'd have our outdoor Christmas tree delivered here instead.'

Everyone cheered and raised their cups in approval.

'When we ordered it, we were going to put it next to the house,' said Jasmine, who clearly had no qualms about talking in front of so many people, 'but then we said that if we put it here everyone would be able to see it all the time.'

'Thank you, Jas,' said Lisa, speaking for all of us, 'that was a very kind thought.'

'So,' said Luke, his eyes searching the crowd, 'let's get it lit, shall we?'

'It's going to look amazing!' said Jasmine, bobbing up and down.

'Where are Freya and Finn?' shouted Luke.

Chloe started to bounce on her toes, looking very much like Luke's eldest daughter in her eagerness to point Finn and me out. Suffice to say, her antics quickly attracted everyone's attention.

'Come on, you two,' Luke grinned, beckoning us over.

'As the two newest recruits, we thought we'd leave the honours to you.'

I knew I had no choice but to step up, but I really didn't want to. Being the centre of attention was the last thing I had expected when I arrived.

'Come on,' said Finn, nudging me in the back. 'Let's get it over with.'

I couldn't tell if he was just plain grumpy or embarrassed like me, or a bit of both. I handed Chloe my cup and walked over to Luke and Kate with Finn following close behind. I really hoped Luke wasn't going to force us to say anything. Public speaking was definitely not my forte.

'All you have to do is press this down,' said Luke, pointing to a switch on what I guessed was some sort of external power pack. 'Okay?'

'Okay,' Finn and I said together.

'Here we go!' Luke shouted, turning back to the group while Finn and I got ready to hit the button. 'Ten, nine, eight . . .'

As soon as everyone shouted 'one' we pressed together as instructed, our gloved fingers briefly touching, and the tree became a beacon of brightly lit bulbs. Everyone cheered and clapped and we took a step back to admire the festive view.

'It's beautiful,' said Kate, coming to stand next to me while Luke went to the opposite side and nudged Finn out of the way because he was blocking the view for at least half of the crowd. 'Isn't it pretty?'

'It's gorgeous,' I told her.

'Happy Christmas, Freya,' she smiled, kissing me on the cheek.

'Merry Christmas, Kate,' I said back, 'and thank you, for everything.'

And then everyone was kissing and hugging. Somehow, I managed to avoid both of the Stanton brothers and made my way back to Chloe to admire the green, blue, red and yellow lights which reflected on to the baubles and bathed the whole square in a bright and seasonal glow.

'Isn't it wonderful?' said Chloe.

There was something in her tone which made me look at her properly and I was shocked to find her eyes filled with tears.

'I'm all right really,' she said, sniffing hard and shrugging off my attention with a watery smile as she handed back my cup of wine. 'It's just Christmas, you know. It's tough.'

With her usual gusto and get-up-and-go enthusiasm, it was all too easy to forget that she was a widow harbouring a broken heart.

'Yes,' I said, carefully pulling her into my side so as not to crush our drinks, as I felt sympathetic tears prickle my eyes too, 'I know.'

We stayed like that while Luke delivered the rest of his speech, filling us all in with a quick update on Winterfest.

'Practically every spot for every session is filled now,' he announced, with a big smile. 'Which shows us that there's definitely a demand for this sort of thing and if it doesn't get us all in the mood for Christmas, then nothing will.'

'We're already in the mood!' called John, making everyone laugh.

'Well, that's good,' said Luke, 'let's see if we can keep that feeling going right the way through to spring, shall we?'

We all had enough to do to keep us occupied and I couldn't image Graham, who was standing next to Carole and looking flushed from the wine, would have time to feel anything like as low as he had the winter before. At least, I hoped he wouldn't. If push came to shove in the garden, I still had every intention of drafting him in to help.

There might still have been over a month to go before the official opening on December twentieth, but I could have quite easily filled double that time with what I wanted to achieve, and that was even before we had worked out where to place Finn's sculptures. Without thinking, I swallowed down a mouthful of wine as I ran through the long list of jobs which still had the power to make my heart canter and my nerves prickle.

'I'm going to be checking through everything tomorrow,' Luke finished up, 'and if any of you who are involved could come along, I'd really appreciate it.'

Everyone seemed happy with the request and I thought it was a good idea to get us all together to share our plans and give a flavour of what to expect. I was really looking forward to Winterfest now, even the part that I was going to play in it.

'It's exciting, isn't it?' I said to Chloe, who I was happy to let go of, now I had banished my nerves again and she had recovered from her understandably emotional moment.

'It is,' she agreed. 'Hannah and I have signed up to do one of the sessions.'

'Hannah?'

'My friend who works in The Dragon.'

'Of course, which one are you doing?'

'The bread- and chutney- making that Mark and Poppy are running.'

'That sounds wonderful,' I nodded, my mouth watering at the thought of warm crusty bread topped with local cheese and a spoonful of chutney.

'And what about you, Finn?' Chloe asked, as he walked by. 'Are you excited about Winterfest? Have you signed yourself up to make a needlefelt robin or a festive cake?'

'No,' he said, sounding gruff. 'I haven't.'

'You don't sound very enthusiastic,' I commented, looking up at him.

His hair was tied back properly for once and I could see the whole of his face. I hadn't noticed before but his cheekbones really were beautifully defined.

'I thought you were on board with it all,' I swallowed, quickly regrouping.

Given that Zak had let slip that Finn had gone ahead and offered to run a session himself, I thought he would have sounded far keener.

'It just seems to be getting out of hand,' he grumbled, shoving his hands deep into his pockets, 'I had no idea it was going to be so popular.'

I couldn't understand why he felt so aggrieved. Surely,

the more people the event attracted, the more would see his work if we got it out in time and possibly offer him a commission.

'None of us did,' Chloe pointed out.

'You aren't going to back out of doing your workshop, are you?' I asked.

'No,' he snapped. 'Of course not.'

'Well, there's no need to bite our heads off,' Chloe shot back.

'Sorry,' he muttered, scuffing the grass with the toe of his boot. 'I'm just worried about how it's all going to impact on my studio time. I only get to work in there properly during the weekends at the moment and there's still loads to do. It's going to be hard to work if the grounds are heaving.'

'It's not going to be that busy,' I said, my own mood deflating a little in the face of his persistently grumpy one. 'And if you keep the door shut and your music belting out like you usually do, then you won't even know it's happening.'

'Maybe,' he muttered.

Chloe looked at me and shrugged, clearly, she was as confused by his apparent change of opinion as I was.

'I just need to be able to get on,' he elaborated. 'I've got a lot riding on this.'

When he said that, I realised his mood was more the result of fear than grumpiness. He was doubtless mindful of his professional future and worried about hitting the Winter Garden deadline rather than having to cope with a few extra people milling about. Given the way I also felt about the fast-approaching official opening date, I could empathise with that.

'Just keep in mind that the garden's a work in progress,' I said, as much for my benefit as his. 'You'll be able to add to it as we go and I'm sure Luke won't be expecting you to have *everything* ready all at once.'

'Because that's not how creativity works, is it?' Chloe cleverly pointed out. 'You can't just sculpt on demand. You can't rush it, can you? I would imagine it's a lengthy process.'

I can't say I'd given much thought to the nuts and bolts, either figurative or real, but Chloe was right. It wasn't all about hammering and welding, the planning and preparation had to come first.

'Jesus!' Finn suddenly shouted.

For a moment I thought he was shouting at me and Chloe, but then his hair fell loose around his face and Zak appeared from behind him, waving a band about.

'Are you having a little arty-farty temperamental moment, bro?' he teased, tossing the band into the air for Finn to catch.

'Fuck off,' Finn snapped.

Chloe and I exchanged a look and I realised that Finn's bad mood was most likely aggravated by his half-brother's unwanted presence as well as his concerns about his work.

'Not that you can call welding a few bits of junk together, art,' Zak carried on, obviously determined to get a reaction.

'Actually,' I said, thinking of the beautiful cat Finn had put together for Jasmine, 'I've seen one of Finn's pieces and his work is exquisite. It's definitely art.'

Zak looked shocked that I had sprung to his brother's defence. Perhaps he wasn't used to having someone stand up to him.

'Well,' he said, 'whatever. I've only really come over to ask if you lot fancied a trip to the pub?'

'And yet you couldn't resist trying to get a rise out of your brother while you were about it?' I pointed out.

There was no way I'd be going to The Dragon with him, and not only because it was far too soon after my switch-on hangover.

'Crikey,' Zak grinned, looking me up and down. 'She is a feisty one, isn't she? You said as much.'

'Shut up, Zak,' Finn warned him.

'Good looks and a bit of spirit,' Zak carried on anyway. 'I get the feeling you're going to be more of a challenge than Poppy, Freya.'

'I think you'll find we're both unconquerable, Zak,' I snapped.

'Oh well,' he shrugged, 'you can't blame a fella for trying.'

Chloe looked at me and shook her head. The risk of running into Zak was the only thing I didn't like about living in Nightingale Square and I hoped Luke was going to take up Finn's offer to finish off any outstanding jobs.

'Well thanks for that, Freya,' Finn said tartly, once Zak was out of earshot.

'What?' I frowned.

'She only spoke up for you,' Chloe pointed out.

I wondered if Finn had mentioned her to Zak too.

'Exactly,' he rumbled, 'and I'll never hear the bloody last of it, will I?'

'So, I should have just stood by and let him talk to you like that, should I?'

'Yes,' he said, 'that's exactly what you should have done.'

He strode away without another word and I was left red-faced and wondering if our relationship was ever going to be plain sailing.

I was looking forward to joining everyone at Prosperous Place to discuss our Winterfest plans, but I didn't make it over very early because I had a call from my mother to contend with first, followed by a very quick soul-soother with Peter.

'Freya!' Mum said by way of greeting, 'I've found you at last.'

'I did message Dad last week,' I reminded her, 'so you knew I was okay.'

'Oh, I don't mean that,' she said with a tinkly laugh and I imagined her waving her hands about.

'What do you mean then?'

'I mean I've found out where you actually are. It's that Prosperous Place in Norwich, isn't it? Owned by that luscious Luke Lonsdale.'

'How do you know that?'

'I spotted you in the background of one of the photographs advertising this Winterfest thing he's so keen on and then you were named in the article too. Can you believe it made the national press? I take it you're managing the garden?'

'Yes,' I confirmed, inwardly cursing the efficiency of the photographer and his zoom lens, 'yes, I am.'

'I don't know why you didn't just tell us that's where you were going,' she said, sounding a little sulky.

'Because, like I've already explained, I wanted to get settled first.'

It was ridiculous that I didn't feel comfortable telling either her or Dad my whereabouts, but the turn the conversation then took more than justified my reason for not saying anything.

'Well, whatever,' she said, dismissing my explanation without further comment. 'It says here that you're working with him on this new Winter Garden project?'

'That's right.'

'You'll have to let us know if you need any professional input,' she offered.

'I am the professional input,' I said indignantly.

'Well, of course, you are,' she laughed, 'but you know what I mean.'

Unfortunately, I knew *exactly* what she meant. First Jackson had made out that I wasn't up to the job his aunt had employed me to do and now my own mother was implying the very same thing. Either that, or she wanted to make sure she wasn't missing out on a business opportunity.

'Thank you for the offer,' I said, biting my lip, 'but I'm managing just fine, more than fine actually. You'll be able to see for yourself when the garden is officially opened in a few weeks' time.'

I knew there was no point pretending there wasn't going to be an official opening because Luke was bound to have mentioned it in the interview.

'Not before then?' she wheedled.

'Absolutely not,' I said firmly. 'Luke's very protective of his privacy.'

'Um,' she said, 'I had heard that about him.'

I was surprised by that, because I hadn't. I'd only said it to keep her and Dad at arm's length for a bit longer.

'In that case,' she said, 'I suppose we'll have to wait for December twentieth. Now, Freya, let me give you an update on what's happening at Broad-Meadows. You won't believe—'

'No,' I said, cutting her firmly off. I wasn't at all interested in hearing what Jackson was up to. 'Sorry, Mum, but I have to go. I have a work meeting to get to.'

'On a Sunday?'

'We never stop here,' I said briskly. 'Let's catch up again in a few weeks.'

I ended the call before she could say anything else and rang Peter for a quick video chat. I didn't really have time, but I didn't want to turn up at Prosperous Place carrying an aura tainted by the aftermath of a conversation with my mother.

'Hey, Freya,' he said, answering with a smile.

'Hey,' I said, my jangling nerves settling a little as I took in his familiar face.

'How's it going?'

'Good,' I said, perhaps a little too quickly. 'Great.'

'Are you sure? You don't sound it.'

'I've just got off the phone with Mum.'

'Ah.'

Peter knew full well that was enough of an explanation, but I elaborated anyway.

'She told me to ask if I needed any professional input with the Winter Garden.'

'That will account for the frown then.'

I ran my fingers over my forehead, trying to smooth my brow.

'Yeah,' I swallowed. 'Look, I don't actually need any help to do this.'

'Of course, you don't.'

'And practically everything's already been approved, but if I email you my plan and proposal would you just have a quick read? Confirm that I'm on the right track.'

'That Jackson guy really undermined your confidence, didn't he? And your mother obviously hasn't helped either, has she?'

I didn't say anything. I didn't want to agree out loud. It was enough carrying the evidence around in my head. The Mum and Jackson combo really had struck quite a blow.

'There's no doubt in my mind that everything you've planned is perfect, but by all means send it,' Peter said kindly. 'I'm really interested to see what you're working on.'

'Thanks, Peter,' I said, feeling better.

I took a moment to look at the detail around him. He obviously wasn't at his place.

'Are you in a restaurant?' I squeaked, the second I realised I had interrupted what appeared to be an evening out.

'I am,' he nodded, turning the phone around so I could see a yacht-filled harbour and a very pretty woman sitting opposite him. 'I'm actually on a date.'

'Oh my God,' I said, cringing as he turned the screen back to his face, 'I'm so sorry. Why did you answer?'

'It's fine,' he laughed.

'Of course, it isn't,' I hissed. 'I'm going now.'

'Okay, but before you do, tell me, how's that Finn fella you mentioned? Still an interesting character?'

'Oh yeah,' I said, rolling my eyes. 'He's getting more intriguing by the day. I'll email you later and please apologise to that lovely woman you're with.'

I hung up before he handed the phone over so I could say sorry myself. At least one of us had got our love lives back on track, that is, assuming she'd forgive him for taking a call from an ex in the middle of their dinner date.

Nell and I jogged across the road, arriving hot and flustered in the Prosperous Place kitchen and full of apology for not getting there sooner. I noticed there was no Finn either.

'Where's Finn?' I whispered as I slid into the empty space next to Chloe, and Nell headed for a spot in front of the range cooker with the cats. 'I thought he said he wasn't backing out.'

'He's not. He was here,' she whispered back, 'you're sitting in his seat, but he spoke first and then excused himself so he could get back to work. His session is still going ahead.'

'And what are you doing here?'

'You'll find out in a minute.'

Having waited until I was settled in my seat, Carole then told us all about her grand cake and pudding plans. She was followed by Mark and Poppy and their delicious-sounding chutney and bread proposals. There was also a needlefelt session being run by Heather who had sorted childcare, planting up winter garden containers with Graham and making a woodland-inspired wreath, which was where Chloe came in.

'I didn't know you could do that,' I said to her, once she had finished talking.

'I'm full of hidden talents,' she smiled. 'I'm hoping you might give me a hand. But only in an assistant's role,' she hastily added.

So that must have been the extra session Carole had signed me up for!

Lisa and I were up next. Just like the others, we ran through what our schedule was going to include, timings for each section and what each attendee would need to bring. Had I not been helping out; I would have signed up to take part myself because it sounded wonderful. It all did.

After a quick coffee break, Luke went through the formalities and handed around the contact details of each attendee to the relevant session leader – Lisa in my case – and we drafted out emails which we then read out, before all pressing send at the same time. It might sound silly, but it was very exciting and I wished Finn could have hung on to join in with the rest of us. Being in the thick of things might have lifted his spirits again, assuming they were still sagging.

When I walked back to the square, I was tempted to knock on the studio door, but I didn't. To be honest, I didn't think he would have heard me anyway, because the radio was on full blast and it was accompanied by the sound of grinding metal. Even though he was cross with me for sticking up for him, I was still kind enough to hope that meant he had hit his creative stride and was happy in his work.

It can't have been easy to keep his dream alive when faced with Zak and his father's steady stream of disparaging remarks. Jackson's snide comments about my lack of qualifications had ensured I could empathise with some of what he was feeling and then there was my mother's offer of *professional input* which hadn't made me feel any better either. Perhaps I should point all that out to Finn. It might be a comfort to know that he wasn't the only one striving to fulfil his dream in the face of adversity.

Chapter 13

That evening I emailed my plans, proposals and plant lists for the Winter Garden off to Peter, including further apology for interrupting his harbourside date, and went to bed early, wondering what the next few days would bring.

The beginning of the week got off to a flying start, and I was able to indulge in one of the aspects of my job that I love the most. Luke had taken delivery of a huge plant order including shrubs, bulbs and a couple of small trees, and it was up to me to decide where they would be best placed.

By Monday lunchtime I had everything marked out and was able to take him around, explaining why I had chosen to put things where and describing for him how it would all look, paying particular attention to the Winter Garden borders, in just a few weeks' time.

There was a certain irony in that I had just got on with it, rather than waiting to find out what Peter thought of my ideas. That clearly meant I had more confidence than I gave myself credit for and that, in reality, Jackson's undermining (and to a lesser extent Mum's) had no lasting power over me.

In my mind's eye, as Luke and I went around, I could already envisage the additional seasonal pops of colour that the new shrubs would bring and my nose was practically picking up the sweet scent of the sarcococca, which would start flowering soon after the new year. The viburnum x bodnantense with its tiny pink flowers was already providing a smell of what was to come and Luke was delighted with it all.

'Winter is so often underrated,' I enthused as we made our way back to the office, 'but it only takes a couple of tweaks to keep real interest in the garden all year round.'

Luke grinned as he held the door open for me.

'What?' I asked.

'I thought I was enthusiastic about the project,' he laughed, 'but you're taking it to a whole new level, Freya.'

'Well,' I said, feeling my face flush with more than cold, 'that's what you've employed me to do so I might as well make a decent show of it.'

'More than decent,' he praised, joining in with my banter.

I was delighted that he was so happy with the way it was all coming together and for me it was a relief to feel my creative spark burning brighter again. My former passion was finally back after its period of grieving for Eloise which had made it vulnerable to attack.

'I'm going to start planting this afternoon,' I told him, 'and carry on with Chloe tomorrow.'

'And I'm happy to help out,' Luke said. 'I was also wondering if we could get the girls out here to plant a few of
the bulbs? As long as it won't interfere with your schedule.'

'That would be wonderful,' I told him. 'In fact, I have a
bit of a trick up my sleeve when it comes to bulb planting.'

It wasn't my trick, but it was a good one nonetheless. I
was a massive fan of gardening enthusiast Beverley Nichols,
who wrote passionately and prolifically about his horticultural endeavours, between the 1930s and 1960s. Eloise had
introduced me to the books he had written about his various
homes, gardens, friends and cats, and I had been hooked
ever since.

She had gifted me her exquisite hardback copies shortly
before her death and they were my most prized possessions.
He had not only written at length about his love of winter
flowers and how a garden should have enough interest to
tempt you from your fireside during the colder months, but
also about his fun ways when it came to planting bulbs.

'I'm intrigued,' said Luke.

'Good,' I laughed, 'I'm pleased, and I can guarantee you'll
be thrilled in a few months.'

'You aren't going to tell me what you're planning to do
with them, are you?'

'Nope,' I said, shaking my head.

If I told him Mr Nichols' methods for bulb planting now,
there would be no surprises to come. As well as filling a
wooden tray with bulbs, tossing them into the air and planting them where they fell to achieve a naturalistic look, he

also liked to give his visiting friends a handful or two, along with a trowel and instructions about planting depth. Then, he would turn his back, send them out into the garden and eagerly look forward to the following spring when he could indulge in a treasure hunt in his own grounds to discover where they had ended up.

That was what I intended to suggest to Kate. 'Just bring Kate and the girls out tomorrow as soon as Jas gets home from school, and then go back into the house.' I instructed Luke, my heart thrumming at the thought of playing the game Mr Nichols had invented.

'You don't want me to help?'

'Nope,' I told him firmly, 'and I certainly don't want you looking out to see what we're up to.'

'Fair enough,' he laughed, catching my enthusiasm, 'I'll stay hidden until you're finished then.'

'Perfect,' I grinned.

Thankfully, Jasmine was home early from school the next day. She'd had an afternoon dental appointment which meant going back to class was hardly worth it and was able to join me, along with Kate and Abigail and Chloe, just after half past two which gave us enough daylight to carry out my bulb planting plan.

The sisters loved taking part and thought it was going to be great fun keeping it all a secret from their father, and Kate was keen too. It was almost dark when they finally headed back to the house and Chloe cycled home and most of the bulbs had been well hidden. I was going to plant the daffodils in what Luke called 'the meadow lawn' myself, and there were just a random few others left to distribute.

There was no sound coming from Finn's studio, but there was a light on and I wondered if I dared to knock and ask if he fancied taking part. If not in the dark that evening, then perhaps tomorrow or later in the week.

I knew I was using the idea as an excuse to work out whether or not he had forgiven me sticking up for him in front of Zak, but it had all been preying on my mind and I really did want to try and explain to him that, with regards to family at least, we truly were paddling a pretty similar boat.

I was also interested to discover what exactly he had said about me to his family. Zak had implied that he'd said something, but given that Finn had a complicated relationship with his father, I thought mentioning me at all was unnecessary, so it was most likely something and nothing, inflated by his half-brother to arouse Finn's annoyance and my curiosity, and that of course had worked because I desperately wanted to know.

The only problem was, you never knew which version of Finn you were going to be faced with. Would it be Dr Jekyll or Mr Hyde who opened the door? Would I be treated to a warm welcome or a glowering scowl? I'd had a truly lovely afternoon, and the surly Mr Hyde would be a total mood killer. If I was still in Finn's bad books, then I was really going to regret disturbing him, even though I would have been doing it with the best of intentions.

I'd literally just decided not to take the risk when the

studio door was wrenched practically off its hinges and Finn peered out.

'I thought I heard someone loitering,' he said gruffly, and I took another step away, swallowing down the gasp which had shot into and then out of my mouth.

'I was just passing,' I swallowed, readjusting my hold on the bulb bag and trying to sound placatory for fear of further rousing Mr Hyde from his lair. 'I didn't mean to disturb you. I'm just about to pack up for the day.'

'In that case,' he said, stepping out, reaching for my sleeve and pulling me in before I had a chance to free myself from his grasp, 'come and give me your opinion before I bottle it and start to take them all apart again.'

I had barely time to draw breath, let alone object to his gentle but nonetheless forceful manhandling, before I was over the threshold and the door had closed behind me.

'Where's Nell?' he frowned, releasing me and thankfully putting a little space between us.

'Asleep in the office,' I told him.

'Good,' he said, biting his lip, 'because I haven't had a chance to sweep up yet.'

I could see that. The place was littered with all sorts of sharp-looking odds and ends.

'So,' he said, puffing out his cheeks and raising his eyebrows, 'what do you think?'

He nodded towards the back of the studio and I followed his gaze. Another gasp rose unbidden in my throat and this time I did nothing to check it.

'Oh, Finn,' I cried, abandoning the bag of bulbs and rushing over, all thoughts of our crossed swords, my good intentions and determination to wheedle out of him what he had said about me, instantly forgotten, 'they're incredible!'

He came to stand next to me.

'You really think so?' he asked, running a hand through his wild hair and staring at me intently, a frown etched so deeply across his forehead it looked like a freshly furrowed field.

'Of course, I do,' I told him. 'How could I possibly think anything else?'

His shoulders dropped, the frown cleared and his expression was transformed. The biggest smile lit up his face and he looked like a completely different person. Dr Jekyll was definitely in the house. Or studio in this case and as far as being miffed with me for sticking up for him was concerned, I was pretty certain I was forgiven.

'They're for the meadow lawn,' he told me.

The huskiness of his tone told me he was clearly touched by my reaction.

'They should be in a gallery,' I said back, and I meant it too.

'Well,' he said, cocking his head as he started to study them again, 'I don't know about that.'

All of the tension in him had disappeared and his tone was softer. It really would have been heresy if he had 'bottled it and pulled them all apart again'.

'Well, I do,' I insisted, moving to admire them from another angle. I felt tears gather behind my eyes and knew my emotive reaction was not only the result of admiring his outstanding work, but also because of the dramatic change in him. 'How on earth have you made them look so alive?'

What he had created from various coils, springs, cogs and cylinders were a trio of hares. The first in the sequence was poised to leap, the second was at full stretch and the third had just landed. They were utterly mesmerising and I wouldn't have been at all surprised to see them turn their elegant heads in my direction and blink. They were going to look perfect positioned in the meadow lawn.

'I honestly don't know,' he said with a self-deprecating shrug. 'I just kind of get a feel for the subject and then put together the shapes that I think will work.'

He was utterly self-effacing and it infuriated me to think that Zak and his father were so ignorant and dismissive of his talent. Perhaps once the garden was finished and they could see Finn's art, because that's most definitely what it was, in situ, then they might change their opinions. They'd be stupid not to.

With some difficulty, I tore my eyes away from the sculptures and took in the rest of the space.

'Did you draw these?' I asked Finn, as I walked over to the bench, which was covered with sketches of hares in various poses.

'Yes,' he said, 'I know this guy, Jake, who has a farm over near Wynbridge with hares on the land and I spent some time there, photographing them and then sketching them in the fields.'

'Amazing,' I sighed, meaning both the real hares and the essence of them that Finn had captured in just a few strokes of a pencil.

The marks he had made appeared effortless, but for someone who struggled to come up with so much as a competent doodle, I knew they were incredibly accomplished.

'There aren't anywhere near as many hares there now as there used to be, thanks to the bloody coursers, but Jake does what he can to keep those on his land safe.'

'I thought coursing was illegal,' I said, turning back to look at him.

'It is,' he said sadly, 'but it doesn't stop it happening.'

'But why would anyone want to kill something so beautiful?' I said, shaking my head, my tears not quite banished.

I knew there had been an increase in coursing activity in Suffolk too in recent years, but thankfully not too close to the Broad-Meadows estate.

'Money,' Finn said bluntly. 'It's all about money. And big money too.'

He turned back to the sculptures, squatting down on his haunches to get a closer look and I wished he was always like this. Not talking about cruel blood sports and rural crime obviously, but looking proud of his work and with his inner spark aflame.

But then, perhaps it was his artistic temperament, the soaring highs and deep lows, which enabled him to create such stunning pieces. Maybe he needed the good as well as the bad to balance it all out. He looked then like he did the night we had supper with Luke and Kate. He had come alive when he presented Jasmine with her cat sculpture and, in that moment, he wore exactly the same look as he did studying the hares; his eyes blazing with something close to wonder.

He appeared to all intents and purposes as if he didn't believe he was looking at something he had made, but rather at a vision someone else had been responsible for. It was most endearing and very sexy.

'Talking of money,' I said, dismissing my libido as I walked back over to him, 'I bet you could charge a fortune for these and there would be no suffering or bloodshed.'

'Perhaps,' he said, straightening back up. 'These hares might be cruelty-free, but my hands have taken a bit of a battering.'

They did look rather knocked about, but at least he had come out of his trance far enough to acknowledge that the work in front of us was his own.

'But you know what I mean,' I said, swallowing hard as I tried not to look at his hands. 'They'd sell in an instant.'

'Yeah,' he said, 'maybe, I dunno.'

I could see that he really had no understanding about how unique his work was. He might have been passionate about the creative process, but he was clueless when it came to considering his sculptures financial value.

'I'm being serious, Finn,' I said firmly. 'You could make a proper living doing this.'

Anyone would be able to see that it wasn't just a case of welding a few bits together and coming up with something that resembled the animal he had been aiming for. There was real personality, life and movement in what he had created. I guessed his family's dismissal and belittling of his passion had taken a toll, just like my parents' opinions about me taking the job at Broad-Meadows and Jackson's cruel words had dented my confidence for a while. Perhaps this was going to be the moment to share some of that with him after all.

'Well,' I said, 'Luke's going to be thrilled, along with every single other person who walks through the garden and spots them.'

'I hope so,' he sighed.

'I know so.' I told him.

'I wish I had your faith,' he said, sounding vulnerable.

'You just need a bit of time,' I told him, moving a little closer and laying a hand on his arm.

'Time?'

'Yes,' I said. 'I mean, you've barely started, have you?'

'I've been doing this for a while,' he said, the frown forming again. 'I did tell you that.'

'You did,' I confirmed, 'but you also told me that you were surrounded by people who were hell-bent on chipping away at your dream, didn't you? Given the circumstances,' I carried on, 'it really must have taken some strength to keep going at all, but you did and now you're here and Luke has given you the opportunity to work in a completely different atmosphere and surrounded by people who want to champion your achievements. Believe me, it won't take long for your self-belief to catch up.'

I stopped to draw breath and found he was staring at me.

'Sorry,' I said, removing my hand from his sleeve and feeling my cheeks flush.

I hadn't meant to have such a major soap-box moment.

'No,' he said, 'don't apologise.'

'Sorry,' I said again, without meaning to.

'And certainly, don't apologise for apologising,' he laughed, reaching for my hand and holding it tight in his.

I couldn't have offered a third apology, even if I'd wanted to because his action robbed me of speech, my libido leapt up again and my body tingled as our skin touched.

'It's just that I've been in the same boat as you.' I eventually managed to say. 'My parents hated it when I took the hands-on role at Broad-Meadows and, even though they didn't voice their opinion quite as vociferously as your father and Zak, I felt its impact nonetheless.'

'So,' he said, looking deeper into my eyes as he stepped closer and tucked a strand of hair behind my ear, 'perhaps you and I aren't so different, Freya.'

'No,' I whispered, glancing up at him and remembering how Zak had said he had described me to his family. 'Perhaps we're not.'

Whether it was the feel of his fingers lightly touching my face, the fact that our hands were still entwined or the sound of my name on his lips, I couldn't be sure, but the next thing I knew I was in his arms and he was kissing me and I was kissing him.

Held tight in his embrace I didn't hold back; I didn't think about our professional relationship or Chloe's warm feelings for him. I kissed him long and hard as the flames of desire which had been burning so low in me for so long, sprang up, shooting hot, fiery sparks to every nerve ending and erogenous zone. Pressed tight against him, I could feel his firm body reacting to my mine and as I dipped the tip of my tongue into his mouth he groaned with pleasure.

'Freya,' he breathed, as I twisted my hands into his hair and then felt his tongue gently meet mine.

As one we took a step towards the workbench and he lifted me up on to it. I was just about to wrap my legs around him and pull him in again, when the sound of the *Gardeners' World* theme tune filled the air and I realised my phone was ringing.

'Is that your phone?'

'Don't worry about it,' I breathlessly replied, reaching for him.

'I think you'd better answer it.'

'It'll stop in a minute,' I insisted, determined not to have our passionate moment doused.

'I don't think it will,' he said, a few seconds later.

He gently lifted me down and, feeling furious to have been interrupted, I wrenched my phone out of my pocket and accepted the call without checking to see who it was first.

'Freya?'

'Hey,' I swallowed, my annoyance slightly scotched as I realised who it was, 'Peter.'

Finn took a step away and I checked my watch. He was the last person I would have expected it to be.

'Why are you ringing so early?' I asked him. 'Is everything okay?'

Some speedy mental maths told me it must have been before dawn in New Zealand.

'Everything's fine,' he told me, 'but I've got an early start and a long drive. I'm going away for a couple of days and wanted to talk to you about the stuff you sent before I set off. Is now a good time? Why are you breathing so hard?'

'Actually,' I said, taking a moment to try and slow my breathing back down as I looked over at Finn who had moved further away, 'it's not a great time.'

He was standing with his hands on his hips, his breath shallow like mine, but I couldn't have guessed what he was thinking.

'It's fine,' he said, in a low voice.

'Who's that?' asked Peter.

'No one,' I shot back, which made Finn's eyebrows shoot up in response.

'It's not Finn, is it?' Peter laughed. 'I reckon you wrote more about him than your plans for this Winter Garden.'

'No,' I said, pressing the phone harder against my ear in the hope that Finn wouldn't hear what was being said, 'it's not.'

I suppose I had gone a little overboard telling Peter about what had happened since mine and Finn's first unfortunate encounter, but it had felt cathartic, writing it all down. Peter would have been mightily amused by the sequel, not that I would be telling him about it.

Now the moment had passed and I had come back to my senses, my face burned with shame as thoughts of Chloe and her feelings for Finn filled my head. Some friend I had turned out to be.

'Look, Peter,' I said, 'can I call you back? Now's really not a great time.'

'Don't hang up on my account,' Finn said gruffly.

'Are you sure that's not him?' Peter persisted.

'I'm really sorry,' I said to Finn as I gathered up the bag of bulbs, I had dumped on the studio floor. 'But I think I'd better go.'

'It's fine,' he said tersely.

'I'll see you tomorrow,' I insisted. 'We'll . . .'

'What?' he said, his chin held high. 'Pick up where we left off?'

Had it not been for Chloe's obvious interest in him, that was *exactly* where I would have liked to have picked up, but I really did have to factor my friend into the equation and embarrassingly, Finn sounded far from thrilled at the prospect. He was obviously regretting the moment already, which made me feel even worse about allowing it to happen.

'I thought we could look at the meadow lawn and work out where to put the hares,' I therefore suggested instead.

He shrugged his shoulders and turned away.

'Freya?' came Peter's voice in my ear again. 'I'm sorry, but I really do need to get on.'

I suppose I could have told Peter that I'd catch up with him when he got back from his trip, but given that he had taken the time to read through what I had sent him and had kindly made the effort to call, I could hardly cut him off and so I left Finn brooding over his trio of beautiful hares, and walked back to the office, all the while wishing that Finn hadn't invited me to look at his sculptures and cursing that we had got caught up in the moment and let our artistic emotions get the better of us.

Chapter 14

Needless to say, I wasn't looking forward to having to face Finn the next day and spent the morning hoping that he hadn't been paying attention when I had suggested that we should look over the meadow lawn, but luck wasn't with me and he turned up at the office just as Chloe and I were finishing lunch.

I had given Chloe a morning full of jobs on the opposite side of the garden from where I was working, for fear of blurting out what I had done. Keeping quiet didn't make me feel any better about betraying her, or less embarrassed that Finn hadn't requested a repeat performance, but it did save me from hurting my friend.

Peter, full of praise for my plans and proposals, had soon winkled the details of my heated moment with Finn out of me and said I should just come clean with Chloe, like I had with him when I had broken our engagement, but I just couldn't bring myself to do it and opted instead to pretend it hadn't happened.

That wasn't an easy mindset to maintain when I could still feel the imprint of Finn's lips on mine and when faced with him, standing just behind where Chloe was sitting in the office, it became even harder. My already flimsy denial bid a hasty retreat, and left me floundering, which was probably no less than I deserved.

'I'm just going to take Nell back to the square,' was all I could think to say. 'It's chilly this afternoon and she'll be more comfortable at home with the heating on.'

I knew I was taking the coward's way out, but I thought that if Finn wanted Chloe to know what had happened between me and him, then he might take the opportunity to mention it himself. She wasn't going to hate me any less, finding out like that, but at least I wouldn't be the one having to say the words.

The pair of them were coming out of the studio when I arrived back and Chloe was looking more than happy, so I knew he hadn't spilled the beans. Perhaps like me, he was going to pretend it hadn't happened. It would certainly make our lives simpler, and perhaps it really hadn't been a memorable moment for him, but I was still full of mixed emotions.

I'd never experienced a kiss like it, the heat between us, to my mind, had been scorching and there was a part of me, quite a large part actually, that would have very much liked to experience it again.

'The hares are amazing,' Chloe beamed when she spotted me. 'You should see them, Freya.'

'She has,' Finn said bluntly.

'They certainly are,' I agreed with a smile and making a gargantuan effort to pull myself together.

'You didn't say,' Chloe frowned, looking at me.

'Well,' I said, 'we've hardly seen each other all morning, have we? Now, let's get on. It looks like it might be gearing up to rain and there's loads I still want to get done today.'

'You haven't forgotten I need to leave early, have you?' Chloe asked.

'Bunking off now it's getting cold, are you?' Finn tutted. 'You didn't strike me as a fair-weather gardener.'

'Not at all,' she said primly, swatting him with the end of her scarf. 'I have a meeting at school about a student who came to us recently and is struggling to settle in.'

'You're in demand, Chloe,' Finn smiled.

'All the more reason to cut the chat and get on then,' I butted in, striding off with the heavy tray of daffodil bulbs under my arm.

'Fair enough,' said Finn, sounding equally crotchety as he relieved me of the tray. 'Let's get it over with, shall we?'

'Whatever's the matter with you two?' Chloe demanded.

'Nothing,' we said together, before sharing a glance which told me very little about how Finn was feeling, other than that he didn't really want to be anywhere near me.

Chloe didn't look as though she believed us and I could hardly blame her.

'I'm just feeling the pressure,' I elaborated, as she came to link her arm through mine. It wasn't a lie; I still spent plenty of time worrying that I wouldn't hit the open day deadline. 'And it's making me jittery because I desperately want it all to be perfect.'

'It will be,' she said, squeezing me close. 'We're a team, right?'

'Of course, we are,' I swallowed.

'Absolutely,' Finn reluctantly joined in.

The area which formed the meadow lawn had been cut at the end of the summer which made it easier for us to negotiate. We looked at it from all angles before carefully marking the spots where Finn's trio of hares would be most admired. Thankfully, focusing on the task had eased some of the tension between us and it didn't take long to plot the prime positions out.

'They'll be great here now,' I said, adding covers to the tops of the cane markers for obvious health and safety reasons, 'but when the grass starts to grow up around them in the spring, they'll look even better.'

'And if the grass gets too high in summer,' Chloe suggested, 'we could trim it, but just around the bases.'

'That's a good idea,' I agreed, feeling better for being out in the fresh air again.

'And what about this lot?' asked Finn, pointing at the bulbs. 'Are they going in here too? There's an awful lot of them.'

'Yes,' I told him, 'they are. You need a lot if you want to make an impact.'

'We've forgotten the planter,' Chloe tutted. 'I'll go back and get it.'

I'd added the short-handled one to the tray but forgotten its long-handled cousin which kept bending to a minimum and saved a fortune in muscle soak.

'You can go, if you like,' I said to Finn, suddenly self-conscious now that it was just the two of us.

'No, it's all right,' he said, picking up one of the bulbs and rubbing its papery skin. 'I'll stay and give you a hand. How are you going to decide where to put them?'

'I have a trick up my sleeve,' I told him.

'Ah yes,' he smiled, making my heart melt, 'Luke mentioned that you have a way with bulbs, but he couldn't tell me what it was because you had insisted on keeping it a secret even from him.'

'I want it to be a surprise,' I told him, 'so if you are staying, you can't go blabbing.'

'I won't.'

'Promise?'

'Scout's honour,' he said seriously. 'I'm good at keeping secrets.'

I was just about to suggest keeping our kiss a secret when Chloe came back and the moment was lost.

'Right,' I said, 'you two stand back.'

I carefully stepped up on to a tree stump and then used all of my strength to launch the bulbs from the tray on to the grass where they fell in exactly the haphazard muddle that I had been striving for.

'Beverley Nichols?' Chloe grinned, clapping her hands together.

'Beverley who?' Finn frowned, looking from her to me and back again.

I think he thought I'd gone a little mad.

'Yes,' I gasped, looking at Chloe who was laughing and shaking her head. 'How did you know that?'

'My nan was a huge fan,' she told me. 'She loved his books and had loads of clippings from his magazine column.'

'Well, I never,' I smiled back.

Other than Eloise, I'd never met anyone else who'd even heard of him.

'Him?' Finn frowned, looking more confused than ever.

'Yes,' I said, stepping down and handing him the long-handled planter because he was the tallest, 'come on, I'll show you what to do.'

Finn soon got the hang of it, which was just as well as there were quite literally hundreds to plant.

'Some of these have fallen quite close together,' he pointed out. 'Do you want me to space them out a bit?'

'No,' I said, rushing over, 'clumps are fine.'

Planting exactly where they landed was going to ensure they looked naturalistic rather than regimented. We were striving for swathes of colour not municipal park planting.

'Are they all the same?' he asked. 'There are loads of daffodil varieties, aren't there?'

'There are,' I confirmed, 'but these are all the same sort. I've used them in a scheme before. In fact,' I added, remembering and then thinking aloud, 'they became a bit of a trademark for Peter and me.' We had used them to great effect on at least three occasions and I couldn't wait to see them swaying in the spring breeze at Prosperous Place. 'And when they come up,' I told Finn, 'you'll see why I asked Luke to get just one variety – and remember, no blabbing about what we've been up to.'

'Are you talking just about the bulbs, or something else?' he asked darkly.

Taken aback, I quickly turned away and got my foot caught in one of the planting holes he had made, but not yet filled.

'Shit,' I swore, dropping everything as the ground came up to meet me.

Finn swung into action and, before I knew it, I was safely enfolded in his arms and had been saved from the pain of a twisted ankle. I clung to him as I carefully lifted my foot out of the hole and gingerly set it down on the grass. Thankfully there was no harm done. Other than to my dignity, which had taken another battering.

'I don't remember that being part of the Nichols technique,' Chloe laughed. 'You're supposed to be throwing not catching, although Freya is a rather lovely catch.'

I kept my eyes focused on Finn's broad chest, let go of his sleeve and put a little distance between us, embarrassed that Chloe had commented.

'You all right?' Finn asked.

When I risked a glance, there was a smirk playing around his lips and I supposed I could hardly blame him. I daresay I had looked hilarious, but I couldn't see the funny side.

'Yes,' I said, 'no harm done.'

'What a hero,' Chloe carried on, too far away to see my face as she pretended to swoon. 'Although I would imagine women are always falling at your feet, aren't they Finn?'

Now it was his turn to look uncomfortable. His face was almost as red as I imagined mine to be.

'Not exactly,' he said, turning his attention back to the job in hand.

'Remind me,' she said, wandering over, 'what exactly is your current relationship status?'

I could feel my heart starting to beat faster and it had nothing to do with the tumble I had just taken. I didn't like the turn the conversation was taking and knew I had to stop it.

'If you want to ask him on a date, Chloe ...' I blurted out, but stopped when I spotted the change in her expression.

Her eyes were wide and her rosy glow was dialled down to deathly white.

'No,' she stammered. 'That's not what I ...'

She bit her lip and her eyes filled with tears as she fumbled to pull back the sleeve of her coat to check her watch.

'I have to go,' she said, rushing off. 'Otherwise I'll be late for school.'

'Nice one,' said Finn, as soon as she was out of earshot.

'I was worried you were going to say something about what happened yesterday,' I said, my own eyes filling with tears, just like Chloe's had.

'Why would I want to tell anyone about that?' he snapped back.

211

My analysis of the situation was right then; he hadn't felt the same level of heat as I had, and I felt even more foolish than when I'd fallen over.

'And I don't think Chloe actually was trying to ask me out, was she?' he said pointedly, making me feel even worse.

'I'll go after her,' I said, my tears spilling over as I realised what I had done.

Chloe hadn't been asking about Finn's love life for her own benefit. Of course, she hadn't. If I hadn't been so stupidly jealous of their friendship and insisted on reading more into it, then I might have worked that out far sooner and stopped myself from making such a stupid mistake. All this time she had been trying to matchmake him and me, not him and her.

'No,' said Finn, catching my arm, 'leave her. There's nothing you can say right now that will make her feel any better.'

I hated to admit it, but he was right.

I sent Chloe a text that evening, apologising for my silly comment and making her promise to meet me in The Dragon Friday night so I could buy her a drink and say sorry in person. Had it been anybody else, with any other past, my silly faux pas most likely wouldn't have mattered anywhere near as much. But dear Chloe, widowed so young, certainly didn't need me accusing her of looking for love when all she really had going on with the man in question was an easy-going friendship.

I felt a bit jittery as I left the square and headed for the pub. The last thing I wanted to do, especially as the new girl on the block, was upset anyone and I hoped my new friend would accept my explanation when I told her in all honesty that my silly comment was the result of me feeling totally blindsided by my unexpected feelings of attraction for Finn which shouldn't have impacted on her at all.

The last thing I had been expecting was to fall headlong for the fella who had bitten my head off when I first laid eyes on him, but that's what had happened, and our passionate kiss had confirmed it. Why else would he be constantly on my mind? Why else would I be factoring in his thoughts and opinions when considering my own? Why else would I care so much that he had been annoyed when I stuck up for him? Why else would my eyes turn green every time I saw him with Chloe?

It was all a mortifying mess, especially now I knew for certain that he was keen to forget all about the best kiss I'd ever had. I would just have to tell Chloe that as kindly meant as her matchmaking was, it was very definitely misplaced.

'Just a Coke for me please,' I said to Chloe's friend Hannah, who was serving behind the bar, 'and what do you think Chloe would like?'

'No idea,' she said bluntly, 'but she sent me a text a minute ago asking me to tell you that she's not coming.'

'Oh,' I said, reaching into my jacket pocket for my phone.

'She said she tried to call you but you didn't answer.'

After Peter's timely interruption, I'd switched my phone to silent and hadn't felt it vibrating in my pocket, but sure enough, there was a missed call listed on my log.

'Damn,' I said, feeling worse than ever, especially when I realised that from the look Hannah was giving me, she knew what had happened. 'Did she say anything else?'

'No,' Hannah shrugged.

I paid her for the drink she had already poured and found myself a table tucked around the corner from the open fire. I would drink up, head home and work out what I was going to say to Chloe when I called her from the more private confines of my sitting room.

'All on your lonesome?'

'Zak,' I said, 'hi.' He was the last person I wanted to see. 'Yeah, I am, but I'm about to head off actually.'

'But you've only just arrived.'

'I wasn't planning on staying long.'

'You've not been stood up, have you?'

'No,' I said, trying to keep my patience.

I didn't think it actually counted as being stood up if the other person had let you know they weren't coming. Not that I had any intention of sharing that summation of the situation with Zak.

'I thought you might be waiting for my brother,' he smiled, 'but as you're not, would you mind if I sat with you?'

'I would actually,' I told him as I quickly drained my glass.

'Fair enough,' he shrugged. 'I just wanted to have a quick word, but I'll come and find you next week.'

Something in his tone made me look at him properly and I can't deny, I was surprised by what I saw. Clad in a shirt which wasn't two sizes too small and with considerably less product than usual, attempting to sculpt his closely cropped hair, he was almost unrecognisable. He was a much more attractive proposition, toned down and covered up.

'Too cold for a T-shirt tonight?' I asked, unable to resist.

'I know, right,' he grinned. 'Who'd have thought it? But actually,' he went on, 'this is your doing, Freya.'

'Mine?'

'For the most part, yes,' he said, taking the chair opposite. 'You really took the wind out of my sails the other night.'

'Did I?'

I felt myself tense up, waiting for the punchline, chat-up line, or any other line he might be about to deliver. But apparently, he was in earnest.

'Yeah,' he said, rubbing a hand around the back of his neck and looking uncharacteristically sheepish.

'I think you'd better explain.'

Truth be told, I'd rather hear it when I was already having a rough night, than next week when I was enjoying a day's work.

'The thing is,' he said, putting his glass on the table and fiddling with the cuffs of his shirt.

I imagined it was an unusual feeling, having his whole arms covered.

'You might not have realised it, but what you said at the square switch-on really hit home.'

'Which bit?'

'All of it, to be honest. I've spent so long taking the piss out of Finn that I'd forgotten what it might feel like if I stopped. For years, I've been going along with Dad's opinion of him . . .'

His words trailed off as he looked around him, but there was no one paying any attention to us.

'Go on,' I encouraged, still not convinced his words weren't part of some elaborate prank.

'Promise me you won't breathe a word to anyone else, Freya, especially not Finn.'

'I won't,' I told him. 'Scout's honour,' I added, echoing his half-brother's words.

'Well,' he swallowed, 'the truth is, I'm jealous of him.'

'Jealous?'

'Shush,' he pleaded, looking around again, 'yes, jealous. I've spent my entire life looking for Dad's approval by doing and saying everything he wants and expects, but Finn's had the balls to carve his own path and be his own man, even when it's been difficult, nigh on impossible, at times.'

The words escaped him in one long rush and I took a moment to study his face.

'I'm not bullshitting,' he told me, clearly reading my thoughts, 'although I totally get why you might think I am.'

'I don't think you're lying,' I reassured him, because I didn't. There was absolutely no trace of mischief about him and I was pretty certain he wasn't clever enough to deliver those lines with such commitment if he didn't truly mean them. 'I'm just in shock.'

'You and me both,' he smiled. 'It's taken a lot for me to say out loud what I've secretly been feeling.'

It wasn't a direct comparison, but it had taken me a while to break off my engagement with Peter, even though I had been harbouring feelings of doubt practically from the moment he slid the solitaire diamond on to my finger. In fact, if Eloise hadn't happened to come into my life when she did, then I might never have found the courage to do it. Given that I now thought what Zak had just told me was true, then I had bestowed upon him (and in turn Finn), the ultimate 'pay it forward' moment.

'So, why now?' I questioned. 'Finn was really annoyed with me for sticking up for him and, to be honest, I assumed you were going to use it against him.'

Zak shook his head. 'To tell you the truth,' he laughed, 'initially so did I, but it didn't work like that. Your words struck a chord, Freya, and I realised that it was time that I grew up and started acting my age. I even sneaked into the studio when Finn was upstairs in the flat and had a look at those three rabbits he's been working on.'

'Hares.'

'What?'

'They're hares, not rabbits.'

'Same difference,' he shrugged.

There was plenty of difference, but it wasn't the moment to explain them.

'And what did you think of them?' I asked instead.

'They're amazing,' he said. 'You'd have to be stupid not to be able to see that.'

As I recalled, when I first set eyes on the trio, that was exactly what I thought Zak and his dad were.

'They are spectacular,' I agreed, 'and we've found the perfect spot for them in the garden.'

'I don't know how he does it,' he said, wide-eyed. 'How can he take a pile of scrap and see that potential and those shapes?'

'I have no idea,' I said. 'Not a clue.'

A beat of silence fell but then I couldn't resist asking. 'So, does this mean you're about to reveal a secret ambition, too?'

'Nah,' he said, 'I'm happy being a builder like my dad, I just don't want to be a tosser like him anymore, that's all.'

'Well,' I said, 'I think that revelation is more than enough to be going on with and I like the new image,' I added, nodding at the cover-all shirt.

'It's all right, isn't it?' he said, looking down at his chest and smoothing the fabric. 'I'm not into the kind of stuff Finn wears, all those symbols and stuff, but I'm sick of being a carbon copy of Dad. I always thought he was the strong one in the family, but actually that's Finn. I've realised now that it's taken a lot for him to stick to his guns and follow his heart, especially when he didn't even have me in his corner.'

'Are you going to tell him any of this?'

I really hoped he was.

'You must be joking,' he laughed. 'He'll think I'm taking the mick.'

'He might not,' I told him, 'especially if you say it all to him just like you've said it to me.'

'I'm not sure I could do it again,' he grimaced, puffing out his cheeks, 'and you gave me your word that you wouldn't tell, remember?'

'I remember,' I smiled.

'Not a word to Finn or anyone else, all right?'

'Of course, I said so, didn't I?'

'That's all right then,' he said, standing back up, 'people will soon get the idea that I've changed when I stop being a—'

I was pleased that he didn't finish that sentence, even though there were many and varied words he could have called upon to describe his former self, most of them anatomical and none of them flattering.

'I bet Jacob will be first to see that you've turned over a new leaf,' I laughed.

'You reckon?'

'Absolutely. If you can get through the next few weeks without flirting with Poppy then everyone will know that you're a changed man.'

'That's a big ask,' he said, shaking his head, 'but I'll do my best. She's a cracking girl though, and so are you, Freya.'

'Thanks,' I said. 'I think.'

'I'm surprised Finn hasn't snapped you up by now,' he grinned, a little of his former puckish self peeping through the shiny new façade. 'You're just his type, but then ...'

'Then what?'

'No,' he said, holding up his hand, 'not my place to say. The old Zak would have done, but the new Zak knows it wouldn't be right to go around talking about Finn's disastrous love life.'

I was intrigued and he was halfway there already. Perhaps I could coax a little more out of him.

'Has it been that disastrous then?'

'Just a bit,' he said, shaking his head. 'He's definitely damaged goods.'

I wished I could shake his head hard enough to make the memories fall out so I could take a look at them.

'But then, given what Finn's said,' Zak then shockingly carried on, 'you haven't fared much better yourself, have you? Although at least you were doling it out rather than being on the receiving end. It's got be easier that way around, right?'

I was poised to quiz him about exactly what Finn had said, when a group of lads came bursting in and carried him off.

'See you next week, Freya!' he called as they dragged him away, leaving me choking down an unpalatable cocktail of shock, annoyance and confusion.

Chapter 15

I felt really put out that Finn had been going around sharing what he thought he knew about my romantic past, especially when I ran our former conversations through my head during the chilly walk back to Nightingale Square and realised that he didn't actually know anything of consequence.

He might have heard enough from me during our time in The Dragon after the city switch-on to furnish him with the broadest details of my broken engagement, but that didn't give him the right to discuss it, especially in his brother's presence. I hoped he hadn't jumped to any conclusions about what had happened, and if he had, then I was going to have to set him straight.

I also hoped that he hadn't been playing fast and loose with the details of our passionate clinch in the studio. His apparent indifference to the experience did make me think that he'd prefer to keep that to himself, but then again, it hadn't ever crossed my mind that he would talk about my former love life either.

I had promised to go over to the Grow-Well the next day but as it was Saturday, I didn't have to be early, so I took a cup of tea and a bowl of porridge back up to bed for a lazy start. I had just finished the porridge and was rehearsing what I was going to say to Chloe when she beat me to the punch and called me.

'You're up early for a Saturday,' I cautiously said, hoping that she hadn't had a sleepless night.

I knew that she liked to lie in at the weekend.

'I couldn't sleep,' she told me.

'And that's my fault, isn't it?' I groaned.

'In part.'

'I'm so sorry, Chloe.' I told her, a lump in my throat. 'I didn't mean to be so spiteful about Finn. It just kind of slipped out and I really hate myself for it.'

'Hate's a bit strong,' she said, and I clung to the hope that there was the hint of a smile in her tone.

'Well, I do,' I insisted. 'And you certainly didn't deserve to be on the receiving end of my stupidity. I'm so sorry.'

'I know you are,' she carried on, 'and I also know why you did it. It's obvious that you really like Finn, which is why I was trying, not very discreetly I suppose, to set the pair of you up.'

Had we had this conversation the night before in the pub as I had planned then she would have been in full receipt of my confession that I *was* harbouring feelings for Finn, but thankfully that hadn't happened and I could refute her assumption with a clear conscience.

True, I did still have feelings for my scrap-sculpting colleague and yes, the kiss we had shared was the most arousing I had ever experienced, but, thanks to Zak, my feelings for Finn had morphed into rather different ones now.

'After you'd gone on Thursday,' I told Chloe, 'I realised that's what you were trying to do and it made me feel even worse.'

'I wouldn't have done it as a rule,' she said, 'but it's obvious that you two are into each other and I wanted to help because, left to your own devices, I don't think you'll ever get there.'

Had she caught a glimpse of us kissing in the studio, she wouldn't have said that.

'But the pair of you will be great together,' she carried on, blissfully unaware of the seismic shift my emotions had been subjected to, 'you just need a little encouragement.'

'Please don't take this the wrong way, Chloe,' I cut in before she became completely melded to her matchmaking cape, 'but I'd really appreciate it if you didn't say or do anything else.'

'But why?'

She sounded both crestfallen and frustrated, and I knew I had to nip her enthusiastic endeavours in the bud. Given that I hadn't had the opportunity to tackle Finn about what he had been saying behind my back, I didn't want to go into details, but I did want to stop Chloe from trying to shove us along the happy ever after path she so obviously had her heart set on.

'I am right about you liking him, aren't I?' she asked. 'That is why you're always a bit sulky when you've seen me talking to him.'

I was embarrassed to think that she was observant enough to have worked that out.

'I do think he's nice,' I tentatively admitted, 'but the thing is, Chloe, I'm new to the area and settling in to a brand-new job, a new home and a completely different way of life and, for now at least, I really don't need the extra complication of a relationship too.'

That was all true. I was still acclimatising to the changes my life had gone through and getting used to the lie of the land, both in the garden and out. My life in Norwich was different to the rural isolation I had been used to in Suffolk in every possible way.

'But you do like him, like him?' Chloe asked again, this time with added emphasis.

She was like a dog with a juicy butcher's bone.

'And besides,' I added, 'I found out last night that he has emotional baggage of his own which he's no doubt trying to deal with and as my love life hasn't exactly been plain sailing, I think your plan to get us together, however kindly meant, is best forgotten.'

'Oh,' she said, 'I see. What sort of baggage might that be then?'

'I don't know the details,' I said truthfully, revealing that I didn't know anything of consequence about Finn's while carefully managing to share nothing of my own, 'but he was described to me as damaged goods, so what he probably needs right now more than anything else is friendship.'

'And what's been so complicated about your relationship history?' Chloe further probed. 'What sort of choppy seas have you had to negotiate?'

'I'll tell you another time. It's a coffee and cake conversation, rather than a quick phone call run-down.'

'Not that's it's any of my business,' she then said, with a sigh. 'Given my past and how often I don't want to share it with anyone, the last thing I should be doing is sticking my nose into other people's affairs.'

'But you meant well,' I said softly. 'And given what you've told me, I shouldn't have said what I did about your intentions towards Finn.'

'That's true,' she shot back, but I could tell she was teasing.

I was forgiven, although I did still feel bad about it all.

'Hannah at the pub made it pretty clear that she thought I'd behaved badly too,' I told her. 'She wasn't best pleased to see me last night.'

'Oh,' Chloe squeaked, her voice a hundred octaves higher than it had been. 'What did she say?'

'It wasn't exactly *what* she said,' I recalled, 'it was the *way* she said it.'

'Well,' Chloe quietly said, 'I can't say I'm surprised. She has a vested interest, you see.'

'How so?' I frowned, moving my legs because they had gone to sleep under the weight of Nell's lean body.

The sudden silence was so complete I thought the call had been cut off.

'Chloe?' I said, moving the phone away from my ear to look at the screen, 'are you still there?'

'Yes,' she said, 'I'm here.'

'What's this about Hannah having a vested interest in my stupid comment?'

She let out a long breath.

'You promise you won't tell anyone,' she eventually said.

'I promise,' I said back.

I was fast getting used to keeping secrets.

'Well,' she swallowed, 'Hannah asked me out on a date a few weeks ago . . . and to begin with I said no.'

'I see.'

'Not because she's a girl,' Chloe hastily added, 'and that's not why I don't want you to tell anyone. It's just because . . .'

'You haven't been out with anyone, since . . .'

'Exactly.'

'I can understand that,' I told her, although really, I couldn't begin to imagine the turmoil she was in.

'But then she kept asking and, in the end, just last week in fact, I said yes.'

'But that's great,' I told her, because it was.

It was a huge leap and I was delighted that she'd made it.

'I know,' she said, before adding, 'but then the guilt that I was moving on with my life really began to eat away at me. Just the thought that I was even starting to consider doing all the things again that Ade couldn't, stopped me in my tracks.'

'And then I said what I did and tipped your survivor's guilt into a whole new stratosphere and made you cancel your date with Hannah.'

'I couldn't have put it better myself.'

'Shit,' I said. 'No wonder she was so pissed with me. When was this date supposed to happen?'

'Tonight,' she said sadly.

'All right,' I said, sitting up straighter in the bed. 'There's still time. Here's what you have to do.'

'I don't have to do anything.'

I ignored that.

'Send Hannah a text right now,' I carried on, 'telling her that your date is definitely back on and then get yourself up to the city to buy a new outfit.'

'I can't do that,' she laughed.

'Yes, you can,' I said firmly. 'You must.'

'Why?'

'Because otherwise I'll never forgive myself and you'll feel guilty about that too.'

'That's a low blow,' she scolded.

'I know,' I told her, 'but has it worked? Will you text her?'

She was quiet again.

'Chloe, will you text Hannah and tell her that you'll go out with her tonight?'

'Yes,' she eventually said, 'yes, I'll do it.'

I let out a cheer, making Nell jump.

'And you'll let me know how it's gone, won't you?' I smiled into the phone.

'Surely, you won't want the full kiss-and-tell, will you?'

I rather liked that she was so invested in her evening that she thought there might be a kiss to tell me about.

'No,' I said, 'I'm not that nosey. I'll just want to know that I'm going to get a warmer welcome when I go back to the pub again, that's all.'

Having properly cleared the air with Chloe, I felt much better, but the feeling didn't last when I crossed the road and walked by Finn's studio. There was no sign of life, so there was no point in knocking and, given my continued annoyance with him, that was probably no bad thing. Zak had given me no reason to think that his personality change hadn't been the real deal and that I should doubt his words, but I knew I would be better off tackling Finn when I'd got my temper reined back in.

'What's with the long face?' Lisa asked when I arrived at the Grow-Well.

'Nothing,' I said, pasting on a smile. 'I'm all right. Just a bit tired after a hard week, that's all.'

'I don't know how you do it,' she said. 'The garden is already beginning to look so much better and the new planting is beautiful, but how you can work outdoors in all weathers is beyond me.'

'I'm used to it,' I told her, 'and I like being outside.'

'Me too,' agreed Graham, who was arranging some planted seasonal containers around the bothy. 'A bit of fresh air every day is a great mood lifter, Lisa.'

'I suppose,' she said, but I could tell she didn't really get it. Not like Graham and me.

'These look great, Graham,' I told him.

'I wanted to get a few established ahead of my Winterfest session,' he said. 'And I'm really rather pleased with how these have turned out.'

'What would you like me to do?'

I could see Poppy's brother Ryan, and Lisa's eldest, Tamsin, were cleaning out the hens and I could hear Carole singing along to the radio as she swept out and tidied the bothy.

'There's some sowing to be done,' Graham told me. 'Broad beans in double rows are to go in that bed over there and there's a net cover to go over the top after they're in, to keep the cats off and we could do with another sowing of winter salad. That's doing nicely in the cold frame in front of the bothy.'

They were both jobs I was more than willing to take on.

'We could do with a slightly bigger greenhouse here really,' I pointed out.

'Luke's promised to put the Winterfest profits, if there are any, towards one,' Graham explained. 'And he's mentioned restoring the main garden glasshouses next year too.'

I was pleased to hear that. I really would have to make a point of talking to him about it. I had meant to, but with everything else that was happening and with my main work schedule focused on planting up the Winter Garden, it had slipped my mind.

'That will be a great help,' I smiled. 'We'll save a fortune raising plants for the garden from seed, won't we?'

'Every little helps,' Graham smiled back.

'Exactly,' I agreed then, deciding to grasp the nettle, asked, 'and while we're on the subject of helping, I was wondering if you might have a spare hour or two available to help me, Graham?'

'What, in the house garden?'

'Yes,' I nodded. 'There's still so much to do and I daresay Chloe and I could get it ready in time, but an extra pair of hands, especially a pair as competent as yours, would ensure everything got finished to the standard that I'm aiming for.'

'I see,' he said, straightening up.

'I know you mentioned that Luke had been reluctant to ask, but—'

'I'd be honoured to help,' Graham cut in. 'I can easily manage a couple of hours every day. Mornings would be best, if that suits you?'

I don't think I'd ever found anyone so keen to work for free. That said, Chloe was always willing to work hard for no financial reward. The garden at Prosperous Place had a truly dedicated team and it was a real labour of love.

'Mornings would be great,' I nodded. 'Thank you.'

It was a weight off my mind knowing that he was eager to pitch in. Professionally, everything was coming up roses and if I could just get my private life to follow suit, life in Nightingale Square would be practically perfect.

I let my mind wander as I sowed the rows of broad beans in the raised bed and then the winter salad in the cold frames. Seed sowing was one of my favourite tasks in the garden.

The excitement of knowing that my hands were the ones responsible for starting the alchemy, the magic of turning a dry, hard seed into something either beautiful or in this case, edible, never waned and I was already looking forward to watching the bright green shoots and leaves emerge and grow. It was the most satisfying cycle imaginable and I loved that my neighbours in the square had such a beautiful garden in which to be a part of it too.

After lunch, Lisa and I went up to the house where Kate and Luke had been busy arranging the dining room for those Winterfest sessions which wouldn't take place either in the kitchen, the Grow-Well or the garden outbuildings.

Luke and I had a quick chat about Graham putting his name down as another Prosperous Place garden volunteer and then about the glasshouse restoration schedule, before he headed to his office, leaving Lisa and me with Kate to finalise the plans for our Winterfest session.

'We can start outside, can't we?' Lisa asked me. 'And then come in here.'

'Absolutely,' I agreed. 'A tour of the garden will be the perfect kick-start for our session and it will be much more practical to work in here in case it's a breezy day.'

Lisa had sourced pretty notebooks made from recycled paper in a variety of sizes for those attendees who had specifically asked for her to supply their journal and I had been collecting more brightly coloured leaves for pressing and preserving as I spotted them.

The plan was for the participants to collect their own

leaves during the morning garden tour which would, hopefully, inspire them to start their nature diary during the afternoon, but if it was raining then the leaves would be no good, so I had a dry supply, just in case.

'And these are great,' I said to Lisa as I read through the list of writing prompts she was using for her creative writing session. 'I might even be tempted to write something myself.'

'You should,' she grinned. 'You'd be amazed where your imagination would take you.'

'And I can imagine exactly what the hot hero of your piece would look like, Freya,' said Kate, with a wink.

'Oh yes,' giggled Lisa, 'me too.'

Clearly Chloe wasn't the only person who had picked up on my feelings for Finn. Unless they'd assumed that as we were both single and living and working in close proximity to each other, then we were the perfect match? I wasn't about to ask and find out.

'Right,' I said, gathering my leaf collection together again, 'I'm going to draw a line under this conversation and head for home.'

I said it with a smile on my lips so they knew I could handle their banter.

'I'm planning an early night, tonight.'

'Sweet dreams,' Lisa couldn't resist calling after me.

I reckoned she was worse than everyone else put together.

I hadn't really got a plan for Sunday, but as soon as I woke, I knew what I was going to do and Nell was happy to accompany me. The drive down to Suffolk was as uneventful as the weather, and I had time to stop on the way to buy some beautiful winter blooms to lay on Eloise's grave.

My excitement to visit her was short-lived, however, as it was immediately obvious that no one had visited or tended her grave since my last visit. It might only have been a few weeks since I was living close enough to pay my respects regularly, but within that time the spot had become overgrown and the last lot of flowers were understandably well past their best and not looking at all how I remembered them.

'Freya!' A voice rang out from the church.

I shielded my eyes from the winter sunshine and spotted Samantha, the vicar, waving from the porch.

'Hello,' I waved back.

The morning service having finished and the few members of the congregation gone, she strode across to meet me, as brisk and efficient as ever.

'I thought it was you,' she smiled. 'How's it going? I heard you'd moved.'

I told her all about my new life in Norwich and how much Nell and I were enjoying it. The amused twitch of her lips left me in no doubt that she had heard all about my dognapping escapade.

'It's all wonderful,' I told her, 'but I feel like I'm leaving Eloise behind. I've not been thinking about her or Broad-Meadows quite so much recently and now I come here and find her grave looking like this and it makes me feel awful.'

'And what do you think Eloise would say about that?' Samantha asked, her eyebrows raised.

I pursed my lips, but didn't comment.

'Exactly,' she said stoutly. 'That smile tells me that you know as well as I do that our dear friend would be delighted that you've moved on.'

'But she'd be less than happy to know that I intended to keep coming back here, wouldn't she?' I sighed.

'That she would,' Samantha agreed.

'But the flowers,' I swallowed, pointing out the horrid mess in the vase.

'Are dead,' Samantha shrugged, 'and they make the grave look uncared for.'

'You're right,' I said. 'I should get rid of them and the vase.'

'It would be a great help to the mower man if you did.' Samantha told me, making my decision sound a little less harsh. 'It's far easier for him to keep the grass looking smart and in check if he hasn't got to weave around vases of dead flowers.'

I knew that wherever Eloise had gone, she was most likely surrounded by flowers and she certainly wouldn't want me feeling obliged to keep the vase at her grave freshly filled as well, especially now I was living that much further away.

'Jackson isn't going to come at all, is he?' I swallowed.

'Of course, he isn't,' Samantha laughed, 'and don't tell me you were foolish enough to think that he would?'

'No,' I said, 'no, I wasn't.'

'And never mind him,' she said dismissively, bending to stroke Nell, 'you will always carry Eloise in your heart and that's all that matters. You already know you don't have to keep coming back here to find her, don't you?'

'Yes,' I nodded, looking at the bouquet, I had stopped on the way to buy.

'I'll even take those off your hands and put them in the church so you aren't tempted to leave them,' she helpfully added, whisking them away.

I thought about our conversation on the journey back to Nightingale Square and glanced down at Nell. She looked thoroughly depressed again, curled up in the footwell and emitting the occasional heavy sigh. I had looked forward to visiting Eloise, but my decision not to return was the right one. As Samantha had pointed out, I carried my friend in my heart and I always would and thankfully that was enough for both of us.

Chapter 16

It didn't take Nell long to get her Nightingale Square mojo back again. A couple of laps around the green at full pelt with Gus after work on Monday and she was like a dog with two tails, and she wasn't the only one with a spring in her step.

Graham had applied himself with gusto to the garden tasks assigned to him and I was feeling much more settled in my mind that we would be ready to open on time. If only my mind felt as content every time it flitted to Finn, which it often did, but I was beyond busy and sorting things with him would just have to wait.

'Morning, boss,' beamed Chloe when she waltzed in, earlier than usual on Tuesday morning, and pulled a cardboard tray bearing two takeaway coffees and a bag from Blossom's bakery out of her basket. Clearly, she was as enamoured with life as Nell and Graham. 'As the weather's so miserable I thought we'd start the day off with a little sustenance and some self-care.'

The weather was rather dismal; foggy, damp and very dull, and I had to admit I was rather intrigued by the idea of practising self-care because I'd never been very good at putting myself first when it came to the work-life balance conundrum.

I was either at work or at home, and doing little else in between, and living on-site quite often meant the lines between the two were blurred. I supposed now I wasn't actually situated *quite* so close to my workplace, I should make more of an effort to distract my mind from planting schemes and weather forecasts and the tempting bag from Blossom's looked as good a place to start as any. I was making more of a success at keeping busy at the weekends now, so there was no harm in the occasional mid-week treat to back it up and keep the momentum going, was there?

'Someone's in a good mood this morning,' I smiled, reaching for the bag and peering inside.

Nestled snugly together were four breakfast pastries, still warm and emitting the most delicious buttery smells.

'I'm not going to go into details,' giggled Chloe, 'because you said you didn't want to know everything and besides, we haven't got all day, but,' she dreamily added, 'what I will say, is that you will *definitely* find you receive a much warmer welcome the next time you go to the pub.'

Suddenly shy, she ducked her head and reached inside the bag, pulling out a pain au chocolat which was generously studded with dark chocolate chunks and topped with toasted almond flakes.

'Oh Chloe,' I sniffed, delighted at the sight of her obvious happiness, 'I'm so pleased for you.'

Admittedly, I was almost as relieved for myself as I was happy for her and Hannah. I'd felt awful when she told me I'd messed things up, not that she'd put it quite as bluntly as that, but now everything was sorted and my new friend was thrilled to have found the courage to make her fresh start. It was a great start to the day, in spite of the inclement weather, and the delicious pastries made it even better.

Nell, very sensibly, decided to stay in the office, when Chloe and I pulled on our wet-weather gear and, full of carbs and good, strong coffee, reluctantly ventured out.

'I'll be glad when the glasshouse is restored,' Chloe sighed after I had filled her in on Luke's plan, 'and we can work somewhere dry on days like this.'

'I couldn't agree more,' I told her.

'I'll happily second that,' said Graham, walking up to join us.

I might have said to Lisa that I enjoyed working outdoors, but there were limits. There was so much moisture in the air that morning that, although it wasn't raining, we would have been soaked through within minutes, had we forgotten our waterproofs. I knew we could have stayed in the office and cleaned and oiled the hand tools, but I was saving that task for when winter really bit.

'Are you still happy to have a go at fixing the ride-on?' I asked Graham.

Having looked at the forecast together yesterday, I thought

it wouldn't be a bad use of his time. He'd already told me he'd got some mechanical experience and if we could get the mower working, then Luke wouldn't have to keep calling in a contractor.

'Gladly,' he grinned, ducking into the shed.

'And don't worry,' I said to Chloe, before loading tools and buckets into the wheelbarrow, 'what I've got lined up for us should protect us from the worst of it.'

We spent the morning in what had fast become one of my favourite spots in the garden. The fern garden was a secretive little place located next to the boundary wall, surrounded by established shrubs and trees and entered via a weather-worn brick arch. It was an original, but slightly scaled-down, garden feature, and in spite of its city location, had a very otherworldly feel.

'This place is going to be even better with some of Finn's dragon sculptures dotted around for people to find, isn't it?' commented Chloe as she followed my lead when I started to cut back the huge hosta plants which thrived in the shady, damp conditions.

'Yes,' I agreed, 'this is an ideal spot for a treasure hunt.'

I focused on the job in hand and refused to allow my mind to become too distracted by fantasies of exploring this secret place on heady, summer evenings with Finn. I was supposed to be cross with him after all.

'Not the ferns,' I said as I came to and spotted Chloe starting to make inroads into trimming those too. 'We'll leave those until the spring,' I added, brushing thoughts of

Finn more firmly away. 'It's the hostas we need to focus on because they'll harbour slugs and snails over the winter and that's the last thing we want.'

Luke had given me a comprehensive planting plan for this part of the garden and as well as my particular favourites which included ferns, Japanese anemones, cyclamens, bluebells and hellebores, there were many other lovely species and even two tall tree ferns which he had planted himself.

'And what are we supposed to do with these?' Chloe asked, once we had worked our way along to where they stood. 'It was quite mild here last winter,' she told me, 'so Luke just left them, but aren't you supposed to protect them somehow? They look pretty fragile to me.'

I'd never looked after tree ferns before, but had read up about them online.

'They're hardier than you might think,' I said, 'but they do need a bit of cosseting if there's a really cold snap. According to what I've read, you pack the top with straw, to protect the crown and then fold last year's leaves over the top and secure it all with twine. They're pretty sheltered in here, but if the temperature drops too much, we'll definitely need to do that.'

The weather hadn't cleared at all throughout the morning and it was still grim after lunch. Graham had signed off at our arranged time, but left a note in the office saying he thought he'd found the problem and was going to read up about how to fix it. That lifted my sagging spirits a little, but by three o'clock, what light there was, was fading and I'd had enough.

'Let's call it a day,' I said to Chloe, who had started to shiver.

'But it's only three,' she said, her teeth chattering.

'I know,' I said, gathering everything together, 'but at this rate you'll catch your death and there's plenty of admin I can be working on at home.'

'Well, if you're sure.'

'I am,' I told her. 'This is horrid and it isn't going to get any better now, is it?'

Chloe decided to cycle back home in the gear she had been working in and, after I'd made a trip to the compost heap, I cleaned up the tools, grabbed my files of paperwork, whistled to Nell, who hadn't budged from under her blanket and headed back to the square.

I was thinking about what I was going to cook for dinner when I pushed my key in the lock. I'd got a half a bottle of red wine left from the weekend and a couple of sausages from the butchers. A comforting sausage and onion casserole beckoned, with plenty of buttery mash. My stomach growled in response, but as I opened the front door, my excitement to be home shifted to concern because I could tell there was something wrong.

I slipped off my wellies and deposited my files on to the hall table before flicking on the light. Everything looked exactly as it should, but there was definitely something amiss, even if I couldn't see it.

'Oh shit,' I swore as I stepped into the kitchen and found my socks soaked in cold water. 'Shit,' I said again, stepping back.

I looked up at the ceiling and was relieved to find there was no damp patch or bulging plaster. The leak was at ground level I realised and most likely from under the sink. It was annoying, but it could have been a whole lot worse.

'Hey, Luke,' I said, having quickly called his mobile, after shutting Nell in the sitting room.

'Hi, Freya, what's up?'

'I'm really sorry to bother you,' I apologised, because I knew he and Kate were having a couple of days away ahead of Winterfest and without the children who were staying with Carole and Graham. 'I was just wondering if you happened to know where the stopcock is in Harold's place, my place, I mean.'

'Why? What's happened?' He sounded rather panicked.

'There's a bit of a leak,' I told him, 'but nothing to stress about. It's just on the kitchen floor, most likely from under the sink, but I want to get the water shut off, just in case.'

'Oh crikey,' he fretted. 'Um, hang on.'

I heard him say something away from the phone and then Kate took over.

'Freya?'

'Yes.'

'It's Kate.'

'Is Luke all right?' I asked her. 'It's really nothing major. I didn't want to stress him out.'

'He's fine,' she said, 'he fusses that's all. We had a ceiling down last year and he's had a bee in his bonnet about water pipes ever since.'

'This is absolutely nothing like that,' I told her. 'I just need to know where the stopcock is and thought asking you guys might save me some time.'

Given the fuss, I would have been better off looking for it myself. It was most likely located under the kitchen sink, but I didn't fancy paddling through the chilly water, until I absolutely had to. My feet had been cold enough at work all day as it was.

'I can't believe we don't know this,' she said, 'but neither of us do. Have you got a number for Harold? I'm sure he'll be able to tell you.'

'Yes,' I said, wishing I'd gone straight to him instead. 'Yes, I have his new number. I'll call him.'

'Great.'

'Okay,' I nodded, 'and please don't worry.'

'I'm not,' she said over the noise in the background which sounded very much like Luke having a mini meltdown.

'I'm really sorry,' I apologised.

'It's fine,' she told me. 'Ring or message later to let me know how you're getting on.'

'Will do.'

As predicted, Harold did know where the water cut-off point was and after assuring him that turning the water off was just a precaution and that the only harm done had been to the kitchen lino, I took a deep breath and prepared myself to seek the stopcock out.

'This,' I muttered, as I opened the understairs cupboard door and peered inside, 'is just my luck.'

The cupboard was dark and musty and it was well over half a metre from the door to the tap. It might not have sounded far, but for someone who hated dark enclosed spaces as much as I did, it looked more like a mile.

'What on earth's it doing there?' I had accusingly asked, when Harold told me where to find it.

'It's an old house,' he quite reasonably pointed out, 'and I never had the need to move it. What's the problem with it being there?'

I hadn't told him about my claustrophobia of course. Had I gone through the explanation I had given Finn, then I never would have plucked up the courage to pin back the door using practically everything within reach and step inside.

I squealed as a cobweb brushed the top of my head as I bobbed down. Thankfully the tap wasn't too tight and it only took a couple of seconds to shut off. That said, I still kept one eye on the door, just in case it somehow mysteriously started to close.

'Ow,' I groaned as I rushed back out, banging my head on the frame. 'What a perfect end to an already wet day.'

Standing on the watery threshold, I contemplated putting my wellies back on, but then decided it wasn't worth the muddy footprints, or the damp jeans. I quickly stripped them off so I could kneel down and get a proper look under the sink without soaking them.

'Crikey,' I shivered as I made a recce of the situation.

There wasn't actually all that much water, it had just spread a long way so it looked worse than it was, but that didn't make it any warmer. From what I could make out the pipe-work had come loose, probably as a result of me knocking it when I filled the space with my cleaning products, and the seal around the plug looked as if it had seen better days too. Everything in the cupboard was well soaked so it must have been my morning washing-up water which had stealthily escaped into the room rather than down the plughole.

'Damn,' I muttered as I realised that I hadn't needed to shut the water off or disturb my boss and his wife. In fact, neither of them had needed to know about it at all because this was something I could sort myself.

'Freya?'

I screeched in shock and banged the back of my head hard on the cupboard, which set Nell barking.

'For God's sake,' I cursed again, mortified that someone had just wandered in and found me on all fours, in my pants, with my head under the sink. 'Ow,' I groaned, rubbing the back of my head which now ached as much as the front.

'Are you all right?'

'Of course, I'm not all-bloody-right,' I snapped, reversing out, while at the same time attempting to pull my jumper far enough down to cover my practically bare bottom.

I knew it was Finn standing in the doorway, no doubt smirking at the ridiculous sight, because why wouldn't he be? It must have been an even more amusing spectacle than when I'd tripped on the lawn. I was dreading having to turn around, even though facing him would hide my arse.

I supposed I should have been grateful that it wasn't Zak.

I was pretty sure he would have captured the moment on his phone and zoomed in for good measure. Or maybe not, given that he'd supposedly turned over a new leaf?

'What are you doing here, Finn?' I demanded, resting on my haunches to avoid a further soaking.

'Luke called and asked me to come over,' he told me. 'He was in a bit of a flap, said there was a flood.'

'Well, as you can see,' I told him, 'it's a bit of a leak, not a flood, and nothing I can't handle.'

'Evidently,' he said, and there was definite amusement in his tone which further infuriated me.

I put one hand on the cupboard door to steady myself and rubbed the back of my head with the other. It hurt worse than the front and that was all his fault.

'Here,' he said, 'let me help you up.'

I was just about to tell him I didn't need his help and ask him to leave so I could recover my dignity in peace, but he stepped into the room before I had the chance. The second his foot touched the floor, it shot out from under him, sending him high into the air and then crashing back down in a spread-eagled heap, on to the wet floor.

'Ow,' he groaned, gingerly pushing himself upright. 'Ow.'

At this rate there wouldn't be anything left of the house by the end of the day because the place had literally shook on its foundations when he hit the deck.

'As I said,' I couldn't resist commenting, 'I can handle it myself.'

He nodded but didn't say anything. At least his jeans were

doing a decent job of soaking up the water. I reached for the hand towel and covered my lower half with it as best I could before struggling to my feet.

'I'll let you get yourself up,' I said, sliding towards the door, 'I'm just going to grab some dry clothes.'

I might have still been annoyed with him for gossiping behind my back and shrugging off our kiss, but there was no way I could let him walk back to the studio in soaked trousers. I'd most likely go out the next morning and find him halfway back and frozen to the spot. Having just cleared my conscience over Chloe, I couldn't replace her with Finn's frozen assets.

'Here,' I said, throwing him a bath towel, 'take your jeans off under this and I'll stick them in the dryer for a few minutes.'

He looked at me and raised his eyebrows.

'What?' I snapped. 'I don't see why I should be only one who's suffered total humiliation, do you?'

'Turn around then,' he grumbled.

I walked out and went to check on Nell. I had no desire to stay and watch him strip off.

He sat at the table in sullen silence and wrapped in the towel while I mopped and tidied around him, before bracing myself to go back into the cupboard and turn the water back on. As I ducked into the space, having propped the door open again, I could imagine how useful it could be.

There was room for all sorts to be tucked away out of sight and I felt determined to try and use it. After all, it wasn't the cupboard that had been the problem all those years ago, was it? It was my spiteful cousin and, as long as she wasn't around to lock me in, then perhaps I could finally conquer my fear.

Had Finn not been sitting in the kitchen, I would have let out a whoop of delight at my moment of enlightenment but he was, so I settled for a mental high five instead.

Back in the kitchen, I wrote a note reminding me not to tip anything down the sink and stuck it on the tiles before retrieving Finn's jeans from the dryer.

'Here you go,' I said, handing them back.

'Thanks,' he muttered, still clearly hacked off.

I knew why I was in a bad mood with him, but had no idea why he was apparently fed up with me. If he was still miffed over what had happened with Chloe then he needed to get over it, because we had. And if he was regretting our kiss, then he needn't be fretting over that either because as wonderful as it was, it was just a couple of minutes out of my whole life and I had no intention of telling anyone about it.

As he eased his legs into the trousers, I couldn't help but notice a bruise was already blooming on the back of his leg. His unnecessary heroics had caused us both bodily harm.

'I'll be off then,' he said, handing me the towel.

'Before you go,' I said, knowing that as we were both grumpy already then mentioning it couldn't possibly make things any worse, 'can I ask you something?'

He shrugged in response as he bent to pull on his rigger boots.

'Why have you been talking about me behind my back?'

He took a moment before standing straight and when he did, there was a deep-set frown creasing his brow. It was the look I had now come to associate with him most, which was a shame because he looked far more attractive when he smiled, like he had the day he showed me the hares. I only had to close my eyes to remember the effect that had had on me.

'Who said I've been talking about you behind your back?'

'It was—'

'No wait,' he interrupted, 'let me guess. It was, Zak, right?'

'Yes,' I testily said, 'it was actually.'

'And you believed him?'

I had no reason not to, especially as he'd sworn that he'd turned over a new leaf and had consequently given me no cause to doubt him. Not that I could tell Finn that, not after the promise I had made to let people work it out for themselves and, given the look on Finn's face, he wouldn't have believed me anyway.

'It's not really the fact that you've been talking that's hacked me off,' I carried on, 'it's more the fact that you've been talking about something that you don't even know the details of.'

'Well you're a fine one to talk,' he laughed. 'Talk about hypocritical!'

'What's that supposed to mean?'

'You told me everything I needed to know in the pub,' he said, roughly brushing past and making for the front door. 'And backed it up with that phone call in the studio and anyway, aren't *you* the one who's been going behind *my* back and asking my brother about me? He told me that you were very interested in my past when he bought you a drink in the pub Friday night.'

'He didn't buy me a drink,' I said, although that was hardly the point.

'But you did ask him about my relationship history?'

'Well, yes,' I admitted, 'but he didn't tell me—'

'Like I said, that's totally hypocritical when you've just lectured me about not knowing the full story about yours. Don't you think you would have been better off talking to me, rather than Zak?'

We seemed to have reached an impasse and glared at each other, neither wanting to be the one to ask for details first. Not that I was much in the mood for sharing and I daresay he wasn't either.

'I don't honestly think I care enough to carry on with this conversation,' I told him as he reached for the door.

'Fine by me,' he ranted, slamming it behind him and making the house rock again.

Chapter 17

Even though I still hadn't got to the bottom of what it was that Finn had assumed he knew about me, as I tossed and turned in bed that night, I came to the conclusion that I was just going to have to accept the fact that we were never going to get along.

Whatever the barrier was between us, it had been there from the second we met, and not even a spontaneous moment of passion had been able to shift it. It was hugely inconvenient that I still felt so attracted to him, but I would just have to work harder on getting over that.

It had perhaps been naïve of me when I moved into the square to think that I was going to become friends with everyone, and if it was only him who rubbed me up the wrong way and vice versa, then I supposed that was still pretty good going, given the number of people who lived in the close-knit community.

I would do what Luke had asked of me, and work with Finn when it came to deciding where best to place his sculptures around the garden, but beyond that I would avoid him.

'So, what exactly was the problem then?' Chloe asked as I relayed to her the details of what had happened after she left on Tuesday.

I hadn't mentioned the part Finn played in the farcical proceedings, just the watery welcome home bit, and me resorting to crawling about in my underwear to find the source of the problem to add a comedic twist to the tale.

'A worn-out sink seal and some knocked pipework,' I précised. 'I haven't used the sink since so it will be dry when I come to mend it at the weekend. I would have sorted it sooner, but what with things being busy here and Saturday to prepare for, I haven't had time to even get the sealer in yet.'

'So how are you managing to wash up?'

'I'm doing it in the bathroom.'

'And do you know how to fix the problem?'

'Yes,' I told her. 'It's hardly rocket science, but a plumber would charge plenty to sort it and as it was my fault the pipe got knocked, I feel responsible for the repair. My finances can't run to a plumber, so ...'

'You're opting to do it yourself.'

'Exactly,' I sighed, for some reason wondering how Finn's bruise was faring. 'And I wish I'd never said anything to Luke because ...'

My words trailed off as I heard someone crunching along the gravel path. Given my failed conviction to not think about him, I hoped I hadn't now conjured up Finn's physical form.

'Morning, Freya,' beamed Zak as he appeared around the corner. 'Morning, Chloe.'

'Hey, Zak,' I replied, ignoring the pang of disappointment his appearance didn't deserve. 'What are you doing here so early?'

What I really wanted to ask was what he was doing here at all. Given that he'd all but finished work in the house, he was still maintaining an extremely strong presence in the vicinity. Stronger than his brother anyway, and he actually lived on site.

'Just a couple of things for Luke,' he told me, 'including sorting out your dodgy sink.'

'There's no need,' I told him, exasperated that Luke hadn't believed me when I had told him that it was all in hand. 'I'm doing it at the weekend.'

'It's not my call,' he said, picking up the bulb planter and scrutinising it. 'I told Luke you were more than capable of dealing with a little job like that, but he's got a bee in his bonnet about water.'

'Oh yes,' I said, biting my lip as I remembered. 'Kate did mention that he's on high water alert after a burst pipe incident last year.'

'That did cause one hell of a rumpus,' said Zak, turning the planter up the wrong way. 'What is this?' he frowned.

I gave him a quick demonstration, much to Chloe's amusement but only because it was easier for him to see it in action, than explain.

'Cool,' he beamed, kneeling next to me so he could have a go himself. 'So how about it then?'

Chloe looked at me and rolled her eyes.

'Fixing the sink, I mean,' he quickly qualified without so much as a smirk, which made Chloe's eyebrows shoot up.

'Can you come over about four?' I asked. 'We're packing up early this afternoon, at Luke's insistence, so we can make the most of the Christmas carnival.'

The street next to Nightingale Square was holding a full-on festive event that evening. The road was going to be completely closed to traffic, apart from Santa's sleigh and, as well as the shops staying open late, there would be street performers, food carts, carollers and market stalls, all with a seasonal twist.

Lots of us were going to walk down together and I had been looking forward to it all week. It was about time I started my Christmas shopping and I was excited to be getting in the mood.

'All right,' Zak agreed, standing up and handing back the planter. 'I'll see you in the square at four. Nice scarf by the way,' he added, addressing Chloe, who was wearing a very bright and colourful knitted creation of her own making. 'Very striking.'

He strode off, whistling and with a spring in his step, and Chloe looked from his retreating figure to me and back again, her mouth moving like a marionette who had lost the puppeteer who supplied her voice.

'Oh well,' I said, 'that saves me the hassle, I suppose.'

'Saves you the hassle,' she eventually repeated, sounding incredulous. 'Is that all you can say?'

'What else is there to say?' I shrugged, pushing the barrow along a bit.

'But,' she said, pointing to where Zak had disappeared, 'we just had a completely normal conversation with Zak Stanton.'

'And?'

'And,' she said, 'there were no bulging muscles, no bravado, no flirting and no cringeworthy innuendo.'

'Is that really what a standard conversation with him is always full of then?'

'You know it is,' she said. 'You've seen, and heard, him in action.'

I had been privy to some of that, but I had to play it down in view of my recent promise.

'Well,' I shrugged, 'I've hardly known him any time at all, have I? And I did have a feeling that he couldn't be like that all the time. Especially the bulging muscles bit. It's freezing today so he could hardly strut about in a T-shirt, could he?'

'But he didn't even strut,' she pointed out, still sounding gobsmacked.

'Like I said,' I nodded, rubbing my hands together, 'it's too cold for all that and we need to get on. We've got loads to get through if we want to finish early again.'

'So, how did I do?' Zak asked, later that afternoon when he was ensconced in my kitchen with a mug of tea, a plate of biscuits and Nell's head perched on his knee.

She wasn't usually so demonstrative when it came to showing affection, especially to men she barely knew. Eloise and I had always speculated that she must have been mistreated in the past and that made her wary, but she was more than happy to cosy up with Zak. Unless it was the biscuits she was after, but I didn't think it was.

'Do?' I frowned, sitting opposite him.

'This morning,' he elaborated. 'Talking to you and Chloe. I reckon the compliment about the scarf might have been a step too far.'

I couldn't help but laugh as I remembered Chloe's expression after he had gone.

'That and the sight of you in a jumper,' I told him. 'The poor girl didn't know what had hit her.'

He patted Nell's head. 'I'm still trying to get the balance right,' he told me with a smile. 'And anyway, I'm about to lose the jumper.'

He stood up, reached for the hem with crossed arms and pulled it over his head, taking the T-shirt underneath almost completely with it. Given the taut, toned and tanned torso I was faced with, I thought that it was hardly surprising that he liked to show it off. Creating and maintaining a body which looked like that had to be a full-on commitment. I quickly looked away before he caught me staring.

'Don't strip off on my account,' I told him, gathering the mugs and then putting them back down again when I remembered I had nowhere to deposit them.

'Don't worry,' he said, reaching for his workbag. 'I'm not.

I just won't have time to go home and change before the carnival, and I don't want to mess it up.'

'I see,' I blushed.

'And between you and me,' he winked, getting down on all fours, 'I'm actually happier keeping it on. For one thing, it's much warmer than a T-shirt and I've recently discovered that women seem rather fond of a well-built fella in a chunky knit.'

'Is that right?' I laughed.

'Sure is,' he said seriously while carefully pulling on a head torch so as not to mess up his hair which had grown out a bit. 'I should have been layering up years ago.'

It took him no time to sort the sink and he stressed again that it was a job I was more than capable of and that he hoped I didn't mind him muscling in.

'Not at all,' I told him. 'You were only doing what Luke asked after all.'

Nell had shuffled over to him and had a paw resting on his leg.

'You,' he said, leaning over to her to kiss her head, 'are an absolute sweetheart, aren't you?'

'She's certainly fond of you,' I told him, 'but she's wary around men as a rule.'

'Even Finn?' Zak asked.

'Especially Finn,' I sighed, thinking how differently the two brothers had behaved in my kitchen.

Finn had been all about the crashing, groaning and shouting whereas Zak had been slow, steady and quiet, not to mention tender and kind to Nell. Given his flirtatious in-your-face reputation, I could have been forgiven for assuming it should have been the other way around.

'And how is my brother?' Zak asked. 'I've been staying out of his way. I thought it best to put a bit of time between our last encounter and the next so it might not come as quite such a shock when I don't carry on acting like the cock, he quite rightly thinks I am.'

That was further proof that Zak was in earnest about his fresh start and I was pleased he had thought it all through.

'I have no idea,' I told him. 'I haven't seen him for a couple of days.'

'But I thought you were working together on some project for the garden.'

'We are,' I said, looking away, 'but we haven't had much to do yet, so . . .'

'Do I sense trouble in paradise?' Zak asked, without a trace of his former teasing.

'Not at all,' I told him, with what I hoped was a non-chalant shrug. 'We just don't seem capable of getting on, so I've decided to keep our relationship on a strictly professional footing.'

'Aside from the fact that you've both expressed curiosity about each other's current relationship status and past loves, it's all work, work, work,' Zak astutely pointed out.

'I know what you're getting at,' I shot back, 'but that was just because we were getting to know each other and now we do, we've come to the conclusion that we don't like each other all that much.'

'I think that's just because you don't *properly* know each other,' Zak interrupted. 'I daresay you've got more story behind you than a jilted groom, and if you knew why Finn—'

'I have no interest in knowing why Finn anything,' I snapped.

Peter had hardly been the jilted groom, standing at the altar surrounded by family, friends and overblown floral displays. The reality was that he'd barely got the ring on my finger before I'd decided to take it off again, and as for Finn's reasons for objecting to my life choices, well, I didn't want to know what they were.

'I just think—' Zak tried again.

'Well, don't,' I said, throwing him his jumper. 'Where your brother and I are concerned, please don't think at all. Now come on, otherwise we'll be late for the carnival.'

'And we can't have that. I'm never late to a party.'

The street was already packed by the time we, and practically everyone else from the square, congregated on the green and walked down together. Exactly as the posters had advertised, the whole area was alive with festive music, extra decorations and a whole host of mouth-watering smells.

'Here,' I said to Zak, handing him a soft bread roll from Blossom's which was crammed full of sliced turkey, pigs in blankets and cranberry and gin jelly.

'What's this?'

'A thank you for sorting out my sink,' I told him.

'Luke's already seen me right for that,' he pointed out.

'Just eat it, will you?' I told him, as I swallowed down the first delectable bite of mine. 'I can't manage two.'

He followed my lead and was soon making yummy noises of his own. We tried the deep-fried brussels sprouts next, which were far tastier than I could have imagined, and washed it all down with orange and cinnamon infused mulled wine. Last on the festive food list was Christmas pudding ice cream, which Zak insisted on paying for.

'I've got to head off,' he said, bending his head so I could hear him above the Salvation Army band which was belting out a rousing rendition of 'The Holly and the Ivy'. 'I'm meeting a mate, but maybe I'll see you later, in the pub.'

I nodded in response and he kissed my cheek before wandering off, leaving me feeling rather shell-shocked.

'Was that Zak you were with?' shouted Chloe, who then appeared arm in arm with Hannah.

'Yes,' I told her. 'I owed him a bite to eat after fixing my sink.'

Chloe didn't say anything.

'Nice to see you again, Hannah,' I said. 'I'm so, so sorry about last week.'

'Doesn't matter,' she said, pulling Chloe closer. 'It all got sorted in the end.'

The pair grinned at each other and I was pleased my silly comment had been forgotten.

'Have you seen anyone else?' Chloe asked.

'Everyone except for Finn,' I told her. 'I don't think he's coming. He certainly didn't walk up with the rest of us.'

I had wondered if he would be here already. His height ensured he would be easy to pick out in a crowd, but there was no sign of him. Not that I had really been looking.

'Are you going to buy anything?' Hannah asked me.

'Yes,' I said, holding up my reusable shopping bags. 'I'm hoping to get most of my present-buying done tonight.'

'Shall we look around together, then?' Chloe suggested.

'No,' I said, 'I'm all right on my own. I'll see you in the pub.'

'As long as you're sure,' she frowned.

'Of course,' I insisted. 'Go on.'

It didn't take long to fill my bags with homemade edible treats, handmade crafts and unusual gifts, the likes of which you'd be hard pushed to find online. Considering the weight of the bags, versus the few people I had to buy for, I couldn't help thinking that the person I had treated most was me. It didn't happen all that often though, so I wasn't about to feel guilty about it.

When I had reached the point where I had so much crammed in my bags that I couldn't put them down to look at anything else, I decided to call it a day and head for the pub. A lot of my neighbours had already decided to do the same and I squeezed into a seat at the table with Poppy and Jacob, Mark and Neil, Harold and a lady I hadn't seen before, and Heather and Glen, who had managed to bag babysitters for the evening and were making the most of their child-free time. Lisa and John had already taken their three home and Graham, Carole, Luke, Kate, Jasmine and Abigail had gone with them. There was no sign of Chloe and Hannah or Zak and Finn.

'So,' said Neil, who had kindly squeezed closer to his husband, Mark, to make room for me, 'how are you settling into life in Nightingale Square, Freya?'

'Very well, thank you,' I told him, 'and I absolutely love working in the garden.'

'Luke was saying earlier,' commented Mark, as he leant around Neil, 'how pleased he is with it all. He said you were bringing it back to life and that the new Winter Garden is already looking amazing.'

I felt my face flush with pleasure. I hadn't said as much, but I thought that it was looking good too, and it was wonderful to know that Luke was happy enough to be talking about it to other people. Deciding to get Graham on board had been a good call. Not only had he fixed the ride-on but he could keep pace with Chloe, and that had made a big difference to what we could achieve within the limited time we had before the official opening.

'It's all coming together really well,' I told Mark, with a smile. 'Give it a season or two and it will be even better.'

'And how's the kitchen?' Harold shouted across the table.

'All sorted,' I told him, 'and no harm done.'

He gave me a thumbs up and went back to talking to his companion.

'Let me go and get you a drink,' Neil kindly offered.

I looked over to the bar, which was at least three deep with people waiting to get served. If he joined them, he'd be there until closing time.

'No, I'm fine,' I said, 'but thank you for offering. I really should be heading home.'

'Are you sure, Freya?' said Heather, catching the tail end of what I had said.

'Yes,' I said, 'I've got a really early start tomorrow.'

'Do you want us to walk with you?' Glen generously offered.

'No,' I told him, gathering up my bags. 'It's not all that far. I'll be all right.'

I said my goodbyes and pushed my way back out into the chilly night air. The carnival was still in full swing, but suddenly I wasn't enjoying it. The lights, music and laughter couldn't lift my spirits as I made my way home, the faces of my neighbours around the pub table and those who had already left, swimming in front of me.

I never usually took any notice of the fact that I was on my own, and I certainly wasn't the sort of person who needed a relationship to complete me, but I can't deny that, in that moment, I felt an unexpected pang of loneliness. I was the only one among us that evening who had been alone.

It hadn't bothered me when I was shopping, but suddenly I couldn't stop thinking about it. Even Nell had Gus to keep her company and Peter who had sent me photos of his few days away, had a new love too. The woman from the restaurant, Rebecca, had featured, smiling and happy, in almost all of the images.

As I made the final turn into Nightingale Square and looked across the road to Prosperous Place, I wondered if that was why Finn had decided not to join in. Was he lonely too? He always came across as pretty self-contained to me – alone, but not lonely – there was a very definite difference between those two states and I went to bed feeling sad to realise that for some reason I was suddenly experiencing the latter.

Chapter 18

The next day dawned bright, sunny and crisp, but I struggled to raise my spirits high enough to match the effort the weather was making. The evening before had started off so well and I had thoroughly enjoyed the larger part of it, but I couldn't shake off the feeling that it would have been all the better if I'd had someone to share it with.

I had told myself time and time again that I wouldn't concern myself with thoughts of Finn but I couldn't stop wondering if he hadn't attended the carnival for the same reason. I wasn't supposed to be worried about finding any common ground between us, but was this it?

Were we actually more in tune than we first thought, and after our kiss, increasingly aware that we were very much on our own? However, it didn't take me many minutes at work to stop speculating because that clearly wasn't the reason behind why he had missed out on the festive fun.

As was my habit, on the last morning of every working week, I made a tour of the garden, mentally ticking off all the things which had been achieved and committing to memory all those which still needed addressing. However, my list-making went rather awry when I reached the fern garden.

Tucked away, but not so hidden that you wouldn't notice them, I found two dragon sculptures. The first caught my eye as I entered, because the light bounced off it. It was attached to the wall, had its wings outstretched and was looking over its shoulder to check that whoever had spotted it wasn't in too hot pursuit. The second was harder to find, but having discovered one, I knew there'd be another and I eventually found it, menacingly crouched in an alcove in the wall at the furthest end of the little secret place. It was close enough to the path to admire but not so close that it would be subjected to inquisitive hands.

Just like the one scaling the wall, it was made from all manner of metal materials, cogs, coils and springs. There were no softened or rounded and smoothed edges like there were on the hares. These were far more ferocious-looking beasts; all raw edges and sharp points. The real deal, straight from the pages of Tolkien and Carroll.

As mesmerising and enchanting as they were, I was annoyed to find them. Finn and I were supposed to be working out where to put his sculptures together and I hadn't even been aware that he'd already created this pair. I abandoned my recce of the garden and made straight for the meadow lawn. Just as I suspected, there were the three hares.

So, this little after-dark mission was the reason why Finn hadn't put in an appearance at the Christmas carnival. He wasn't worried about feeling lonely amongst a crowd at all, he was just feeling petty. After our crossed swords at the house I had been resolved to let my efforts at friendship go, but I was still willing to maintain our professional partnership, but not now.

He knew how passionately I felt about the hares, he had been moved enough by my reaction to seeing them for the first time to take me in his arms and quite literally sweep me off my feet. He had kissed me with a force I'd never before experienced and now, because for some reason he was going out of his way to pretend it hadn't happened, he had snuck out in the night and positioned the sculptures without me. He had known full well that I had been looking forward to placing them and he'd done it on his own. It was as if he didn't want me to be a part of the magic.

I squatted down to look at the hares through the grass. It wasn't as long as it would be during the summer, but my hunkered-down position gave an idea of how it would all look in a few months' time. Pretty spectacular was the conclusion I grudgingly came to. Even Nell was admiring the trio, with her head cocked to one side or, given her doggy genetics, perhaps she was sizing them up for another reason?

'What do you think?'

The voice calling from further along the path belonged to my boss and he sounded impressed, as well he might.

'I spotted them from upstairs in the house,' he beamed, shoving one arm into his tatty old gardening jacket as he juggled a slice of jammy toast. 'The light catches them beautifully, don't you think?'

'They're stunning,' I agreed, because I couldn't deny their beauty.

'And this is just the spot for them,' Luke carried on, now striding backwards and forwards to look at them from all angles as he bit into his toast. 'Well done to the pair of you for picking it.'

'Well . . .' I began, 'I might have . . .'

'And facing them that way,' he chewed and swallowed, 'I never would have thought to put them that way around.'

He was going to have indigestion at this rate.

'That part really was all down to Finn,' I said, no doubt sounding a little sulky.

We might have decided *where* the hares were going to go, but I had played no role in the final positioning of them.

'I suppose that's fair enough,' Luke grinned, rubbing his crumby hands down his jeans. 'After all, the artist knows his work better than anyone else, right?'

I didn't comment.

'And there's no damage to the grass or paths,' he carried on, looking around, blissfully unaware of my bullish mood. 'How did you manage that?'

'I wasn't here,' I shrugged. 'I'm as surprised to find them here as you are.'

The sculptures were heavy and yet there was no evidence as to how they had been transported from the studio. How had Finn managed that? Perhaps he'd employed some kind of levitation spell. He certainly looked like a god, maybe he really was one?

'Finn!' Luke shouted, spotting the deity himself. 'Oh mate,' he enthused. 'These look spectacular. They're even better than I could have imagined, and you know I had pretty high expectations.'

Finn ducked his head, unaccustomed as he was to hearing his artistic efforts praised.

'They've not turned out too bad, have they?' he said, not meeting either of our eyes.

'Not turned out too bad,' Luke tutted as he clapped him on the back. 'They're a bloody triumph, man. Praise where praise is due, isn't that right, Freya?'

'Absolutely,' I agreed, smiling tightly. 'They look really great.'

Finn and I stood next to each other in silence, not that we could have got a word in edgeways as Luke walked up and down, giving us a running commentary on his thoughts.

'It's weird,' he said, 'I know they're not real, obviously, but you've managed to give them so much life, Finn, that I wouldn't be at all surprised to find them turn their heads and stare right at me.'

It was funny that he should say that because I had thought the very same thing when I first saw them in the studio. I bit my lip and looked at my feet. I wasn't going to think about what had happened after I had been introduced to them.

'Zak said that last night,' Finn then shocked me by saying.

'Zak,' I frowned, my head snapping up again, 'when did you see him?'

'He called around late, just as I was finishing up and, as he was here, he offered to help me move them. It was perfect timing really because I wanted it to be a surprise.'

'A surprise?' I echoed.

I don't think I could have felt more surprised if the hares came to life and started leaping about the place.

'Yes,' Finn carried on. 'As you and I had decided where they should go, I wanted to get them in place under cover of darkness so that it would just look like they'd hopped here themselves. I knew it was going to be a job to manoeuvre them, but had you and everyone else been here to help me do it, then some of their magic would have been lost.'

I looked at him and took a deep breath. Not the petty-minded sod I had labelled him then.

'I know that sounds ridiculous,' he said, turning red and scuffing the edge of the path with his boot.

'No,' I swallowed, 'it's not that . . .'

I stopped and shook my head. I had assumed that he had gone to all this trouble out of spite, but actually he had just wanted to surprise everyone.

'What then?' he frowned, his grey eyes darker than usual, his scrutiny impossible to shrug off.

'Well,' I said, 'I was already surprised to find them here and now you're telling us that Zak helped you move them, I'm even more amazed. It's all a bit much, isn't it, Luke?'

I purposefully pulled him back into the conversation and thankfully it did the trick.

'Yes,' Luke gaped. 'Zak, of all people. He would be the last person I would have expected to lend you a hand, Finn!'

'I know,' said Finn, sounding equally baffled.

'So, how did that come about?'

Finn shook his head. 'He said he was heading home after the carnival,' he explained, 'and realised he'd left some tools here that he was going to need for a job today. Then he spotted the studio light was still on and thought he'd check that I was all right.'

That sounded about as 'un-Zak' as you could possibly get, if you weren't privy to the new and improved version that is.

'He thought he'd check that you were all right?' Luke frowned in response. 'What, no mickey-taking or brotherly baiting?'

'Nope,' said Finn, shoving his hands deep in his pockets. 'Nothing like that. When he saw me struggling to load the sculptures on to the platform truck, he offered to lend a hand.'

'I was wondering how you'd got them out here,' said Luke, again looking at the path.

'I probably could have managed on my own,' Finn carried on, 'but having Zak's brawn was a real boost and we had them set out in no time. He even helped rake the gravel once we'd finished, and did it quietly so we didn't disturb anyone.'

'Did Zak say if he liked them?' I couldn't resist asking, as I tried to coax Nell out from behind my legs, which was still her go-to spot whenever Finn was around.

'He did actually,' Finn said, scratching the back of his head. 'Though he did keep calling them rabbits rather than hares, until I pointed out the differences.'

'I bet he loved that,' Luke laughed.

'He took it all with good grace,' Finn carried on. 'He even hung about to help me with something else.'

I bet that was fixing the dragons in the fern garden.

'And the even weirder thing was,' Finn finished up, still sounding amazed, 'that when he left, he didn't take any tools with him at all.'

'So, what was all that about then?' frowned Luke. 'What was he really doing here?'

'I don't know,' Finn shrugged. 'I just hope he wasn't up to something. Snooping around with an ulterior motive.'

I was annoyed that was where his mind had immediately sprung to. The purpose of Zak's visit was obviously to check his brother was okay, having noticed his absence from the carnival.

'I hardly think he would have purposefully sought you out if he was up to no good, would he?' I pointed out. 'If he was snooping, as you so kindly put it, then he wouldn't have made an effort to alert you to his presence, would he?'

'I suppose not,' said Finn, looking a little embarrassed that I had called him out.

'Perhaps you should give him the benefit of the doubt,' I carried on, 'and accept his help as the act of kindness that it was no doubt intended to be.'

I stopped talking before I said too much.

'If you knew Zak as well as we do, Freya,' Luke said, 'then you'd understand Finn's scepticism.'

'I see,' I swallowed.

'You aren't falling for the charms of my burly builder by any chance, are you, Freya?' he teasingly added.

'No, of course I'm not,' I shot back.

Luke laughed at my hasty and vociferous denial, but Finn didn't.

'But he is handy with a spanner,' I said, more equably, 'so that does give him a certain appeal I suppose.'

'He sorted your sink, didn't he?' said Luke, readily abandoning the subject of attraction for his preferred topic of faulty pipework.

'He did,' I agreed. 'It's all as good as new.'

'I thought you said you could handle it yourself,' Finn said gruffly.

'I could,' I snapped, 'but my landlord called in the professionals before I had a chance to do it.'

I was annoyed to find my tone matching his.

'I don't think it would be a bad idea to come and have a proper look around the house before the winter really sets in,' Luke carried on, not picking up on the rising tension. 'I know we had a survey done, and Harold's never had any problems, but that burst pipe last year caused absolute chaos here, so it would give me some peace of mind. Would that be all right do you think, Freya?'

'Of course,' I told him. 'Whatever you want.'

'Great,' he said, 'I'll get it sorted for next week then.'

'Super,' I nodded.

'Now, Finn,' he smiled, 'what was the something else that you said Zak had stayed to help you with?'

The question seemed to go some way to pulling Finn out of the fug he had fallen into after I'd sprung to his brother's defence.

'Come on,' he said, 'I'll show you.'

He strode off, as was fast becoming his habit when he had finished any sort of interaction which involved me.

'You coming, Freya?' asked Luke.

'No,' I swallowed, 'I've seen already.'

Finn turned to glare at me while Luke rushed to catch him up. I didn't think I'd really said anything to warrant such a look, but if I wasn't careful, he'd be doing a Medusa and turning me to stone.

Chapter 19

I didn't have time to fret over mine and Finn's most recent interaction because the next day Lisa and I were hosting the first Winterfest session and, as much as I had been looking forward to it, I found myself feeling increasingly nervous as the time to welcome the attendees ticked relentlessly closer.

As soon as I finished in the garden on the Friday afternoon, I rushed around to the house where I was meeting Lisa to set everything up in the dining room Kate and Luke had already cleared for the occasion. There wasn't all that much to do, but we checked, checked and checked again, ticking everything off and making sure everyone would have what they needed and also that we had spares of a few things, just in case.

'Here's hoping for some sunshine,' said Lisa, chinking her mug of tea against mine in a toast to our adventure, once we had finished laying everything out.

'And plenty of inspiration,' I added for good measure.

We needn't have worried about lacking in either because

it was an extremely clear and frosty start the next morning, which meant sunshine was guaranteed, and when we walked back into the dining room, having deposited Nell in the kitchen, we found that Santa's elves had been at work overnight and the room had been transformed into a veritable grotto, complete with a real tree, swags of greenery and enough warm white twinkling lights to illuminate Blackpool.

'I hope you don't mind,' said Kate, following me and Lisa into the room, 'but after you'd left yesterday we thought that, as lovely as the room looked with all your bits and pieces set out, it wasn't feeling very festive so we decided to put some decs up.'

'Of course, we don't mind,' said Lisa, flinging her arms around Kate's neck.

'It's breathtaking,' I added, taking in the details as I set down the bag of books I'd brought along, 'and so in keeping with the themes of Winterfest.'

'That's what I thought,' said Kate, once she was free of her friend's embrace. 'I told Luke we shouldn't just throw everything at it, but keep it styled to the sessions we've got coming up.'

She'd certainly achieved that. From a nature-loving, gardening fanatic's point of view, it couldn't have been any more perfect. There was holly, ivy and mistletoe in abundance and the real tree smelt divine.

'Finn helped,' Kate told us, her eyes alighting on the ball of mistletoe hanging above the door.

'Why am I not surprised?' Lisa laughed.

'He's got such a great eye,' Kate carried on.

'Two, I think you'll find,' said Lisa, giving me a nudge.

'Come on,' I said, resisting the urge to award her comment the eye-roll it deserved, 'let's get ready. Everyone's going to be here soon.'

In total, there were nine attendees. One person had called to say that they couldn't make it because of illness and Luke had kindly promised they could switch to another session if any gaps came up. It settled my nerves somewhat to see a couple of familiar faces looking eagerly up at me as Lisa and I took our place standing at the head of the long table.

Jacob, Poppy's other half, had signed up, keen to learn a few tricks he could later use in the classroom, along with Heather, who had a child-free day and was keen to do something completely for herself and quite rightly so. There was also a mum and daughter, the daughter there at the mother's behest, two guys in their thirties, two middle-aged women who had been friends forever and a much younger woman, called Sara.

She had heard Luke talking about his SAD diagnosis on the radio not long after she had been diagnosed herself and as a result, quickly signed up for everything. She said that just the thought of doing something proactive had started to lift her low mood, which was very encouraging indeed.

'So, welcome, everyone,' said Lisa, her voice surprisingly shaky for someone who ordinarily oozed self-confidence, 'to this, the very first Winterfest session here at Prosperous Place. Today we're going to be exploring how to banish the winter blues by using nature to kick-start our creativity through a creative writing session, making a nature diary and learning how to preserve leaves through a variety of methods, with lovely Freya, who manages the gardens here at Prosperous Place.'

Fortunately, I didn't have to do anything beyond offer a smile at this point, and by the time we had given everyone the chance to share a little about themselves and their reasons for signing up, my legs had stopped shaking and I was feeling much better about leading them into the garden.

'Do wrap up really warm,' I advised, as I handed out the jute bags in which they could stash their finds. 'We might be in the middle of the city, but there are spots in the garden which really hang on to the frost.'

I knew there was going to be an extra surprise waiting to warm everyone up when we came back inside and the chill in the air made me feel grateful for it. Kate had cleaned and set the open fire, ready for lighting when we headed out. Graham was going to get it roaring while we toured the garden and then come back throughout the day to keep it stoked.

'Ready?' asked Lisa.

'Ready,' I smiled back.

It was bitterly cold, but it didn't take many minutes before everyone had forgotten the arctic temperature and was eagerly engrossed in looking for leaves and cones, seeking out the scents in the freshly planted winter garden and ardently admiring Finn's formidable sculptures.

'Beguiling grey eyes *and* handy with his hands,' Lisa sighed. 'What a combo.'

'And don't forget the sense of touch,' I told the group, ignoring her and rubbing my gloved hands around the nearest tree. 'It helps to engage all the senses when you head out for a winter walk. Although perhaps not taste,' I hastily added, not wanting them to go too far.

'You can indulge that one when we go back in and sample some seasonal delights from Blossom's bakery,' Lisa quipped and everyone laughed.

The fire was much appreciated, as were the warm pas tries, and everyone was enjoying the hygge atmosphere as they emptied their treasures on to the table and Lisa flitted around the room asking questions relating to the walk. She was going to use everyone's answers along with her ideas to kick off the creative writing session.

I took my time moving among the group and chatting. Everyone had gathered lots of lovely things, including snail shells, still bright leaves, lichen-covered twigs and even a few feathers.

By the time the group was primed and ready to start, everyone was eager to get going, even the people who had been worried about getting it wrong because they'd never done anything like it before.

'Okay,' said Lisa, about twenty minutes later. 'Pens down.'

A collective sigh echoed around the room.

'Well, that was easier than I thought,' said the daughter, who had insisted on telling us when she arrived that she was only there because her mum wouldn't come without her. 'I've written loads.'

They all had, and after more time spent sharing ideas, Lisa set them off again, which took things nicely up to lunchtime.

'I've had some great ideas for a children's story,' Sara told me, her tone full of excitement. 'I can imagine a whole host of little characters living in secret in the fern garden and I'm going to write all about them when I get home.'

'And when the Winter Garden's officially opened,' I told her, 'you'll be able to come back to keep the inspirational well topped up and your ideas flowing.'

'Oh yes,' she said, 'I hadn't thought of that.'

I was pleased to see her so stirred and hoped that my afternoon activities would buoy her up further still.

'Help yourselves to bread,' said Carole as we filed into the kitchen. 'The plates either end are all gluten free.'

While she and Kate ladled out bowls of thick, hearty homemade vegetable soup, I asked the group what they would like to do with the leaves they and I had collected. I had plans to show them how to press, sketch, laminate and preserve with a view to embellishing the nature diaries, or journals, to make them even more memorable.

The most popular option, everyone having admired my own set of leaves which I had arranged down the centre of the table, was to try out the glycerine preservation technique. I hadn't been expecting them *all* to pick that one, and even when I said they'd have to come back to collect them later in the week in the hope of putting a couple of them off, they still stuck fast.

'How's it going?' called a voice behind me, when I ducked out to take Nell back to the square and see if I had enough spare baking sheets of my own to add to the few I had already lined up.

Nell had been looking a little perturbed by the sudden influx of strangers and so I was using her as an excuse to pop home. I hadn't wanted to ask Kate if she could help bolster my supplies, for fear of looking disorganised, not that she probably would have thought that, but she was busy enough sorting lunch, without me presenting her with a problem.

'You aren't doing a runner, are you?' It was Chloe. 'It can't be that bad.'

'What are you doing here?' I asked as she walked across the courtyard with Finn.

'I had to come and get my wellies,' she said, holding up her bespoke boot bag. 'Hannah and I off to the coast tomorrow. We fancied a run out to Wynmouth.'

'Oh, right,' I nodded, mindful that I only had a few minutes. 'Well, have fun.'

'Hang on,' she laughed, 'you haven't told me how you're getting on.'

I didn't much want to say in front of Finn.

'Great,' I said, because the morning had been. 'Lisa's a natural. She's had them all writing ninety to the dozen.'

'I saw you all walking around the garden,' said Finn.

'I hope we didn't disturb you,' I said, then quickly added for fear of sounding churlish, 'Your sculptures were much admired.'

I didn't want him to think that his hard stare had upset me and therefore, much like his reaction to our kiss, I carried on as if it hadn't happened. That said, I wasn't prepared to boost his ego by telling him that Lisa had been admiring *him* too.

'Really?' he asked.

'Really,' I said back, 'everyone said they look amazing.'

'Which they do,' beamed Chloe, clearly as impressed as the rest of us. 'And this afternoon you're in the spotlight, Freya.'

'I will be if I get Nell dropped off in time, and I need to pick something up.'

'You can't have forgotten anything,' she laughed. 'You've been going through your lists all week!'

'I'm on the hunt for more baking sheets,' I then felt I had to explain. 'because I'm not going to have enough. Everyone wants to have a go at preserving leaves in glycerine and I've only catered for about half of them picking that option.'

'I can go to the pound shop and grab you some if you like,' Finn offered, quickly stepping up. 'They've got stacks of them.'

'Really?'

'Yes,' he said. 'they're not all that big, but they're only a quid each.'

'If you wouldn't mind, and you can spare the time, that

would be really great,' I said, pulling my phone out of my jeans back pocket, as the weight of worry lifted a little.

I always kept a ten-pound note stashed in the back of my phone case for emergencies.

'We'll settle up when I get back,' Finn insisted, as I tried to juggle the phone and Nell's lead.

She wouldn't usually be on one, but given her tense reaction to the extra bodies in the house, I was worried she might be a flight risk.

'Thanks, Finn,' I said, suddenly feeling heaps better. It was a genuinely kind gesture, especially given that we'd been snapping at each other just the day before. 'I really appreciate it.'

'And if you give me your house key,' Chloe kindly offered, once I had told them why I was taking Nell home, 'I'll take her back and get her settled so you can go back in.'

'Are you sure?'

'Of course,' she insisted. 'I'll drop your key over when I've got her sorted.'

'I really do appreciate this you guys,' I said, feeling a little choked that they had so readily offered to help.

'That's what friends are for,' Chloe told me.

Given our complex karma, I still wasn't sure I could call Finn a friend, but I felt truly grateful that he was willing to help me out of the tricky situation.

'Come on, my love,' said Chloe as I handed her the lead and she and Nell wandered off.

'I'll be as quick as I can,' said Finn, rushing after her.

I went back inside, grabbed a buttered roll and headed back to the dining room to set out my nature diary and the books I had brought along. Looking at those first would be a slight change to the schedule, but I was sure Finn, with his long legs and lengthy stride, wouldn't be all that long.

'Could you write the names of the books down?' asked one of the group, as they passed my treasured tomes amongst them.

Along with my own diary, I had given them my copy of *The Country Diary of an Edwardian Lady* by Edith Holden, along with Emma Mitchell's books about the healing power of nature and how to survive winter, (one of which described how to preserve leaves using the glycerine technique we were going to be trying), and another two by Simon Barnes, one of which advised how to go about making nature more visible. They formed the larger part of my required reading list, when it came to connecting with the great outdoors.

'I've written out a suggested book list,' I said, handing them out and feeling pleased they had asked and even happier that I'd had the foresight to prepare something. 'There are lots of titles on here but if you don't want to buy them, I know there are copies of most in the local libraries.'

'Not for long,' grinned one of the guys. 'We'll have these all checked out by next week.'

Everyone nodded in agreement and while I was still waiting for Finn, we made a start on recording the morning's walk in the journals. It made for a wonderful first entry and although some were nervous about finding the right words, or adding a less than perfect sketch, Lisa and I coaxed and encouraged and they were all soon industriously working away.

'Sorry,' said Finn, puffing in the doorway, far later than I had expected him to be.

Fortunately, everyone had been engrossed by the pressing demonstration I had just given and a few were now, under Lisa's supervision, giving laminating a go, courtesy of Luke's office laminator, so there was no harm done. Finn looked relieved when I told him.

'But why are you out of breath?' I asked, as he handed over the bag, which was heavier than I would have expected. 'I thought you were just popping to the pound shop up the road.'

'I was,' he said, running a hand through his tangled hair, 'but then I realised that if you hadn't got enough sheets, then you probably hadn't got enough glycerine either.'

I hadn't even thought of that. I peered into the bag and found a big bottle of the stuff leaning against the trays.

'I tried to ring, but your phone's off,' Finn further explained.

I had turned it off before the session started.

'And I didn't want to waste time coming all the way back to check, so I went to track some down. It's not easy to find, is it? I got this from the chemists. They only had one bottle. This is the stuff you're going to be using isn't it? Chloe seemed to think so when I called her. Did you need it?'

I listened to the words rush from his lips and I could have kissed him. Again. I very nearly did.

'Yes,' I said, 'I definitely need it. I haven't got nearly enough to go around, but I hadn't even thought of it.'

I had been just minutes away from looking like a right numpty, but Finn had thought it through and saved my blushes.

'Well, that's all right then,' he puffed, squeezing into the doorframe as Carole came to announce that there was coffee and cake available in the kitchen. 'I'll leave you to it.'

He was gone before I had a chance to either thank him, pay him or kiss him and while everyone went back to the kitchen for some mid-afternoon refreshment, Lisa and I hastily rearranged things so everyone had their own tray, which would actually make things easier as we could name them and make sure they all got the right leaves back.

'Oh crikey,' I grimaced, as my stomach gave the loudest rumble, 'that's embarrassing.'

'Did you not have lunch?' Lisa frowned.

'Half a roll,' I told her, 'I didn't have time for soup.'

'That's no good,' she scolded, 'go and grab a scone or something. I can finish up in here.'

'Are you sure?'

'Yes,' she said, ushering me out of the room. 'We can't go the rest of the afternoon with your guts providing musical accompaniment, can we? It's hardly "White Christmas", is it?' she giggled, as it rumbled again.

She was right of course, and I did feel much better after

I'd eaten a scone laden with the thickest clotted cream and lashings of Carole's excellent homemade strawberry jam. With two cups of sweetened tea to wash it all down, I was feeling far more human by the time I went back to show everyone what to do with their leaves and thoroughly enjoyed the rest of the day, as did everyone else.

I was still buzzing when we waved them all off, and I wasn't the only one. The group had all swapped numbers and email addresses as we worked out when they could come and collect their leaves, and they were all planning to meet up on a monthly basis, either in the garden, or somewhere a little further afield to keep their nature connections topped up.

'I don't think that could possibly have gone any better, do you?' beamed Lisa, after we had walked everyone back to the garden gate.

'It was amazing,' I agreed. 'And,' I yawned, 'absolutely not worth the sleepless night spent worrying about it. I loved it.'

'I hope my session goes as well as yours,' said Carole, when I went back to the kitchen to collect my key which Chloe had dropped off.

'I'm sure it will, Carole,' I told her. 'I'm tired out from today, but I'm really looking forward to it.'

She had got me enthused when she explained that she was going to show everyone how to scale recipes down as well as up and I was looking forward to making my own pudding the next day, even if it most likely wouldn't last until Christmas because I wouldn't be able to resist it. Not that that really mattered because I could always make another one.

My job had always meant that I stayed on the slim side, but living now in such close proximity to Carole and Blossom's Bakery I wasn't sure I would be the same svelte shape for much longer.

'It's going to be a busy day,' she said, 'that's for sure.'

I knew she was even more organised than Lisa and I had been and that she would be keeping everyone on their toes and sticking tightly to the schedule. I'd bet good money that she hadn't underestimated anything, like I had. Thank goodness for Finn's act of kindness.

'Are you staying for the debrief?' Carole asked as she handed me my keys. 'Luke said it will be quick so I can get things set up in here.'

'To be honest,' I told her, stifling yet another yawn, 'I just want a long, hot bath and an early night, but I'll hang on. It will be useful to share our experience from today, won't it?'

'Absolutely,' she agreed, 'and Luke will really appreciate it. He's been like an expectant father all day.'

'Has he?' I laughed. 'I don't think I've seen him.'

'He's been trying to stay out of the way,' she grinned. 'He didn't want you and Lisa thinking that he was looking over your shoulder, but he's been about, believe me!'

I left her chuckling and went to fetch Nell, who I knew would be more relaxed among people she knew.

There were just a few of us gathered for the 'debrief' as

Carole had named it, but it went on longer than expected because Luke had arranged delivery of a Chinese takeaway for everyone to share. Lisa, John and their brood were there, along with Carole and Graham, and even Heather popped in, to say how much she'd enjoyed taking part. It was good to get another perspective on the day, and Lisa and I were both delighted it was being heralded such a success.

'Would you consider running it again?' asked Kate as she passed me a bag of mini spring rolls and a lager.

'Definitely,' Lisa and I said together.

'So, how did it go?'

Everyone's eyes swung to the door and the hulking great figure looming there.

'Finn,' I beamed, before I could stop myself.

Without his help, the afternoon would have been tricky for me to pull off, but his generosity and quick thinking had saved the day.

'Like a dream,' said Lisa.

'Excellent,' he nodded. 'Graham, I've stacked a load of logs by the back door. I know you wanted to fill the baskets again and that'll save your back a bit.'

Crikey, he was sprinkling magic everywhere. It really was a shame that we couldn't seem to get along for five minutes together because this version of him was rather wonderful.

'Come in,' said Luke, pulling out a chair, 'and help us out with some of this food. I think I might have over-ordered.'

'Sorry,' he said, 'I can't. I'm expected somewhere and I'm already running late.'

He did look very smart in a collarless, linen shirt and black jeans.

'In that case,' I said, jumping up, 'let me give you this now, before I forget.'

I handed him the ten-pound note from my phone and tried not to stare at the collarbone and little bit of his chest that I could see where the shirt wasn't done all the way up. He smelt wonderful too and I realised that, wherever he was headed, he'd made an effort to look his best.

'Is it enough?' I swallowed, secretly hoping he wasn't going on a date, even though I knew I shouldn't have cared.

'Ample,' he smiled. 'Thanks.'

'No, thank you,' I smiled back, quickly returning to my seat and away from his seductive scent. 'You really saved the day.'

'Getting paid for services rendered now, are you, lad?' John quipped and everyone laughed.

'Something like that,' he laughed back, meeting my eye for just the briefest moment. 'Well,' he said, 'I better be off. See you all tomorrow.'

'Bye,' everyone called after him.

'Don't be late,' Carole added.

'I can't wait to see him in an apron,' giggled Lisa and I realised that he had signed up for the baking session too. 'He's going to cause quite a stir, isn't he?'

'The only thing he'll be stirring is his pudding mix,' tutted Carole disapprovingly. 'Now, eat your chow mein. I want to get cleared up in here in a minute.'

I finished my last few mouthfuls of special fried rice and mulled over the session to come. If Finn and I were going to be ensconced in close proximity in a hot kitchen all day, then our freshly formed truce was most likely going to get pretty stirred up too!

Chapter 20

It was just as well that Carole's cake and pudding session wasn't reliant on the weather because the next day was nowhere near as sunny and bright as the Saturday had been. In fact, I couldn't help thinking that the sky had that yellowy, grey kind of tint to it, the one that usually heralded snow, but none was forecast.

'I'll see you later,' I told Nell, who I couldn't take with me, for obvious reasons. 'I'll come back at lunchtime.'

She huffed in response and I tried not to feel guilty as I locked up and then gasped in surprise as I turned from the door to find Chloe on the path.

'Crikey, you gave me a fright,' I scolded. 'What are you doing here? Aren't you supposed to be paddling in the icy North Sea today?'

'I was,' she shrugged, 'but there's been a change of plan. Hannah's been asked to work an extra shift and the weather's not all that great anyway, so I've asked Carole if she has room for a little one.'

'And does she?'

'Yes,' Chloe grinned, linking her arm through mine. 'So, you're going to have to help me out, because I could burn a cup of tea!'

I had been looking forward to the day already, but having Chloe there would make it really fun.

'You know Finn's coming too, don't you?' I said.

'No,' she giggled, 'I didn't. My goodness, I wonder what he'll look like in an apron?'

Pretty damn good, we soon discovered when we arrived at Prosperous Place and found him in the kitchen, acting as Carole's competent sous chef. Chloe looked at me and raised her eyebrows.

'That hair though,' she murmured dreamily, and I felt pleased that she and Hannah had got together because had they not, then her rapt expression would have awoken my green-eyed emotions again. 'Tied back like that,' she carried on, 'you can really appreciate his bone structure, can't you?'

'All right,' I told her. 'That'll do. It's going to get hot enough in here as it is, without you cranking up the temperature before we've even started.'

Had I filled her in on how soft yet firm Finn's lips felt at close quarters and how the tips of his fingers could elicit enough electricity to light every Christmas tree in Norwich, she would have swooned on the spot. Fortunately, I'd kept that knowledge to myself, so we weren't in trouble on that front, but her observations about him had warmed me up a bit.

We went to stand behind our places at the table – which were helpfully named – and waited for everyone else to arrive. Like yesterday, there were ten spots in total, but unlike yesterday everyone who filed in looked pretty serious. With the exception of one older gentleman, it was all women, including Sara from the day before, who gave me a little wave.

'Crikey,' Chloe whispered, 'this lot look at bit competitive, don't they?'

'Right,' said Carole, making me stand up a little straighter as I began to wonder what I'd let myself in for, 'welcome, everyone. We might be a week late for stir-up Sunday, but I can promise you that by the end of today, you'll all have a wonderful cake to take home and ice as well as a delicious pudding to celebrate the season with.'

A loud sniff from one woman drew my attention and I felt Carole bristle in response.

'Who do you reckon the woman with the too heavily sprayed hair is?' Chloe hissed as we took our turn at the sink to wash our hands.

'I can tell you who she is,' said Finn, who had crept up behind us.

Perhaps he wasn't a god after all, rather one of Tolkien's light-footed elves. I focused on my hand hygiene while my sense of smell was again hijacked by his aromatic and arousing aftershave.

'Who?' demanded Chloe.

'That's Daphne Pemberton,' he said, bending low so his breath almost tickled my ear.

He wasn't the only one who had had to tie their hair up and my ears and neck felt exposed and not at all prepared for the gentle caress of his hushed tones.

'She's Carole's baking nemesis at the local Women's Institute. From what I can make out, there's a far from friendly rivalry between them.'

'Oh goodie,' beamed Chloe. 'This'll be fun.'

Had it been anyone else, I would have felt sorry for them, but I knew that Carole's recipes, techniques and end results were top-notch, so she had nothing to worry about and I didn't feel at all guilty as I eagerly agreed with Chloe's summation of the situation.

'Come on, you three,' Carole's voice now rang out, 'We've lots to do and a schedule to stick to.'

Chastened, we hurried back to our spaces and began the wonderful alchemy of turning ingredients into food heaven.

As promised, Carole scaled her recipes both down and up. I opted to make three mini puddings as well as her speedy Christmas cake which would bake in a couple of hours, while the puddings cooked in a tray of water in the oven and would need to be heated in the same way again when I wanted to eat them.

Just as I had predicted it was soon hot and busy, with everyone doing different things at different times to make sure we all had a spot at both the hob and in the oven. It could have been chaos, but Carole was everywhere and, I was delighted to note, had a ready answer for everything Daphne threw at her, which was quite a lot.

'That smell though,' Chloe sighed dreamily.

I wasn't sure if she was referring to Finn's aftershave or the heady mix of fruit, spices, citrus, brandy and chestnuts. The latter combination was playing havoc with my tummy which was rumbling again, in spite of the breakfast I had provided it with, and when Finn leant between us to set down the teas and coffees he had helpfully made, the addition of his own seductive scent almost tipped me over the edge.

'Any special requests?' he asked, his voice close again.

'I can think of a few,' Chloe smiled.

'I meant for music,' Finn told her. 'I'm going to play some festive tunes.'

'I know,' said Chloe, swaying a little, 'that's what I meant too.'

'Chloe,' tutted Carole, 'are you sure you added all that brandy to your mix?'

Chloe hiccupped, which suggested possibly not.

'Shall we have some John Rutter, Carole?' Finn hastily suggested. 'Or would you prefer a bit of Wizzard and Slade?'

Thankfully that was enough to distract Carole, and I rolled my eyes at Chloe who was looking a little flushed.

'Do you know,' she said, looking bright-eyed, 'this is the first time in what feels like forever that I'm thinking I might actually enjoy Christmas?'

'That's wonderful,' I told her. 'And I'm delighted for you, my darling, but if you don't rescue your pan from the hob, you and Hannah are going to end up buying a cake, rather than eating your own.'

As promised, I popped back to check on Nell at lunchtime, but I made sure I had something to eat first. I didn't want a repeat of the day before and the seasonal smells had made me far hungrier than usual. When I got back, the group had been joined by Neil.

'Mark insisted I came over,' he told me, Chloe and Finn. 'He says he's not doing all the cooking this year, so I needed to come and get some pointers. Is it hard?' he asked, wrinkling his nose as he took in what, to the uninitiated, probably did look quite complicated.

'It's simplicity itself,' said Carole brusquely. 'I'll squeeze you in somewhere and make sure you have at least one thing to take away with you by the end of the day.'

Neil looked doubtful, but dutifully followed Carole's lead and got to work and I helped Finn wash up the cups and mugs ready for the next round of drinks. We even shared a tot of brandy once we'd finished and I felt delighted that our entente cordiale had extended so far into the day. We weren't out of the woods yet, but it was something of a record that we still hadn't fallen out, and I hoped it would continue.

I put the fact that I was beginning to find it easier to forget that he'd talked about me when I wasn't around, down to the escalation of Christmas spirit, but I hadn't forgotten that I had been in the wrong too. By quizzing Zak about him, I'd been equally as guilty of the crime I'd accused him of.

'I know I've said it before,' said Chloe when I joined her back at the table, 'and I daresay, I'll say it again, but the pair of you really do look good together.'

She was watching Finn help the formidable Daphne manoeuvre her cake tray, so I was in no doubt who she was talking about.

'Yes,' I said, 'you have mentioned it before, but I wouldn't get your hopes up, Little Miss Matchmaker, because he went out last night, looking and smelling lush, so I'm pretty certain he was on a date.'

'Yes,' she surprised me by saying, 'he was.'

'Well, there you go then,' I sighed, as my spirit sagged deeper than the centre of any of the cakes baked that morning.

'I saw him,' she carried on, 'in the pub. He was there until almost closing.'

There was no need for her to rub it in and, more to the point, if she was still harping on about us being the perfect match, then why was she waxing lyrical about his date?

'And having, what looked to me, like a surprisingly good time.'

'Right,' I said tightly. 'Well, good for him.'

'You'll never guess who he was with,' she whispered.

'Who?' I huffed.

'Zak.'

'Zak?'

'Shush,' she admonished. 'Yes, Zak.'

'What as in the most annoying half-brother in the world, Zak?' I asked, just to be absolutely sure.

'That's the one.'

'Well, I never,' I smiled, feeling better about life again.

'I don't know what's going on,' Chloe finished in a rush, 'but something is.'

'What do you mean?'

'With Zak,' she hissed. 'I know you said you don't really know what he's like because you haven't been here all that long, but in the last few days he's seemed completely different and the fact that he and Finn were drinking together last night . . .'

She didn't get to finish her sentence because Finn was in earshot, but I knew where she was heading. Zak was being true to his word and I was pleased about that. He was fast becoming a completely reformed character.

It was dark by the time Carole was ready to send us off, our bags weighed down with impressive puddings and cakes. Even Neil had something to show for his afternoon's efforts.

'I can't believe it,' he beamed. 'I don't know what Mark makes such a fuss about.'

In view of his delight, none of us pointed out the carnage he had left behind in the kitchen or the fact that his husband is up in the early hours every day baking our daily bread.

Finn and I stayed to help Carole tidy up and then chatted with Luke during the day's debrief. He was delighted with how the weekend had gone, as well he should be. It had been a huge success, although I wasn't completely convinced that everyone in attendance today was there to stave off the winter blues.

'Right,' I said, as I gathered my apron and keys. 'I'd better get back. Nell will be wanting her walk.'

'At this time?' commented Finn. 'It's pitch black out there.'

He had already made Chloe, who was on her bike, well-lit and wearing both helmet and high-vis, promise to text him when she got home, and now he was furrowing his brow at the thought of me heading out on my own too.

'That's as maybe,' I told him, 'but she still needs her walk.'

'In that case, I'll come with you,' he said, not giving me the chance to turn him down. 'I'll go and grab my coat from the studio and meet you on the green. It'll do me good to stretch my legs.'

It hadn't got any warmer, but the sky had cleared and I could even pick out the odd star, in spite of the streetlights. There were worse evenings to be out and Nell was delighted to be getting some fresh air. She gave a low growl as Finn approached but stopped when she realised it was him and even wagged her tail when he patted her head. Things were definitely looking up.

'So,' said Finn, who had now, like me, let his hair down, and pulled on a woolly beanie hat, 'where are we headed?'

I didn't have a definitive route, so we wandered where our feet took us and after about half an hour ended up at a church gate. The windows were beautifully illuminated and we could hear the strains of the organ and far more voices than I would have expected for a chilly Sunday evening service. It was really rather lovely.

'Oh,' I said, just remembering the date, 'it must be the first service of advent. That's today, isn't it?'

Finn frowned. 'I've no idea,' he said, 'church isn't really my thing.'

'Nor mine,' I smiled, 'but I do remember the story from school and my friend Eloise used to talk about the *Blue Peter* advent crown which was made from coat hangers, candles and tinsel.'

'That sounds like a fire hazard,' Finn laughed. 'Do you want to go in?'

'Not with Nell,' I said, 'but we could sit in the porch.'

It was cosy out of the wind and with the muffled sounds of the service reaching us through the heavy wooden door.

'I don't think I've ever been to a church service,' said Finn as we made ourselves as comfortable as we could on the wooden bench.

'What never?'

I hadn't been to all that many myself, but I knew my way around an Easter and Christingle service.

'Not a proper one,' he smiled. 'But I do love the architecture,' he admiringly added. 'Did you know Norwich has two cathedrals?'

'No,' I said, 'I didn't.'

'The Catholic and the Anglican,' he elaborated. 'There are green men carved into the Anglican. Maybe I'll take you one day and show you.'

'I'd like that,' I smiled, amazed that he had suggested it. 'I'd like that very much indeed.'

We sat in silence then, listening to the music, and I felt happy that we were going to make it through the entire day without falling out.

'It's been a good day, hasn't it?' I eventually said.

'A great day,' he smiled, leaning forward and blowing on his hands.

I hadn't realised he hadn't got gloves on.

'Here,' I said, wedging Nell's lead under my leg and holding out my hands.

He turned a little and put his hands in mine and I rubbed them briskly, trying to keep the action as far from intimate as possible.

'How's that?' I asked after a few seconds.

'Better,' he said, removing one and putting it in his pocket, but not the other. 'Much better, thanks.'

I swallowed and carried on staring at his hand in mine.

'You know, I'm not very good at this sort of thing, Freya,' he said, gripping my fingers.

Given how he had shrugged off our kiss, I wasn't at all surprised to hear him admit that.

'And I find it pretty excruciating when everyone keeps implying that we'd be a good match, like we're a couple out of an Austen novel or something.'

I couldn't help but smile and squeezed his hand in response.

'But I do like you,' he told me. 'Really like you, I mean.'

It took me a minute to take in what he had said. Our kiss must have had some impact on him after all.

'And I really like you too,' I quietly responded, my voice catching a little as I realised that the attraction wasn't all one way. 'I was kind of hoping that you'd say something like that after what happened in the studio.'

I risked a glance and found his eyes trained on mine.

'It was what happened in the studio that made me back

302

off,' he then said. 'You've no doubt worked out that I have trust issues, Freya.'

I remembered how Zak had said he was damaged goods.

'And I just can't risk getting involved with someone who is already—'

His explanation abruptly ended as the church door opened and the porch was filled with light. Nell leapt to her feet and gave a bark and I dropped Finn's hand as I made a grab for her lead. In spite of the location I inwardly cursed, frustrated to have our moment interrupted and my chance to explain a few things lost.

'Hello, you two,' said Kate, who was part of the throng. 'What are you doing here?'

'Nell needed a walk,' I told her, 'and Finn kindly offered to accompany me as it was so dark.'

'Hey, you two,' grinned Luke, as he caught Kate up with the girls in tow.

'Are you heading back now?' Kate asked.

Finn and I looked at each other and Nell strained keenly towards the gate and away from the crowd.

'Yes,' I said, 'I suppose we are.'

'In that case,' said Luke transferring Jasmine from his hand to Finn's as he picked Abigail up, 'let's walk together, shall we?'

And that was the end of that.

Chapter 21

Shocked to have heard Finn say, that he liked me, *really* liked me that is, and knowing that I could no more keep my feelings for him on a professional footing than I could fly to the moon, I started the new week determined to sit him down and talk properly, with no interruptions and no misunderstandings. I'd had enough of those to last me a lifetime.

I had no idea where Finn and I would be headed after that, but at least we could move forward with a clean slate and a relationship based on firm and honest foundations. On my part anyway. Whether or not he decided to share with me the reasons why he had trust issues would be up to him.

Well, that had been my plan. Unfortunately, the weather, and life in general, had other ideas and the week kicked off in unexpected ways.

'Don't worry about coming in tomorrow,' I told Chloe, when I called her Monday evening, and I had said the same to Graham earlier in the day. 'This snow is only going to harden overnight and we'll end up doing more harm than good if we go anywhere near the lawns, and digging's going to be impossible.'

Not much of the white stuff had fallen, it was more of an icing sugar dusting than a '*do you wanna build a snowman*' layer, but with the drop in temperature, it was enough to stop any practical outdoor work happening. It was very pretty though and, sticking to the paths, Graham and I had walked around the garden taking photographs to capture the icy beauty and frosted effect.

The old bandstand looked particularly lovely, as did Prosperous Place itself, surrounded by a white haven of peace and tranquillity. The road beyond the confines of the garden wall was definitely quieter and the only birdsong we heard came from a robust robin, who was keen to share his annoyance with the world through his shrill persistent outbursts.

Together, using straw brought in for the Grow-Well hens, Graham and I had cosseted and wrapped the tree ferns and there wasn't much more we could do after that, besides wait it out.

'Well, if you're sure,' said Chloe, who had already told me her school was closed because of heating issues.

'I am,' I insisted, 'have another day at home.'

'To be honest,' she confided, 'it couldn't be better timed. What with my wreath-making session scheduled for Saturday, this is the perfect opportunity to finalise my plans and make sure I've got everything.'

'There you are then,' I smiled, 'make the most of it.'

'I intend to, and you're still up for helping, aren't you?'

'Absolutely.'

Given how wonderful the first Winterfest weekend had been, I was very much looking forward to it. Saturday I would help Chloe, and maybe even make something for my own front door and Sunday, Poppy and Mark were going to be sharing their chutney- and bread-making skills.

I hadn't formally signed up to that one, but Poppy had called to ask if I would like a spot which had become available in exchange for helping tidy up. Her friend Lou, who runs the vintage shop nearby, had offered to help but now had to duck out.

'And how are things between you and Finn?' Chloe asked. 'Did you manage to go the entire day on Sunday without falling out?'

'We did,' I told her, but I didn't go into details about our chat in the church porch. 'I even went to talk to him today.'

'That's good.'

'But he wasn't about.'

'Oh,' she said. 'Not good then. I can't imagine he was working for his dad today. A building site wouldn't be much fun in this weather, would it?'

'About as much fun as the garden,' I sighed, hoping we weren't down for another sprinkling of snow any time soon.

There was still plenty to finish ahead of the official Winter Garden opening and sub-zero temperatures and more snow would only hamper the schedule.

'Well, let's keep our fingers crossed for better weather,'

Chloe said, 'and I'll see you on Thursday and in the meantime, keep on the right side of Finn, okay?'

I didn't see how I could to do that when I couldn't find him, but at least his absence limited our opportunity to argue.

'And don't forget to put up your advent calendar,' I reminded my friend. 'It's the first tomorrow.'

'So it is,' she tutted, 'where have the months gone?'

I mulled her question over as I hung up my two calendars. It was astonishing to think that so much could happen in such a short space of time. I was delighted with my decision to be brave and take up Luke's offer to move to Nightingale Square. I loved living in the house and working in the garden, and my neighbours had been more than welcoming.

I had barely been here five minutes before I was feeling like a part of the community, so my courageousness had definitely paid off, but I still missed Eloise, and that morning I hadn't been able to stop myself from wondering if Broad-Meadows had woken to snow and what it all looked like.

The decision to not keep visiting Eloise's grave had been a difficult one, even though I knew that it was the right thing to do, for Nell especially, but I missed the estate too. I often pictured the magnificent vistas and wide-open spaces, both with and without snow, but that was only to be expected, I supposed, especially as I didn't know what was happening to them. Had Jackson sold the place yet? And if he had, were the new owners planning to flatten everything?

Nell pushed her cold nose against my hand and I stroked her head.

'No peeking,' I told her, and she woofed in response.

One of the calendars was for her and filled with doggy treats. The other was a hand-stitched and embroidered fabric beauty which Eloise had passed on to me. The pockets were just big enough to hold a wrapped chocolate.

'Well, now, would you look at that,' I said to Nell as I unwrapped a strawberry crème and popped it in my mouth, 'I must have picked up one too many.'

She didn't look impressed, but then I'd counted out exactly twenty-four doggy treats for her.

Just as I expected, the ground was frozen solid the following morning and after a tour of the garden and a detour to see if Finn was at the studio, (he wasn't), Nell and I retreated to the warmth of home and spent the day indoors. After lunch, I was working my way through some paperwork at the kitchen table when there was a sharp rap on the door.

'Zak,' I frowned, 'what are you doing here?'

'Catching hypothermia,' he shivered.

'Sorry,' I said, quickly stepping aside, 'come in. The wind's got up, hasn't it?'

'Just a bit,' he said, rushing over the threshold and bringing a wonderfully crisp smell of cold air in with him. 'It's enough to freeze your bits off out there. I thought the walk here would do me good, but I'm not so sure now.'

'It's hardly brick-laying weather, is it?'

'Definitely not,' he said, nodding to the toolbox he was holding, 'which is why I thought it would be the perfect time to check out your pipework. The house's pipework, I mean, as Luke requested. I've brought a few bits with me in case anything crops up.'

'Of course,' I said. 'You're far better off in here than out there and it would be good to get it done. Luke keeps asking if you've had a chance to take a look. Let me make you a drink first though and you can thaw out a bit.'

Nell was delighted to see him and we chatted over tea and biscuits before he headed upstairs to make a start. I had no idea what it was that he was going to do. I didn't think there were any leaks, although the cold water tap in the bathroom sink did have a tendency to drip.

'Let me know if you need anything,' I shouted after him up the stairs

'Another tea wouldn't go amiss.'

I set the kettle to boil before carrying on with my admin, but I'd barely started before there was another knock on the door. I looked at Nell and rolled my eyes. Perhaps it would be best to abandon my work altogether.

'Finn,' I laughed when I opened the door and found myself faced with the biggest bundle of willow whips, 'I take it that is you behind there?'

My heart cantered at the sight of him, even though he looked more like an extra from *The Wicker Man* than a Norse god.

'It is,' he confirmed, his broad smile appearing around the side. 'I wondered if these might be any good for Chloe's wreath-making session on Saturday.'

'I'm sure they would be perfect,' I told him. 'They'll make the ideal natural base. Where did you find them?'

He propped the bundle against the wall, making sure it was in a spot where the wind wouldn't catch it, and followed me into the kitchen.

'I've been to see my mate at Skylark Farm again,' he told me, which explained his absence from the studio, 'and then I had to go to Wynthorpe Hall.'

'Why does that name ring a bell?' I frowned, reaching for another mug.

'It's the place where Luke got his Winterfest idea from.'

'Oh yes,' I said, 'I remember. What were you doing there?'

'Angus, the patriarch of the Connelly family who live there, wanted to talk about a potential commission. Jake had shown him the pictures I sent him of the hares and dragons and he wanted to talk through the possibility of creating something for the hall.'

'Oh wow, Finn,' I smiled, relieved that we had eased straight into a conversation, 'that's amazing.'

'It could be,' he swallowed. 'If I can pull it off.'

'I'm sure you will,' I told him. 'Your work is phenomenal, and with an endorsement from this Angus, it could really be the start of something, couldn't it?'

'But this is a much bigger project,' he frowned, not catching my excitement. His reserve echoed some of what I'd felt when I found myself fretting that I'd bitten off more than I could chew with the Winter Garden. 'Anyway, I've promised to submit some sketches but advised him that if he would like to go ahead, then I need to complete the work for Luke first.'

'Will that be an issue, do you think?'

'Oh no, he didn't mind at all, and when I explained about what's happening here with the Winterfest, he offered me the bundle of willow whips for Chloe, free of charge.'

'He sounds lovely.'

'They all are,' Finn laughed, 'and it's not just the family living in the hall. There's the handyman, cook, housekeeper and groundsman and someone else in the cottage in the woods. From what I could make out, they're from all walks of life and backgrounds. Anna, the partner of one of the sons, told me that if you go there for even just a few weeks, it's most likely that you'll fall in love and never leave. It's a fairy-tale place.'

'A bit like here,' I suggested.

I felt my face colour, but thankfully Finn didn't seem to notice. I had meant fall in love with the place as opposed to anyone living in it. I wasn't ready to admit that just yet.

'Yes,' said Finn, running a hand through his windswept hair. 'Luke might not have the acreage that Wynthorpe Hall has, but he's definitely creating the magical urban equivalent, isn't he?'

'It's beginning to feel that way.'

We were quiet for a second and I wished Zak wasn't working upstairs so I could pick up our conversation from Sunday. It would have been the perfect time to properly clear the air, what with Finn's exciting news and me, comfortable in my own home.

'Would you like a tea or coffee?' I offered, knowing our talk would have to wait.

'Coffee please,' said Finn. 'It's freezing out there. I could do with warming up.'

'So why have you carried the willow over here?' I asked, as I splashed milk into the mugs. 'Chloe's going to love it, but it'll be better off stacked in the garden.'

'It was just an excuse really,' he huskily said, coming to stand next to me.

'An excuse,' I blinked up at him, my breath tight in my chest.

'Yes.'

'For what?'

'Coming to see you.'

'Did you need one?'

'I just thought it would make turning up on your doorstep a bit easier.'

'And why did you want to turn up on my doorstep?'

'To carry on the conversation that we started on Sunday of course.'

Off went my heart again, galloping about all over the place.

'Well,' I said, trying to sound relaxed, 'you didn't need an excuse to do that. You could have just turned up without a horticultural accompaniment.'

'I tried that before I left,' he said, turning endearingly red, 'and I didn't even get through the gate.'

'I see,' I smiled.

'Don't laugh,' he tutted. 'It's not funny.'

'I'm not laughing, I'm just smiling.'

'Well, whatever,' he said, a smile of his own tugging at the corners of his luscious lips, 'I realised that I was going to need an excuse to come over and Angus Connelly kindly provided me with one.'

'And I'm very glad that he did,' I told him, giving him a nudge.

'Are you really?'

'I am really,' I whispered.

'Well,' he sighed, reaching to tuck an unruly strand of hair behind my ear in a gesture that now felt achingly familiar, 'that's all right then, isn't it?'

I was just about to tell him that it was more than all right when there was a thud from upstairs which was accompanied by some extremely blue expletives.

'Oh,' said Finn, as he looked up at the ceiling and took a step back, 'I'm sorry. I didn't realise you had company.'

'I haven't.'

The racket upstairs suggested otherwise.

'Well,' I elaborated, 'not company, company.'

The swearing then morphed into heavy footfall and Finn stepped into the hall to find himself faced with the source of the rumpus.

'Hello, bruv,' said Zak, who had almost collided with him in his eagerness to get to the kitchen. 'What are you doing here?'

'I could ask you the same thing,' Finn shot back.

Personally, I was more interested to find out why Zak was topless.

'I'm here to—' Zak began, but Finn didn't wait to hear his explanation.

'Oh, forget it,' he angrily said, pushing through and making for the door. 'I'll let Chloe know about the willow.'

He crashed out, slamming the door behind him and making the whole house shake. Again.

'Earth to Freya,' said Zak, clicking his fingers in front of my face. 'Can you hear me?'

I came back to earth with a bump. 'What?' I dazedly asked.

'Where's your stopcock, my love?'

Chapter 22

'So, what happened then?' Chloe asked wide-eyed as I relayed the details of what had happened on Tuesday when she came in on Thursday.

'Zak came tearing down the stairs, naked from the waist up and crashed straight into Finn.' I told her, cradling my head in my hands.

'No wonder he seemed in such a temper when he called to tell me about the willow,' she said, eyeing the bundle which was now in the office, protected from the still breezy weather. 'Finn, I mean.'

The snow had all gone and the temperature had lifted a little, but it was unlikely that Chloe would be holding her Winterfest session in the Grow-Well as originally planned. Making wreaths wasn't the tidiest of tasks, but it was going to have to take place in the Prosperous Place dining room if we didn't want the attendees to freeze.

'At least the floor is tiled,' Luke had said to Kate when he told her about the change in venue, 'which will make sweeping up easier than if the room was carpeted.'

Kate had looked as unsure about Luke's reasoning as Chloe had about my description of Zak's half-naked appearance in my kitchen.

'So, why *exactly* did he have his top off?' she asked, leaning in. 'You don't suppose he was planning to entice you upstairs for a bit of—'

'No,' I interrupted, and she grinned, 'of course not.'

'What then?'

'The silly sod was trying to change a tap washer in the bathroom sink without turning the water off,' I tutted, thinking of the unnecessarily drenched room. 'He thought he could be quick enough to switch them, but even with all those muscles, he was no match for the square's water pressure and then he found the isolation valve was jammed.'

'And he was shirtless, because?'

'Because he'd got a sudden soaking, the water was freezing and he'd whipped his top off and dumped it in the bath before running down the stairs.'

'That sounds feasible enough,' Chloe shrugged.

'Of course, it is,' I shot back, still not able to see the funny side, 'not that Finn thought so. You should have seen his face.'

'I'm rather pleased I didn't.'

'He took one look at Zak, made what I suppose was the most logical assumption and legged it out the door.'

I was a bit put out that he had jumped to the wrong conclusion, but I was willing to overlook it. I had to if I didn't want to take us straight back to square one and I daresay

I'd have reacted in exactly the same way had I turned up at the studio expecting to have a heart to heart and found a half-naked girl in the flat.

'Oh dear,' said Chloe, 'and just when you two were starting to get on.'

'I know,' I groaned, 'that's the worst of it.'

'So, what are you going to do now?' she asked.

'I don't know yet,' I said, 'but I'll come up with something.'

I was going to have to if I wanted to feel Finn's strong arms around me again and the touch of his lips kissing mine and I *really* did want to feel both of those things. I might have been trying to convince myself otherwise, but it was no good. My body gave an involuntary shudder as I again remembered the stirring sensation of our spontaneous embrace.

'You all right?' asked Chloe.

'Yes,' I said, clearing my throat and turning my attention back to my list of jobs. 'I'm fine. The wind really cuts under that door, doesn't it?'

The shops were open late again that evening and, although there wasn't the same carnival atmosphere, Chloe convinced me to join her and Hannah for a little retail therapy followed by a drink in The Dragon.

Nell and I had been making inroads into our respective advent calendars, but the festive spirit that I had felt building had come to a grinding halt in the face of what had happened with Finn.

All of my thoughts were now focused on finding a way to explain to him why Zak had been shirtless in my house as well as picking the right moment to sort out our former misunderstandings. If I could manage to do that, it would be the best Christmas gift ever!

'Right,' I said, coming back from the bar and banging three pints of Christmas Cracker down on the table, 'I've made a decision.'

'About what?' asked Hannah, dipping into Chloe's bowl of chips.

'Finn,' I told them both. 'I'm going to take charge of the situation once and for all.'

'And how are you going to do that?' Chloe frowned, pinching a chestnut from the bag Hannah had picked up from one of the food stalls outside in response to the chip pillaging.

'I'm going to stage an intervention,' I said, drinking down a mouthful of the festive ale. 'I'm going to get Finn on his own—'

'Impossible,' Chloe cut in.

'So, it's just the two of us,' I soldiered on, ignoring her scepticism, 'landline unplugged, mobile's off, doors locked, curtains closed, that sort of thing.'

'Nice,' nodded Hannah, with a cheeky grin.

'And I'm going to force him to listen to what I have to say.'

'I suppose that could work,' said Chloe.

'You could tie him up,' giggled Hannah, clearly quite taken with the idea.

Chloe gave her a sharp nudge.

'What?' she protested. 'It might come to that.'

'It won't,' said Chloe, a smile tugging at her lips.

Hannah looked disappointed and I couldn't help but laugh before drinking more of my pint. This proactive show of force was going to be the right way to go about it; I just knew it.

'I'm going to own this situation,' I told the pair, putting my glass back down with a thump. 'No more buggering about.'

'It's the only way,' Hannah agreed, pinching another chip.

'Actually,' said Chloe, nabbing a second chestnut for good measure, 'I think you might be right.'

My stirring speech in the pub had further fuelled my determination to reach a resolution and, as luck would have it – which must have been a positive portent – the perfect opportunity to put my forceful plan into action presented itself the very next day.

I had finished work and was locking the garden office, when I heard Finn crashing about in the studio. Because of the cold, Nell was wearing her dog socks. She hated them really, and still hadn't worked out that her feet felt better for having them on, but at least Finn wouldn't be able to object to having her in the studio if he hadn't swept up. I didn't want to run the risk of taking her home before I tackled him, in case he sloped off before I got back.

'Come on,' I said to Nell, giving her head a rub. 'Let's get this done.'

I purposefully marched the few steps to the studio and hammered on the closed door, allowing myself no time to think or run through what I was going to say.

'Freya,' said Finn, when he opened the door, thankfully before my courage failed me.

'Can I come in?' I asked, sliding past him before he could say no, 'and don't worry about Nell. She's got her socks on, so her feet will be fine.'

After a look at Nell's feet, which made his eyebrows shoot up, Finn closed the door and I leant around him, slid the bolt across, crossed the studio floor and ran up the stairs which led to the living space above.

'What the hell,' he gruffly objected, as I took the steps two at a time and didn't look back. 'Freya?'

'I won't keep you a minute,' I told him, as he rushed to follow me. 'I promise I'm going to make this really quick.'

I didn't focus on the finer details of my surroundings, but 'functional' and 'basic' would have been the best words to sum up what I did notice. Cosy home comforts were few and far between and I couldn't see a phone handset anywhere.

'Do you have a landline here?' I asked.

'What?' said Finn, frowning.

'A phone,' I reiterated, as I mentally ran through my intervention checklist.

There was no need to draw the curtains because we were

high up and no one could physically get in now because I had barred the only entrance.

'No,' said Finn. 'No landline. What the hell's going on?'

'Mobile then?' I said, pulling mine out of my jeans pocket.

'You know I have a mobile,' said Finn, waving the ancient model about before I swiped it out of his hand. 'Hey!'

'Trust me,' I told him, feeling the adrenaline pump through my veins as I marched to the bedroom, or the space where the bed was. 'I'm going to put it here with mine and if it rings, ignore it.'

Finn stood with his hands on his hips and a less than amused expression on his face.

'Here, Nell,' I said softly, 'lay down.'

She ignored me and crawled under the table, circling twice before settling with her head on her front paws.

'Good girl,' I praised.

Now the scene was set, I wasn't sure what to do next. The initial influx of adrenaline was starting to wane but I couldn't give up. Not when I'd completed phase one without a hitch. I might not get another chance.

'Will you sit down?' I said to Finn.

'Are you asking me to, or telling me to?'

He sat on the sofa before I could answer, his long jean-clad legs stretched out in front of him and one arm resting along the back. He wasn't such an imposing prospect sitting down. In fact, he looked almost relaxed. I wished I was.

'Look,' I said, moving to stand right in front of him to make sure his attention didn't wander.

'How about I go first?' he suggested.

'Absolutely not.'

I know I sounded rude, but I couldn't risk any interruption. It might have been happening on Finn's turf, but this was my intervention; my way, my rules, my words first.

'Right,' I said, 'I know this might seem a little unorthodox ...'

'A little,' Finn snorted, 'you've all but kidnapped me in my own home, Freya!'

I dismissed the 'tied-up' image which had appealed to Hannah in the pub.

'I know,' I said, 'and I'm sorry about that.'

'You don't look it.'

'Please,' I begged, 'please, just listen because I'm here to clear the air between us once and for all.'

Finn nodded and thankfully didn't say anything else.

'You told me that you liked me last week,' I swallowed, 'and I told you that I liked you back.'

He was most likely wondering why now.

'Right?'

'I did,' he confirmed.

'And you also said that you have trust issues.'

He began to move and I held up a hand to stop him standing up.

'I haven't come to ask what they are because that's your business, not mine, but what I do want to do is dispute the conclusion that I think you jumped to when we talked about relationships in the pub.'

It felt like forever ago now.

'I told you,' I carried on, 'that I had broken off my engagement at the wedding venue and I think you assumed that I had left the poor, broken-hearted groom at the altar.'

Finn frowned, but didn't comment.

'Didn't you?' I asked, wringing my hands.

'Yes,' he said, 'what else was I supposed to think?'

'I daresay, it was a logical assumption,' I swallowed again. 'But it was wrong. My fiancé and I *were* at the wedding venue when I broke off our engagement, but it wasn't our wedding day, nowhere near it in fact, and it wasn't the self-ish act on my part that you're thinking it was, at all.'

'Go on.'

'On the day it happened,' I told him, reaching for a dining chair because my legs were shaking, 'we were both beginning to realise that our so-called romantic relation-ship had materialised purely as a result of us working in such close proximity and we were going along with a union which would benefit us professionally, but had absolutely nothing to do with falling in love.'

'I don't understand.'

'Our families are both highly esteemed landscape archi-tects and they were keen to have more than a business merger. We had successfully worked together on high-profile projects before, and our parents, noticing this, took the opportunity to push us closer together. They thought they were giving us the nudge we needed to take things from professional to personal.'

'I see,' Finn frowned.

'However,' I carried on, keen to ensure that he really did, 'when I met Eloise at Broad-Meadows, I talked to her about the relationship, and she told me some blunt home truths before asking me some probing questions. The answers I gave her made the scales fall from my eyes. I realised I wasn't in love and so I sat my fiancé down and told him what I'd worked out.'

'And did he understand? Did he agree with you?'

'Totally,' I sighed. 'What we were planning to enter was a marriage of convenience, a business transaction really, and deep down it wasn't what either of us wanted. We were a dream team when it came to work, and it was our professional compatibility which had seduced us into believing that we were right for each other in love, but we weren't.'

'So, if it was a mutual decision to end it,' Finn asked, 'then why did you say it was you who broke off the engagement?'

'Because I was the one who instigated the break. I was the one who got the ball rolling and as I wanted to stop working with my parents and return to a more hands-on horticultural role and he wanted to carry on in the industry, it was easier to explain it that way. I guess it's just kind of stuck.'

'I see,' Finn said again.

'*Do* you?' I implored him. 'Do you really?'

'Yes,' he said, his eyes meeting mine. 'Yes, I do.'

I felt a tidal wave of relief rush over me, but I couldn't submit to it yet. There was still more I wanted to tell him.

'Eloise was the person who helped me reconnect and find my way back to what it was that I had started out loving. She was the one who encouraged me to get my hands in the earth again and I haven't looked back since.'

'I think I would have rather liked your friend, Eloise,' Finn smiled. 'I thought that when you talked about her before.'

She would have liked him too. His clever sculptures would have been the perfect fit for Broad-Meadows.

'And what about your ex?' he asked. 'What's he doing now?'

'Oh, Peter's living the dream.' I smiled. 'Working in New Zealand.'

'New Zealand, wow,' Finn sighed. 'Hang on, did you say, Peter?'

'Yes.'

'The guy you were engaged to is called Peter?'

'Yes,' I said again. 'It was him who interrupted us . . . before . . .'

'In the studio,' Finn carried on, 'when we were . . . kissing.'

'Yes.'

'The one who you described me to as no one.'

'I only said that because I didn't want him to start teasing me,' I hastily explained. 'Peter and I have stayed good friends and I'd already mentioned you to him by then and he annoyingly thought I had a bit of a thing for you.'

Finn raised his eyebrows.

'Which was right.' I swallowed, my cheeks starting to glow.

325

Finn grinned.

'I take it that you are still happy about that, then?'

'Which bit?'

'Me having a bit of a thing for you.'

'Of course, I bloody am,' he laughed, clearly delighted to have made me say it again. 'And it's a relief to find out your ex is called Peter. You've mentioned his name more than once and I was beginning to think he might be someone . . . current.'

'Oh,' I said, feeling hurt.

'Not that I had you down as someone who would just kiss another person when they were already in a relationship,' he quickly went on, a rush of colour suddenly flooding his face and matching it to mine. 'But I was the one who instigated that kiss and when Peter's call came through, I felt as guilty as hell.'

I wondered whether he was the one who had instigated it, but perhaps that was a conversation for another time.

'Is that why you've been pretending it never happened?' I asked him, 'Because you thought that not only had I left a groom crying at the altar but I was also in some sort of long-distance relationship?'

'I wasn't sure what I thought, to be honest,' he admitted, raking a hand through his hair. 'I couldn't really see you as being that sort of girl, but I got it all messed up in my head. That said, there was never any doubt that I was severely smitten with you, Freya, but I've had a rough time relationship-wise, and after our kiss and Peter's call, I just thought it would be best all round if I tried to keep things between us on a purely professional level.'

'And now?' I asked, standing up again, 'Now you know that I've never been a Bridezilla, I'm completely single and that Peter's a friend, are you still going to try and keep things professional?'

'How can I?' he said, leaning forward and pulling me down on to his lap. 'You're utterly irresistible.'

Before I could say another word, his mouth had covered mine and more of those passionate, forceful, hard and exciting kisses rained down. I kissed him back, every bit as forcefully. His hands were in my hair, my fingers were under his shirt and I lost all sense of propriety.

The dam that had been bricked up between us after our first embrace had well and truly burst and I had no intention of plugging it. It was time to set aside the cocktail of misunderstandings and conclusions we had jumped to and embrace a completely fresh start. After all, that had been the purpose of my intervention and Finn's kisses felt very much like mission accomplished.

'Oh, and about Zak,' I gasped, my nerve endings tingling.

'Do you have to mention him now?' Finn groaned.

'Yes,' I said, my back arching as his fingers grazed my skin with the lightest touch. 'It's important.'

'Go on then.'

'He was just changing a washer,' I whispered. 'That was all.'

'Actually, I know,' he said, and I could tell he was smiling. 'He told me.'

'He told you?'

'Yes,' he said, pulling away slightly, 'and if you hadn't come and found me today, then I had every intention of finding you and staging an intervention of my own.'

I couldn't help but laugh, but the sound soon changed to a groan as someone began hammering on the studio door and my plan of action came to a far less intense ending than the one I had set my sights on.

Chapter 23

By the time Finn had rearranged his clothes and rushed down the stairs, leaving me to tuck my dishevelled shirt back in, the hammering had stopped. I coaxed Nell out from under the table and followed him down.

'Cheers, mate,' I heard him say, before he closed the door and turned around holding a cardboard box. 'Delivery that needed signing for,' he said, rolling his eyes. 'Do you want to come back up?'

'Best not,' I said, lightly kissing him over the top of the box. 'Sure?'

'I'm sure,' I swallowed. 'Some things are worth waiting for.'

'Haven't we waited long enough?' he seductively whispered.

'Almost,' I whispered back, before quickly slipping out in case my resolve crumbled.

Earlier than requested, the next morning I headed back to Prosperous Place with a spring in my step and a smile I couldn't seem to get rid of. Not that I particularly wanted to, but if Chloe noticed me looking so chipper so early on a Saturday, then she was bound to guess I'd staged my intervention and put two and two together, and I wanted to avoid her speedy calculations.

I might have staged a successful intervention and Finn and I might have indulged in another knee-weakening kiss as a result, but I still didn't know what our relationship was destined to be, and therefore it definitely wasn't time to unwittingly share any details or purposefully go public about it. But as it turned out, it wasn't my smile that Chloe noticed.

'What have you done to your face?' she frowned, when I met her trying to negotiate the door to Prosperous Place while juggling yet more wreath-making supplies.

She'd come equipped with enough bits and pieces to adorn every door within a five-mile radius, but I didn't comment. There was something about her frown which suggested that it wasn't only whatever she'd spotted wrong with my face that was causing it. My friend was clearly feeling the pressure of what lay ahead and, even though I knew she'd be fine once the session started, she didn't look in the mood to listen to my reassurances, no matter how kindly meant.

'Nothing,' I therefore cringed instead, knowing exactly what she'd noticed. 'Why, what's wrong with it?'

'All around your mouth,' she said, 'it's really red.'

'Oh yes,' said Luke, who then appeared and took some of the bags from Chloe's laden arms, 'it looks ever so sore, Freya.'

I felt my cheeks glow bright enough to match the skin around my mouth.

'Windburn,' I said, thinking on my feet. 'I've always been partial to it and working here in the city I thought I'd get away without wearing my usual moisturiser to prevent it, but apparently not.'

Thankfully, the pair seemed to accept this answer and neither suggested beard burn, which I was certain it actually was.

'Oh wow,' said Chloe when she entered the dining room and found the fire already lit and the lights twinkling away. 'I thought it looked lovely when I'd finished setting up last night, Luke, but this is wonderful.'

The room smelt even better than when Lisa and I had used it thanks to all the extra greenery which had been arranged into separate piles on the covered dining table. There were long lengths of green ivy, holly studded with the brightest red berries and fecund bunches of mistletoe. Bowls of small pine cones, cinnamon sticks and satsumas added a forest, spiced and citrus tang to the air and it smelt almost good enough to eat.

'This all looks amazing,' I said, wondering if I needed to remind Chloe to tell the attendees that mistletoe berries were poisonous.

'Luke sorted delivery of most of it,' she told me. 'Didn't you?'

'It was more Finn really,' Luke nodded. 'It's all from the Wynthorpe Hall estate near Wynbridge, that the Connelly family owns. They supply some of the seasonal greenery for their local auction every December and as they've had a bumper year, they were happy to supply us at cost after Finn mentioned what we were doing here today to another friend who lives nearby.'

The friend was doubtless Jake from Skylark Farm and I daresay Finn had mentioned the need for greenery to Angus Connelly himself when they were talking about his sculpture commission. I felt my temperature rise at the mention of Finn's name. If we did end up together, I was going to be in constant danger of combustion!

'Right,' I said, reaching into my battered Barbour pocket to check the time on my phone, 'tell me what I can do to help.'

My phone wasn't in its usual spot and I realised I must have left it at Finn's. That gave me the perfect excuse to go back, not that I needed one, but I didn't want him to think I was hounding him.

'I reckon a bite of breakfast might not be a bad idea,' Luke suggested. 'I bet you haven't eaten yet, have you, Chloe?'

After a hearty breakfast with the family in the kitchen, Luke left Chloe and me to it and we ran through the schedule she'd drawn up and checked through her supplies again.

'I know it's silly, to feel so nervous,' she told me, as she wiped her clammy hands down her jeans. 'And I was fine until this morning but then the alarm went off and I realised just what I'd let myself in for.'

'I was the same,' I smiled, 'but once you get into the swing of it, you'll be fine.'

I left her in peace and went to find Kate to ask if everyone had now collected their preserved leaves which I had rinsed and separated into named bags. There was only one bag left and that belonged to Sara, the young woman who had signed up to do everything.

'So, how's it going, Sara?' I asked her, once Chloe had registered the day's attendees and we were taking a quick tour of the garden.

'Really well,' she nodded. 'I've been keeping up with my nature journal and planning the children's stories and a group of us met up for our first walk last week.'

'That's great,' I said, thrilled that they were making good on the promise to keep in touch and do things together throughout the winter.

'We went to Whitlingham Lake,' she told me with a shudder. 'It was absolutely freezing, but that said, we did feel better for the fresh air and exercise.'

'That's fantastic,' I smiled, noticing Chloe was waving to get my attention, 'I'm so pleased you've all kept in touch. I'll have to add the lake to my list of places to visit.'

Finn had already suggested a tour of the cathedral, perhaps he'd fancy joining Nell and me for a walk around Whitlingham too. Or was I getting ahead of myself, imagining us strolling hand in hand, wrapped up in scarves and cosy layers, before settling down to supper in front of a roaring log fire?

'It's definitely worth a look,' Sara smiled, unaware of my fireside fantasy, 'but do wrap up warm.'

After helping Chloe, who was already feeling more confident, with the tour, which included admiring the hares in the meadow lawn and seeking out the dragons in the fern garden, I then acted as assistant while my friend gave a competent demonstration in the art of wreath-making. I found my helping hands were much appreciated as everyone twisted, formed and secured their wreath bases.

As I rushed around handing out wire and helping to weave willow ends into place, I realised that was the trickiest part of the process and it took a while to get it right.

'There's no point skimping on the base,' Chloe told everyone as she checked their progress. 'Think of this as your foundation. The tighter and more solid it is, the better the end result will be. Time spent on this now will pay dividends when it comes to longevity and impressing your neighbours.'

A ripple of laughter ran through the group and they carried on with renewed vigour. By the time we were ready to fill up on the lunch Carole, Kate and Luke had been preparing, and the smell of which was making our stomachs grumble, everyone had the firm foundation Chloe had insisted on and were looking forward to embellishing their efforts during the afternoon session.

'Here's one I prepared earlier,' Chloe said, *Blue Peter*-style, as she handed me another base from her bag. 'This is for you,' she smiled. 'Everyone will be able to manage to wire in on their own this afternoon, so I thought you might fancy making one for your front door.'

'Oh, thank you, Chloe,' I smiled back, taking the tight and tidy wreath from her. 'I'd love to have a go.'

As before, lunch was homemade soup, and bread from Blossom's, and everyone was in fine spirits as they sat around the big kitchen table, talking about their festive plans and how Luke's Winterfest was making them view the season with fresh eyes. The expression on his face told me that he was well-pleased and Graham, who joined us to check the log basket and stoke the fire, looked equally happy. I knew he was loving Winterfest too, but it was his time helping me in the garden which had really given him a sense of purpose.

'You've got a visitor,' he said, as he drew level with me.

I followed his gaze and spotted Finn in the doorway, holding a big bunch of eucalyptus. It was so noisy in the kitchen that I hadn't heard him come in. Chloe spotted him at the same time and went to stand up.

'I'll take it,' I told her, meaning the extra greenery, 'you finish your lunch.'

She gave me a knowing smile, which I pretended not to see.

'I didn't get to eat much the day I worked with Lisa, and I felt a bit grim as a result,' I quickly added, more to justify my rush to spend a moment with Finn than in concern for her blood sugar level.

'Of course,' she grinned, turning her attention back to the lady sitting next to her.

Finn followed me into the dining room, set the stems down on the table and quickly pulled me into his arms. I was delighted that he was as keen to see me as I was to see him.

'And there was me thinking that you turning up here was purely to bolster supplies,' I laughed, once we had kissed a very warm hello.

It was a truly wonderful, if risky greeting. Anyone could have walked in, but with eyes only for each other, we hadn't thought to close the door.

'I haven't been able to stop thinking about you, Freya,' he said huskily, which had the effect of weakening my knees again so he had to hold me tighter, 'and I'm not just talking about after last night either. You really have been in my head from the moment I first set eyes on you.'

'Shouted at me you mean,' I cheekily reminded him, and he kissed me again. 'You've been on my mind a bit too.'

'A bit,' he laughed, letting me go.

'A lot then,' I admitted. 'And I was hoping I'd see you today.'

'How about I come over to yours tonight, when you've finished up here, and we have a takeaway or something,' he suggested.

I didn't know about the takeaway, but I was already looking forward to the *something*.

'There's something I want to talk to you about,' he then said, which rather took the wind out of my sails. 'It's important.'

That didn't sound like the sort of *something* I'd had in mind.

'All right,' I swallowed, hoping it wasn't another complication which would call a halt to our romantic progress. 'I'll see you tonight.'

'Don't look so worried,' he grinned, 'it's nothing bad.'

That was a relief.

'Promise,' I whispered.

'Scout's honour,' he laughed. 'And if you give me your keys, I'll pop over and check on Nell if you like. Let her out in the garden for a bit if you haven't got time.'

'Thanks,' I said, reaching for my coat, 'I am almost out of time so I'd appreciate that.'

I knew Nell still wasn't all that struck on Finn so this might be an ideal bonding opportunity for the pair without me hovering about and fussing.

'Oh, and I almost forgot,' said Finn, pulling my phone out of his pocket, 'you left this in the flat.'

The sound of someone clearing their throat caught our attention and I nearly dropped the phone as he handed it over and we sprang apart.

'Windburn, my arse,' Chloe laughed, looking from one of us to the other.

In spite of my preoccupation with how Finn and Nell were getting on and what it was that he wanted to talk to me about, I did still manage to be of some use to Chloe and produce a very pretty wreath for my front door.

Everyone was delighted with their day's work and left happily weighed down with wreaths which they promised to photograph once they were in situ and share online, tagging Luke and Winterfest, which made him very happy indeed.

'There's not as much left as I thought there'd be,' I said to Chloe as we swept and tidied. 'I thought you'd got far too much stuff, but you hadn't, had you?'

'No,' she said, 'thank goodness. I didn't want anyone having to skimp.'

I bundled together a few stray cinnamon sticks and a partly clove-studded satsuma and added them to the bits Chloe said she could make use of.

'You might as well get off,' she said to me. 'You're helping Poppy and Mark tomorrow, aren't you?'

'Yes,' I said, stifling a yawn, 'I am.'

'You'll be shattered by Monday.'

'That's why I'm giving her the day off,' said Luke, who had come back to help.

'No, that's all right,' I told him, shrugging the suggestion off, even though it was rather appealing.

'I insist,' he said firmly. 'By the looks of the forecast, it's not going to be great gardening weather anyway. In fact, take Monday and Tuesday off and Chloe, you come in just on Thursday next week. You've both been flat out and I really appreciate it.'

'But there's still loads to do ahead of the Winter Garden opening,' I protested, but he wouldn't hear of it.

'You've got an extra pair of hands now, thanks to enlisting Graham, *and* you were the one who told me that it was going to be a work in progress, weren't you?'

'I was,' I admitted.

'There you are then.'

He wouldn't be swayed and I went home looking forward to the lazy start to my working week as well as the evening ahead. The only thing hampering my mood was Finn's insistence that he had something to tell me. I really hoped it wasn't going to be anything that would throw us off course again.

Chapter 24

Nell was in a buoyant mood when I arrived home and opened the door, having hung my pretty wreath on a hook which had conveniently appeared at some point during the afternoon. I guessed that was Finn's doing. I also guessed that Nell was so happy because someone – Finn again – had been extremely generous with the treats I usually saved for walks which I knew were going to test her recall. Not that I really minded. He'd clearly been determined to make an effort with her and my guess was that she'd love him forever now.

I'd just finished soaking in a hot bubble bath when my phone pinged with a disjointed text saying he'd be with me in half an hour, that he'd already put the plates to warm in the airing cupboard and that he'd bring a Chinese takeaway with him. I wasn't sure if his decrepit phone was the cause of the message arriving in separate chunks or if Finn was more proficient at wielding hand tools than texting, but it didn't really matter.

'I didn't know what you fancied,' he said, when I answered the door, 'so I've got a bit of everything.'

'I'm not fussy,' I told him, resisting the urge to point out that if he was concerned about that, then he could have come over empty-handed and I would have been happy.

Neither of us wanted to sit in the kitchen, so we set everything out on the coffee table in the sitting room and dipped in and out of the containers with trays on our laps.

'This is *so* good,' I said. 'I can't remember the last time I had a takeaway at home.'

'This place is only up the road,' Finn told me. 'Two doors along from The Dragon.'

'I still haven't got my head around how close everything is,' I laughed. 'When I was living at Broad-Meadows there was no such thing as home delivery or a quick wander down the road for a pint of milk.'

'Did you mind that?'

'No,' I said, remembering how beautiful the place was, even if it was rather isolated, 'not at the time. But I could definitely get used to this.'

'We'll have to make a habit of it then,' he grinned, leaning over to refill my glass of cola.

'I'd like that,' I smiled back.

I was really falling for this guy and I hoped that whatever it was he was gearing up to tell me wasn't going to send me crashing back down to earth with a bump. I rather liked the feeling of walking on air.

'What is it?' he asked, his smile turning into a frown.

'What do you mean?'

'You looked so happy a second ago,' he said, taking in my expression, 'but then your face changed and now you look sad.'

'I'm worried about what you're going to tell me,' I said, meeting his gaze.

We'd spent so long not saying the things that we should that I didn't want to waste more time hiding our feelings or pretending that everything was fine when it wasn't.

'I thought you might be,' he sighed. 'I shouldn't have mentioned it earlier. I knew you were going to fret over it as soon as I'd said it. Come on,' he said, taking my plate, 'I'll put this lot in the kitchen and then I'll tell you.'

I sat and faced him, my legs drawn up beneath me and my damp hair free from the band I had tied it back with while I was eating. The weight of it fell around my face and I pushed it behind my ears. I could feel it was already curling out of all control, but that was nothing new.

'I wasn't going to tell you any of this,' Finn eventually began, 'but after what you did and said last night, and what happened after you'd done it, I was more aware than ever that I'm *really* falling for you, Freya and in order to do that properly, there's something I need to share with you, even though it pains me to do it.'

'Okay,' I whispered.

'And Zak said I should too.'

'Zak?'

'I know,' he said, looking at me and shaking his head.

'Who would have thought my pain in the arse half-brother could actually turn over a new leaf *and* offer words of wisdom?'

'Words of wisdom?'

'Well,' Finn conceded, 'perhaps not wisdom, but some plainly spoken home truths.'

We both smiled and I felt some of the tension which had been building ebb away.

'He said that I owed it to you to explain why I thought the worst of you when I assumed you had jilted someone at the altar.'

'Well,' I said, 'that doesn't really need explaining. Jilting someone at the altar would be a pretty shitty thing to do.'

'Oh, I *know* it's a pretty shitty thing to do,' he said with a rueful smile.

'How?' I quietly asked, even though his words practically guaranteed I'd guessed.

'Because I was the sad sod waiting for the bride who'd had a change of heart but not quite mustered the courage to tell me before I was standing in front of family and friends on a distant sun-drenched beach.'

Yep, that was exactly what I'd just worked out that he was going to say. Apart from the beach bit. I didn't have Finn down as a sunshine wedding type at all.

'Oh, Finn,' I breathed, trying not to picture his heartbreak and humiliation.

'No wonder I have trust issues, right?' he said gruffly.

'Especially,' I sighed, 'when a girl comes along who you

like, but who you think has done the very same thing to someone else as you've had done to you, yes?'

'That's about the size of it,' he said, lacing his fingers together and biting his lip. 'I'm sorry I jumped to that conclusion, Freya.'

'It's okay,' I told him, because I could hardly hold it against him when what I said in the pub had made it sound very much like that was what I had done. 'And please don't feel obliged to say any more about what happened to you.'

'But I want to,' he insisted. 'I want you to know everything. I think it's important that you do.'

He then proceeded to explain how he'd met this girl and started a relationship with her while building an extension on the property she was living at.

'She told me the guy who owned the place was her uncle. I only met him once and given his age that was totally believable, but after she left me at the altar, I discovered that he had been her partner. It turned out she'd had a few older men in her life.'

'Did no one guess about their relationship while you were doing the building work?'

'No,' he shrugged. 'We were there to build an extension, not get to know the ins and outs of the personal dynamics of the client. Besides, the bloke was never around when we were and Erica never did or said anything to arouse any suspicion.'

'But she must have loved you,' I pointed out, only defending her to save Finn's feelings, 'otherwise she wouldn't have agreed to marry you, would she?'

'Oh, she didn't want me,' Finn laughed.

'Then why . . . ?'

'She thought I was going to inherit Dad's business,' he cut in. 'She'd been looking at the family portfolio and assumed I was going to receive a secure and wealthy future.'

'So, if you knew that, why did you want to marry her?'

'I didn't know she'd set her sights on the family fortune until after she disappeared.'

'I see,' I swallowed. 'Had you not told her about your ambition to become a full-time artist?'

'I had,' he nodded, 'but Erica only listened to what she wanted to hear and she said my plan to make a living from my sculptures was just a phase.'

'What on earth made you fall in love with her?' I frowned. 'It doesn't sound to me as though you had anything in common at all.'

'I wasn't in love with her,' he quickly said. 'I know that now.'

'So, what attracted you to her then? What made you want to marry her? She must have had something going for her if you were prepared to enter into a life-long commitment.'

Mine and Peter's relationship had been all about business and work connections, but clearly that wasn't the case for Finn and Erica.

'If I'm being completely honest,' he said, ducking his head, 'then I have to admit that it was one-upmanship. Having someone in my life that someone else wanted. Someone who I truly believed had picked me over them.'

'What's that supposed to mean?'

'Zak,' he said, letting out a long breath. 'It was the way Erica spoke to Zak which turned me on to her.'

As soon as he said those words, it all became clear.

'She was always putting him down and shrugging his attention off in favour of mine. For the first time in my life I had something that he wanted, something he couldn't take away from me. That was what I built the foundation of our relationship on.'

'I see.'

'I know it wasn't healthy and I know how awful that makes me sound,' Finn carried on, 'but that's the way it was. I'm just being honest with you.'

'Believe me,' I quickly told him, 'I'm not judging you. Peter and I hardly had the right foundations to build a romantic relationship on, did we?'

'I suppose not.'

'So, what happened next?'

'Well, almost before I knew it, I had proposed and the date was set. Zak tried to warn me off but I ignored him, assuming he was jealous. However, the night before the wedding I did have a taste of what was to come, even though I didn't see it. Erica and I argued again about my plans to leave the business.'

'She still couldn't accept your decision?'

'Not to begin with, but before she left the room, she apologised for not taking me seriously, which was a shock because she never said sorry for anything, and then she promised to do whatever she could to make me happy.'

'And then the next day, she left you at the altar,' I said, shaking my head.

'Exactly,' said Finn, his tone suddenly lighter. 'So, she did come good in the end.'

'How do you mean?'

'Well, I've been thinking about it more rationally recently, and she did fulfil her promise, didn't she? I might have felt like the biggest fool standing there waiting for a bride who was never going to arrive, but at the end of the day, she had done whatever it took to make me happy. She didn't marry me.'

That had to be the most positive spin I had ever heard anyone put on anything.

'I suppose ...'

'And now,' Finn said, making both Nell and I jump as he stood up and rushed from the room, 'I want to celebrate.'

He quickly reappeared, carrying a bottle of champagne in an ice bucket and two flutes.

'Where did you spring that from?' I gasped, as he popped the cork.

'I brought it over this afternoon and hid it in the cupboard under the stairs,' he grinned. 'Are you using that cupboard by the way? It's full of stuff.'

'I am,' I told him proudly. 'I think I've finally conquered my claustrophobia demons, or some of them anyway.'

I'd still made sure the door was properly propped open before I stacked my bits and pieces inside.

'But never mind that now,' I said, shaking my head, 'you were saying about the champagne.'

'I've been saving it for the perfect moment.'

'And this is it, is it?' I laughed. 'What exactly are we toasting?'

We clinked glasses and he looked at me intently.

'Well,' he said, 'I'd like to raise a glass to Erica.'

I raised my eyebrows, which made him laugh.

'Because,' he hastily explained, 'had she not left me, I wouldn't have found out that Prosperous Place, or you, existed and that would have been a tragedy. Erica's desertion helped me find the courage to become the man I am today, and I'm very grateful for that.'

'When you put it like that,' I laughed again, 'I feel I should be the one making that toast myself.'

'I thought you might want to raise a glass to Eloise.' Finn smiled.

I noticed Nell's ears twitch at the sound of her former mistress's name.

'Had it not been for her, you might have gone through with a disastrous wedding and not made it to Nightingale Square either.'

Tears pricked my eyes, but they were happy ones.

'To Eloise,' I said, raising my glass. 'And Peter, because he was saved from a miserable marriage, too.'

I wondered what he was going to say when I told him that he'd been right about how I felt about Finn all along.

'To Erica, Eloise and Peter,' said Finn, joining me on the sofa and kissing me firmly on the lips before draining his glass in two gulps.

'Thank goodness for Erica and Eloise's timely intervention in our lives,' I added, before emptying my glass so it matched his.

What happened after that became a little hazy. I do know that we emptied the bottle far quicker than the person who lovingly made it would probably have thought respectful, and I can remember smooching on the couch. I could also recall waking a little after two on Sunday morning with a crick in my neck to find Finn had gone, but he had thoughtfully covered me with the throw from the sofa to stave off the night's chill.

I negotiated the stairs up to bed, content in the knowledge that the day had ended on a real high and feeling the happiest I'd been since I'd moved to Nightingale Square.

Chapter 25

Feeling dazed, I slammed my hand down on the alarm clock, but it didn't make the noise stop. It took a few more seconds for my brain to work out that it wasn't a weekday morning and the cacophony I was being subjected to was coming from my phone, not my bedside clock. Groaning, I pulled a pillow over my head and tried to drift off again, but it was no good. Nell was pawing at the duvet, needing to go out and I was awake just enough to register that my head was pounding.

'Oh, for pity's sake,' I groaned, catching sight of myself in the wardrobe mirror as I pulled on my dressing gown and shuffled to the bathroom.

My hair was absolutely wild and I had no idea what I was going to do to tame it. I was supposed to be helping Poppy and Mark with their Winterfest session, but there was no way I'd be able to do that with the unruly mop on my head. I was a health and safety nightmare and I would need to sort it before I could go anywhere near the Prosperous Place kitchen.

'Come on then,' I said to Nell, letting her down the stairs ahead of me, for fear of tripping over her.

I let her into the garden, checked over the plants from Broad-Meadows which were thriving in the porch, flicked on the kettle (the boiling of which was an assault on my eardrums), rammed bread into the toaster and swallowed down two painkillers.

Accusingly, I stared at the empty bottle of champagne which was the cause of my hangover, but then I remembered kissing Finn and some of the pain in my skull receded and the heavy weight of my hair lifted a little. I wondered if he was feeling as rough as I was? Probably not, given the size of him and certainly not yet, because he didn't have a Nell to tend to and was doubtless still asleep.

I could hear my phone ringing upstairs again and knew it would be Mum. Rather than rush to answer it, I forced down a few mouthfuls of toast to stave off the nausea and waited for her to call again.

'Morning, Mum,' I said brightly, determined not to give her even the merest hint that anything was amiss when she rang the third time. 'How are you?'

'It's Peter, actually and I'm really, really good.'

'Peter,' I laughed, reminding myself that checking caller ID was never a bad idea. 'You sound very merry.'

'I'm a little tipsy,' he hiccupped.

I checked the clock on the wall.

'At six in the evening? Have I got the time difference, right?'

'You have,' he told me and I could image him woozily nodding, 'we had a *very* long lunch and we're celebrating.'

'Celebrating what exactly?'

'I asked Rebecca to marry me and she said yes! She was the beautiful woman I was wining and dining when you called me before, remember?'

'That's fantastic news,' I smiled, hoping I hadn't interrupted more than just a meal out. It would have been awful if he had been gearing up to propose then and was halted by a call from an ex. 'Congratulations to you both. I'm truly thrilled for you.'

'You will come out for the wedding, won't you?'

'I'll try my best,' I promised. 'Where's Rebecca now?'

'She's phoning her parents. I told mine a little while ago.'

I was flattered that I featured so high up on his list of folk to call.

'And what about you?' he asked. 'Any joy with that Finn fella?'

'Lots,' I grinned, thinking of the evening before.

'Oh, really?' said Peter, sounding deservedly smug. 'So, I was right then?'

'As it turns out.'

'I knew it!'

'I know you did,' I said, shaking my head and regretting it, 'now, go and find your fiancée. We'll chat again soon, okay?'

'All right,' he agreed.

'Congratulations,' I said again, but the tipsy fool had already hung up.

I had barely put the phone down before it buzzed again. This time I checked and it was Mum.

'Morning, Mum,' I said, feeling genuinely brighter than before, buoyed up as I was by Peter's wonderful news. 'How are you?'

'I'm fine, thank you, Freya,' she said, 'but what's wrong with you? You sound all croaky?'

'I've had a cold,' I told her, amused that Peter hadn't noticed and grateful that she was miles away and couldn't see my hungover state. 'It's almost gone now,' I sniffed to prove the point, as I rifled through my drawer of hair accessories. 'I've just been left with a bit of a croak. How are things with you and Dad?'

'Busy,' she said, just as I knew she would.

She and Dad were *always* busy.

'And I have news,' she added.

'If it's about Jackson and Broad-Meadows, I don't want to hear it,' I interrupted.

'There's no need to be rude,' Mum tutted. 'I do have news about Broad-Meadows, and lots of it, because you wouldn't let me tell you the last time we spoke, but I'm actually calling about Peter.'

'Peter,' I repeated, trying to keep the smile out of my voice, because I already knew what she was going to say.

'It's a bit delicate,' Mum carried on, 'especially if you still have feelings for him. You don't, do you, darling?'

'Not the sort you're implying,' I said. 'And you know I never did. I thought we'd established that a long time ago.'

'Well, as long as you *really* mean it and you aren't just

353

saying it,' she went on, making me bristle a little, 'then that's something I suppose.'

'Oh, just spit it out, Mum, for heaven's sake,' I goaded, spurred on by the bedside clock which seemed to have fast-forwarded at least half an hour.

'He's engaged.'

She accompanied the two words with a sigh of such magnitude that she must have sucked in every last drop of air in her orbit in order to release it so dramatically.

'Well, that's wonderful news,' I said happily.

I had no intention of telling her that I already knew. Had in fact heard the words from the man himself, because that would only lead to a barrage of questions.

'If you say so.'

'Of course, I say so,' I said, with a very genuine smile, 'I'm absolutely delighted for him. Do you know his fiancée's name? I'll have to send a card.'

'It's Rebecca,' Mum said airily. 'No idea what her last name is. Peter's parents called earlier with the news, but they didn't say who she was. She's no one significant, I'm sure.'

'Well,' I said, bristling again, 'she's pretty significant to Peter, isn't she? Otherwise he wouldn't have asked her to marry him. And that's all that matters.'

'I suppose.'

I was quiet for a moment, imagining Peter happy and drunk in New Zealand and my pounding head stilled a little. I wasn't sure if it was the painkillers kicking in, or if I was still drunk too – on love, that is – but whatever it was, I was happy for him and for me. The year was going to end on a high for both of us. If someone had told me that just a few months ago, I wouldn't have believed it.

Unfortunately, Mum misconstrued my momentary quiet for disappointment.

'Oh, you are upset,' she sympathised. 'I shouldn't have said anything.'

Her voice drifted away and I knew she was saying something to Dad who, as always during these Sunday morning calls, was lingering in the background.

'Freya?' came his voice.

He sounded concerned and I daresay Mum had told him I'd collapsed and was having a crisis.

'Hey, Dad,' I smiled, 'I'm guessing Mum's—'

'We've just put you on speakerphone,' he cut in, saving my blushes. 'We're sorry about, Peter,' he carried on.

'Well, don't be,' I said, my mind full of Finn, 'because I'm not. I'm happy for him. Truly delighted.'

If Peter was as love-struck as I was, then he was feeling very content indeed and I couldn't have wished the feeling on a lovelier bloke. We might not have been right for each other, but I was genuinely thrilled that he had found the right fit with Rebecca.

'That's good then,' said Dad, sounding relieved. 'And don't you worry, you'll find someone. You won't be on your own forever.'

'I'll tell her about Jackson's plans,' I heard Mum loudly whisper, 'that might help.'

'Thanks, Dad,' I said, then, in a desperate bid to put her off, blurted out, 'but actually, I'm not on my own. I have found someone.'

Mum shrieked and there was scuffling as she unnecessarily took back control of the handset.

'What was that, Freya?' she pounced. 'What did you just say?'

'I said, I've met someone,' I smiled. 'I'm in a relationship, Mum. A wonderful one with a man I'm very much in love with.'

I knew I should have mentioned that to Finn before my parents but, bursting with bonhomie for Peter, I wanted to shout about my own feelings. That said, I knew I was going to regret shouting them to Mum because she was bound to keep pestering me for details.

'Well,' she said, 'that's lovely news.'

She didn't make it sound like it was lovely news.

'So, when do we get to meet this man you're so besotted with?'

That wouldn't be happening any time soon.

'Will he be at the Winter Garden opening?'

I'd forgotten she and Dad were coming to that.

'No,' I lied, crossing my fingers, 'he's nothing to do with the garden.'

'Is he not?'

'No,' I lied again as my head started to thump. 'Look, Mum, I'm ever so sorry to cut you off, but I'm working today, so—'

'On a Sunday?'

'Yes, with a Winterfest event in Prosperous Place so I need to get ready.'

'But I haven't told you about Broad-Meadows yet,' she said, sounding disappointed.

'You know I don't want to hear about Broad-Meadows,' I tersely reminded her. 'But I do need to get on. We'll speak again soon.'

And with Dad shouting goodbye in the background, I ended the call.

Channelling Helena Bonham Carter circa 1985, I managed to pin my hair into submission, settle Nell and arrive at Prosperous Place just as Poppy and Mark were welcoming everyone to a day of 'seasonal and fulfilling foodie heaven'.

'You all right?' Poppy asked as I helped distribute the ingredients which were going to be transformed into her chuck-it-all-in chutney.

I had felt fine, out in the fresh bracing air, but the vinegary tang which was already filling the kitchen, made my stomach roll a little.

'You do look a bit peaky,' Mark chimed in, arching an eyebrow from his side of the table.

'I'm all right,' I told them both.

'Saturday-night hangover,' they said together, with a little chuckle.

'How do you know that?' I tutted, knowing denial was futile.

'You're displaying all the classic signs,' quipped Mark, clearly delighted that his and Poppy's observation skills were up to scratch. 'This vinegar must be playing havoc with—'

'Don't,' I swallowed, cutting him off.

'Funnily enough,' Poppy carried on where Mark had left off, 'I saw Finn earlier and he was looking a little green around the gills too. Coincidence?'

'Must be,' I sniffed.

'Talk of the devil,' said Mark, with a nod to the door.

'Finn,' I sighed, his name escaping my lips before I could stop it. 'I'll be back in a sec,' I told the terrible two as Finn beckoned me over.

'Take your time,' they said, again in perfect synchronicity.

Finn reached for my hand and led me back into the corridor next to the kitchen.

'I had a great time last night,' he said, pulling me gently into his arms, once he'd checked there was no one else around.

'Me too,' I said, laying my head against his broad chest and feeling thrilled that, thanks to a timely intervention, some secret sharing and a hefty dollop of honesty our relationship had been totally transformed. 'Did we only drink one bottle of fizz, though?' I asked, looking up at him, 'because I've got one hell of a hangover this morning.'

'We did,' he laughed, the sound resonating through his chest, 'and I'm feeling it a bit too.'

Given the size of him, that was a surprise. I had assumed

his physical bulk would have made him immune to the thumping head and churning tummy I was enduring.

'Which is not what I need today,' he added. 'I've got to be on top form.'

'Why? What have you got planned?'

'Sunday dinner with the family.'

'You're going back?'

The last I'd heard; he had sworn off Sundays with the family for good.

'Yep,' he said, puffing out his cheeks. 'Zak's talked me into it. But I've told him, if Dad even hints that he's starting on me, then I'm out of there.'

'Well, good luck,' I smiled, reaching up to kiss him and hoping that Zak's personality change would ensure he'd take Finn's side if there was any trouble. 'I've had my weekly dose of family this morning. Trying to find the right thing to say to Mum is exhausting!'

'Poor you,' he said, kissing me back. 'Did you hit on the right thing to say?'

Given that he was already stressed about the prospect of dinner with his dad, I didn't think it was quite the right moment to tell him that I'd told my parents I was in love with him.

'I'll tell you later,' I said. I'd fill him in on Peter's news then too. 'I better get back to the kitchen. Mark's preparing some dough that he wants me to bash about.'

'Rather you than me,' Finn grimaced. 'I'll come and see you in the garden tomorrow, shall I?'

'Oh, I won't be there,' I said, only just remembering. 'I've got tomorrow and Tuesday off.'

'In that case,' he said, 'how about we spend it together? I could take you to the cathedral like I suggested before and there's a Christmas market in the city centre. We can look around that too, if you fancy it?'

I fancied it very much indeed and went back to the kitchen light of step, with my hangover practically forgotten and feeling buoyed up for the chutney- and bread-making marathon.

Chapter 26

The following morning, I was up long before it was light. The bread-and-chutney Winterfest session had been every bit as successful as those which went before it, but I couldn't say, in all honesty, that I had felt particularly present during any of it.

Finn's brief visit, along with his suggestion that we could spend my days off together, had pretty much banished my post-fizz sickly feeling, and I was very much looking forward to the start of my week.

'Come on,' I said to a surprised but delighted Nell, as I rattled her lead that Monday morning. 'Let's get an early walk in, shall we?'

The stars were still shining and I was pleased I'd layered up because it was more than a little crisp when I stepped outside. Nell, resplendent in her tweed and moleskin fleece-lined coat, trotted ahead, as keen to start the day as I was.

'Couldn't you sleep either?'

My hand shot up to my chest and even Nell, usually so

aware of everything around her, was caught off guard, but then she realised who the voice belonged to and her tail thumped against my leg.

'Crikey, Finn,' I gasped. 'You made me jump.'

'Sorry,' he said, quieter than before, so as not to disturb the neighbours.

Aside from those in Lisa and Heather's houses, there were no other lights on in the square and I reckoned they were only lit up because kids tended to be early risers, especially in the run-up to Christmas.

'So where are you going so early in the day?' Finn asked, falling into step as Nell tugged on the lead in her eagerness to be off.

'I thought I'd get Nell walked early as you and I are going out. We are still going, aren't we?'

'Definitely,' he said, taking my free hand, giving it a squeeze and then not letting go. 'I could hardly sleep for thinking about it.'

'Excellent,' I said, as my heart kicked hard in my chest, both the result of us holding hands and Finn being as excited about our festive trip as I was. 'So where are you headed?'

'I'm going to Blossom's.'

'Blossom's?' I echoed. 'At this time?'

'Yes, she does the most amazing filled breakfast rolls, but you have to be up really early to get them. I was planning to get us some and surprise you with them.'

'I rather wished I'd stayed at home now,' I told him. 'Breakfast almost in bed would have been most welcome.'

Finn chuckled.

'So, what does Blossom fill these rare rolls with?'

'Pretty much everything from the traditional full English range,' he explained, making my tummy rumble. 'My favourite is the classic eggs and bacon. It might sound basic, but it's packed full and keeps me going till long after lunchtime.'

'In that case,' I said, quickening my pace, 'shall we step it up a bit? I'd hate to miss out.'

'Definitely,' Finn agreed.

'I'll have the same as you, if that's all right,' I requested. 'Why don't you go and get them while I whizz Nell around the block and I'll meet you back at the house?'

'Sounds good to me,' he said, lingering to give me a soft, sweet kiss before letting me go. 'I'll see you in a bit.'

'Oh my God,' I groaned, 'you weren't wrong, were you?'

Blossom's breakfast rolls were every bit as delicious, full and tasty as Finn had described and I had been hard-pushed to finish mine. Even Nell was in seventh heaven because he'd got her some cooked sausages to snack on.

'They're good, right?' Finn smiled, wiping his mouth with a sheet of kitchen roll.

'So good,' I groaned again.

'And just what we need to keep us on our feet, because I have a packed itinerary for today.'

We both stood up to get ready to go.

'I can't wait,' I told him, wrapping my arms around his waist and kissing him again. Blossom's roll might have sated my hunger, but I still had plenty of appetite for Finn. 'By the way, how did lunch with the family go yesterday?'

'Do you know,' he said, his voice full of wonder, 'it was actually all right. Dad kept the digs dialled down and he couldn't believe it when Zak whipped his phone out to show him what I'd been working on. Mind you, I was pretty shocked by that too. I had no idea he'd taken such an interest.'

It was a total turnaround, but a most welcome one.

'And what about you?' Finn asked. 'You were going to tell me what you said to your mum.'

'Oh, I'll tell you later,' I swallowed, quickly diverting the focus of our conversation from family to friends. 'But Peter rang too and his call was much more exciting.'

'Oh.'

'He rang to tell me he's engaged.'

'Well, that's lovely news.'

'It is,' I agreed, 'and he wanted to see if I still had the hots for you, of course.'

'And what did you tell him?' he grinned, kissing me softly. 'Did you tell him that you had to carry a fire extinguisher with you everywhere now?'

'Something like that,' I chuckled, between kisses.

'And did you tell your mum about me, too?'

'You might have got a mention.'

I still didn't go into details, but then, given the way our kiss quickly deepened and my body melded itself to his, I couldn't have focused on details even if I'd wanted to.

*

364

It was only just after nine, but the city seemed to be waking up earlier and earlier in the run-up to Christmas. With just a couple of weeks to go until the schools broke up, harassed-looking parents were striding out with lengthy lists, all wearing stern expressions and carrying multiple reusable shopping bags.

They weren't exactly exuding festive joy, but fortunately for us, Finn and I had the luxury of unlimited hours and could take things at a more leisurely pace when it came to enjoying the sights, sounds and scents of the season, of which there were many.

'Let's start at the market,' he suggested. 'The Christmas one,' he hastily added, 'not the permanent one.'

'I don't mind either now I'm coping with my claustrophobia,' I told him, keeping tight hold of his hand as we wove our way through the rapidly growing crowds. 'And it doesn't feel quite so tight for space there during the day.'

Both the area in the front of the Forum and outside the shopping mall were packed with little wooden stalls selling festive treats. My favourites were the wreath and garland stall (the orange and pine scent of which you could catch from metres away), the one selling quirky and kitsch festive decorations, and the German Schokokuss, or chocolate kisses, stand. Neither Finn nor I could resist those and we both purchased a few, even though we were still full of Blossom's breakfast.

'Have you decided when you're going to put your decorations up yet?' I asked Finn, as we made our way along the wonderful cobbled Lanes, which housed a variety of unique artisan shops and boutiques.

'I'm not sure I'll bother, to be honest,' he told me. 'As you know, the studio flat isn't exactly all that roomy.'

'But you have to have something,' I insisted.

'Even if it's just a bunch of mistletoe?'

'Absolutely,' I said. 'Any excuse for a Christmas kiss, right?'

'I don't need mistletoe for that,' he said, pulling me to one side and proving the point.

'Apparently not,' I blushed.

'What about you?' he asked, taking my hand again.

'What about me, what?'

'We were talking about decorations.'

'Oh yes,' I said, 'well, I've got a few bits and pieces, so I'll probably get a tiny tree, or even a few branches of something from the garden to display them on. And lights, I definitely need twinkling lights.'

I was rather looking forward to decorating the house and wondered what Harold used to put up. I'd have to ask him next time I saw him.

'Where are we?' I asked, looking about me.

After the lingering kiss and criss-crossing lanes, I was completely disorientated.

'Why are we heading towards a church?' I frowned as Finn led us down an even narrower path. 'I thought you weren't the religious type, or are there more green men in here, like the ones you've spotted in the cathedral?'

'It's not that sort of church,' he told me. 'Not anymore, anyway.'

And he was right. St Gregory's was now an antique and vintage emporium selling everything from furniture to fancy ornaments, vinyl to vases. I could have spent the entire day exploring the stands and stalls. Some parts were a trip down memory lane, packed full of 'we used to have one of these when I was little,' moments and others were full of far more unique treasures. There was one thing in particular which caught my eye.

'What have you found?' Finn asked, as he looked over my shoulder.

'Just a brooch,' I said, lightly running my fingers over the exquisite detail.

'Wow,' said Finn, 'that's beautiful.'

'It's art nouveau, according to the label.'

It was a beautifully handcrafted bunch of snowdrops made in silver. It was in pristine condition and the perfect reproduction of my all-time favourite winter flower. If I'd had cash to spare, I would have definitely been wrapping it up and putting it under my tree.

'Snowdrops are my favourite,' I smiled, 'all that delicate and fragile beauty springing up during the worst the winter storms can throw at us. I don't think there's a more hopeful little flower in the whole of the world.'

I know everyone had their own ideas about that. Eloise favoured the yellow primroses which grew in abundance and lined the ditches along the edges of the fields around Broad-Meadows, but it was the snowdrop which struck a chord in me.

'Come on,' I said, as the grandfather clock next to the tills began to chime and alerted me to how long we'd spent browsing, 'we've still got the cathedral to explore before the end of the day.'

'I'll meet you outside,' said Finn. 'I just want to ask the guy how much he wants for that suit of armour.'

I had thought he'd been joking when he fell into raptures over that, but as he called to the stallholder and walked back over to it, I realised I was wrong.

'Why don't you grab that table,' I suggested to Finn when we arrived at the cathedral refectory after our walk through the city, 'and I'll get the tea.'

Our breakfast had, as predicted, sustained us for a good long while and the lunch rush had long since gone so we could take our time over our still-warm scones, thick cream and locally made strawberry jam.

'I hope this counts as one of my five,' I laughed, layering the jam on. 'We've hardly had the healthiest of days, have we?'

As well as the bacon and egg breakfast, we'd also shared the Schokokuss on our walk down to Tombland.

'In terms of calorie intake, perhaps not,' said Finn, 'although we've walked a fair few miles, and mentally it's been a real boost.'

'You're right,' I said, smiling across as him as I licked the luscious jam and cream combo from my lips.

Even though I loved life in the square and my job in the garden, it was a treat to go somewhere else and do something a bit different, and in such great company. Every second I spent with Finn, the harder I found myself falling for him.

I risked another glance as he poured us both a cup of tea, too engrossed to notice my scrutiny. His hair was tied tight back from his face which showed off his jawline and made him look even more warrior-like than usual. I let out a long breath as I realised that I'd never been in love before. I couldn't have been because nothing I'd ever experienced had felt like this. I adored everything about the man sitting opposite me and that covered so much more than just the way he looked. I loved his bravery and his ambition and . . .

He looked up and caught me staring.

'What?' he asked, making my cheeks burn as brightly as if I'd been caught saying the words out loud. 'Did you want the tea poured before the milk? I can never remember which way you're supposed to do it.'

'No,' I said, my voice catching as I quickly looked away, 'milk in first is fine.'

We walked the length and breadth of the mighty cathedral and Finn pointed out his beloved green men before buying postcards of them from the well-stocked shop.

'Do you want to come to mine for supper?' I asked, as we hopped on a bus which would take us most of the way back to the square.

It was already getting dark and, weighed down with our various purchases, we didn't much feel like making the trek back on foot.

'I would,' he smiled.

'Fantastic.'

'But I'm not going to.'

'Why not?'

While we had finished drinking our tea, I had been devising great plans to make the end of the day as memorable as the rest of it had been.

'Because I want you to have an early night,' he told me.

'I was planning to,' I huskily replied.

What was he doing to me? I'd never sounded so wanton.

'Not that sort of early night,' he grinned, 'as much as I would love that.'

'Then why don't we?'

'Because,' he said, leaning around me to ring the bell for our stop, 'I've got another busy day planned for tomorrow and both you and Nell will need to be ready early.'

'Nell?'

'Yes,' he said, standing up and taking more than his share of the bags, 'I feel bad that she's been home alone, so tomorrow we're taking her with us and she's going to have a whale of a time.'

Kind, considerate, caring and with an eye to the welfare of my beloved Nell, Finn really was the stuff of dreams.

He was true to his word, and early the next morning he arrived to take me and Nell, complete with an overflowing picnic basket, packed full of treats and cooked sausages, off on our next adventure.

'I'm sorry we've got to take your van,' he said, once we'd eaten more rolls from Blossom's and everything was packed.

'That's all right,' I told him, tossing him the keys, 'as long as you're happy behind the wheel.'

'More than happy,' he said, jumping into the driving seat.

I knew he hated not having his own vehicle, so the evening before, in lieu of the early night, I'd added him as a named driver to my insurance so he was covered to chauffeur me about. I was looking forward to taking in the scenery, assuming there was going to be some. I still had no idea where we were headed.

'So,' he said, as he pulled to the side of the road and pointed at the view about an hour later, 'what do you think? Any good?'

'Very good,' I nodded, clapping my hands together.

'I know it won't be warm, but there's a great pub we can thaw out in. It's dog friendly and they do a really decent lunch.'

'Let's go for it,' I grinned. 'It's been ages since I've been to the seaside.'

'Wynmouth has a stunning beach,' Finn told me, 'and I've checked the tide times so we should be able to explore the rock pools if you've packed enough clothes to keep out the wind.'

It was a bit on the breezy side, but Nell had a great time tearing up and down the beach and the rockpools were surprisingly busy. Not in terms of visitor numbers – we had the whole stretch of sand to ourselves – but the pools were full of activity, the occupants seemingly unaware of the bitter temperature above their watery world.

'Have you had enough?' Finn asked Nell, once she had finally run out of steam and flopped down, panting at our feet.

'I don't know about her,' I said, rubbing my hands together, 'but I'm starting to feel it.'

Looking at the colour of Finn's nose, I guessed he was chilly too.

'Right,' he said, 'let's head to the pub. This sea air has given me an appetite.'

I was in complete agreement and more than happy to while away the afternoon in The Smuggler's, the only pub in the village and which had a roaring fire, a surprisingly exotic menu (Finn and I both had steaming bowls of curried crab) and a landlord with the most beguiling green eyes.

All too soon, and because Wednesday was a workday for both of us, we climbed back into the van with a very sleepy Nell and headed back to Norwich.

'Are you all right?' I asked Finn, who had been quiet on the drive home.

'Yes,' he said, throwing me a smile. 'I'm fine.'

I really hated that word, because it always meant anything other than fine, but I didn't push him further. Like me, he was most likely sad that our two days together had come to an end. At least, I hoped that was what had caused the dip in his mood.

Back in the square, he followed me into the house. By the

time we'd unpacked the picnic basket, he was sporting the oddest expression and I realised there was something on his mind other than going back to work.

'What?' I said, as he closed the gap between us and my back was pressed against the wall. 'Whatever is it?'

'I know I shouldn't be saying this,' he swallowed, as he pulled off the woolly hat I was still wearing and released my curls.

'Saying what?' I breathed, drinking the scent of him deep into my lungs.

He was a heady cocktail of fresh sea air and aftershave. It sent my heart rate soaring and I could imagine my pupils dilating in response. His were wide and dark and I had no doubt that mine matched them. Surely whatever was on his mind couldn't be bad, if he was looking at me like that?

'We've only known each other for a few days,' he said huskily.

'It's nearer six weeks actually,' I whispered, thinking of the first time our paths had crossed. 'I've been here since Hallowe'en and, in spite of all the ups and downs and mis-understandings, we've been in each other's lives since then.'

'That's true,' he said, leaning in so our bodies came together as he placed his hands on the wall either side of my head.

I gasped at the contact, feeling my body respond. We were the perfect fit.

'And as it's been *that* long,' he sighed, resting his forehead against mine, 'then it can't be too soon to say I love you, Freya, can it?'

I felt my world shift on its axis.

'No,' I whispered, 'it's not too soon, because I—'

He didn't give me the chance to say it back because he was kissing my lips and his hands were in my hair.

'Don't say it,' he whispered urgently, 'I don't want you to say it just because I have.'

I was going to tell him that I was saying it because I meant it, not because he had gone first, but his hand slid under my shirt and his fingers began caressing my bare skin, making the words die in my throat.

'Oh Finn,' I gasped, as the seductive movement intensified.

After that I was speechless and remained so for the rest of the night.

Chapter 27

The middle and end of the week was in every conceivable way as perfect as the beginning. In fact, it was all so wonderful that if Richard Curtis happened to be looking to set a future romcom in the east of England – be it festive themed or otherwise – then I was in no doubt that Finn and I could have provided plenty of inspiration for the leading roles.

After that first exquisite night together, we knew we were going to struggle to keep our hands off each other and so settled on an agreement whereby we stayed apart during the day and kept after work and after dark strictly for each other. I still hadn't told him I loved him, but given the passion and heat between us, I was pretty certain that he knew that his feelings were in every way reciprocated.

I hadn't told any of my friends about the seismic shift in mine and Finn's relationship, not even Chloe. Although, given my constantly happy demeanour and wide smile, along with the evidence of my former beard burn, I'm sure she must have had her suspicions.

'Freya,' Luke beamed, when he came into the garden after lunch on Thursday afternoon, 'how on earth have you managed to do all this in just a day and a half?'

He was accompanied by Jacob and a few children from the school where he worked and who formed part of the new Bird and Wildlife Club they'd recently started. They had come to position some of the hedgehog homes Finn was so adept at making, as well as set up a few bird feeding stations. It was too late to get any hogs hibernating in the homes, but I had no doubt the feeders were going to be very much appreciated and there were plans to put up bird boxes in a few weeks' time.

'I'm capitalising on the weather,' I told him. 'It's just over a week until the official opening and, as the ground has thawed, I'm making the most of it. And don't forget, I've got Graham on the case, too. I might have taken a couple of days off this week, but he hasn't. He's been forging ahead.'

'Making hay while the sun shines, hey?' Jacob beamed.

'Something like that,' I agreed, my shoulders tensing a little as I remembered the last time I'd heard the expression. It was Jackson who had said it.

I couldn't be sure if Jacob was talking about getting ahead in the garden or if he'd seen Finn popping in and out of the square. His house was only a couple of doors away from mine and he and Ryan often walked Gus together in the evenings, so it was a possibility.

'Well, whatever the reason,' Luke continued, 'it all looks even better than I could have imagined. It's amazing that we're only a few weeks into the project and so much has happened.'

'I'm truly delighted you feel that way,' I smiled, before turning my attention to the children who had started to shiver. 'Now, let's work out where to put everything, shall we?'

With so many eager pairs of hands, the operation didn't take all that long and Luke promised to get the special wild-life cameras, which the school had raised funds for, trained on to the feeders the following week. The livestream was to be beamed straight into the classroom so I would have to make sure Finn didn't track me down for a clandestine kiss in full view of the local kids. That wasn't the sort of wildlife they were hoping to see!

'Are you coming to the carol concert tonight, Miss?' asked one of the boys, as he helped carry the tools back to the shed.

'Oh, I'd forgotten about that,' I told him, 'I'll see what I can do.'

'I'm going to be singing a solo,' he proudly told me.

'In that case,' I promised, 'I'll definitely be there.'

The church was packed, and I was pleased to see Harold in a pew just ahead of me. I would ask him after the service about how he used to decorate the house.

'This isn't quite what I thought you had in mind when you said we were going out,' Finn, who was sitting tight up against me because there was such little space, said quietly. 'I hope you aren't expecting me to sing.'

'Can't you sing?' I asked, pressing my thigh against his.

'I can,' he whispered back, 'I just choose not to.'

We quietened as the lad I recognised from earlier walked down the aisle and then turned to face the congregation. There was total silence as he sang the first verse of 'Once in Royal David's City' without any musical accompaniment. His voice was confident, strong and pure, and when the congregation joined in with the second verse there were more than a few moist eyes being dabbed with crumpled tissues and neatly pressed hankies.

After the service, throughout which Finn had sung with gusto I was amused to note, everyone stayed on to drink tea and enjoy the mince pies supplied by the school kitchen and the local Women's Institute.

'Are you keen to get off?' I asked Finn.

He'd sat down again once he'd collected his pie, because he took up so much space standing up.

'No,' he said, 'I'm in no rush. I'll wait for you and we'll go back together, if you like.'

'All right,' I smiled. 'That would be lovely.'

I ignored the knowing looks coming from certain neighbours and friends and waved to Harold.

'Just the person,' he said, as he made his way over and Finn shuffled up so he could sit down too. 'I was hoping I'd see you, Freya.'

'Likewise,' I told him. 'I have a question for you, Harold, but you go first.'

'Age before beauty, hey,' he chuckled, slapping Finn's knee. 'It's about my Christmas decorations.'

Finn looked at me and smiled. He knew that was what I wanted to ask about and was clearly amused that Harold had got in first.

'They're all still in the loft,' Harold explained. 'They're the only things up there, and in all the excitement of moving, I completely forgot about them.'

'Don't worry,' I told him, 'I can drop them round to you in my van. It's no bother.'

Given that his family had lived in the house since it was built, I knew there were bound to be some vintage treasures among the tinsel and tree decorations. I wondered if he would mind if I had a peek in the boxes when I dropped them off.

'Now, that would be grand,' he said, 'but to tell you the truth I only really want the wooden nativity set my father made and the angel for the tree. She's even older than I am!' he chuckled. 'I was thinking that it might be nice if everything else stayed at the house.'

'I see.'

'But only if you don't mind,' he rushed on. 'You don't have to do anything with them, but if they're taking up too much loft space—'

'Actually,' I quickly interrupted to stop him fretting, 'I was wondering if you would mind if I carried on using them to decorate the house?'

'They're all a bit old-fashioned,' he warned me.

'That's just what I like,' I told him, as his eyes moistened with tears. 'The house is still a bit old-fashioned, isn't it? So, they definitely belong there.'

'Well,' he sniffed, 'that would be wonderful.'

'And when I've got them up, you can come and see them.'

'Only if you're sure. I wouldn't want to intrude.'

'We could have some of the cake I made at Carole's Winterfest session,' I told him, 'and tea.'

'Well I'd like that,' he said, reaching for his handkerchief as Finn looked at me and smiled. 'I'd like that very much indeed.'

'That's settled then,' I said, bending to give him a quick kiss on the cheek.

'Hey now,' he grinned, 'don't be doing that, not with your strapping great fella sitting right next to me. I don't want him getting ideas that I'm trying to pinch his girl!'

Finn and I looked at each other and shook our heads. So much for keeping our relationship under wraps.

Even though I was keen to get ahead in the garden, Harold's kind gift of his family's festive decorations had me yearning to clock out on Friday. I was planning to get the decorations down and start going through them before buying a tree at some point over the weekend.

It was going to be a busy couple of days, what with helping my beloved with his Winterfest session on Saturday and saying a few words of horticultural wisdom before the start of Graham's on Sunday, but I was determined to squeeze buying a tree into my already packed schedule.

'Ta da!'

'What on earth?' I gasped.

'It's your tree,' came Finn's voice, from somewhere beyond the mass of beautiful pine branches, filling the porch when I opened the door to him that Friday evening.

'But I haven't ordered one.'

'I know,' he said, sounding more muffled than ever, 'I did. It's a present.'

'Oh Finn,' I laughed, clapping my hands. 'It's beautiful, thank you.'

'It's also heavy,' he said, 'so are you going to let me in, or what?'

'How far have you carried it?' I asked, opening the front door as far as I could in the hope that he could sidle in without knocking off too many needles.

'Only across the road,' he told me, carefully edging in. 'I had it delivered to Prosperous Place so I could surprise you. And it's container-grown, which is why it's so heavy.'

He'd barely got it into the sitting room before I flung my arms around him and kissed him deeply.

'I take it you like it then,' he said between kisses.

'I love it,' I told him, 'almost as much as I love—'

'Come on then,' he said, denying me the chance to say it again. 'Let's get it in position and then we'll get Harold's decs out of the loft.'

The tree fitted the space in the bay window beautifully. It was a little on the tall side, but I didn't mind that. I'd never had such a beautiful tree and the fact that it was going to be returned to the grower to be re-used again next year, by me if I wanted it, made it sustainable too, which was even better.

'Look at this,' said Finn, diving into another box and pulling out a bag of old-fashioned crêpe streamers.

'Harold's saved everything, hasn't he?' I laughed, looking at the eclectic collection we'd unearthed so far.

There were seasonal treasures of all styles, spanning many decades, contained within the cardboard boxes we had lifted down. Even some of the carrier bags that the foil ceiling decorations and streamers were stashed in were historical artefacts. It had been a while since Woolworths and C&A had graced the high streets, but in the loft their names lived on.

'And this,' Finn rushed on.

He sounded as excited as a child diving into their Christmas stocking.

'This must be the nativity set Harold's father made.'

We set that carefully to one side along with the fragile angel which, according to a quick online search, must have been at her best in the 1930s.

'There's far too much here to put up, isn't there?' I said, looking again at the lengths of tinsel, bright glass baubles, garlands and lights.

Most of the lights weren't wired up to current standards so they were easy to set aside, but as for the rest, it was going to take forever to choose.

'Why don't you pick a theme or decade?' Finn suggested, kneeling next to me. 'That'll narrow it down a bit. Or even a colour. There's enough here to fill the house, just using red decorations alone.'

He was right; I needed a plan. I wondered which things Harold favoured. Probably those pieces he remembered from childhood which, I guessed, most likely narrowed it down to the thirties and forties. There were plenty of glass baubles and even some small crêpe crackers which I reckoned originated from then. Another online search would help.

'That's a good idea,' I said, 'I just wish I had more time to get stuck into it.'

Nell had finally shuffled into the room. She hadn't been sure about the tree, but now it was in place and not moving, she'd made her peace with it. She laid her head on my lap and I bent to kiss the top of it.

'Oh, I meant to say,' said Finn, reaching to fuss her too. 'If you don't want to help with my session tomorrow, you don't have to.'

'I wasn't angling to bunk off,' I told him. 'I can finish decorating next week.'

'Well, it's entirely up to you,' he said, 'but I've got some extra help lined up now, so if you change your mind I won't struggle.'

'Are you just saying that because you know I can't hammer a nail in straight?' I pouted, giving him a nudge and making him almost topple over.

'No,' he grinned, 'and it was almost straight . . .'

'If you looked at it with your head bent at a right angle,' I giggled, nudging him even harder.

He took hold of my hand and we fell together while Nell skittered about.

'I wasn't going to mention that,' he laughed.

'You're only saying that because I've got you in compromising position,' I said, as I sat astride him and pinned his arms either side of his head.

'No, I'm not,' he said, looking deep into my eyes. 'I really have got someone else to help.'

'Who?'

'Zak.'

'Zak!'

He took advantage of my surprise to flip me on to my back so he was then on top.

'Yep,' he grinned. 'He said my session fitted his skillset and that it would be a good opportunity for us to bond. Brothers in arms and all that. He reckons if we keep putting up a united front then Dad will have to get off my case.'

Considering what a chip off the old block Zak had been when I arrived in the square, he really had gone all out to stick to the new side of the leaf he had turned over. I might have had my doubts at first, but there was no evidence to suggest that his efforts weren't in earnest and I was as thrilled about that as Finn clearly was.

'In that case,' I said, 'I think I will leave you to it.'

'You can spend the whole day decorating the house,' he said, lowering his lips to mine as I wrapped my legs around his waist. 'Assuming you aren't too tired to get up in the morning.'

'Why would I be too tired to do that?' I asked, kissing him back.

'Because you're in for a very late night,' he smiled, punctuating each word with another kiss.

Chapter 28

The following morning, I was every bit as tired as Finn had said I would be, but it wasn't the bone-weary sort of tiredness which descends after a day of digging, rather an exhaustion that you were thrilled to feel, one that left you with a very big smile on your face.

'Right,' I said to Nell, as she took advantage of my lethargy and jumped up on to the bed. 'What shall we do first?'

Finn's side of the bed was already cold. Before we fell asleep, he had told me he would head back to the studio before it was light, not only because he wanted to avoid subjecting us to gossip, but also because he wanted to check everything was set out in good time for his Winterfest session.

So far, every event had gone without a hitch and it was a testament to how much everyone thought of Luke that they were prepared to go to such lengths, in their own time, to make it a success.

'How about another half an hour in bed?' I suggested to my canine companion.

I turned on to my side and pulled the duvet almost over my head, hoping to tempt Nell into falling asleep next to me, but she was having none of it.

'All right,' I caved, 'I get the message. We'll start the weekend with a walk, yes?'

Given that it was only another fortnight until Christmas, the weather, thanks to a blanket of cloud, was surprisingly mild and I knew Finn would be thrilled about that because he was working in the Grow-Well. I was tempted to call in and find out if Zak had turned up early to help but, not wanting to disturb my beau, opted to send a text instead.

Back at home I fired up the slow cooker before returning to the boxes of decorations. I had promised to feed Finn that evening and knew that a hearty stew, accompanied by a bottle of rich red wine, would be just the thing to revive him after a day spent outdoors instructing people in the art of wildlife home building.

My thoughtful preparations all felt rather domestic, but I didn't mind that. Finn was the kind of guy who was happy to do his share in the kitchen, so having a fortifying dinner prepared for his return didn't feel too 1950s housewife, even if the house's festive theme suggested otherwise.

'Oh Freya,' gasped Harold, when Luke escorted him to pick up his angel and nativity set later that day. 'You've taken me right back.'

He had looked thrilled when Luke helped him out of the

car and he had spotted the tree positioned in the window and once inside his enchantment had continued to grow.

'This is just how I remember it from when I was a lad,' he said, shaking his head as he admired the crêpe paper crackers nestled amongst the fragrant branches of the tree and his reflection in the delicate glass baubles.

I'd put the most fragile, irrespective of their size, nearer the top, out of the way of Nell's thumping tail, just to be on the safe side.

'Although,' Harold added, turning to Luke, 'we never had a tree this size. Ours was a piddly little plastic thing. I think we threw it out in the end.'

'This is a real beauty, Freya,' commented Luke.

'Finn gave me it,' I said, instantly regretting the admission, but neither man seemed to take any notice.

I knew that if Chloe, Lisa or even Poppy had been present they would have pounced on that, declaring the gift as a token of love, which in a way I supposed it was.

'Although I think hired would be a more accurate description,' I added. 'It's in a pot and the grower's going to collect it in the New Year.'

'It must be from the same place where I get ours then,' Luke smiled.

'Oh yes,' I said, only just remembering. 'The one on the green is in a container, isn't it?'

I left them chatting and went to make tea. As I filled the kettle, I heard Harold comment on what a lovely job I'd made of everything and my heart swelled.

'And you think it's still all there, do you?' Luke was saying, as I carried through a tray bearing cups and saucers and a plate of biscuits.

'I'm certain of it,' Harold nodded. 'And that thing's only plywood. You could have it down in a flash.'

'What's this?' I asked, passing around the cups.

'The fire,' said Luke. 'Harold tells me that the original tiled fireplace is still in situ, behind that board.'

'When that thing was fitted,' Harold told me, pointing at the ineffective electric fire with disdain, 'what was behind it just got boxed in. It wasn't fashionable anymore, but it would have been expensive to have it ripped out so it was just covered up and the board painted over.'

'Oh wow,' I said, eyeing the fireplace with fresh eyes and imagining the room properly warmed by logs burning in the grate.

'The tiles have got some sort of leaves and flowers on if I remember correctly,' Harold mused. 'They go all the way around and the hearth's the same.'

'Is the chimney blocked?' Luke asked.

'Only by old newspapers and the like,' Harold told him. 'It would be easy enough to pull it all out and get the flue swept.'

'What do you think, Freya?' Luke asked me. 'Would you fancy reinstating the original fire?'

'I'd love to,' I told him. 'As long as it wouldn't be too expensive.'

'I'd bear the cost,' he said, 'although I daresay we could do most of it ourselves.'

'You could even use Lisa and John's youngest to sweep it,' Harold chuckled. 'I bet the little rascal would fit up there a treat!'

'I daresay he would,' Luke laughed.

'Do you think we could get it done before Christmas?' I asked.

'I don't see why not,' said Luke. 'It's not as if a modern sweep makes a mess, is it? You wouldn't need to clear the room or anything.'

'The electric fire only needs unplugging,' Harold pointed out. 'It's not wired in.'

'And I could get the board off tomorrow,' I said, keen to make a start, 'after I've finished helping Graham with his Winterfest session.'

'And first thing Monday I'll ring around and find a sweep,' Luke nodded.

'I'd leave the papers stuffed up there until the sweep comes,' Harold advised, 'just in case there have been any birds nesting. You won't a mess coming down and spoiling your lovely decorations.'

'Your decorations, Harold,' I reminded him.

'I think they've switched allegiance,' he said happily, while making a fuss of Nell who was scouting for crumbs. 'They're all yours now, Freya.'

Luke cleared away the tea things while I thanked Harold and gave him another kiss on the cheek and promised to look after everything just as he always had.

'Everything all right?' I asked Luke, who seemed to be taking ages.

'Yes,' he said, quickly closing the sink cupboard door as I walked into the kitchen.

'Were you checking the pipework by any chance?' I laughed.

He nodded, looking very much like he'd been caught doing something he shouldn't.

'Zak's done a great job,' I told him. 'Down here and upstairs. There's nothing to worry about.'

'That's good,' he said. 'And a weight off my mind. What do you make of his personality change? He's helping Finn out today and they seem to be getting on really well.'

'I know Finn's delighted,' I told him.

'But do you think Zak's going to revert to his formerly flirtatious and mischievous self?'

'No,' I said, 'I don't. I know I didn't know him for all that long before his conversion, but he's neither said nor done anything to make me doubt him.'

'A peaceful Christmas might be in the offing after all, then,' Luke smiled.

'I'm certain of it, and we've got the official opening of the Winter Garden to look forward to, haven't we?'

'Yes,' he said, 'and I'm looking forward to that more than anything else.'

'Don't let Jas and Abigail hear you say that,' I laughed. 'I think the appearance of a jolly gent in a red suit is the thing we're supposed to be most excited about at this point in the year!'

*

Finn arrived, fresh from the shower, just in time for dinner and carrying a beautiful handcrafted bird table which was yet another gift for me.

'You really are a man of many talents, aren't you?' I said, wrapping my arms around him once he'd carried it through the house and set it up just outside the kitchen window.

'Oh yes,' he said, making my knees buckle as he gave me a kiss which demonstrated his artistry perfectly, 'and you don't even know about half of them yet.'

I was very much looking forward to discovering what else he had up his sleeve.

'And given the gorgeous smell in here,' he smiled, 'I'm guessing you've got few more strings to your bow for me to find out about, haven't you?'

'Oh, definitely,' I nodded, 'and not all of them confined to my skills with the slow cooker.'

While we ate the stew, which was a melt-in-the-mouth triumph, Finn told me about his day. Everyone had taken something away with them, be it a more complicated hedgehog home or a simple bird box with a slightly skew-whiff lid.

'It was harder than I thought though,' he said, helping himself to the last ladle of gravy and grabbing some bread to soak it up with. 'I'd pre-cut all the kits so it was just a simple construction production line, but some people still managed to make a hash of it.'

'But you got there in the end,' I pointed out, 'and everyone enjoyed themselves, didn't they?'

'They did,' he said, 'but I was shocked that some of them

found it such a challenge. Zak was brilliant though, especially with the kids. Turns out he's got more patience than I have.'

'It's your artistic temperament,' I teased. 'You're used to working on your own now and doing things your way.'

'Are you taking the mick?'

'A bit,' I grinned. 'I think it's brilliant that you offered to do the session though, even if you wouldn't want to repeat it.'

'Oh, I don't know about that,' he then surprised me by saying. 'I've told Luke I'd do it again and Jacob said he'd love me to go into school to do some workshops with the kids. I reckon I'll have to get Zak to help out with that though.'

I shook my head and laughed.

'What?'

'Nothing.'

'Tell me about your day then.'

I told him how thrilled Harold had been with the decorations and the plans to uncover the sitting room fire. Finn was all for making a start on it that night but, utilising some of my other skills, I managed to convince him to leave it.

Finn rolled on to his side, opened one eye and looked at me.

'Morning, gorgeous. Are we late?' he asked, his voice thick with sleep.

I'd been awake a little while, watching him and trying not to disturb him. It hadn't been easy as I took in the steady rise and fall of his broad chest but I'd known how tired he'd been and thought it kinder to let him sleep. Even if I did have some interesting ideas about how I could wake him up.

'No,' I whispered, 'it's still early.'

'Good,' he said, sidling closer, 'because I know the perfect way to start the day.'

Later, we threw caution to the wind and walked over to Prosperous Place, with Nell, together. I found it impossible to stop smiling and happily let my hand sit snugly in his. I couldn't remember a time when I'd felt so complete and content.

My job was a dream, my house, although not mine, was perfect, I had more friends than I'd ever had before and now I had a wonderful relationship with a man I loved. And even though it was a new relationship, it wasn't all physical. Finn was such a fascinating person. I loved his bravery and his creativity and the way we could talk for hours about all sorts of things. My life was richer for having him in it and even though we'd got off to a rocky start, everything had finally fallen into place and fit seamlessly together.

Thanks to Eloise's timely beyond-the-grave radio re-tuning, everything had literally come up roses and I very much hoped it was going to stay that way.

'Are you all set then?' I called to Graham, having left Finn at the studio door and walked over to the Grow-Well with Nell, who quickly abandoned me in favour of the cosy bothy and the cats.

'I think so,' he said. 'What do you make of this lot?'

Graham's contribution to Winterfest was going to be a morning spent planting up containers with plants that were guaranteed to lift the spirits, even if you only had a tiny courtyard garden or even just a doorstep. He had sourced trays of pansies, violas and polyanthus in a riot of colours, as well as delicate cyclamens and trailing ivy and a variety of grasses to add structure and texture.

'Absolute perfection,' I told him. 'If this lot doesn't raise a smile, then nothing will. What about containers?'

'I've got some for people to use,' he explained, 'but the majority are bringing their own and, if the emails are anything to go by, they've been quite inventive.'

As the group arrived and unloaded their pots, I realised what he meant. The repurposing and upcycling ethos was clearly thriving in Norwich and I was delighted to see it.

'These are gorgeous,' I said to Sara, who was looking even happier than the last time I saw her. 'Where did you find them?'

'I got them from my brother,' she told me, handing over a mini keg beer barrel. She had already removed the top and added holes to the bottom for drainage. 'He had a party in the summer and got through a few of these. He was going to dump them, but I thought they'd be ideal for planting up.'

'They're brilliant,' said Graham, coming over for a closer look, 'and someone over there has got an olive oil container, but we're going to have to find a way to adapt it. Do you think Finn might have some tools to help with that, Freya?'

'I'm sure he does,' I said, hoping that he wouldn't mind the interruption. I knew he was hoping to add the finishing touches to his latest creation.

When everyone was settled, Graham asked me to step up to say a few words.

'As you all know,' I began, 'Luke Lonsdale, who owns Prosperous Place, set up Winterfest this year with a view to helping us cope with the long winter months and short dark days.'

The sky was all cloud, which demonstrated the point beautifully.

'He's also created a Winter Garden.'

'With your help, Freya,' Graham quickly added.

'And yours and Chloe's,' I nodded, 'and for everyone to enjoy. It's going to be officially opened soon, but today is all about creating something cheering to have closer to home. It's been scientifically proven that getting outside in nature, looking at green things growing and vibrant colours, such as those in the flowers Graham has found for us to plant today, releases all sorts of feel-good chemicals in the brain and therefore a container on the doorstep, or dotted around your garden, could make all the difference to your mental health.'

Sara gave a little cheer and a couple of the others clapped.

'So,' I finished up, 'before we all start to freeze, let's get planting!'

I very much enjoyed helping with the plant selection and colour co-ordinating. We soon discovered that the most impactful combinations seemed to be those which didn't match at all.

'I'll just pop to see Finn about this container,' said Graham, once he was happy everyone was occupied.

'You don't want me to go instead?' I offered.

'No,' he winked. 'There's no telling how long you'd be!'

When he came back, he had a couple of people with him. I knew they couldn't be Winterfest late arrivals as all the spots were taken, but Graham looked delighted as he left them at the gate and rushed back over to me.

'They're here to see you, Freya,' he excitedly told me as I looked up from the bag of compost my hands were immersed in. 'I recognised the woman straightaway,' he elaborated, 'she's a famous landscape architect. In fact,' he added, 'now I think of it, her last name's Fuller. She isn't a relative, is she?'

'Yes,' I swallowed, my shocked heart beating a sudden tattoo as I looked over to where she was standing, 'she's my mother.'

It took me a moment to realise that she wasn't with Dad, but Jackson. I had no idea why they'd come, but the sudden appearance of a shaking Nell at my side told me that she'd seen Jackson too. There was no way I was going to subject her to a reunion.

'Would you keep an eye on Nell for me, Graham?' I asked. 'And I'll get rid of them.'

'Of course,' said Graham, 'but don't do that. Take your time, show them around.'

Obviously, he had no idea about my family set-up, and it was hardly the time to enlighten him, so I just smiled and strode over to where the pair were standing.

'Freya, darling,' said Mum.

She leant in to offer me her cheek but, noticing the grubby state I was in, she recoiled.

'Have you come to plant up some polyanthus?' I asked, smiling sweetly.

'Hardly,' she grimaced.

Bright bedding was the last thing she'd put in a winter-flowering container. Not that she would ever actually do any planting herself.

'Well,' I said, still ignoring Jackson, 'that's what I'm doing, so—'

'We won't take up much of your time,' she cut in. 'We just want a quick word. Jackson has something to tell you.'

'Hello, Freya,' he said, stepping up and giving me the kiss Mum had shied away from.

'Jackson,' I said, my stomach rolling because I hadn't managed to move away quickly enough to ward him off.

He had never, in spite of his early efforts, managed to kiss me before, and I was annoyed that he had caught me off guard. I was also perturbed to find that, in spite of the manner in which I'd left Broad-Meadows, thwarting his cruel plan for Nell, he still had the power to unsettle me.

'You're looking well,' he added, appraising me in a way that I didn't appreciate.

'You'd better follow me,' I said, heading for the garden office.

'Aren't you going to take us to your house?' Mum asked, refusing the seat I offered her as I scrubbed my hands at the cracked Belfast sink.

'No,' I said, 'I'm not. I haven't got time.'

I knew Graham wouldn't mind if I took a minute or two, he'd already said as much, but I didn't want either of them, particularly Jackson, crossing my threshold and tainting the cosy ambience I had created.

'Well, I have to say—' Mum began, but Jackson interrupted her.

'It doesn't matter,' he said. 'We thought you might be busy and we really don't want to hold you up.'

'What do you want then?' I demanded, determined not to let him know he had unnerved me.

'I just wanted to tell you, in person, that I've decided not to sell Broad-Meadows.'

I felt my temperature shoot up and my hands, which I'd just dried, turn clammy. I closed my eyes and swallowed.

'Not sell Broad-Meadows,' I repeated.

'That's right.'

Jackson sat in the chair I had offered Mum and I dumped myself down in the one behind the desk.

'I tried to tell you the last time we spoke,' Mum piped up, 'but you never let me get a word in edgeways these days.'

Jackson bit his lip and I guessed he found my mother every bit as trying as I did. Had I not been reeling from shock, I might have found his expression amusing, but as it was ...

'You're now keeping Broad-Meadows,' I repeated.

'Yes,' Jackson smiled, showing off his perfectly aligned too-white teeth.

He really was the all-American dream. Even on a Sunday he was dressed for business; come to that, so was my mother. Was there something else they had driven all the way to Norwich to tell me?

'What made you change your mind?' I asked.

'I decided I couldn't part with it, after all.'

That was something, I supposed. I wondered what Eloise would make of his dramatic turnaround.

'And I was kinda hoping,' he carried on, fixing me with a penetrating stare, 'that you might come back, Freya?'

'To Broad-Meadows?'

'Yes,' he nodded, 'and to your cottage in the grounds.'

I had loved that little place. It was cramped but quirky and full of character, but then so was where I was living now, and in Nightingale Square I was surrounded by friends.

'But what about your tenant?' I frowned, remembering my speedy eviction.

Jackson seemed to think he was offering me something special, and had conveniently forgotten the circumstances of my departure from my once beloved home.

'Decamped,' he shrugged. 'So, the place is yours, if you want it – unless you were happier in the house.'

'You know I was never happy in the house,' I reminded him.

He laughed then, which infuriated me and ruffled my mother's feathers. Clearly, the meeting wasn't going how she had planned.

'Jackson wants you to manage the garden again, Freya,' Mum pointedly remarked.

I'd already realised that, but the way Mum said it told me that we were now getting to the crux of their unexpected arrival. I saw Jackson's jaw tighten, just a little, but it was enough of a tell to warn me that something else was afoot.

'Well,' I smiled, 'you know I always loved the gardens.'

Jackson went to say something, but Mum got there first.

'And now,' she rushed on, waving a bejewelled hand about, 'they're going to be even better.'

'How so?' I asked, my eyes flitting between them. 'Are you making some changes, Jackson?'

'You could say that,' he said tightly, clearly annoyed that he'd been forced to say as much so soon. 'I've submitted plans to turn the house and estate into a luxurious country house hotel complex.'

There it was. My stomach rolled again as I imagined the workmen moving in and the character of the place being hacked out.

'And the gardens,' I steeled myself to ask.

'Total remodelling,' said Mum, looking delighted. 'Cutting edge, modern, exciting. Jackson has already awarded your father and me the project and we want you to manage it.'

I couldn't believe that was something that she, or Dad, thought I would want to be a part of. They were both aware that one of the main reasons I had wanted to move on when Jackson put the estate up for sale was because I couldn't cope with the thought of it all being changed. Surely, she hadn't forgotten that?

'Imagine it,' she said, looking dreamily off into the middle distance.

'Oh, I am,' I told her, my eyes fixed on Jackson.

'You'd be back at Broad-Meadows and back in the family firm,' she pressed on. 'You'd have the best of both worlds, my darling. Everything you could possibly want.'

Except for the garden that I loved. The garden that Eloise and previous generations of her family, had spent their lives creating and perfecting. I couldn't bear to think of it being ripped out and replaced with something contemporary and cutting edge.

'But you seem to have forgotten that I'm very happy where I am,' I said, turning my gaze back to Mum. 'I'm settled here.'

'But for how much longer?' she asked. 'The Winter Garden must be all but planted now, what with the opening happening so soon, and then you're going to be twiddling your thumbs just maintaining the place. It's hardly going to be a challenge, is it? From what I've seen it's no size at all. You need to be thinking long-term, Freya, and much, much bigger.'

I knew it would be a waste of time trying to explain to her that Nightingale Square and Prosperous Place were about so much more than the size of the garden.

'But then I'm forgetting that you've started something with one of the locals, aren't I?' she laughed, as if my feelings for Finn meant nothing. 'You can't really be in love with him, Freya. You've only been here five minutes.'

'I think you'd better go,' I said, standing up. 'I'm astounded that either of you could possibly think that inviting me back to Broad-Meadows to see it all being ripped apart was something I'd even contemplate.'

'Don't make a decision now,' said Jackson, following Mum through for the door. 'Think it over.'

Exactly how dense was he?

'We're going to make the place great.'

'I know you haven't noticed,' I snapped, following him out and feeling his previously negative effect on me dwindle to insignificance, 'but it already is. Now, you found your own way in here, so I'm sure you can find your own way out.'

Chapter 29

There was no time to answer any of Graham's questions about my unexpected, and unwelcome, guests because by the time I returned to the Grow-Well, Nell was decidedly off-colour.

'I heard her behind the compost bays,' Sara told me with a concerned frown. 'I don't think she's eaten anything she shouldn't, but she's looking a bit sorry for herself, isn't she?'

She was right. Poor Nell was looking very green around the gills and I was certain it wasn't because of anything she had eaten. Her pallor – if a dog can have one – was the result of seeing Jackson. She might have only had the briefest glimpse, but it was enough to upset her and further proof, not that I needed it, that going back to Broad-Meadows would be damaging for both of us.

'I think you'd better take her home,' said Graham.

'But I'm supposed to be helping,' I reminded him. 'I don't want to let you down.'

'I can manage,' he said stoically. 'Everyone's off and running now.'

'And I can help too,' offered Sara, who felt like a regular visitor now, which I supposed, given that she'd attended every Winterfest session, she was.

'Take Nell back to the square and get her settled in the warm,' Graham insisted.

'All right,' I agreed as my poorly pooch began to retch again. 'She's not setting quite the tone we were aiming for, is she?'

We had a slow walk home and I settled my little love, who was trembling, in her basket in the kitchen. It wasn't the warmest room, but it did have a tiled floor and once I'd put a jacket potato in the oven for my dinner, it soon heated up.

I sent Finn a text asking if we could give our planned evening a miss and then returned my attention to reassuring my nervy companion that all was well and she had nothing to worry about.

Unfortunately, my words didn't soothe her and it was a long night for both of us. I spent much of Monday flitting backwards and forwards from the square to the garden and trying not to think about what my parents were planning for the gardens at Broad-Meadows or what Jackson had in mind for the house. I wasn't going to play any part in it, but that didn't stop it dominating my thoughts.

'How's Nell?' Luke asked, as I loaded tools into a wheelbarrow after lunch. 'Graham said she was poorly yesterday.'

I wondered if he'd talked about my visitors too, but as Luke didn't ask after them, I didn't mention them either.

'Yes, she was,' I sighed, 'and she still is. I've left her wrapped in a blanket at home feeling very sorry for herself.'

'Then why are you here?' Luke tutted. 'You should be with her.'

'I can't take the day off just because my dog's sick.'

Luke clearly didn't agree.

'It's not as if she's a child,' I pointed out.

'As good as,' Luke smiled. 'Take the rest of the day. And tomorrow.'

'But I can't.'

'I'm the boss,' he said firmly, pulling rank, 'and I'm ordering you to go home and look after Nell. I don't want to see you back here until she's well enough to come with you. Got it?'

'Got it,' I smiled, pushing the barrow back into the shed. 'Thanks, Luke.'

'Oh, and about the fireplace,' he said. 'I've got a sweep lined up to come and take a look at the chimney, but I'll put him off for a few days.'

'I'd appreciate that,' I told him, 'and so would Nell.'

The last thing my little bag of nerves needed was a strange man, with scary, noisy equipment, coming into the house. It was frustrating to think that all the progress she'd made in the last couple of months had been undone in moments, but it had happened and I would just have to help her bounce back. Still feeling unsettled myself, I knew it was going to take me a little while to bounce back too.

*

'Is that it then?' Chloe asked the next morning when she popped in to collect the list of jobs I had collated for her and Graham to work through in my absence.

'That's it,' I said. 'That should keep you both out of mischief, shouldn't it?'

'I should think so,' she agreed, 'and how's the patient?'

'Much better,' I said, looking over at Nell who was watching our every move.

She hadn't been sick overnight and had wolfed down, and thankfully kept down, the dry food I'd put out for her that morning.

'Was it the virus that's doing the rounds?'

'No,' I said. 'She got a bit stressed at the weekend and that's what set her off.'

I had spoken to the local vet, just to be on the safe side, and she was in agreement with me. Had Nell caught the nasty bug that was currently plaguing dogs everywhere then she'd have been knocked off her feet for far longer.

'Poor little mite,' Chloe tutted nonetheless.

She knew all about Nell being a rescue with a less than happy start in life and therefore felt kindly sympathetic towards her fragile mental state.

'Do you want a coffee?' I offered, holding up a mug.

'Just a quick one,' she said, glancing at the clock. 'I don't want the boss thinking I'm slacking and I know Graham will be itching to get on.' She pulled out a chair at the table and sat down. 'Nell wasn't the only one across the road who was stressed out at the weekend, was she?'

'What do you mean?'

'When I dropped my wellies back late Sunday night, I heard a godawful row going on in Finn's studio.'

'Did you?' I frowned.

'Yes,' she said. 'Didn't you know?'

'No. Who was it?'

'Well, to begin with, I wondered if it was the pair of you, having your first lovers' tiff.'

'What?' I gasped.

Chloe rolled her eyes. 'Oh, come off it,' she tutted, 'we all know that you're together now.'

'All of you?'

'Yes,' she laughed. 'We're taking bets on how long it'll be before you go public.'

'I see,' I said, focusing on making the coffee.

'Anyway,' Chloe continued, 'it wasn't you, obviously.'

'Why obviously?'

'Because it was two guys shouting.'

'Oh crikey. I hope it wasn't Zak.'

The brothers had been getting on so well, it would be a shame if they had a setback and had to start all over again.

'I thought of him too,' Chloe frowned, 'but it didn't sound like him.'

'Do you think Luke and Kate could hear it?'

Luke hadn't mentioned anything about it to me, but then why would he?

'Probably,' Chloe sighed. 'They were really going for it.'

I hadn't seen or spoken to Finn since we'd exchanged text

messages late on Sunday afternoon. He was fine then, happy to put our plans off under the circumstances. I had told him Nell was unwell, but not why, and he told me that he was going to carry on working in the studio. As we were both so busy, we'd agreed to catch up later in the week, and I knew how immersed he got once he was in the creative zone. As we'd sorted everything, I hadn't given his subsequent silence any further thought, but now . . .

'And Finn's not at the studio this morning. The place is locked up and looks deserted,' Chloe elaborated further. 'It's all very mysterious.'

'I see,' I said, handing her a mug. 'It is a bit, isn't it?'

'I take it you don't know anything about it at all then?'

'No,' I said. 'Nothing.'

'Curiouser and curiouser,' she mused.

On Wednesday, Nell was well enough to walk from the square to the garden office, where I tucked her up, with a hot-water bottle, while I ran through my to-do list.

I'd knocked at the studio, and tried the door, but the place was still locked. There was no sign of life and Finn hadn't responded to any of the texts I'd sent him after my chat with Chloe either.

'Is he not about?' came a voice as I was eating my lunch and checking invoices.

I looked up to find Zak standing in the doorway and watched in amazement as Nell climbed out of her basket and trotted around the desk, her tail wagging, to greet him.

'Well, I never.'

'Well I never, what?' Zak smiled, stroking Nell's head.

'She's been ill and basket-bound since the weekend,' I told him. 'That's the first bit of enthusiasm she's shown for anyone in days.'

'What can I say?' Zak sighed, looking very pleased with himself. 'I'm irresistible to the female sex.'

'Don't start that again,' I snapped.

If he'd reverted to being bad old Zak then he might well have been the person Chloe had heard Finn arguing with.

'I'm only kidding,' he frowned. 'What's up?'

'I take it it's Finn that you're looking for?'

'Yes, I just tried the studio, but it's all shut up. Do you know where he is?'

'No,' I said, the uncomfortable feeling I'd been brewing settling more firmly in my stomach. 'No, I don't. No one's seen him since Sunday.'

'Oh right.'

'You didn't see him then, did you? Only he was heard having an argument with someone.'

'Not me.'

'And not your dad?'

He was the only other person who I thought it possibly could have been when I'd lay awake wondering.

'No,' said Zak, shaking his head. 'We've all been okay recently. It's a bit weird, isn't it?' he added, once he'd taken a few seconds to let the situation sink in.

'Just a bit,' I agreed, chewing my bottom lip.

'Have you messaged him?'

'Of course, I have,' I tutted. 'A dozen times, but he hasn't replied.'

'That's even weirder then, because surely he would have told *you* where he was off to if he was going away,' Zak said pointedly.

'Why me?'

He rubbed a hand around the back of his neck and I guessed that Chloe had made a bet with him about mine and Finn's coming-out party too.

'What with you two being so close and everything,' he grinned.

'I see,' I sighed.

Our relationship was clearly common knowledge.

'I'm really chuffed for the pair of you,' Zak continued as my phone vibrated loudly in my pocket. 'I honestly didn't think you were ever going to get yourselves sorted, but I'm pleased you got there in the end.'

'Thanks, Zak,' I said, knowing there was no point denying it.

'I'll bet that's him now,' he said, nodding towards where the noise from my phone had sprung. 'Can you ask him to give me a call?'

'Why don't you call him yourself?' I asked. 'I thought you were worried about him.'

'Nah,' he shrugged. 'Finn can look after himself. We're no doubt making a fuss over nothing.'

I wasn't so sure.

'Do you want to wait and find out?'

'No, but you can send him a kiss from me.' He grinned.

'Idiot,' I muttered as he left, pulling the door shut behind him.

He was right about the message being from Finn, but there was no mention of Christmas, or where he'd gone. Just the unsettling words,

> I had the pleasure of speaking to your former
> boss Sunday night and he told me you're
> going to be heading back to Broad-Meadows
> to be with him in time for Christmas …

All of a sudden, and in spite of the chilly temperature, I felt far too hot to be wearing a coat. I shrugged it off as my head spun with all manner of nauseating thoughts.

It didn't take many seconds for me to work out that Jackson had somehow established, most likely via one of Mum's many sources, that Finn was the man I was in love with, and then, because I hadn't fallen in with his plans, after I'd dismissed him and Mum on Sunday, he'd spitefully gone all out to sabotage my new-found happiness.

This had to be the reason behind Finn's sudden and unexplained disappearance. He had believed what Jackson had said and then left Prosperous Place wanting to put as much distance between us as he possibly could.

'Mum,' I gasped, my breath tight in my chest, when she eventually answered her phone. 'I have to talk to you.'

'I'm in the middle of something right now, Freya,' she responded tersely.

'I don't care,' I told her. 'And don't hang up, because I'll just keep calling.'

I heard her rustling papers and excusing herself from whatever meeting she was in. Was she with Jackson?

'What happened on Sunday?' I demanded.

'You know exactly what happened,' she said, sounding slightly less sure of herself. 'You turned Jackson's offer down and then threw us off the premises.'

'But Jackson didn't leave, did he?'

She was quiet for a moment.

'No,' she admitted, 'he stayed in Norwich.'

'And went back to Prosperous Place to stir up trouble.'

She didn't answer.

'Didn't he?' I shouted, making poor Nell flinch.

'I honestly don't know what he did,' Mum said, sounding ruffled, 'but I wouldn't have put it past him. He was in a foul mood when we parted company.'

'You could have warned me,' I said bitterly. 'He's caused a lot of trouble for me here, Mum.'

'I'm sorry.'

'What?'

Had she really just apologised?

'I said I'm sorry, and I really am.'

A lump formed in my throat, adding its bulk to the band around my chest and the weight in my stomach.

'I saw a very different side to that man after we left you,

413

Freya,' she continued with a sniff, 'and I told him he could keep his precious contract. The firm won't be working on the Broad-Meadows project in any capacity now.'

I didn't know what to say. Obviously, I was delighted about that, but why hadn't she let me know? If I'd known she and Jackson had fallen out, I could have worked out who Finn had argued with the second Chloe mentioned it and acted far sooner.

'Subsequently,' Mum carried on, 'I've found out that there's a lot of local objection to Jackson's plans and I've advised the chap in charge of rallying the troops to officially lodge everyone's complaints, and their desire to protect the gardens, through the appropriate channels.'

I could hardly believe it.

'So, your beloved Broad-Meadows might be saved yet.'

'That's wonderful,' I swallowed, feeling shell-shocked.

'I think your Eloise would think so too, wouldn't she?'

'She certainly would.'

'And I really am sorry if Jackson has messed things up for you, Freya. From what I saw, the Prosperous Place gardens are actually very lovely.'

'Thank you,' I said, thinking more of Finn than the flowers.

'I hope it all gets sorted without too much heartache.'

'So do I,' I told her, still feeling floored. 'So do I.'

Everything that had happened – from Mum and Jackson's visit, right up to Finn's text – kept running on a loop in my head as I tried to get on with my work. I was astounded that

Mum had pulled out of the project. She'd never done any-thing like that before, not even when she didn't think much of the client. Jackson must have been especially foul to her, but I couldn't fret over that. My sole priority was to find Finn and set him straight about the lies Jackson had told him.

Every few minutes, I stopped to call his mobile but it must have been turned off and, until he turned it back on, I had no way of finding out where he'd gone or the amount of damage Jackson had selfishly done.

Chapter 30

During the next couple of days, I thought long and hard about telephoning Jackson, or even driving down to Broad-Meadows to see him in person. As I worked in the garden, putting the finishing touches in place for the grand opening on Sunday, I played through the *conversation* that I would have with him. It was always loud and very one-sided.

Somehow, I resisted the urge. I didn't call and I didn't visit. For every fibre that wanted to rant and wipe the smug smile off his face, there was a counterpart, refusing to allow him the satisfaction of knowing that his selfish actions had had such a devastating impact on my new life in Nightingale Square.

With Nell thankfully recovered and able to accompany me in the garden again, I worked from before dawn to after dusk, making sure everything was as perfect for the grand reveal as it possibly could be. I didn't let on to either Chloe or Luke that anything was amiss. I knew I could confide in my new friends, but found I didn't want to.

If I asked Chloe for more details, or Luke if he'd heard anything, the thought that I'd lost Finn, having only just found him, would become real and I simply couldn't cope with that. It was difficult enough sending texts and hanging on for replies that never came.

'So, how's it all looking?' Luke asked, as I was getting ready to leave long after it had turned dark on Friday. 'Shall we have a look at these lights?'

I couldn't help but smile, in spite of my turmoil.

'I thought you wanted it to be a surprise?' I reminded him.

I'd had a feeling he wouldn't be able to wait. He'd had a company in to install some strategic lighting to highlight certain parts of the garden, impressive specimen shrubs, trees with interesting bark and the like. I knew how spectacular the illuminations looked because Maddie, the woman heading up the installation, had secretly shown me when Luke was out, but he was supposed to be waiting until the open-day evening before he saw it all.

'I do,' he said, rocking back on his heels, 'but it could be a surprise that I have now, couldn't it?'

'No,' I said, ushering him out of the garden office where the main control panel had been installed. 'Wait until Sunday. I promise it will be worth it.'

He looked a little sulky but I resisted telling him that he could operate some of the lights independently, from the switches next to the chosen trees and shrubs, because I knew he would have been off around the garden and most likely blowing the bulbs in his excitement.

'Oh, all right,' he relented. 'I'll wait. We'll see you in the morning, yes?'

It was the last Winterfest session – making a needlefelt robin under Heather's competent guidance. The little collection of felted woodland animals and garden birds she made were exquisite. So exquisite that we'd all told her she should be selling them. That said, I had no idea how she found the time to craft them with three tiny tots under her feet, so perhaps running a business, even a small one, might have been a bit of an ask.

'Yes,' I nodded, 'I'll be there.'

'I can't believe it's the final session,' Luke said wistfully. 'The last few weeks have flown by, haven't they?'

'Just a bit.'

'This time next week it'll be Christmas Day,' he pointed out. 'The end of Christmas Day!'

I still hadn't decided how I would be spending mine. Not with Finn, obviously, but I wasn't sure I could face a return to the family fold. I knew I would be made to feel welcome, but still thought I'd be better off, with Nell, home alone. I didn't want my mood ruining anyone else's seasonal celebrations.

'Right then,' said Luke when I didn't bemoan the fact that in just one week's time it would all be over. 'I'd better get back. See you tomorrow, Freya.'

'Yes,' I swallowed, 'see you tomorrow.'

The Prosperous Place dining room looked as beautiful as ever the next day and it was a full house *and* a couple of last-minute additional Nightingale Square attendees who greeted me as I took my place at the table. I tried to focus on the demonstration Heather was giving which would enable us, allegedly, to replicate the jolly round robin she had provided for each of us so we knew what we were working towards, but I couldn't take it in.

Once she had distributed supplies, I began stabbing at the wool with my needle, which was surprisingly cathartic, and my mind wandered.

'Don't rush, Freya,' Heather told me as she made her way around to check on everyone's progress and monitor their technique. 'The more time you spend getting this bit right, the more solid the little chap will be.'

I nodded and she moved around to where Lisa was working, most likely to tell her something similar. For some reason our friend seemed to be more adept at stabbing her finger than her creation and she was being most vociferous about it. That said, Lisa was generally vociferous about everything, so that was nothing new.

During the mid-morning coffee break, Kate asked if it would be a help if Luke popped over to let Nell out at lunchtime.

'You're always rushing about,' she told me. 'It would be lovely if you could have the whole day here without any interruptions, wouldn't it?'

'Do you know,' I said, pulling my house keys out of my pocket and handing them over, 'you're right. It's been quite a week and it would be nice not to have to leave at lunchtime.'

419

I knew that Nell was fond of Luke, so there would be no issue about him letting himself in and, if I stayed with my fellow felters, there was less chance that I would spend the time, scrolling through my phone in the hope that I would hear something from Finn. I hadn't managed to magic him up so far, so I might as well cut back on trying. He'd been gone for the best part of a week now and it was time I started coming to terms with the end of our brief, but wonderful, time together.

It soon became apparent that everyone else's cheerful little felt birds seemed to be much sturdier than mine and far more tightly packed, but I soldiered on, determined to make the best of it while I mulled over what Mum had said when she and Jackson had turned up the weekend before.

I might have turned down a return to Broad-Meadows, but perhaps I should consider moving on once I was sure the Prosperous Place grounds were back in fine fettle and the Winter Garden was the success Luke had wanted it to be.

Of course, my maudlin meanderings weren't really about my job. I absolutely adored the place, my home and my many new friends in Nightingale Square, but the thought of living and working in Norwich, without Finn, wasn't something I wanted to face long-term. I had only managed to carry on that week because he wasn't actually there and I was under such a tight deadline. Trying to function with him in the vicinity when the pressure was off was going to be impossible. I would wait the winter out and then search for a new position in a different county in the spring.

The thought made tears spring to my eyes and I yelped in pain as the needle missed its mark and ended up embedded in the side of my finger.

'There,' said Lisa, shooting Heather a look. 'You said I was being over the top, Heather, but it does bloody hurt, doesn't it, Freya?'

'More than I would have ever thought possible,' I sadly replied.

At the end of the session we all had a look at each other's efforts. There were some fine specimens amongst the flock, but unfortunately, mine wasn't one of them.

'I know,' said Heather, reaching into her sewing bag as I tried and failed to make my ornithological effort stand on his feet for the umpteenth time. 'I'll sew a loop at the back of his head and then you'll be able to hang him on your tree.'

She'd hit upon the perfect solution and I wondered if she'd be able to sort out my love life with a flash of her needle and a length of thread. Perhaps she could sew my poor broken heart back together?

'Your keys, Freya,' said Luke, handing the bunch back, while I waited for Heather to work her magic.

'Oh, thanks,' I said, taking them from him. 'I'd completely forgotten he still had them. 'Was Nell all right?'

'Absolutely fine,' he smiled. 'She's completely recovered, hasn't she?'

'Thankfully, yes,' I said. 'She's back to her lovely self.'

I wished I could say the same for me.

I slipped out while everyone else was still pulling on their coats and wishing each other a merry Christmas. I was keen to get away because I would have to be up early the next morning to help prepare for the crowds. The weather was forecast to be crisp and bright which I knew would swell the numbers and Luke had been on the radio again and featured in the local newspaper too, so interest in the grand opening was high.

I walked back through the garden, just to make sure everything was in place. I was tempted to turn on a few of the lights, but couldn't risk drawing Luke's attention so made my way carefully along the paths with the torch on my phone just about lighting my way.

'What the—' I gasped as I came around a corner and found myself faced with one of Finn's stunning sculptures.

It was of a much larger dragon than those hidden in the fern garden and we had originally planned to work out where to put it together. How had it got here? And more to the point, when? I rushed back along the path to the studio, thinking he must be back, but he wasn't. The place was silent and in total darkness and I was still none the wiser as to where he had gone. Luke must have drafted in some help to move and site the sculpture while I was ineffectively felting during the day.

The smell of smoke lingered in the cold night air and I shivered as I crossed the road back to the square with an even heavier heart before stopping to look at my lovely little home. Luke had left the hall light on which lit up the stained-glass panel above the door and the Christmas tree lights were twinkling too, which made the place even more idyllic and welcoming.

I quickly stepped up to the door, before my emotions got the better of me, and turned my key in the lock.

'I'm back,' I called out to Nell as I stepped inside and realised that something was amiss.

She barked in response and the broad bulk of Finn suddenly filled the sitting room doorframe.

'And about time,' he smiled, making my heart clatter against my ribcage. 'Come and see what we've done.'

Feeling numb, but not from the cold, I followed him into the sitting room, my eyes alighting on the biggest fire burning in the grate. Finn stood one side and Nell the other, both keen to claim a spot next to the heat which I could feel warming the room even though I was barely inside it.

'Luke and I wanted it to be a surprise,' Finn told me. 'That's why he's had your keys for so long today. He told me what he was planning when I got back and we moved the sculpture and I said I'd give him a hand.'

I looked from the bright flames to the pretty polished tiles, the brimming wood basket and the various accoutrements required to keep the home fire burning and then back to Finn again.

'Do you like it?' he asked, sounding less sure. 'It is all right, isn't it?'

I tried to blink them away, but the effort was in vain and two fat, salt-laden tears rolled down my cheeks. They were quickly followed by a deluge.

'Freya,' said Finn, rushing across the room and taking my hand before leading me to the sofa. 'What is it? What's wrong?'

As soon as I was sitting, I let go of his hand. I didn't want to remember what it felt like in mine if I wasn't going to be able to hang on to it forever.

'You left,' I said, my voice barely audible as I tried to sniff and stem the long-unleashed flow. 'You disappeared and then you messaged to say that Jackson had told you . . .'

I couldn't bring myself to verbalise what it was that my ex-employer had said.

'Wait,' Finn swallowed, reaching for my hand again and not letting it go even when I tried to pull away. 'I don't understand—'

'I got your message,' I said again.

'But that's impossible.'

I wrenched my hand free and pulled my phone out of my pocket.

'Here,' I said, bringing up the text and shoving the screen under his nose.

He took the phone and read what was displayed.

'Oh, for fuck's sake,' he choked, wide-eyed. 'This is only the beginning of what I typed, and I didn't even know my crappy phone had sent that!'

He put my phone down and pulled out his ancient relic.

'It's dead,' he said. 'Finally gave up the ghost when I tried to text you and I haven't had a chance to buy another. Not that I'd know what to go for.'

I'd teased him plenty about his decrepit phone and his severely lacking tech skills. Why hadn't I thought about that before? In my panic I'd latched on to the implications of the text I'd received suggested and never entertained the idea that what had landed on my phone wasn't the whole story.

'I had no idea the bloody thing had sent anything,' Finn said again, sounding desperate. 'I thought it had snuffed it before I pressed send.'

'So, you haven't seen any of my messages?' I huskily asked.

'No,' he said. 'Not one. I spent ages typing out a really long message explaining what happened on Sunday night,' he carried on. 'I knew my phone would deliver it in parts, but I thought that would be okay. Or at least I did until it presented me with the black screen of death and no clue that any of it had been sent.'

'I see.'

'After that, I decided I might as well wait to tell you in person because you were bound to appreciate the outcome.'

'Which was?'

'Basically, that I'd called Jackson a wanker and sent him away with a flea in his ear.'

'You did what?'

Finn looked at me intently. He was still frowning as it dawned on him that I had been through emotional hell during the last few days.

'You've been thinking that I believed him, haven't you?'

'What else was I supposed to think, after that message landed on my phone?'

'Oh, Freya! Of course, I didn't believe him! I might not have known you long, my darling, but I know you better than that.'

'I thought you'd gone because you didn't want to see me,' I said, more tears gathering. 'I thought you believed that I was moving back to Broad–Meadows.'

'Oh hell, Freya,' he swallowed. 'If I'd had even an inkling that something like this had happened, I would have got another phone, or called from a landline, or something. I didn't even know you were aware that this Jackson idiot had been trying to stir up trouble.'

'Chloe said she'd heard you arguing and I worked out who with,' I sniffed. 'So, where have you been?'

'Never mind that,' he said, chucking down his phone. 'Come here, for pity's sake.'

I flung myself across the sofa and into his waiting arms.

'I thought I'd lost you,' I sobbed.

'Of course, you hadn't lost me,' he said, squeezing me closer. 'I'm so sorry any of this has happened.'

'Don't you apologise,' I blubbed. 'It was Jackson's fault.'

'I wished I'd laid him out when I had the chance.'

I rather wished he had too.

We stayed locked together, feeling the warmth of the fire and watching the flames lick up the chimney. With every breath I could feel my frozen heart thawing again, but that had nothing to do with the coals glowing in the grate.

Eventually I sat up so I could look at him, but I didn't move away and I didn't let go of his hand either.

'So, where were you then?' I asked. 'Where did you disappear to?'

He softly kissed the back of my hand before answering.

'Wynthorpe Hall,' he said with a smile. 'The Connellys have decided they want to push ahead with creating the sculpture trail through their woods and they've commissioned me to make a few of the pieces.'

'Oh Finn!' I said, throwing myself back into his arms. 'That's amazing! Congratulations.'

'Thank you,' he smiled. 'I'm really pleased.'

'And so you should be. What a perfect end to the year.'

'It is rather, isn't it?' he said, ducking his head. 'And being back with you again makes it even better. You do know now how much I love you, don't you, Freya?'

I felt an overwhelming rush of relief and was just about to tell him how much I loved him too, but he kissed me with such passion and conviction that the words were lost. I happily melted into his embrace and my world slipped seductively back into focus.

Chapter 31

Waking, wrapped in Finn's warm and strong arms the next morning, it genuinely felt as though Christmas had come early. I looked at him briefly, taking in his features, softened by sleep, the tangle of his hair and the steady rise and fall of his chest, before closing my eyes, ready for sleep to claim me again, but they sprang straight back open the second I remembered.

It might not have really been Christmas Day but it was as good as. It was finally time to open the Winter Garden and find out what the rest of the world, or at least a small part of it, thought of the horticultural efforts I, along with my team of two, had made since arriving in Nightingale Square just a few short weeks ago.

I mentally ran through Luke's plan for the day and then gently, and reluctantly, manoeuvred myself further from Finn's warm reach.

'No,' he sleepily muttered, pulling me straight back again, 'just five more minutes.'

'I can't,' I told him, 'I need to get the garden ready.'

'The garden *is* ready,' he said, his eyes still closed. 'Five minutes.'

'There's no time,' I weakly protested, as he rolled on to his side and then on top of me. 'I've got to do something with my hair.'

I didn't need to look in a mirror to know that it was going to need some attention.

'I'll do it for you,' said Finn, kissing me lightly on the lips.

'Will you?' I asked, my head instantly filled with that delicious hair washing scene featuring Robert Redford and Meryl Streep in *Out of Africa*.

'Yes,' he said, kissing me again.

'In that case,' I giggled, 'let's take ten minutes instead of five.'

After a very seductive fifteen minutes, Finn was true to his word and tamed and plaited my tangled tresses in no time at all.

'You can do this every morning,' I told him as I admired his handiwork in the hall mirror as we were getting ready to leave.

'That can be arranged,' he smiled.

The loose side braid he had nimbly created was boho heaven but perfectly practical in my line of work.

'I can never reach right round the back,' I said, squinting to get a better look. 'My arms give up on me.'

'We need to work on your upper body strength,' he grinned.

'No, we don't,' I said, clipping on Nell's lead, 'I'll just take advantage of yours.'

By the time we crossed the road from the square to

Prosperous Place there was already quite a crowd gathered and when we dropped Nell in the kitchen, where she was going to spend the morning with Gus and the cats, the excitement was palpable.

'When I looked out earlier,' said Luke, who was doling out a cooked breakfast to Kate and the girls, 'there were already a couple of people queuing.'

'There's more than that,' said Finn, pinching a rasher of bacon from Jasmine's plate and earning himself a stern glare in the process.

'There's nearer a dozen now,' I said, pulling Finn away from Jas's plate and into an empty chair.

'Have you not come from the studio?' Kate then asked Finn.

'No,' he said, 'I came over with . . .'

His words trailed off and his face turned bright red, as did mine.

'You did have an early start,' Kate grinned at us both.

'No doubt you'll be wanting breakfast then?' Luke said teasingly, adding more bacon to the pan.

'Yes,' said Jas. 'Finn's *really* hungry, aren't you?'

'I have got a bit of an appetite this morning,' he admitted.

'I'm just going to do one last tour of the garden,' I quickly swallowed.

I did want to check that everything was as it should be, but I wanted to get out of the steamy kitchen too.

'Everything's perfect,' Luke told me. 'I've already been out and looked, so there's no need.'

'But even so,' I said, heading for the door. 'Just a quick check, won't hurt, will it?'

'Take this then,' he said, thrusting a bacon roll into my hands, 'and don't start fiddling about with anything.'

Practically everything was perfect, but I still wasn't completely satisfied with the arrangement of the containers we were using to show off winter planting combinations for small spaces. Chloe and Hannah were in charge of sales and the plants had all come from a nursery near Wynbridge which was run by two women Finn had met through his friend, Jake.

If sales were strong enough, we were planning to strike a deal which would mean we could set up something similar for each season, possibly with Graham and me heading up a container planting masterclass like the one he had organised for Winterfest. I refused to allow my mind to track back over that fateful day as I pulled everything out of place and then back into a much more satisfactory set-up.

'What are you doing?' Finn called.

'Nothing,' I said hastily stepping away.

'The evidence on your clothes suggests that's not quite true,' he laughed.

'Oh damn,' I swore, when I looked down to find my jumper streaked with compost. 'I'll have to go back and change.'

'You'd better be quick then,' he said, shaking his head, 'it's almost time to open.'

I would have been far quicker had he not come back with

me and insisted that I really needed help stripping off and re-dressing to settle my nerves. We were out of breath when we rushed back again, which was slightly embarrassing, especially when I spotted two familiar faces in the queue.

'Mum,' I said, pulled up short by her appearance. 'Dad. I wasn't sure if you were still going to come.'

The pair looked as impeccable as ever, but they were more casually dressed than usual. They were even wearing wellington boots, but not just any old wellies, of course. The matching Le Chameau boots they were sporting were way out of my price range and I was amused to see that they were completely spotless. Most likely fresh out of the box that morning.

'I know we talked about today,' I carried on, trawling back over our telephone conversations, 'but I did wonder—'

'We wanted to come and lend you our support,' Dad cut in, kissing me on the cheek and neatly stopping me from mentioning Jackson as I lost sight of Finn in the crowd.

'And I really wanted to come because I'm thinking about going back to my roots and doing a bit of gardening myself,' Mum said.

My eyes swivelled from searching for Finn back to her again.

'I'm serious,' she said, flushing a little as she took in my shocked expression. 'I think it will do me good.'

'In that case,' I told her, 'you need to come to the plant sales area when you get inside, unless you want to come in with me now?'

'No, no,' she said, shaking her head. 'We're happy to wait. It's nice listening to the buzz about the place along with everyone else.'

I left them standing in line and went back inside.

'What's up with you?' Finn asked, when he took in the look of shock Mum had picked up on too.

'What's up with you more like?' I countered.

He was looking bright red and wide-eyed himself.

'Zak's convinced Dad to come,' he said, wringing his hands. 'He's out there with my step-mum. He wants to see what I've been working on.'

It was a red-letter day for both of us then, but there was no time for an attack of the vapours because Luke was ready to let everyone in.

Once the gate was open, the people who had been waiting so patiently rushed inside and congregated around the steps which led up to the main door of the house. Luke threaded his way through them, pulling me along with him. I had hoped I was going to get away with hiding in the background while he said a few words, but apparently not.

He talked briefly about the house and his connection to it and then turned his attention to the renovation of the garden and the creation of the Winter Garden, reiterating all he had said on previous occasions about the importance of embracing nature and getting outside, even on the most bitter winter days.

'As you walk around,' he said, by way of introducing me, 'please be aware that the garden is very much a work in progress. As all gardens are. That said, there's already plenty here to delight the senses, and there will be more as the winter moves on, but Freya is more qualified to talk to you about that than I am, so I'll hand you over.'

Thankfully, plants were my forte and it didn't take many seconds for my voice to stop shaking and for me to get into my stride listing everything to look out for that day as well as sharing the details of what would be popping up throughout the next few months.

'And of course,' I finished up, easily spotting Finn because he was so tall, 'we also have the work of a very talented local artist to enjoy. I'll hand back to Luke, to tell you more about that, and perhaps Finn could join us up here too?'

Finn's face was aflame as we passed each other and Zak could be heard whooping and cheering. I knew I was going to be in trouble later for forcing him to step up, but I was rather looking forward to that.

'So,' said Luke, once Finn had got everyone fired up with the promise of hidden dragons, 'all that remains for me to say is that I hope you enjoy your first trip around the Winter Garden and that there are plants for sale near the garden office and mulled wine, soft drinks, along with homemade soup and pizzas available in the Grow-Well, so please stay as long as you can and don't forget that we'll be illuminating the garden at dusk.'

Everyone cheered and began to disperse. Some people headed straight for the garden, while others peeled off to the Grow-Well. I opted for the garden, keen to eavesdrop on a few conversations and see if I could get a feel for what people thought.

'Have you smelt this?' was the first comment I heard and it made my spirit soar. 'It's so sweet!'

I stopped and had a few words with the family who had discovered the sarcococca, which looked as good as it smelt.

'I hope this is on sale?' asked the guy who had smelt if first.

I reassured him that we had a few plants in stock and then moved on, smiling to myself as I heard children squealing in the fern garden, no doubt having found at least one of Finn's fabulous hidden dragons.

And thinking of Finn.

I could see him standing on the path ahead of me with his dad, step-mum and Zak. They were looking at the hares in the meadow lawn. I was just about to take a different path when Zak turned and gave me a thumbs up and Finn's dad clapped his eldest son firmly on the back. It might not have been a particularly demonstrative moment, but it was a very definite seal of approval and I knew Finn would be thrilled. He might have found the strength to stick to his guns and follow his heart even without his father's understanding, but I knew the man's approval still meant the world to him.

'Freya!' Finn called, when he spotted me loitering. 'Come and join us.'

With all eyes on me, I walked to where they were standing. Finn reached for my hand and in a rush told them that I was his girlfriend.

'Bugger,' Zak grinned and I knew he was only acting up for the sake of it. 'What, like officially and everything?'

'Officially and everything,' Finn said firmly, kissing the back of my hand before properly introducing me to everyone.

The day absolutely flew by and it took a while for me to catch up with Mum and Dad. I worked my way around the garden in my capacity as head gardener, stopping to talk to the visitors and offering advice when asked, and I was keen to find out what my parents thought of the place.

'Isn't that them?' said Finn, pointing when we gave up in the garden and walked round to the Grow-Well.

'It is,' I nodded, easily picking the pair out. 'What's Mum eating?'

She was tucking into a slice of the pizza John had made in the garden oven and deep in conversation with Graham about the joys of pea sticks versus metal stakes. Dad was looking a little unfocused and I guessed he had been sampling the mulled wine Carole had been warming in the bothy. They still looked like my parents, but they didn't sound much like them. I was rather pleased about that.

'And here she is,' Dad beamed, 'our clever girl.'

Finn and I stepped forward before Dad stood up. He was definitely a little tipsy, a state I had never seen him in. Mum, on the other hand, was high on life.

'And this is Finn,' I said, keeping introductions brief.

'Well, Freya,' Mum smiled, taking in Finn's handsome face. 'I can certainly see why you're so smitten.'

'The gardens are gorgeous, aren't they?' I swallowed.

'The what?' asked Mum. 'Oh yes, the gardens. Yes, the gardens are glorious.'

I couldn't swear to it, but I think she actually winked at Finn. The way he started to laugh told me that I was right, and I didn't know what to feel more shocked about – her and Dad turning down Jackson's project, the realisation that they had bought up half the plants and Mum was intending to get her hands (or at least her gardening gloves) dirty, or the fact that the pair of them had finally taken a long hard look at my life and applied the lessons that I had learned to their own!

There was a bit of a lull in the afternoon so Finn and I collected Nell and took her back to the house. I wanted to put some potatoes to slowly bake in the oven, so we would have something to eat after the illumination event, and while I did that Finn cleaned out and remade the fire.

'Your mum's a card, isn't she?' Finn laughed when he came back to the kitchen to wash his hands.

'If you say so,' I laughed back, thinking that he wouldn't have said that had he met her the first time she had visited. 'But she's not usually like she was today.'

'I could say the same for my father,' he pointed out.

'Parents are hard work, aren't they?' I sighed, thinking of the metamorphosis both sets had so very recently gone through.

'Just a bit,' he agreed. 'Dad's insisting that the two of us spend Christmas day with them.'

'Oh no,' I gasped. 'My mum wants us to go there. What are we going to do?'

Finn glanced up at the kitchen clock.

'We're not going to worry about it now,' he said stoically, 'because we need to get back over the road.'

I knew I was biased, but the garden really was looking so much better and with the paths packed with friends who were already feeling more like family, a variety of visitors, a group of carol singers and Finn at my side, when the lights came on the whole place took on an even more magical appearance.

'You were certainly right about washing those trees, weren't you?' smiled Chloe as she slipped her arm through mine and we stood admiring the bright bark and lengthy shadows as everyone 'oohed' and 'aahed' over the spectacle.

'Yep,' I smiled back, squeezing her into my side, 'and I hope you know that I wouldn't have been able to achieve anywhere near half of this if I hadn't had your help to get it all done.'

'I haven't done much,' she mumbled. 'And Graham's done loads too.'

'You've done loads,' I told her. 'You both have.'

'And you've taught me so much,' she batted back, unwilling to let the compliment just lie.

'How did the plant sales go?' asked Finn.

'Biggest surprise of the day,' Hannah, who was standing on Chloe's other side, told us. 'We sold out!'

'No way,' I gasped.

'We did,' said Chloe. 'Everyone loved the containers and they were keen to replicate them at home.'

'You'll be doing that again then,' chuckled Finn.

'We certainly will,' I said, shaking my head. 'And there was me worrying that we'd over-ordered.'

'We probably could have sold more,' said Hannah, 'especially of that smelly shrub.'

I made a note of Hannah's description of the sarcococca. If she was going to help out next time, Chloe could get her up to speed on plant names. Although, that said, I bet all those who'd visited and weren't au fait with the official name would have been able to pick out the plant she had described.

'Everyone all right?' asked Luke, coming along to join us, with Graham close behind.

Luke was carrying a tray of yet more mulled wine and we all took a cup, as keen to warm our hands as we were to enjoy the fruity flavour.

'More than all right,' I told him. 'What a day.'

'It's been amazing,' he smiled. 'Definitely one for the memory bank. And I've already got loads planned for next year.'

Why didn't that surprise me? I was very much looking forward to being a part of the plans for the gardens at Prosperous Place and couldn't wait to find out what he had in mind.

'Shall we have a look through them tomorrow?' I suggested, before thanking Graham for all his hard work while I attempted, and failed, to stifle the biggest yawn.

'Absolutely not,' said Luke. 'No work tomorrow. In fact, no work now until the new year.'

'I can't possibly take off all that time,' I told him, and I really meant it.

Luke was generous to a fault, but I couldn't leave the garden for three whole weeks. It was going to be a struggle not coming in on Christmas day. Living on site had made always being at work part of my life and that wasn't about to change.

I might have been a little further off from the garden in Nightingale Square, but it was still just a stone's throw away really. That said, I was pretty sure Finn would be able to come up with ways to stop me constantly rushing back.

'Reduced hours then,' said Luke, stating the fact rather than asking the question. 'Let's say, half nine until half two.'

'Nine until three,' I batted back.

'Half nine until half two,' he said again. 'Tell her would you, Finn?'

'It's nothing to do with me,' Finn laughed. 'Freya knows her own mind. That's one of the many things I love about her.'

Chloe dug me sharply in the ribs and I gulped down a mouthful of wine, not that I needed it to warm me now that Finn had so publicly bandied the 'L' word about. His words had lit me up inside and out.

Chapter 32

Finn was right, I did know my own mind, and it was his acknowledgement of that which gave me the courage to tell my parents that we wouldn't be joining them for Christmas and he then said the same to his. It wasn't something either of us relished doing, especially as we'd only just found some level ground with both sets of families, but we needn't have worried. They were equally understanding and, having got that out of our heads, we were able to enjoy the run-up to the big day without any worries hanging over us.

While Finn focused on his designs for the Wynthorpe Hall sculpture trail, I worked the reduced hours Luke had suggested in the garden. The weather had taken a definite downward turn and I was looking forward to seeing the Winter Garden flourish further throughout the coming months. Discovering hidden and delicate-looking gems, such as Iris unguicularis, when the weather was at its worst was going to be a real treat, as was helping out in the Grow-Well and working on whatever it was that Luke had lined up for the place next.

'You all set then?' asked Chloe, who had called in on the Wednesday as she wasn't working the next day because it was Christmas Eve. 'Got your wrapping all done and a mountain of food in the fridge?'

'The presents are all wrapped,' I told her, 'and the food is coming later this afternoon.' I had no idea I would be able to shop local in the middle of the city and get it delivered. I thought that sort of thing was reserved for more rural towns.

Although, that said, the isolated position of Broad-Meadows often meant that suppliers didn't want to drive all the way out to deliver. Living in Norwich had gifted me the best of both worlds.

I wondered if Jackson had factored any of that into his Broad-Meadows rejuvenation equation. If the weather *really* turned bad, the whole estate could be cut off for days. I bet he hadn't given any thought to weighing up how easy it would be to run a luxury hotel in the middle of another Beast from the East. The weather might well end up giving him as much trouble as the locals, and I felt rather delighted about that.

'What about you?' I asked, quickly pulling my thoughts away from his potential difficulties. His problems weren't mine and they never would be.

'All done and dusted,' Chloe grinned. 'And Hannah and I spent a fortune at the Christmas Fayre in the cathedral.'

'On what?' I laughed. 'I thought you said you didn't need anything else.'

'Gin mostly,' she mused, biting her lip. 'I had no idea there were so many local distilleries.'

'And you thought it was only fair that you sampled and took away a little from each, did you?'

'Exactly,' she laughed along with me. 'Hannah's in the trade after all.'

I wasn't sure about her reasoning but I was delighted to see her so content. She and Hannah were truly kindred spirits (and not only because of their mutual appreciation of gin), and I was extremely happy to see my friend and colleague ending the year in a very different place to where she had found herself twelve months before. Finding our courage and taking the plunge had worked out very well for both of us.

'What have you got for Finn?' she asked me after we had swapped our bags of gifts.

I wrinkled my nose and let out a long breath.

'He told me he didn't want me to get him anything,' I sighed. 'He said there was nothing he wanted or needed.'

'So, does that mean he hasn't got a present for you?'

'I doubt it,' I whispered, 'because I ended up getting him a little something anyway.'

'Oh yes,' she purred, raising an eyebrow.

'And I'm certain he will have got something for me too.'

'You hope,' she nudged.

'He's promised to start work on a sculpture of Nell in the New Year.'

'I suppose that counts then.'

I didn't actually mind whether I got any presents at all. Living in Nightingale Square with Nell, surrounded by my new friends and working somewhere so beautiful in the heart of a wonderful city, was more than enough of a gift for me.

My life had changed beyond all recognition and I was still thanking my darling Eloise for that timely prod from my re-tuned radio.

'Anyway,' I said, blushing as I nudged Chloe back, 'Finn's more than present enough.'

'And I'll bet he takes no time at all to unwrap,' she giggled.

Christmas Eve arrived with leaden skies and, according to the local weather report, the possibility of a falling snow-flake or two. Not enough to give us a white Christmas but enough to ramp up the festive feeling even further, not that we really needed it.

As I stood in front of the bedroom mirror, I turned this way and that, admiring the elaborate plait Finn had created for me, and I could hear him singing carols in the shower. The expression on Nell's face suggested that she didn't think much of his voice, but I thought he sounded pretty good. With the bathroom door firmly shut anyway.

We were getting ready to go over to Prosperous Place for a party and I was very much looking forward to it. I had little gifts for everyone and I knew that Kate had further decorated the house and that all the foodie folk had created a beautiful buffet. It was going to be quite a celebration and of course, pets were included.

'Oh Freya,' Finn gasped, when he finally appeared, still dripping and with a towel draped loosely around his hips.

'I hope that's a good "Oh Freya",' I mimicked as I twisted around trying to do up the zip on my dress.

'It is,' he said keenly, 'it certainly is.'

I had no idea what everyone else was going to be wearing but I had gone all out. I had just one winter party dress and Luke and Kate's seasonal celebration felt like the perfect opportunity to give it an airing. It was deep burgundy, knee-length, close-fitting with long sleeves and a slash neck. A slender diamanté belt was the only embellishment and I felt wonderful in it.

'Well, that's all right then.' I told him. 'Can you give me a hand with the zip?'

Finn stepped up and I tried not to let myself become seduced by his near nakedness.

'The other way,' I laughed, when I realised he was undoing all the work I'd put in so far. 'We haven't got time for shenanigans.'

'I hope there'll be time later,' he pouted, dropping a kiss on my neck. 'I've never seen you all dressed up before.'

'If you think the dress looks good on then why are you so keen for me to take it off again?' I teased, stepping neatly out of his way before he answered. 'Now, hurry up, or we'll be late.'

I finished putting on my make-up downstairs while Finn got ready in the bedroom and I again admired my hair in the mirror above the fireplace. Finn's large hands were extremely and surprisingly dextrous.

'You look incredible.'

I spun around and found him framed in the doorway.

'Wow,' I grinned, 'you look pretty good yourself.'

He was wearing dark jeans and a shirt, the colour of which matched my dress. He had tucked it in for once and I could make out the shape of his body underneath it – broad shoulders, narrowing to a slim waist. I stepped towards him, intent on finding out if he felt as good as he looked.

'No time for shenanigans,' he said, warding me off, 'but there is something I want to give you.'

'Oh yes,' I smiled, hoping my luck was in.

'Yes,' he said, 'sit down and close your eyes.'

I raised an eyebrow.

'Just do it,' he laughed.

I sat and squeezed my eyes closed.

'Hold out your hands,' he said, the smile obvious in his voice, once I had done as instructed.

I felt the weight of something land and opened my eyes.

'What is it?' I asked, my fingers closing around a small velvet-covered box.

'Open it and see,' he said, sitting next to me.

The box opened with a creak and there, resting on a bed of ruby-coloured silk, was the beautiful art nouveau snowdrop brooch that I had fallen in love with the day we went shopping in Norwich.

'The suit of armour,' I swallowed, running my finger lightly over the detail. 'That's what I thought you'd hung around for.'

'Oh, that's coming too,' Finn smiled. 'It's being delivered after Christmas.'

I shook my head, blinking fast to save the eyeliner it had taken a while to perfect.

'Do you like it?' he asked, looking at the brooch again.

'I love it,' I told him as he took the box and carefully unpinned it. 'It's exquisite, even prettier than I remembered.'

He pinned it into place, his hands lightly brushing my skin and making me shiver.

'Thank you,' I said, kissing him on the lips. 'Thank you so much.'

'You are most welcome,' he said, kissing me back.

'So much for your embargo on gifts,' I tutted.

'I know,' he said, 'but I bet you've got me something, haven't you?'

'Of course,' I said, nodding at the presents under the tree, 'but you can have yours tomorrow.'

'I can't wait,' he grinned, looking more like an excited child than a fully grown Norse god.

'Me neither.'

We wrapped ourselves in coats and scarves, clipped Nell's lead on to her collar and made our way across the square to Prosperous Place. It was still light but only just and I could see a few snowflakes falling from the slate grey sky. I linked my arm through Finn's and he squeezed me close.

'Who would have thought we would be ending our year like this?' he smiled, shaking his head.

'I know,' I agreed, as we carefully negotiated the house steps and the sound of a party in full swing met our ears.

'The pair of us didn't exactly get off to the most auspicious of starts, did we?'

'I suppose not,' said Finn, 'but then appearances can be deceiving.'

'What do you mean?'

'Well,' he said, turning to me again, 'I know it didn't look like it after our initial meeting, when I bawled Nell out, but for me, it really was love at first sight.'

I swallowed and leant closer in.

'It was love at first sight for me too,' I said back.

'Really?' he asked, his cheeks flushed.

'Really,' I whispered back, quickly kissing him as the door swung open.

'Come in, you two,' said Luke stepping aside. 'You must be freezing. Come in and get warm.'

Finn and I shared a look as we stepped over the threshold and were treated to a rousing welcome from our many friends as Kate took our coats and scarves.

Everyone was included and the house looked every bit as beautiful as I knew it would. Lisa and her tribe, along with Heather and hers were enjoying the buffet, Chloe and Hannah were deep in conversation with Poppy and Jacob, and Carole and Graham were busy keeping everyone's glasses topped up, while Mark and Neil treated Abigail and Jasmine to a dance as Michael Bublé encouraged us to have a merry little Christmas.

'What do you think of the decorations?' asked Harold, when I went to wish him a merry Christmas.

'They're lovely,' I smiled, admiring the festive haven Kate had created, 'but not a patch on mine.'

He laughed in response. 'I'm so pleased it's you who has moved into my home, Freya,' he said a little shakily.

'So am I,' I agreed, taking his hand and giving it a squeeze.

With the wine flowing and the fires stoked, everyone was the happiest I'd ever seen them, and that was saying something. I caught the scent of sweet perfume as I looked around at my new friends and knew that Eloise was with me.

Feeling her presence made me feel even warmer than the fire and I was happy to acknowledge it, comforted to know that she was there. I had been content at Broad-Meadows and my time there had been, for the most part, happy, but Nightingale Square was where I felt truly at home. It was wonderful to know that she understood that.

'Right!' shouted Luke, pulling me out of my reverie. 'Let's go on a tour of the garden, shall we?'

I expected everyone to object, but they were all willing and we bundled ourselves up again before setting off to explore the cleverly lit garden under the star-studded sky.

We hadn't gone far, however, before Finn pulled me to one side and treated me to a pulse-racing Christmas kiss.

'I love you, Freya Fuller,' he said softly, as a snowflake fell and landed in his hair.

'I love you too,' I whispered back, feeling another tickle my nose.

'Are you cold?' he asked, his grey eyes looking deep into mine.

'No,' I swallowed. 'Never. Not with you to keep me warm.'

Again, he took my hand in his and I knew, that with him by my side, I would never feel the cold.

Acknowledgements

I'm absolutely convinced that the time between sitting down to write the dedication and acknowledgements for each of my books is getting shorter and shorter, even though this year has had every opportunity to drag by.

I hope that by the time you are reading this, the world will have returned to some sort of normality and that you haven't borne the brunt of the devastating pandemic that has kept us locked in its grip, seemingly forever. In fact, I hope that by the time *The Winter Garden* is published you will be so busy enjoying the delights of the festive season, that you won't have time for my ramblings at the end of the book!

So, with fingers firmly crossed, I will, for once, keep it brief . . .

Huge and heartfelt thanks to everyone who supported me through what has been, for so many reasons, a particularly difficult year. Whether you are someone I know IRL or through the medium of social media, whether you are a blogger, a dedicated #swainette, fellow author, member of my publishing team or family, I am honoured to call you my friends and beyond lucky to have you on my side.

Your kindness, support and friendship make me one very happy author and it is *always* appreciated. I wish you all a very merry Christmas and a healthy New Year.

May your bookshelves – be they virtual or real – always be filled with fabulous fiction.

With love, your friend,

H x

If you loved *The Winter Garden*, then be sure to read
Heidi Swain's previous novel . . .

The Secret Seaside Escape

Tess Tyler needs a break. Weighed down by her
high-pressure job and her demanding father, she's left little
time to take care of herself. But after a shocking discovery
sends her spiralling, she flees to Wynmouth, the seaside
town she fell in love with as a child, to escape it all.

With its sandy beaches, stunning rock pools and
welcoming community, Tess feels like she can finally
breathe again. And as she grows ever closer to local barman
Sam, she dares to dream that she might never return to her
real life. But when a familiar face returns to town, Tess
realises that there are secrets in Wynmouth too, and that
her own past may be about to catch up with her . . .

AVAILABLE IN PAPERBACK AND EBOOK NOW

If you're looking for more festive fiction, then be sure
to read Heidi Swain's previous novel . . .

The Christmas Wish List

After being let go from her job, Hattie is feeling lost. Even
more so when her boyfriend announces he's landed his
dream job in Abu Dhabi and asks her to move with him.
Luckily, Hattie's long-time friend Dolly is on hand to help
and invites Hattie to spend one last holiday in Wynbridge,
determined to give her a Christmas to remember . . .

The residents of Wynbridge are preparing for their most
spectacular Christmas yet. But for Hattie, it'll take more
than mince pies and mistletoe to open her heart to the
season once more. Relishing the task of reigniting Hattie's
Christmas spirit, Dolly suggests they create a wish list of
all the things the season can offer. And with the help of
Wynbridge's resident handyman, Beamish, Hattie finds her
frosty exterior is starting to thaw . . .

AVAILABLE IN PAPERBACK AND EBOOK NOW

If you're looking for more festive fiction, then be
sure to read Heidi Swain's previous novel . . .

Snowflakes and Cinnamon Swirls at The Winter Wonderland

Moving into Wynthorpe Hall to escape the town's
gossip, Hayley finds herself immersed in the eccen-
tric Connelly family's festive activities as they plan to
host their first ever Winter Wonderland. But Hayley
isn't the only new resident at the hall. Gabe, a friend of
the Connelly's son Jamie, has also taken up residence,
moving into Gatekeeper's Cottage, and he quickly makes
an impression on Wynbridge's reformed good-girl.

As preparations commence for the biggest event of the
season, the pair find themselves drawn ever closer to
one another, but unbeknownst to Hayley, Gabe, too,
has a reason for turning his back on love, one that
seems intent on keeping them apart.

Under the starry winter skies, will Gabe convince
Hayley to open her heart again once more? And in
doing so, will he convince himself?

AVAILABLE IN PAPERBACK AND EBOOK NOW